Brought to you
by the passage of
ballot measure 6A
in 2019.

Garfield County Libraries
New Castle Branch Library
402 West Main Street
New Castle, CO 81647
(970) 984-2346 • Fax (970) 984-2081
www.GCPLD.org

UNCONQUERABLE
SUN

The Sun Chronicles

Unconquerable Sun
*Furious Heaven**
*Lady Chaos**

Young Adult Novels by Kate Elliott

COURT OF FIVES

Court of Fives
Poisoned Blade
Buried Heart

*forthcoming

UNCONQUERABLE
SUN

KATE ELLIOTT

TOR

A Tom Doherty Associates Book

NEW YORK

UNCONQUERABLE SUN

Copyright © 2020 by Katrina Elliott

All rights reserved.

Edited by Miriam Weinberg

Map on pages 6–7 by Jennifer Hanover
Endpaper maps by Mary A. Wirth

A Tor Book
Published by Tom Doherty Associates
120 Broadway
New York, NY 10271

www.tor-forge.com

Tor® is a registered trademark of Macmillan Publishing Group, LLC.

The Library of Congress Cataloging-in-Publication
Data is available upon request

ISBN 978-1-250-19724-5 (hardcover)
ISBN 978-1-250-19725-2 (ebook)

Our books may be purchased in bulk for promotional, educational, or business use. Please contact your local bookseller or the Macmillan Corporate and Premium Sales Department at 1-800-221-7945, extension 5442, or by email at MacmillanSpecialMarkets@macmillan.com.

First Edition: 2020

Printed in the United States of America

10 9 8 7 6 5 4 3 2 1

There is but one true sun, and each of us
casts nothing more than her reflected glory.

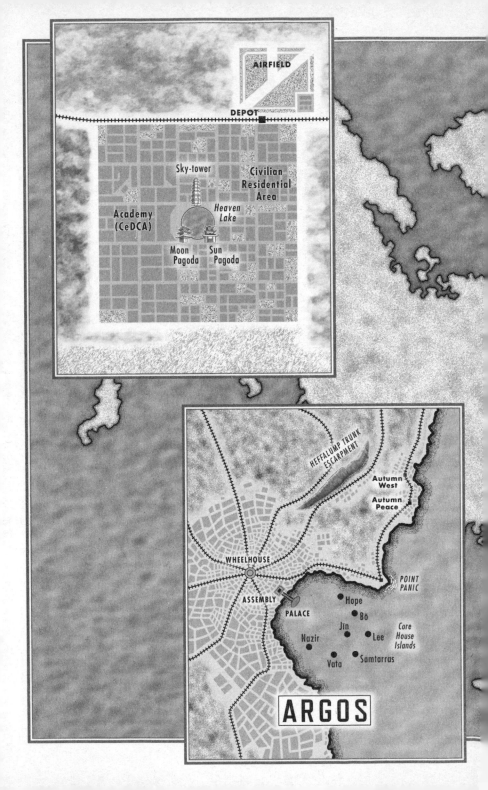

N

CeDCA and
INDUSTRIAL PARK

ARGOS

CHAONIA

UNCONQUERABLE
SUN

1

The Precipitating Action of This Account Begins Here

The battered fleet returned to Molossia System without fanfare or announcement. Military personnel striding across the main concourse of Naval Command Orbital Station Yǎnshī slowed their steps as they looked up. One by one ships slid into view across the threshold of a beacon's aura. The beacon itself was so distant it was no more than a pinprick of light as viewed by the naked eye, so the arriving ships were visible from the station only because their images were being superimposed on the concourse's transparent shell.

A young woman had halted at an optimal distance to get the best angle on the huge curved viewing window. "*Anzû. Kōlea. Asphodel Crane. Alicanto.* That's the . . . the *Bulsajo.*"

"That's not a corvette, Princess," said the burly soldier who stood beside her. Octavian had been making visual sweeps of movement in and out of the gates that connected the concourse to the various rings, nodes, and piers of the station. He tipped his chin up as he glanced at the enlarged image. "It's a corsair. They're both built for atmosphere landings, from the same original Yele design. But—"

"But a corsair has an additional comms bulb on the exterior because it usually hunts alone and can't rely on a task force's greater comms reach as a fleet corvette does." She tilted her head to the left. "I see the extra bulb now."

His lips quirked. "I was worried for an instant there that you hadn't been paying attention in class. The corsair must be one of the local Na Iri militia ships that got commandeered by our fleet before the battle."

"It wasn't assigned to my attack group."

A spontaneous cheer rose from the concourse as a Tulpar-class battle cruiser—much larger than the corvettes and fast frigates in the vanguard—appeared out of the beacon's aura.

"Seems the *Boukephalas*'s part in the engagement has reached fleet ears," observed Octavian, indicating the battle cruiser.

"Will it be enough?"

"Will what be enough, Princess?"

She didn't answer. At first glance she was nothing special: medium height, median looks, and wearing an unobtrusive uniform. Nevertheless, people nudged each other and gestured in surprise as they walked and wheeled past her and her companion. If she noticed, she did not let on, her attention fixed on the returning ships and what their victory meant for the Republic of Chaonia's conflict with the Phene Empire. For what the battle's outcome and her part in it meant for her future.

On the busy concourse, colleagues greeted each other with news of the victory in the hushed tones of people aware the casualty report hasn't yet come in. Many were streaming Channel Idol even though the Ministry of War had not released an official statement.

What's next for the heir to the throne of the Republic of Chaonia? After Princess Sun's bold attack from the flank turned the tide of battle and brought victory to the fleet over the Phene aggressors, will the princess get the duty post she seeks? Or does the queen-marshal plan to tie her close to home? Are the wedding rumors true? Stay tuned to Channel Idol! And now, the farm report. Crop stats from Chaonia Prime are in. It's been a bumper season for 'ulu and squash!

Sun leaned forward to examine a badly damaged corvette coming through. "*There's the* Bulsajo. Look at that debris trail! It's pulling half its guts along."

A flash of gold by one of the gates caught her eye. The steady buzz of conversation died away, choked off as a swirl of unexpected movement entered the concourse. Silence fell except for nervous coughs and the rhythmic hiss of the ventilation system. Octavian released the clip that held a concussion rifle against his back and placed his body between the princess and the densest part of the crowd. The sea of onlookers parted, people stepping out of the way as a man and his entourage carved a path toward her across the gleaming expanse of deck.

"Stand down," Sun said dryly to Octavian. "It's my father."

Prince João was dressed in a cobalt-blue jacket rigged with gold chains, white jodhpurs, and embroidered boots. A glimmering network of lines across his face like a shining neural tattoo marked him as a Royal of the Gatoi. His honor guard identified him as a consort to the queen-marshal. Instead of a respectable contingent of decorated Chaonian marines like Octavian, he traveled with his own personal cohort of Gatoi banner soldiers. There were six of them today, walking with the easy grace of a people trained from childhood to fight to the death if need be and never regret the dying. Everyone in the concourse kept their distance from the perilous Gatoi and guardedly turned so as not to have their backs to them. Those closest made sure to avoid looking directly at their eyes.

Prince João halted in front of the princess as his people set up a perimeter, facing out toward the concourse. First he gave Octavian a nod. Then he surveyed Sun from the bloodred garrison cap perched atop her head to the polished toes of her shipboard boots. His hand flicked out, and she stiffened, face heating with a flush. He intended to adjust some infinitesimal misalignment of her jacket and she could not stop him without appearing rude to her esteemed parent. But just before he touched her clothes he recalled the nature and size of their audience. With a flourish of the hand, as if a theatrical gesture was what he'd intended all along, he indicated her uniform without handling it.

"The drabness and modesty of an unmarked duty uniform is an adept statement. Especially since it will be contrasted with the flamboyance of your successful flanking maneuver. With the way you not only broke and routed the enemy line but used your attack group to surround and destroy the Phene command ship and its escort."

"How does Channel Idol already know the details of the course of the battle and my part in it?" she demanded. "I claimed passage on the fast courier so I'd be first to bring news of the victory to the queen-marshal."

"And has Eirene seen you?"

A familiar churn of frustration tightened her chest. "She has not, even though the palace corvette is docked at Pier 8. I was told she isn't yet on station."

"How like her," João murmured, but his watchful gaze remained on Sun, measuring her reaction.

"Breathe, Princess," said Octavian in her ear. "Don't let your temper control you."

She breathed a slow inhale and exhale and, after making a slight alteration to the alignment of her jacket, was able to speak in something approaching a normal tone. "I was required to give my report to Crane Marshal Zàofù. He only had his son with him. Anas, obviously. Not James."

"Two of the most tediously pompous people in existence," remarked João.

"My *point* is that none of the ministries or palace officials have made a statement about the battle yet. She'll blame you for the leak to Channel Idol and be furious."

The prince raised perfectly sculpted eyebrows. "However shall I manage Eirene's notorious temper? I quake in my authentically detailed boots."

"*Did* you leak it? Because if you did, you must have known it would anger her. When she's angry at you it affects how she treats me."

"No, I did not leak the news. I expect your mother had it leaked as soon as Zàofù pinged her your report."

"Why would *she* leak it? Why not just release the official report? Why pretend she's not here and refuse to see me? What do I have to do, what impossible task must I accomplish, to win a word of praise from my mother?"

"Ah. So that's what's eating you."

Naturally the people on the concourse had already taken it upon themselves to go back about their business, hurrying on their way despite the intriguing scene of the prince greeting his daughter. Channel Idol's ubiquitous camera wasps weren't allowed to roam in military installations, yet images of this piquant public reunion would soon spread across the Republic of Chaonia's confederated solar systems. Prince João might be an untrustworthy foreigner, but no one in Chaonia could fault his absolute devotion to his only child.

"Listen and learn, my unconquerable Sun." The prince started to walk. Sun kept pace, wondering where he was leading her but knowing it would be the right place to go. "Your mother is a complicated person. She'll be thrilled at this evidence of your tactical skills, your boldness and follow-through. But she'll be pricked by envy as well. She was young once too."

"She's not that old."

"Indeed she is not. She has many years left to her, as chance, fortune, the gods, and Lady Chaos allow. Certainly she's packed more accomplishments into the twenty years of your young life than any ten thousand people can manage in a hundred."

Sun said nothing. Queen-Marshal Eirene had achieved what everyone said was impossible. But since she'd done it, that meant it hadn't been impossible.

Which meant the impossible was not just achievable but necessary.

"Youth has a particularly sharp glint of promise," the prince went on with a sidelong glance at her that always seemed to pry into her secret thoughts. "Her silence is good strategy. If she praises her sole viable but ancestrally contentious heir too effusively, her praise looks suspect and self-serving. Citizens might think she cares more about keeping the queen-marshalate in her line of descent than in what's best for the republic. But if the palace releases a dry report noting your accomplishments after the details of your dazzling maneuver have been splashed all over Channel Idol, then her restraint highlights your splendid deeds. Do you see?"

"I wanted my first command to be successful, and it was," said Sun with an edge of impatience for her father's ceaseless spinning of plots and undercurrents. "I wanted our forces to take control of Na Iri and its beacons, to drive out the Phene from that system, and we did."

"Keep the target in mind," he said cryptically.

They reached one of the gates that led out of the concourse onto an array of elevators, transport pods, and slide-ways.

"Where are we going?" Sun asked.

"In her own unpredictable way, Eirene is very predictable."

A ping bloomed into a sixteen-pointed sunburst in Sun's network, perceived just beyond her right eye—a summons from the queen-marshal.

"Just as I expected." João allowed a control panel to scan his retinal signature and flag open a pod that would take them to the station's secure command node.

The pod was big enough to seat sixteen, but only the prince settled onto a padded bench seat. The Gatoi arranged themselves to guard the two sealed doors, while Sun remained standing respectfully in front of her father with Octavian in silent attendance at her back.

"Father, do you know anything about wedding rumors?" A beloved face flashed in her mind's eye, but she pushed the distracting and forbidden thought aside impatiently. "No one has said anything to me about a marriage. I'm not interested."

"I expect that's just Channel Idol sweetening the pot with an extra dab of honey. Pay it no mind. Eirene can't betroth you without my consent. I had a codicil written into our marriage contract."

He licked a finger and leaned over to rub a smear of dust off a nacre pendant nestled amid the embroidery decorating his boot. The pendant was carved into the shape of snake's wings to represent one of the thirteen exalted officials and gracious courtiers who attend the throne of the Celestial Empire of lost memory. Once the nacre gleamed to his satisfaction, he straightened.

"Now, listen carefully. Don't diminish your accomplishments, but don't boast of them either. The evidence of your deeds is the only trophy you need."

Sun sighed, knowing there was more lecture to come. Instead João folded his hands on his lap and nodded with a rare warm smile of heady approval.

"You did well. This is only the beginning."

2

A Fresh and Sharper Thorn of Disquiet

Once the pod sealed and began to race through the interlocking strands of the orbital station, the senior Gatoi soldier relaxed enough to greet Sun.

"Well met, Your Highness."

"Colonel Evans."

Sun acknowledged the other five banner soldiers as well, all known to her from her father's household. She'd spent many an evening playing mah-jongg with them in her father's pavilion, but this wasn't the place or time for less formal interactions.

Octavian offered Colonel Evans a respectful salutation in recognition of their complementary roles, but the two did not converse. Like every marine who had fought in the border wars he did not trust the Gatoi, not then, not now, not ever. Why should he, when 90 percent of Gatoi banner soldiers fought as auxiliaries for the Phene Empire? Yet he had agreed thirteen years ago to become bodyguard to a seven-year-old princess born of an unexpected union between the young and ambitious queen-marshal of embattled Chaonia and a strong-willed prince of the Gatoi who had broken away from his own Conclave of Royals to make a daring alliance.

Was it lust or an exceptional sense of strategy that had driven Eirene's decision to take a second and decidedly controversial consort at a time, twenty-two years ago, when the republic was beleaguered by aggressive Phene raids and arrogant Yele demands? Sun's musings on this perennial question kept her focused until the pod clicked into the airlock on the command node's outer ring.

An intercom chimed, followed by curt words. "Place all weapons on the floor immediately."

Sun tensed, fingers brushing the stinger holstered at her hip. "That can't be for us."

"Standard security protocol, Princess," said Octavian with a tip of the head toward the Gatoi. He calmly unclipped his rifle and set it at his feet aligned so he could grab it quickly.

Prince João looked superficially serene, but by the flicker of his eyes Sun knew he was annoyed. Nevertheless, he gave a languid, downward gesture with his right hand. The six banner soldiers promptly lay facedown on the floor, hands on the backs of their heads. The pose of abject surrender shocked her, but she waited to see what would happen next because she knew her father curated every least interaction.

The pod's door slid open to reveal a line of marines tucked behind guard emplacements in an armored entryway. A middle-aged man with the typical stocky build of a person who has grown up on Chaonia Prime strode forward to halt at the threshold. He did not wear a military uniform, although he moved with the authority of a high-ranking officer. A sunburst badge pinned over his heart identified him as one of the queen-marshal's Companions, born to one of the seven Core Houses and thus equals of Eirene. He acknowledged Sun's presence with a nod rather than a salute.

"Princess Sun."

"Marduk Lee." Sun offered a slight bow, exactly the proper deference in respect of his status as her elder.

"You're still wearing a weapon."

"I am. I'm the heir."

"So you are. Speaking of which, how is my cheerful young cousin Percy? Aren't your Companions with you?" His smirk was a sting. "Not a single one?"

"I believe you know the queen-marshal assigned me to duty on the *Boukephalas* without my Companions," she replied with creditable calm, brushing off a barb meant to remind her that she could not control the movements of her own household. She took a step toward the threshold but, as he did not stand aside to let her pass, was forced to stop.

"I was summoned by my mother."

"So you were." He took a step to one side. The instant she crossed the threshold he stepped back to block the opening, leaving her in the entryway and her bodyguard, her father, and his escort in the pod.

"They are with me," she said.

His gaze examined each of the prone Gatoi before returning to her. "Clearance to disembark has been suspended."

"That's unacceptable——" She broke off when Octavian caught her eye and gave a minute shake of the head.

Her father should not have brought his people this far in, given that most Chaonians saw Gatoi as a hated enemy. Yet this was exactly the sort of provocation João reveled in. Sun resented him placing her in this fraught position almost as much as she was insulted by Marduk Lee's power play, which could not go unanswered.

Before she could decide on a course of action, the far hatch in the entryway cycled open. A large domed chamber lay beyond, an open space used for planning strategy and logistics. Several people moved amid a three-dimensional augmented-reality projection of the battle at Na Iri and its glowing pattern of shifting ship positions. The replay had just reached the point where the enemy line stretched so far it began to lose cohesion. Through the door Sun watched a visual of her attack group with *Boukephalas* in the lead thrusting like a spearhead into the resulting gap. The maneuver had allowed them to surround the enemy's flagship and its escorts while the center and right flank of the Chaonian fleet had driven the remainder of the enemy ships into an ignoble retreat. It was well done, effective, and decisive.

The replay froze, accompanied by a splash of lighthearted banter. A woman walked out of the domed chamber into the entryway as the hatch closed behind her. Sun straightened, shoulders tight, then eased off with a hiss of expelled air. It wasn't the queen-marshal come to greet her triumphant daughter. It was Moira Lee, Marduk's cousin.

Marduk Lee glanced back. "Here you are, Moira. I have a pod waiting for you, as requested."

A prick of instinct sparked in Sun's chest, a sense of a threat hovering just out of sight. Moira Lee was a former Companion to Eirene and now governor and thus senior clan member of the powerful Lee House. So why was she here at a military post instead of back on Chaonia Prime overseeing the crucial ministerial operations for which Lee House was responsible?

Moira and two adjutants wearing Lee House's emerald tree badge made their way around the emplacements. She stopped short when she saw Sun. "Princess Sun. I thought you were on the *Boukephalas.*"

"I was. Now I'm here."

Moira Lee's lips pinched together as she sorted it out. "I see. You must have come on the fast courier with the initial report. I hear congratulations are in order. You did well."

"I did."

Moira dipped her head in acknowledgment and her tone changed to something smoother and icier. "And dear Percy? How is my nephew?"

"I haven't seen him for two months since my Companions were not allowed to accompany me to Na Iri, but his messages are exactly what you would expect."

A harsh smile brushed across Moira's smugly perfect mouth. "Percy always entertains, does he not? Not a deep thinker, our Percy."

"I cherish his good nature."

"That's one way of putting it. I'll see you at the palace soon enough, I am sure."

"Am I not to be given active duty?" Sun asked as a fresh and sharper thorn of disquiet stung in her heart.

"It wasn't a topic Eirene and I discussed." Moira turned to the pod's threshold. Seeing the Gatoi, she took a step back with a fierce grimace of disgust. "How have these . . . creatures . . . been allowed this close to the command node?"

Marduk gestured toward Prince João.

Moira wrinkled up her nose as at a bad smell. "I should have known. Is this exaggerated display of subservience really necessary, Your Highness?"

The prince had remained seated all this time, an arm draped casually along the back of the bench. "We were told to place all weapons on the floor. Each and every banner soldier is a weapon beyond compare, deadlier than any inorganic stock. But of course with Marduk's go-ahead I will give my people permission to stand."

"No need," said Moira before Marduk could answer. "Gatoi should never have clearance to enter the command node. Return to the concourse at once."

João uncrossed his legs and braced both boots on the ground. "Have you forgotten I am father of Eirene's only viable heir?"

"Since you never let anyone forget it, how could we?" said Moira Lee with a cold smile. "Marduk, I need a clean, sanitized pod right away."

The insult was so brazen, Sun could not let it pass. She struck with a frontal assault. "Governor Lee, isn't it true that certain clandestine activities in your past required you to give up your place as Companion to my mother? A place your cousin Marduk then took?"

Moira was too canny and experienced to do more than give Sun a flat look meant to express boredom. "What's your point, Princess Sun?"

"That you're governor of Lee House now, not Companion to the queen-marshal. So you don't have any say about who enters and who leaves her presence." She addressed the man. "Marduk Lee, Prince João accompanies me. My bodyguard, Octavian, will remain behind with the Gatoi cohort, since you're uncertain your own guards are up to the task of managing them."

"A palpable hit," said Marduk with a chuckle, although Sun

wasn't sure if it was the reminder of his cousin Moira's old disgrace or the challenge with respect to his marines that amused him.

Her father rose with his usual prowling grace and blew a mocking kiss to Moira as he walked past her.

Once the pod door closed and the pod detached, the private, secure, untraceable network Sun shared with her bodyguard and Companions pinged open with a message from Octavian: KEEP YOUR TEMPER IN CHECK. STAY FOCUSED ON WHAT LIES AHEAD, AS WE DISCUSSED.

A second pod plugged in and opened. Moira Lee and her adjutants embarked without looking back. It was a relief to have them and their sneers gone.

"Fabulous boots," said Marduk Lee to the prince, still looking delighted by the way the encounter had fallen out. "Aren't they a copy of the famous artifacts on display at the Celestial Shrine on Yele Prime? I studied those artifacts when I did a university year there. I'm sad to say your copy isn't fully accurate."

"I used more authentic source material from the inner sanctum that isn't displayed to the general public," Prince João replied with a bland smile.

The other man cracked a laugh. "That's right. You and Eirene first met in the Temple of Furious Heaven. Quite the coincidence."

A powerful voice broke over them like a sudden storm. "Sun! Why are you dawdling out here? I told you to come at once."

The hatch into the far chamber had opened while Marduk and João dueled. The queen-marshal stood at the threshold with the dome a vast space behind her. Her body was haloed by a gleaming three-dimensional reconstruction of the many solar systems that made up the Republic of Chaonia, making her seem larger than life, a figure burnished through great deeds and illuminated with a cunning and ruthless vision.

And by the look on Eirene's face, she was mightily annoyed.

3

Her Obsidian Eye

Eirene was a robust woman with the typical stocky Chaonian build and a black prosthetic in her right eye. A tiara of optical fiber laced around her short hair tied her into the military network. She wore the red-and-gold uniform appropriate to Chaonia's current Charlie state of threatcon, and a glower to match.

"What is João doing here?" She turned her incendiary glare on Marduk Lee.

Marduk shrugged, untroubled by her anger. "You're the one who gave him clearance to move through all areas up to fifth-level security. Don't look at me, Eirene. Look to how you favor your consorts."

"Come inside," she snapped.

Sun and João accompanied her into the chamber.

"Out," she said to the three officers and two Companions in the chamber.

After they cleared out and all the hatches shut, Eirene crossed her arms and examined her second consort with a hard stare given an ominous shine by the laser embedded in her obsidian eye.

"Why are you here, João?"

"As your consort—"

"None of that. Answer the question."

João smiled in the challenging way he used only on Eirene, leaving Sun to feel personally trapped between two rival sovereignties.

"I am here with my daughter, your heir, after her exceptional performance at the battle of Na Iri."

"I meant here, at the command node. You could have waited on the concourse or in my suite. You know your being admitted inside the node's security for everyone to see puts me in a compromised position. People already say I give you too much rope."

"To hang myself with?"

Eirene smiled sharply. "So they hope. I don't need your provocations right now with the border situation finally looking good for us. People believe you are a foreign agent who I am too weak-kneed to resist."

"I can't help what people think. What matters is you know I am not. Which reminds me——"

"Did you come here on the wings of Chaonia's most recent victory thinking to use my good mood to entice me into agreeing to your cursed project?"

"It's a great gamble that will benefit all involved if it succeeds. You know it is."

Sun took a step forward. "What project are you two talking about——"

"Quiet." Eirene's raised hand cut off Sun's question. She didn't even look at her daughter because she only ever had eyes for him if they were in any room together. "It's too expensive. Too risky. Too much of a long shot. If word gets out, the criticism will fall fast and hard and could destroy us both."

"Oh, come, Eirene. After everything you've done for Chaonia? You survived and thrived after the deaths of your father and brothers in swift succession left Chaonia desperate and vulnerable. You forced the Yele League to the negotiating table and beat them at their own game. You have freed most of the Hatti region from the yoke of the Phene Empire. No one can take your triumphs from you. No one would dare. Your legacy and your position are assured."

He gestured toward the command node's ancestral shrine. Every mission control node and public administrative center in the republic displayed the venerable lineage of the queens-marshal of the Republic of Chaonia. The first queen-marshal, Inanna, had chosen the eight-pointed star as the badge of her authority and passed the device on to her descendants. Her lineage was arranged on a virtual wall as a visually appealing ancestral tree whose queens-marshal were given a doubled and thus sixteen-pointed sunburst halo and whose branch lines had been carefully pruned away so as to be conveniently forgotten.

Eirene's three consorts had been given the courtesy of glowing portraits to remind people of the current queen-marshal's adeptness in crafting political alliances through marriage. The first consort, the inscrutable Lady Sirena of the Alabaster Argosy, who had left Chaonia with her two-year-old son three months after Sun's birth; the second, Prince João, with Sun; and the third, Baron Aloysius Voy of the Yele League, whom Eirene had married four years ago as part of a treaty that sealed the end of hostilities between the Yele League and the Republic of Chaonia.

"Still no child with Baron Voy, Eirene? What are you waiting for?" João's ambiguous smile flickered in remarkable contrast to the welcoming grin seen on the image of the gregarious Baron Voy.

"Spare me your false concern. It's bad enough you've given me a half-Gatoi daughter. Chaonians will never stand for a half-Yele child becoming queen-marshal."

"The long history of relations between Yele and Chaonia is certainly contentious." His smile sharpened to add mockery to the words.

"The Yele are arrogant pricks and always have been. But they bark at my command now."

He chuckled. "The Yele do hate you with such a particular venom, don't they? How lowering for them to be forced into a peace of your making, they who consider themselves the exemplar of all that is best amid the vast reaches of human civilization."

"Father, you don't care about the Yele," said Sun, trying to get a foot into the discussion.

"That's right. I don't care about the Yele. But I do care about my people and this project, which your mother should recognize could break Phene control over the banner soldiers once and for all."

"The Phene have a long-standing alliance with the Gatoi banners and their Conclave of Royals," Sun said. "I thought you two were trying to negotiate treaties with the separate banners to get them to come over to our side one by one."

"It's not that simple. More people need to ask themselves why banner soldiers who serve as auxiliaries for the Phene fight to the death even when they don't need to."

"Honor," said Sun.

"Compulsion," said her father. "Literal, physical, physiological compulsion. Engineered into them by the Phene."

"João!" Eirene snapped. "It's a wild theory, not a proven fact."

"Wild it may be, but I'll say it again and again, until you hear me, Eirene. My obligation and duty as a Royal of the Gatoi is to fight for the well-being of my people."

"Which is exactly why Chaonians don't trust you."

"They ought to, because in this case what would benefit the brave and honorable Gatoi banner soldiers would also benefit Chaonia against the empire. As you know perfectly well."

"What kind of compulsion?" Sun demanded.

"Silence," said Eirene. "Let me think."

Her father caught Sun's eye and tapped two fingers to his lips with a scolding tuck of the head. She could not shake the sense she was merely a potentially useful tool in her parents' personal tool kits, a piece held in reserve within the larger game they were playing. But she knew better than to protest when they were thus arrayed against her.

Eirene studied the images of her consorts' faces with a meditative frown. Something was going on behind Eirene's always-intense expression with its quirks: a pinch of the lips, a squint of her flesh eye, a glance at the deck as her right boot traced a straight line like the path of a thought. But Sun could not have guessed what it was, and the lack of any handle to grab onto irked her mightily.

"After all perhaps you are correct." Eirene took a turn around the room, pacing off a burst of energy.

"I'm correct?" João paused, looking suspicious. "In what way?"

"I've changed my mind. I'm giving your project the go-ahead."

João eyed her suspiciously. "What brings on this abrupt change of heart?"

"The realization that if it's true, and if you manage to do what you claim can be done, then the Conclave of Royals and the Gatoi clans will owe me."

"How like you, Eirene. So be it. Whatever it takes."

"It will have to be done in complete secrecy, totally off the grid. Do you understand?"

"I'll need a venue."

"I know of a venue that will work. I'll release funds from my private treasury. And I'll put out word that our raiders and operatives must send any captured Gatoi to my central authority immediately."

"There's a way to give cover to it, Eirene. You can say it's a prisoner of war camp."

"We're not going to say anything because it's going to be kept secret from everyone except you, me, and the people working there. My enemies in the court and the assembly will have a field day if they find out. To that end, you will disappear. I'll put it about that I exiled you in anger. That way no one will question why you're absent from court. You will vanish. You and your people will be allowed no net presence, no communication with the outside world."

"Not even with me?" Sun demanded. "Am I not the heir? Am I not to be privy to this sort of information?"

Incredibly, her father was nodding so eagerly that he tuned out Sun's question. "You'll see how valuable this is, Eirene."

"It had better be. I'm staking a great deal of reputation on your gamble. Because there's another serendipitous piece that came in with the battle report. An entire arrow of banner soldiers was unexpectedly captured intact and alive on an orbital station above Na Iri Terce."

"I didn't hear about that," said Sun.

"How was that managed?" João asked, still ignoring her.

"They got trapped in an inert engine well and were gassed into unconsciousness. They're still in stasis while the high command decides what to do with them. I'll have them officially declared dead on arrival and delivered to you instead."

He laughed, rocketing from combative suspicion to ecstatic glamour so quickly it set Sun off-balance. She hated being off-balance. "An entire arrow! Lady Chaos smiles on us. And with more to come."

"There won't be many, João. You know they're cursedly hard to capture alive."

"Where are you going, Father?" Sun twined her fingers together as uneasiness washed through her. She wasn't dependent on him while navigating the shoals of court, of course not, but she was used to having him at her back at all times.

"Your mother will explain." Grasping Sun's arm, he kissed her on each cheek, squeezed the hand on which she wore the ring he'd given her, and released her.

The main hatch opened. Eirene followed him to the threshold and, after a moment nailing a stare to his back, shouted angrily into the antechamber in his wake for all waiting in the outer chamber to see and hear. "And don't come back until you've learned not to flout security and my authority!"

The hatch hissed shut. Eirene turned to face her daughter.

"Sit down, Sun."

To remain standing in protest at this high-handed treatment would only provoke Eirene. Sun grabbed a chair set off to one side and guided it to the big oval strategos platform that doubled as a meeting table.

Stay focused on what lies ahead.

"I see you've learned some self-control," remarked Eirene as Sun sat.

"What is this project?"

"Stop asking. I won't tell you. And don't try to cajole your father. I'll instantly withdraw the funding if he tells you or you make any effort to dig out information on your own."

"Why am I not allowed to know? I'm your heir. Haven't I proven myself worthy? Isn't it time for me to be given more responsibilities? Assigned to an active-duty station on a ship like the *Boukephalas?*"

Eirene leaned on the edge of the platform. The pinprick red light in her eye winked a reflection back at itself from the platform's glossy surface. "You followed *my* battle plan well enough to push the Phene garrison fleet out of Na Iri System. *My* plan. That's not the same as being ready for independent action."

"Then what is it ready for?" Sun asked in the evenest tone she could muster as her hands closed into fists.

Eirene looked up. In the domed space above, virtual stars shone. The view zoomed out from the star systems that made up the republic to become a wider perspective.

"Tell me what you see," said the queen-marshal.

Without the beacon network, built long ago by the now-vanished Apsaras Convergence, each star system would be an isolated island of humanity separated by months or years of travel. Sun traced the routes between worlds and alliances—the Republic of Chaonia, the Yele League and various small independencies hanging on its skirts; the Phene Empire, the wealthy city-states of Karnos and their Hatti cousins long under the thumb of the Phene, the fractious Hesjan cartels and shifting Skuda factions; sacred Mishirru and its outlying dependencies; the isolated Ring of Ravenna; and the terminus frontiers. These routes had seamlessly knit together all inhabited systems until an unexpected and shocking collapse had destroyed every beacon in the central region of the network, leaving in its wake what was now called the Apsaras Gap, a vast, beaconless expanse at the heart of inhabited space. At that time, eight hundred years ago, tendrils of destruction like cracks had splintered out along the outer network to randomly rupture individual beacons, which meant some routes were left more or less intact while others had broken links. The now-cut-off star systems weren't wholly lost. They could still be reached by the venerable Argosies, powered by knnu drives and still in motion throughout the region even though their passage times were so much slower than beacon travel. Meanwhile, between the stars, the nomadic Gatoi fleets ran dark and cold, also powered by knnu drives and thus difficult to trace by anyone not born on one of the eleven clan wheelships, as Sun had not been.

"You recite names and histories, as any citizen can do," said Eirene. "But what do you *see?*"

"After the collapse of the central routes, Chaonia's three main systems were left in the most direct path between the Phene Empire and the Yele League. Although they weren't yet an empire and a league back in those days. They grew in power because the changes in the beacon system benefited them more than others."

"We have lived at their mercy for generations," Eirene said, warming to her favorite subject. "Everything the queens-marshal before me have done is to secure Chaonia's independence. This task is our chief duty, the reason for our existence. Our territories have been fought over and annexed by outsiders for long enough."

Sun broke in to forestall a lecture whose content she could quote in her sleep. "Once the Yele League was bound by the treaty you forced on them, you turned your attention to our border with the Phene."

"It was the next necessary step." Where Eirene directed her artificial eye a red laser traced the path of her campaign. "My grandmother retained Troia System when the Phene had to retreat and regroup after their attempts to invade the Yele League failed. Why did she expend so many resources to hold on to Troia?"

Sun managed not to roll her eyes at the question. She'd learned this lesson when she was seven, but it was exactly like her mother to keep treating her as a child.

"Because Troia System is a bottleneck. A gateway that can be reasonably well guarded by a strong network of orbital stations and a garrison fleet. Anyone trying to enter Chaonia from the Hatti region or from Karnos has to go through Troia."

"Yes. Its defensive value is critical to Chaonia's security. It's also a perfect springboard for our fleets. By moving outward into the Hatti region via the Kanesh route we are encircling Karnos one system and one beacon route at a time."

"If we didn't hesitate and instead pushed straight from Troia through our foothold in Aspera System direct to Karnos itself, then—"

"You're always getting ahead of yourself. That's my point. Do you appreciate how long it took Chaonia to get its neck out of the yoke imposed on it when it was annexed by the Phene Empire? How often our ancestors had to bite their tongues when the Yele called us weaklings and collaborators because we didn't have enough strength to evict the Phene when they first occupied us? How many times our people had to accede to the demands of the Yele League when they began strutting around crowing about how they alone had ever defeated a Phene fleet, and against such odds? Their endless speeches! How the Yele love the sound of their own voices! And let us never forget how my father and brothers died one after the next in battle against Hesjan raiders and their Yele instigators. Leaving me young and untried to continue the fight."

"You've told me the story more than once."

"Yes, so I have. I'll continue to tell it until you hear me. You've grown up with what I've built. You've never had to slog through the mud, not as I did. I've got those cursed arrogant Yele under control, for now. Meanwhile the Phene are a behemoth whose heads are only slowly waking to the prod of our tiny spears upon its ass end. With the defeat at Na Iri they'll not slumber any longer, nor blame their setbacks on the incompetence of their regional bosses. They'll come for us, mark my words."

"How far do you mean to go against the Phene?"

"If we take Karnos, we will control a permanent barrier to their aggression."

"If?"

Eirene barked out a curt laugh. "Does *when* suit you better? Karnos is massively protected because of its valuable placement and superb resources. We need those resources to refill our empty treasury. But its seven beacons make it hard to hold without an overwhelming military presence. That means in order to take Karnos we must first rebuild and refit all our damaged ships while also producing more hulls for the campaign. Production, repair, and inventory must double. Triple! The demands on our citizenry will be extraordinary. Campaigns are won and lost on supply. So your next assignment is to tour the industrial parks and the Fleet and Guard training camps on Molossia and Thesprotis—"

"What?" Sun jumped to her feet. "*What?* You're sending me on a show tour, to be trotted out for local banquets and inspect raw recruits?"

"Sit down!"

Sun gripped the edge of the platform.

"If you don't sit down, then I'll know you are unfit for further responsibilities."

Shaking, Sun sat hard, bumping the chair to one side.

"That's better. Your contribution to the victory at Na Iri burnishes you. Right now, we build. You will do your part, exactly as I command you to do. Do you understand?"

Keep your temper in check.

"I understand."

Eirene snapped her fingers. The virtual display of stars and lineages vanished.

"You're dismissed. There's a palace corvette waiting to take you to Chaonia Prime. Once there, you'll gather your Companions and leave for Thesprotis. Imagine how delighted all your hosts will be when the Handsome Alika arrives in town. Zàofù will provide you with the itinerary. It's already been arranged."

As the last word dropped, Eirene blinked on her personal net and turned her attention to a different task. Sun tried to rise but a weight had shocked her legs into immobility. She'd done well; she knew she had. Yet it wasn't enough for her mother. Maybe nothing would ever be enough.

As a hatch opened and two Companions strolled in laughing at a joke known only to them, Eirene caught Sun with the laser edge of her gaze.

"Why are you still here? Go."

History

While Octavian made his security check of their assigned cabin on the palace corvette, Sun settled into a seat and opened a virtual three-dimensional model of Molossia System. She spun the solar system, watching its six planets rotate on their axes and revolve around their star, positions shifting relative to each other.

Five of the planets anchored a beacon. Each beacon was tethered to its planet, caught like a far-flung moon at the farthest limit of the planet's gravity well. A control node attached to the outermost rim of the beacon's spiral coil monitored departures and arrivals. The coils of the still-working beacons had a faint and rhythmically pulsing phosphorus glow rather like a pulse. It was a weirdly soothing but also unsettling sight.

She pushed the view farther out to focus on the triple heart of the republic. The systems of Chaonia, Molossia, and Thesprotis were all scylla systems, each having five beacons although not all were still operable. Most importantly, the three systems all connected to each other, a rare, rich network called a Tinker-Evers-Chance convergence. This interconnectedness had made Chaonia, Molossia, and Thesprotis into natural allies, especially in the long interregnum after the collapse of the Apsaras Convergence. A tendency to trade and ally with each other in the troubled aftermath had caused their once-disparate cultures to meld. Eventually, under the first queen-marshal, the systems united as the Republic of Chaonia.

When Octavian sat down opposite he studied the three-dimensional map, then opened it farther to show all of the territory under the governance of the republic.

"What do you see, Princess?" he asked. She wondered if the words were a deliberate echo of her mother and how he could even have known what the queen-marshal had said.

"I see history." She traced a path with her right forefinger. "I see Chaonia, Molossia, and Thesprotis, the three core systems of our republic. I see the outlying territories brought in system by system by Queen-Marshal Inanna's successors. I see how Great-Great-Grandfather Yǔ kept the peace during the period Chaonia was a vassal of the Phene Empire. How Great-Grandmother Metis managed to retain control of Troia System after the Phene withdrew."

"Why did the Phene withdraw?"

"Is this a test?"

"You're impatient. I understand that. You have a hundred reasons why you should be racing out to the battlefront instead of following the queen-marshal's orders."

"I've earned a chance to be given a command on the front lines!"

"We obey the queen-marshal, Princess. That's my duty, and that's your duty. One day, if you pass the test that is your training for rulership, you'll be the queen-marshal whose orders people obey. But that day is not today. Now, why did the Phene withdraw?"

It was always a test, wasn't it? She squared her shoulders, moistened her dry lips, and proceeded with her usual dispatch.

"The Phene had to withdraw after the Yele League defeated a Phene imperial fleet at Eel Gulf. The Phene retreat left the Yele League as the big boss in our local area. So I also see how my great-aunt and grandfather and uncles fought constantly to maintain our independence from Yele encroachments. I see how the Yele contracted secret alliances with the Hesjan to make trouble for us. An unexpected Hesjan counterattack is how my uncle Nézhā died in battle at Kanesh."

"And then?"

"When the queen-marshalate passed from him to my mother, she decided to pursue a more assertive strategy."

"What strategy is that?"

"Offense, instead of defense. She defeated the Hesjan cartels and forced the Yele League to capitulate at the negotiating table. She increased ship and weapons production throughout the republic. Now she is using our control of Troia to push out via Kanesh and its beacon access into the Hatti region. That way our forces will eventually encircle Karnos."

She used two fingers and a thumb to open up Karnos System enough to see its twelve planets with their orbital ellipses traced in bold lines.

"Karnos has seven beacons, a wealth of resources, and a large military-age population. With the victory at Na Iri, we now control access to three routes into Karnos. Since two of the other beacons lead to the Gap, that leaves only two more functional ones. Both of them are paths into the heart of the Phene Empire. If we take Karnos—"

She broke off, then said, "*When* we take Karnos, we will control passage into the empire rather than the Phene controlling our right-of-way."

He nodded. "Correct. The military that controls the beacon routes will always have an advantage."

"Except the advantage the Phene have that no one else has."

"That's beyond our reach for now."

She pressed her lips together, eyes narrowing. Surely nothing was beyond reach, not for the one willing to risk all and accept no limits.

The pilots' chatter from the cockpit drifted over internal comms as the corvette moved into the traffic lanes. Departing COSY, the fleet's name for Naval Command Orbital Station Yǎnshī, was a slow and reluctant process. The incoming damaged ships needed to disperse to the naval shipyards elsewhere in Molossia System. Everyone had to navigate past a field of massive cargo containers slowly being attached to the Remora freighters that would convey them through the beacon to Troia. From Troia the supplies would be distributed onward via Kanesh to the garrisons and task forces in Maras Shantiya, Kaska, Tarsa, Hatti, and now Na Iri too. Na Iri was her victory. Or, at least, partly hers.

Octavian pulled the visual down to center on Na Iri System with its twin stars. "We've got a thirty-hour transit to Molossia Prime. Let's go back over the battle. See what you did right and what you could have done differently, and what was just the hand of fortune giving you a good set of tiles."

"The queen-marshal would say she laid down those tiles. That without the strength of her hand, none of us would have won at all."

"You can still lose with a good hand if you don't play well. But it is true Eirene has built Chaonia to a position of strength after we were bogged down for years fighting in Kanesh."

"You won your medals at Kanesh."

His wry smile bore the weight of memory. "Everyone my age and older fought at Kanesh at one point or another. The dead deserve medals more than I do."

Victory at Na Iri made her feel she had crossed a river and could now ask personal questions previously denied her according to the complex proscriptions of palace courtesy. "What was my uncle Nézhā like? You knew him."

"I was a marine assigned to the flagship, which isn't the same as knowing a queen-marshal as his Companions would. But still, he spoke to us all with respect and concern, as we expected. He was a good commander who attacked in the right direction at the wrong time. So. Shall we go over the Na Iri battle?"

She laughed. "You never stop."

His answering grin revealed a dimple that gave the graying soldier a mischievous air. "Just doing my job, Princess."

A DISPATCH FROM THE ENEMY

Dear Mom,

There's not much I can tell you given the content restrictions on personal comms.

As expected our graduating cohort has been split apart and sent off to round out understaffed squadrons. I have to admit I've been hoping to be assigned to the Karnos sector so I can fight those upstart Chaonians and their insolent queen-marshal. You'll probably be happy to hear that instead I've been assigned to a backwater station in an undisclosed location. Most likely a typical starting berth on a military cargo ship hauling a pair of lancers to guard against pirates. Lucky me. Quiet and boring. As you can guess I'm not thrilled, but every newly graduated lancer pilot has to work their way up to the big ships no matter how high their scores.

A comms speaker squawked, breaking the writer's train of thought.

"Apama At Sabao, please report immediately to Declarations and Tariffs."

Apama stopped typing as the speaker crackled back into silence. She was sitting on a shaded bench in the arrivals courtyard, holding the keyboard steady with her lower hands and typing with her uppers. Rising, she closed the tablet and stowed it in the outer pocket of her kit bag. There was no one else in the courtyard. She'd been the only passenger on the commercial freighter that had landed on this moon.

There were four doors out of the courtyard, one marked with the double-helix symbol representing the hegemony of the Phene Empire set above the characters for *Declarations and Tariffs*. Crossing the open area offered her a view to the sky. Even in daylight it was possible to see the pinkish-red neon-glow aura, shaped like a spiny malevolent starburst, that surrounded the system's second beacon and rendered it inoperable. The scarily luminous artifact gave this star system its modern name: Hellion Terminus.

The office was slumbering in the afternoon heat with all its windows propped open. Fans gamely stirred up an ice-tinged cooling breeze. Evidently this port was so boring and quiet there wasn't regular air and space traffic. She repressed a sigh. Still, her instructors had emphasized that hard work and high scores would get you a coveted cruiser berthing as long as you didn't slack and get comfortable.

Not that she ever really had a chance to get comfortable except when she was inside a lancer. That autonomy was her escape.

The civilian scribe on duty at the waist-high barrier yawned as Apama handed over the thin ceramic chip that held her duty orders. The scribe scanned Apama's retina, then plugged the chip into a security cube.

"First time here?" the scribe asked as they waited for the green light. A pregnant local woman, she spoke in Yele rather than Phenish.

"It is, thank you." Apama's own Yele was good, drilled into her brain via various accelerated programs.

"It's always everyone's first time here, and their last. It's pretty hush around here, d'y'follow?"

"I'm sure it's lovely."

As the scribe looked blankly at her, Apama racked her brain for any further compliments to make the anodyne comment sound less condescending. No need to create hostility, especially not when she was alone in unfamiliar territory. It wasn't that the Karnos sector and places like Hellion Terminus were the enemy. They belonged to the empire, after all. But they weren't imperial Phene either, not with those spindly two arms and stubby torsos and the impractical ways so many of them wore their hair. These people all spoke the common tongue of the hated Yele League as fluently as their local languages while mangling—some said deliberately—the Phenish taught in schools and required for administration.

She remembered the view from the courtyard where she'd just spent an hour waiting for no obvious reason. "The beacon aura is incredible. I've never seen anything like it."

"People say that all the time, but consider what it means for us. We used to be a busy and prosperous cultural hub on the main beacon route between Karnos and Yele."

"That was eight hundred years ago."

"Long before you Phene got here. We still tell stories about our glory days. Now we're just the end of the line. You must be from one of the bustling central systems, eh? They say the party never sleeps on the Triple As. Isn't that how the song goes?"

"I'm not from there."

The scribe narrowed her eyes, examining Apama in the way of folk who feel you've overstayed your welcome now that you aren't willing to accede to their demands. "Are you one of those shells? Pardon me. I'm not sure if it's an insulting term, but the only other one I know is worse."

Apama had run this gauntlet so many times in the course of her lancer training that she'd developed a special tone and a set of stock phrases. "I don't have an exoskeleton. But my womb mother does. Why do you ask?"

"There's a funny gleam to your skin. They say shells exude mucus constantly to reduce friction between the soft skin and the hard outer shell. Is your matron's skin chitin, or keratin? Or something else?" She lifted her two hands in the gesture of submission. "Pardon. I've never had a chance to ask before, and you seem nice."

What was taking the hells-bound clearance so cursed long?

"It's complicated. A dual endo- and exoskeleton was one of the earliest Phene genengineering projects. That was a really long time ago."

The scribe was nodding, the ribands and feathers of her triple-spined headdress waving in time to her head's movement. "Having a hard shell would be good for certain kinds of dangerous jobs that need extra shielding like shipyard work and ground infantry for planet-side invasion." Her gaze flicked over Apama's four arms, the true mark of imperial Phene. "Surprised to see you down here. Military transfers come in via military transport straight to the orbital station. You getting picked up?"

Apama wasn't sure if it was travel exhaustion that made her uneasy or the weird isolation of this dusty hellscape of a moon. She of her own self with her humble origins wasn't worth spit, but a fully trained imperial lancer pilot? That was another story. Ransom. Forced labor in a Hesjan cartel. Spiteful political murder by anti-empire insurgents. It wasn't common, but it happened.

"Do transfers usually get picked up here?" She wasn't going to reveal she had no orders beyond taking commercial transport to this town on this moon.

"I wouldn't know. Like I said, we don't get military transfers through this office."

A flash of green signaled completion. Apama managed to clamp down on a yelp of joy.

The scribe frowned as she popped the chip out of the cube. "Here's your scrip, Lieutenant. You'll need to clear it for entrance."

Apama pressed the scrip against the node embedded behind her right ear. The scrip initiated contact with a stream of new code from the security cube; her node recognized the official seal entwined with her individual cipher, and the link flashed on the cube. The scribe unlocked the barrier to let her through.

After the barrier closed behind her she set down her kit bag to get her bearings and roll down her jacket sleeves. There was no waiting area here, just two empty desks facing glazed windows along the front, and a lavatory off to the right.

She turned back to see the scribe still watching her. "Is there a base nearby?"

The scribe raised her eyebrows. "They didn't give you a map? There's a post at the east end of the port. It's one klick down the road."

"Is there a mobile connecting them?"

"A mobile? Oh, you mean a tram or a moving walkway. We don't have those here. My cousin runs a lift concession. Reliable and inexpensive."

"I'll walk."

Apama offered the hand sign for *thanks and farewell* and went out through the front entrance into the harsh light of day. There, she halted under the eerie aura of the infected beacon and the blast of a hot sun. The landing pads and stevedore platforms spread to either side behind the arrivals center, punctuated by drab warehouses and a squat control tower painted so dull a beige it was insulting. A hardworking gantry crane refused even a splash of color was at work unloading the *Fake Vestige,* the freighter she'd come in on. She shaded her eyes against the sun's glare and tried to pick out the freighter's crew—Captain Ann and her clan had been a lively bunch who'd welcomed her into their shipboard routine—but the crane blocked her view. They couldn't help her with this anyway.

She started walking along what appeared to be a repurposed runway, glad the moon was big and dense enough to have close to standard 1 gravity. The adaptive fibers in her uniform absorbed and rechanneled the heat, but the light was intense and the air was like breathing inside a furnace. Unfortunately the town was dreary and ugly, with blocky, pragmatic buildings covered in solar soaks and not a scrap of decoration to suggest glory days of any kind. The place didn't even boast a cathedral spire to enliven its torpor. Not a single soul was out and about.

Despite what the scribe had said, in older days this resource-poor system had probably been little more than a nondescript rest and refueling stop for ships on their way to far more interesting places, ones easily reachable across the immense distances of space because of the beacon system. Now it was one of the ends of the line in the extended lattice of the Phene Empire, a lonely military outpost built on an outcast shore of the Gap.

Why *had* she been sent via commercial freighter to the moon rather than being given a place on a military transport that would have gone direct to the main military orbital habitat where she'd be stationed? It was odd to be dumped down here. It almost felt like being abandoned. Like one last piece of nasty hazing for being a shell-born who had the temerity to think she could qualify as a lancer.

She shook off the thought. It was too expensive to train a lancer pilot only to discard them. Nevertheless, she licked her dry lips nervously as she reached the entrance to the fenced-off area. It was definitely a post, not big enough to be a base. The technician first class on duty sat on a tall stool pulled up to a counter. Apparently she was dozing, eyes closed, her chin resting on her cupped upper hands and lowers folded in her lap.

Apama tapped on the guardhouse's transparent shield.

The soldier startled upright as Apama's insignia registered. "Lieutenant!"

A retinal scan and her scrip granted her access past a double set of barred gates. The soldier had straightened her uniform and waited beyond the shield and gates, standing with tense expectation.

"Sorry, Lieutenant. Usually nobody is out and about before planet-rise."

"Do you not have many security concerns down here dirt-side, Technician . . . ?" She checked the insignia. "Ir Bodard."

"I don't make a habit of sleeping on duty, believe me. It's just hmm I have two small children, and they're both sick right now."

"That sounds rough. My best friend had a passel of much younger cousins we spent a lot of time babysitting. But still . . ."

"It won't happen again, Lieutenant." The soldier's bunched shoulders relaxed fractionally. "Anyway it is absolutely dead down here. There's nothing on this rock to interest pirates. All the action is at the margins of the system."

"Chasing smugglers?"

"That's right! And long patrols too, out to neighboring systems."

"Via knnu drive?"

Ir Bodard brightened as at happy memories. "Weeks and even months out in the Gap sometimes."

"Ever tangle with Chaonian ships?"

"Out here? No. Military fleets use the beacon routes. We hunt outlaws and brigands along the old knnu transit lines. Long stretches of boredom alleviated by short sharp shocks."

This was an unexpected development, a wrinkle no one at lancer training had ever bothered to hint at. Apama couldn't decide whether to be excited about its potential to explore ancient pre-beacon trade arteries or horrified by the idea of months stuck in the belly of a ship.

"What sort of shocks?"

"Hmm. You ever serve on a ship with a contingent of Gatoi auxiliaries?"

"No. I've never even seen one in the flesh. Just heard stories."

The technician indicated the healing scar running from the corner of her left eye to down below the left ear, and the braces wrapped around her upper right elbow and lower right wrist. "Don't mess with them. Or even talk to them. They're touchy about their honor."

"That looks painful."

The technician had a cocky grin. "I gave worse than I got."

"I didn't know Gatoi could be beaten in a straight-on fight."

"They can't. But I didn't rely on strength and speed. I'm not a technician first class for nothing."

Apama laughed appreciatively, wanting to ask for details but aware of time passing with her orders still at a dead end.

"So I guess you're wanting the quarterdeck?" the technician added, watching her closely.

"I am. Thanks."

She plugged a map overlay into the scrip. A floating screen popped up in front of Apama's left eye, generated by her imbed, and marked a path.

The post wasn't large, but command hadn't stinted on its construction. For example, it had covered walkways to mitigate the blast of the sun, each support post molded to depict one of the mythical beasts of the long-lost Celestial Empire. The eaves and roofs of the walkways and the building entrances were elaborated with curlicues in a joyful floral style that set her at ease. The building that

housed the quarterdeck boasted sliding entrance doors framed by
an augmented-reality waterfall on each side. Crossing the threshold
prickled her face with a cool breeze like crossing through a guild
portal.

The main room of the quarterdeck's service lounge was silent
and dim except for a figure seated at the welcome desk, reading a
book while snacking on pistachio nuts. When the soldier did not
look up, Apama gave a cough.

The soldier startled, spilling half the container of nuts. "Dyusme! What in the saints-forgiven hells are you doing sneaking
in like . . . Oh. Sorry, Lieutenant." They leaped to their feet and
saluted quite unnecessarily.

"I'm reporting in. Here's my scrip."

"We don't get transfers down here."

"And yet here I am."

The soldier—a specialist by rank—reluctantly accepted the scrip
and slotted it into the security cube with their lower right hand.

"This place seems quiet," Apama said, just to say something.

"It usually is," remarked the specialist in a morose tone, gaze
flicking toward the doors through which Apama had so untimely
entered. "I *usually* get a lot of studying done. Hoping to make senior specialist this go-round."

They waited in awkward silence until the specialist frowned,
opened a virtual keyboard, and tapped into it. "No orders in our
queue for you, Lieutenant."

"There's no orders for me?"

"No. Transfers always go straight to the station. This post is for
local liaison and cargo routings. Are you sure you're at the right
place?"

She wasn't sure at all. Nothing made sense to her about the
cursory nature of the orders or the way they'd been sprung on her
after she'd thought she was headed to a ship squadron like everyone else in her cohort. It had been arbitrary and sudden.

The doors whisked aside. A person hustled in wearing the insignia of a lieutenant senior grade, the swagger of a lancer pilot, and
the welcoming smile of a jolly happy soul.

"Ei! You must be Apama At Sabao. Sorry I'm late. Meant to be here before but I got hung up running errands. Saints alive! Have you ever tried to buy malted barley in a slack-jawed town like this one?" He halted in front of Apama and stuck out his lower right hand. "I'm Abigail Ca Konadu, adjutant to strike squadron leader Colonel Ir Charpentier, who you'll come to know by her call sign, Nails. Sorry I'm late. Oh, wait, I said that already. Come with me, Lieutenant."

Apama grabbed her kit bag and followed him out. Ca Konadu trotted instead of walked, so Apama trotted alongside, kit bag thumping on her back.

"There's a gunship waiting for us. You can call me Gail, by the way. Gale Force is my call sign because I talk a lot. Never mind. Here we are."

They passed into the support zone for a landing pad where a gunship sat in vertical lift position. The mighty rim of the gas giant around which the moon orbited was nudging up over the horizon, an astonishing sight Apama had no leisure to savor.

A senior chief gestured impatiently. "Move! Our lift window is closing."

They pounded up the ramp. Gunships weren't troop transports, and yet a bewildering number of passengers and crew were crammed on board. Apama got split away from her companion and stuck on a bench between the fragrant sack of malt and a rather handsome young Gatoi auxiliary. Even having only two arms he had a lean, powerful symmetry and grace of form. The striking appeal of his facial features was emphasized by the almost indiscernible pattern gleaming beneath his skin. When he caught her checking him out he blushed and turned toward the Gatoi sitting on his other side. He spoke in a language she could not understand, and the other Gatoi glanced at her and laughed. A moment's scrutiny of the hold counted eleven of the savage fighters, who were generally assigned out in eleven-person units called an *arrow*. After what the technician had told her, it seemed rude and also dangerous to try to talk to any of them, much less attempt to examine the fascinating neural patterns all Gatoi had. So she didn't.

Lieutenant Ca Konadu was strapped in across the hold next to the senior chief, the two chatting up a storm as if they were old acquaintances. For Apama, the sack of malt and the auxiliary were equally silent companions as the gunship launched for its five-hour journey to the orbital station. She popped in earplugs and dozed, thankful to be headed at long last for her final destination.

It therefore came as an unpleasant surprise that instead of being ushered off the docking ring to the station's quarterdeck to start intake proceedings, she and the sack were hustled to a different dock and onto a utility shuttle. Her companion shifted the heavy sack into the arms of a senior specialist.

"I got everything. We can launch," Gail announced.

The pilot and copilot turned to give Apama a slow once-over. The pilot drawled, "You're the whole reason we've been sitting on our asses at anchor for three days waiting to leave?"

"I'm transferring in for duty," she said, glancing at Gail for help.

"We are full up on utility pilots," remarked the copilot, lips curling, "so I don't know where you think you're headed. And you don't look one bit like a triple-A fast-track heritage seed, do you? In fact, are you a—"

"I said we can go now," Gail broke in, "and you know who gave me my orders."

"Nails gave the order, yes, we know. This shell is a *lancer* pilot?" the pilot asked with a sneering curl of the lips.

"I earned my place through hard work and high scores, just as you did," Apama said in a coolly neutral tone.

"Nah, his scores weren't that good, which is why he's a utility pilot and not a lancer like us, Apama. I can call you Apama, right?" Gail turned his back on the sour-faced pilots and headed for the passenger benches set against a bulkhead away from the cockpit. "Come sit by me. There'll be a good view out of the porthole."

They strapped in side by side. The senior specialist stowed the sack in a locker, gave Apama a cursory nod of acknowledgment, and exited into the cargo hold.

A comforting exchange with the station control tower initiated. The shuttle disengaged, withdrew from the station, and slotted into a departure lane. Once clear, the shuttle accelerated around the magnificent curve of the striped gas giant, soon leaving the station and the planet-sized moon behind.

Gail talked the whole time, for which Apama was grateful as it became clear he was flooding the silence on purpose. So it was that Gail was telling a long story in a deliberately comic fashion about how he had crashed his first lancer into a shiverpeak wilderness and spent a month hiking to safety with a broken arm and the lover he had just had a nasty breakup with when Apama saw the fleet.

The ships in their tight ready formation were tucked behind a rare triple confluence of three of the gas giant's moons. There were hundreds: assault cruisers, light cruisers on the wings, and an astounding ten dreadnoughts, the jewels of the fleet.

"What are all these doing here?" she asked, shocked into speech. "There's nowhere to go from here except into the Gap."

"We are all destined for death," said Gail cheerfully.

The pilot hailed one of the dreadnoughts. "Bravo Charlie six seven, this is six seven Unicorn three on your nine two niner four mark eight four six one. Checking in with a full tank of mass and five souls on board."

"Six seven Unicorn three, copy your contact on my nine two niner four mark eight four six one with five souls and a full tank. We've got you cleared for hangar five. You're clear to kick to tower. Welcome back. You're the last ones in."

"The last ones in for what? Why no heavy frigates? Where are we going with this boss fleet?"

"Those are the questions we're all asking, aren't they?" Gail replied. "We don't know."

It turns out you won't ever read this letter because we are allowed no mail privileges on this mission. I'm going to keep writing anyway and pretend you'll read it.

I never expected to end up on a high-level assignment like

this so soon out of flight school. If you ask me it's a bit strange. I asked my sponsor, a nice lieutenant senior grade whose name I can't share, if the fleet is short of lancer pilots after our recent losses to Chaonia's military at Na Iri and Tarsa. But he said the *Strong Bull* has their pick of experienced people. So the mystery of why and how I'm here, and why the fleet waited at anchor for three days until I got here, hasn't been answered. Yet.

Meanwhile I was shown to my rack, a tiny cabin sleeping four in two stacked bunks, which is the luxurious accommodations junior officers get. My new friend hustled away because he's adjutant to the lancer squadron commander and has other duties. Now I'm just waiting.

A click and a hiss of air warned Apama that the hatch into the cabin was about to open. She was seated cross-legged on the bottom left rack with her tablet, lowers holding and uppers typing. As the door slid aside she closed the tablet, set it on the mattress, and swung her legs out to stand and face three strangers. They wore gold lieutenant senior grade bars on their flight suits, sleeves studded with combat stars. As they stepped into the cabin the door shut behind them. At once the space felt crowded and intimidating.

Apama interlaced her lower hands and cupped her right upper hand over her left upper fist as she gave the arrivals a nod. They echoed the gesture.

"Our fourth was transferred out very suddenly three days ago," said the one with short, curly black hair. She crossed her upper arms and set her lower-right hand on her hip. "So you're her replacement?"

"Apama At Sabao. Lieutenant junior grade."

The three exchanged glances again, then looked at the photo projection Apama had fixed to the locker end of her rack: an image of her and her mom on the vacation they'd taken to the Grove after Mom finally qualified for her medic's license. They were standing on one of the landings of the Great Helix, the vista behind them blurred by the camera angle. Mom had her arms around little Apama, her only child; there was nothing that felt safer than being encircled by her mother's arms.

Apama had learned to get the obvious out of the way immediately when she was going to have to deal with people over a long period of time, rather than let their curiosity fester. "My mom's a shell. I am too, technically, but my caul was removed after birth so there's nothing to harden into an exoskeleton."

"That's lovely and thank you for sharing, but what we're really interested in is if you passed your lancer training like everyone else in this squadron," said Curly Black Hair.

"I did. Surely command doesn't assign unqualified people to fly combat?"

"I just wanted to hear you say it. I'm Delfina Ba Hill." Her shoulders relaxed as she uncrossed her uppers. "My call sign is Splash. You need to remember it, starting now."

"Okay." Apama tried not to ask many questions because in her experience people would answer what they wanted you to ask, not what you wanted to know.

The svelte blonde said, "I'm Ana Ir Corsária. Call me Cricket when we go out."

"Go out where?"

"I'm Renay Ar Helm," said the one whose hair was styled in a rakish pink-and-purple wedge cut.

"Our own Deadstick," said Ana with an evil grin, elbowing Renay.

"Where's your flight suit?" Delfina gestured to her locker. "We launch in sixteen."

"Launch?" Apama blinked about five times, but she couldn't orient herself to the abrupt shift.

"Our last live field exercises before we leave Phene imperial space for the Gap," explained Delfina. "You do have a flight suit, don't you?"

"Uh, yeah. It's ready to go."

"No time to waste! You'll be my double."

Apama stripped without hesitation, knowing they would notice the nubs at her joints and the unusual glistening of her skin. In such close quarters, they'd see her naked sooner or later so they might as well get an eyeful now. But they politely looked elsewhere.

Delfina tapped a foot like she was the kind of person who got bored easily. "The squadron commanders decided we're going to use the time while the vanguard gets moving to practice maneuvers. It'll take a while to get this boss fleet going."

"Are all the ships in this fleet equipped with knnu drives?"

"That's right. You ready?"

"Ready."

They absorbed her smoothly into their group as they strode along the passageway. She swallowed an adrenaline pulse to keep a bland façade.

Knnu drives on military ships.

A secret mission on the edge of the Gap.

None of this was normal procedure. The situation was so disorienting she didn't try to memorize their route, not yet. Instead, she cooled her mind the way she'd learned to do when young, working through a calming routine like a puzzle falling into place that allowed her to block distractions and just focus.

"A bunch of targets have been laid down out by the dead beacon's control node," Delfina explained. "We launch in our pods and do high-speed runs at them, paint them, and simulate weapon launches. Should be just like combat training back in flight school, basic skirmish tactics stuff. Some kind of mission prep."

"Yeah," chimed in Renay, "but make sure you nail every shot."

"We've got a tally running against the *Steadfast Lion*, and it's neck and neck," added Ana.

"Do you know what the mission is?" Apama asked.

"Only the shadow knows," said Delfina cryptically, "which means no one knows."

"Someone has to know," said Apama.

"You have too high an opinion of the high command," said Renay, and Ana said, "For all we know, we're just hunting smugglers."

"With this size of a fleet?" Apama objected. "That seems unlikely."

They reached the flight deck to find the hum and bustle of a well-trained crew making ready for launch. A heavy cruiser like the *Strong Bull* had a complement of sixty-four lancers divided into four flights of sixteen lancers. Each flight was further divided into four pods of four, and of course each lancer carried two pilots in the back-to-back configuration that gave lancers exceptional maneuverability.

"We're the tailenders," said Renay in an undertone, kindly filling her in. "Lancers fifteen and sixteen in the fourth flight."

"Gale Force is our flight leader," added Ana. "Our flight call sign is Mace. Nails is our squadron commander. Her flight's call sign is Hammer."

"*Obviously,*" said Delfina.

"Second flight is Club," said Renay, and Ana finished, "And third flight is Gurz."

Delfina pushed past pilots toward their assembly position at the port tube. "Let me take the lead, Apama. I don't want you to be the spanner in the works since I'm guessing you've never launched from a heavy cruiser."

"Only in simulation."

"Dyusme," muttered Delfina.

Many of the pilots and deck crew paused for a quick double take, registering Apama's presence with speculative looks that made her feel even more conspicuous than usual. Her hands were sweating, but she locked the nerves away into the puzzle grid and set it aside. A more-experienced pilot had been transferred out in order to make way for her. She had no idea why, but the pressure was on to perform well enough to justify her place here. So she would perform.

A dreadnought had eight launch tubes. The deck crew was so efficient she found herself suited and sealed up into a life-support membrane and dropped into a lancer before she had time to get her bearings on the flight deck. Each lancer was a rhombus, an octahedral diamond able to shift direction quickly. Its nerve center was a back-to-back set of flight chairs surrounded by a flexible te-lemetry lattice that gave its two pilots a 360-degree orientation. Fac-toring in their eight hands and exceptional hand-eye coordination and spatial dexterity meant Phene lancers could turn, adjust, and maneuver with a delicacy and speed that enemies of the Phene respected and feared.

The previous pilot had stuck an icon on the control panel rep-resenting Saint Laranthir, staring right at Apama with his smugly handsome face and perfect leafy-green goatee. The words *I've seen more of the world than most* had been neatly written at the base of the control panel. How annoying.

The internal comm crackled, and Delfina said, "You got a smoke?"

"What is a smoke? Some kind of animal?"

"No one knows, but my bet is it has something to do with ar-tillery. My aunt's an archivist on Anchor, so I got a taste for deep diving into the vaults that contain fragments from the Celestial Empire."

So Delfina was a Triple A, a privileged heritage seed grown up among the well-connected people in the capital systems. Nothing like Apama and her mom struggling at the dregs' end of shattered Tranquility Harbor.

Set it aside.

A burst of bell tones alerted them to launch.

"Here we go," said Delfina.

It was just an exercise, Apama reminded herself. Nothing rid-ing on this except her reputation within this possibly resentful squadron and, of course, the respect of her rack-mates. No big deal. She allowed herself an ironic smile.

"Mace Sixteen, you are fourth in line to launch."

A holographic display bloomed in the transparent lattice that wrapped the pilots' chairs. The lancer clunked as the launch tube rolled it a quarter turn. She lay on her side in the gentle gravity of the cruiser.

"Mace Thirteen, you are go. Mace Fourteen, you are go. Mace Fifteen, you are go. Mace Sixteen—"

Her screens went blue, and the lancer was kicked free as a weight like a juggernaut slammed into her chest. A twist dropped them into space. The weight on her chest eased. She clicked back her controls to let Delfina pilot in the wake of the stream of lancers. That was easy enough.

What surprised her as they raced around the *Strong Bull*'s hull was the sudden, spectacular view of the dead beacon and its radiant halo in high orbit. The beacon's aura had a weird murky texture that reminded her of a poisonous algal bloom that had choked Tranquility's sea harbor in her youth.

"You ready?" Delfina said through their internal comm. "We each need to paint at least two kills to claim bragging rights over *Steadfast Lion*."

Dots marked the position of lancers diving past the outermost coil, laser bursts painting "kills" on shifting ovoid targets that, in their turn, tried to paint hits on the lancers with soft laser fire.

As their pod altered trajectory, falling into line to make their pass, four of the targets made evasive maneuvers to avoid fire and, in the process, passed through a coil of the aura. Lights flared starkly on their bulbous command nodes. The targets swung around, turning from passive pigeons into aggressive bogies as they began firing on the incoming lancers in erratic bursts of full-strength laser cannons.

Chatter flared out on the main comms line.

"It's shooting back, it's shooting back!"

Tower said, "Fail-safes are down. I say again, fail-safes are offline."

A flare of light. An explosion. A lancer spun off at a sharp angle, spewing debris.

"We have lost contact with Targets 13, 14, 26, and 28," said the tower in the tight voice of a person struggling to stay calm. "Trying to reestablish control."

A slab of debris careened through the nearest string of aura, lost to sight in the murky shimmer. Just as she let out a relieved exhale, the slab reemerged at a different and unexpected trajectory. She flinched.

"Dyusme!" Delfina rolled the lancer out of the way, but a glancing blow from the debris sent them tumbling through the outermost finger of the aura.

An uncanny shudder ripped through the lancer.

"Shit, shit, my membrane detached. What in the hells—" Delfina coughed, probably grabbing for an emergency oxygen supply.

"I've got it," said Apama, all hands steady on her controls.

She swung around to get a wider view, manipulating her four controls. As the forward lancers scattered, the rogue targets darted after them, hauling some of the other targets in their wake as if they were linked together, and probably they were. That meant the chained targets were likely going to remain passive.

"Pakshet! My membrane won't reseal! Got to hook up emergency oxygen." More coughing, and a wheeze.

"I've got it," said Apama as the calm of imminent action descended.

The targets were still shooting, spinning with a kind of energetic glee as deadly fire laid out strings like traps. Apama tumbled hard, spinning to get new angle, then thrust toward the rogue targets. Two lancers had been hit, forcing them to roll away. Another pod from the Mace flight was retreating at a hard burn to get out of range.

Her sight narrowed in. She flashed through the telemetry and sorted out the best order. Her first burst took out Target 13. Then 14, flowering into splinters as her laser cannon cut across it in three fierce lines.

"Watch your back, watch your back," said Delfina in a hoarse voice between sucks of oxygen. The ride was too rugged for her to get a clean seal.

Apama tipped into a tight loop. Space was silent so she couldn't hear the shot that almost punctured her lancer, but she could have sworn her lips tasted its heat a breath away.

"Missed us!" hissed Delfina.

Renay and Ana darted past, targeting 28. As it blew up, Apama came all the way around in back of 26 and nailed it.

The debris rattled her shields, knocking their trajectory two degrees sideways. The lancer was flung straight into one of the outermost wraithlike spiral strings of the dead beacon's aura.

The air inside her helmet got suddenly thick like she were breathing sludge. Her vision turned cloudy with speckled spheres and writhing, glowing rods. A scalding spike of pain jammed into the back of her head. Whispers bled into her mind as if the pain were the transmitter.

"The uprising at Sena has been put down and order restored. Unfortunately we have credible reports that one rebel cell vanished without a trace. The threat from the Chaonians looms larger than ever . . ."

"Operation Styraconyx commences . . ."

"The council does not agree with your selfish quest . . ."

A net of stinging prickles flashed across her face, and she shook herself back into focus. Her lips were dry, and it hurt to swallow, like she had caught a cold. Saint Laranthir's handsome face had melted into a smear of green goo, but otherwise the cockpit looked unchanged and undamaged.

"Got my seal!" The comms crackled into life with Delfina's welcome voice. "Holy fire! You were ice, so calm!"

"All lancers return to base. All lancers return to base."

Three repair shuttles raced past her, headed for the crippled lancers. She followed her pod back to the heavy cruiser. Felt an instant's red-hot panic as she targeted her assigned landing slot on the cruiser, but her brain flattened back to its chill as she said, "Can you take us in?"

"Got it," said Delfina.

Apama was glad to give the other pilot this face-saving measure, not that it had been Delfina's fault her membrane detached.

They slid in, were jerked to a halt, and rolled over. The lancer's hatch popped as the membrane unsealed. Hands hauled her out, people speaking to her as she nodded as if nothing out of the ordinary had happened. The pain in back of her head had vanished as thoroughly as the rebel cell in Sena . . . and what was that even? A fuzzy memory of a teledrama half recalled from her childhood?

She found herself ringed by her grinning pod, standing in front of a woman wearing a commander's wings and triple bars augmented by an impressive number of combat stars. Colonel Wulandari Ir Charpentier was expostulating at a dour-looking engineering officer. The engineer was a true exoskeleton-enhanced individual, whose Tadeian-infused and age-hardened caul encased his body in what resembled a skin-hugging but still flexible sheath of armor.

"And how in the hells did that fail-safe cascade collapse happen?" the colonel demanded of the engineer.

"Those targets have never malfunctioned before. Not on my watch. I can't vouch for the civilian contractors. They're a local hire. Besides them the only anomaly in this exercise that I know of was the presence of the dead beacon's aura."

"It's just particulate debris."

"I'm as baffled as you are. We won't rest until we figure it out." The engineer saw Apama and gave her a long, searching look followed by a curt nod of recognition.

"Get it done," said the colonel. As the engineer hustled away, Ir Charpentier turned to frown heavily at her. "Lieutenant At Sabao, I presume."

"Ma'am."

"Seems you have ice in your veins. Well handled, Lieutenant, especially given the way your double got disconnected. Three lancers were damaged, but we suffered no casualties because of your quick action."

"Thank you, ma'am."

"Welcome aboard, Ice. Get cleaned up. I'll debrief you and your pod in an hour."

Apama looked down, surprised to find her flight suit spattered with green speckles of drying ooze.

"Hey hey," said Renay, leading them through the postexercise bustle of the flight deck. "The last becomes the best. Don't you all forget it."

Pilots slapped her on the shoulder. Deck crew clapped. One

cluster of pilots gave her a long, nasty once-over complete with matching sneers. They'd be trouble. But right now she let it go and said to her companions, "We've got a long voyage ahead of us. Please tell me the mess hall has sorbet."

"Ice for sure," said Ana with a laugh. "You've got your call sign."

6

A Flower in Full Bloom

Sun was dozing in one of the recessed bunks aboard the palace corvette when the warning bell chimed.

"Set beacon stations. Transition in ten minutes."

She rolled out of her rack and up to her feet. Octavian looked up from where he was cleaning two guns commonly called *stingers*. He stayed where he was while she remained standing, opening a virtual porthole. The famous marble-blue glamour of Molossia's fourth planet shone in the distance, but it was the spiral coils of its beacon that drew her eye. Some people claimed they could see shadow and light moving deep within the coils. Some said a little piece of your human soul was torn out of you each time you passed through a beacon, and that this growing congestion of fragments of spirit was why the partial system collapse eight hundred years ago had happened. Beacon engineers knew how to keep the surviving beacons running, but no one fully understood how they worked, or why some had failed while others had survived.

"Five minutes. Take all weigh off the ship."

Octavian was already strapped in, but he did pin down the disassembled gun parts with a mesh slung over the tabletop. She hooked her feet through a stability rail.

The gravity cut. Her unbound hair rose off her shoulders.

The transition bell rang. The ship rolled once, and everything vanished.

No sight. No sound. No breath of circulated air on her face. No shadow or light. Only a void empty of sense and existence like a presage of death and defeat.

Then they dropped out of the beacon and, engines firing, slid into Chaonia System above Chaonia Prime. She was home. Victorious but not satisfied.

She pinged her Companions to let them know she was arriving. It took hours longer for the corvette to descend and land in the military airfield on the shoreline of the capital city. Once there, she and Octavian took a Hummingbird out to the palace complex in the bay. A ping from her father dropped in as she was flying, but she ignored the message rather than give the controls to Octavian. The bodyguard kept, an eye on her technique but did not interfere as she landed the 'bird on the restricted airstrip that served the residential wing with its multiple nested gardens and courtyards.

The Honorable James Samtarras was waiting for her on a stone bench in the shade of a portico overlooking the landing pad. As the rotors wound down and Sun and Octavian disembarked carrying their duffels, he pulled his flatcap off his head and waved it enthusiastically.

"All hail the conquering hero! Alika is writing you a song."

Sun swatted him on the shoulder in greeting, then indicated the complicated three-dimensional virtual spreadsheet he was building up from the half of the bench he wasn't sitting on. "What are you doing?"

"As soon as we got the news Hetty told me to make a list of the various installations, factories, assembly halls, and workers' guilds we're likely to tour on Molossia and Thesprotis." He closed a hand into a fist, and the interlocking web of lines and points vanished. "What is up with that anyway, Sun? It sounds dreadful. Did you lose your temper with your mother?"

"I did not lose my temper, James."

"A little touchy about that, are we?"

She added a dart of her own. "I saw your father and your brother."

"That's punishment enough! I'm so sorry you had to endure His Officiousness and His Pompousness." He jumped up to offer Octavian an exaggerated mock salute. "Welcome home, Sergeant

Major. You've done well to keep our scamp of an heir out of trouble, and alive."

"I haven't received your training report yet, Honored James," said Octavian.

James gestured with his cap toward an open gate where an older woman with the weathered face and upright posture of a combat veteran had placed herself on guard. "You can't fool me. Isis sends you my reports."

"I did see them," Octavian admitted, "and it looks to me as if you and I will be taking extra sessions in small-arms fire."

"Why this torture?" James groaned with eyes cast to the heavens in supplication.

Sun started walking. "Let's go."

As they strode toward the gate a miniature pteranodon sailed into sight from over the tiled rooftops to land on Isis's shoulder.

"Your Highness, welcome back." Isis fell into step behind Sun and James as the pteranodon tucked in its wings and cheeped at the new arrivals. "Early reports suggest you did well at Na Iri."

"I accomplished the task I was given."

With the queen-marshal out with the fleet Sun had expected to find a bare-bones staff at the palace compound, like the single pair of guards on duty at the landing pad. But where were the rest of her Companions? It wasn't the lack of Alika and Perseus that fretted her. Why hadn't Hetty been waiting for her at the landing pad alongside James? She refused to ask, and instead cast her thoughts back to the unexpected encounter with Moira Lee.

"James, I need you to do a deep dig into Lee House," she said in a low voice.

"What do you mean?" He glanced up and down the long outdoor passage that led past half-deserted administrative offices to the residential wing. No wasps were allowed within the palace precincts. Since Sun's private ring network allowed her and her Companions to communicate beneath a sophisticated cloak of white noise that was usually impossible for spybots and tracking devices to penetrate, he was checking for physical eavesdroppers.

"I want to know why Moira Lee was visiting my mother at

COSY. Seeing her there raised a tickle down my spine. Something is going on."

"I know that tickle. How many times did it get us into trouble when we were young?"

"Good trouble."

He swept a high flourish with his cap. "You'd say so."

Isis remarked, "You're still young, you sprouts."

"Don't argue with me, James," Sun added.

"Why would I bother, since I'd never be allowed to win?" He tugged the cap on over his curls. "So what exactly are you looking for? Moira Lee was one of Eirene's Companions in their youth. After her older sister Nona Lee died, Moira was appointed governor of Lee House and had to give up her place as Companion."

"Actually," said Octavian, who was walking in front but always listening, "Moira Lee had to give up her place as Companion before Nona Lee died. She was having a sexual affair with Queen-Marshal Nézhā. Favoritism of that kind between rulers and Companions is quite against court protocol, as Moira knew perfectly well. Nézhā's consort found out about it and demanded Moira's removal from Eirene's household, as was within her rights."

"The same Hesjan consort who betrayed Nézhā and was responsible for his death?" Sun asked.

"No one saw that coming, it's true, and we could never prove it," answered Octavian. "But get your events in the right order and you'll have a better chance of figuring out if there's something to the instinct that's nagging at you."

"Do you have any other insights, Octavian?"

"No, Princess. That was all common knowledge on the flagship back in the day. Anything more would have been above my rating."

"Isis, how about you?"

"I'm just an average grunt who wasn't near the court then," said the much-decorated Isis, not that she wore her medals any more than Octavian ever did. "But we are approaching the sixth anniversary of the death of the eight-times-worthy hero Ereshkigal Lee. Maybe Lee House has plans to honor their daughter's sacrifice with a procession and wants the queen-marshal's imprimatur."

"Maybe. James, start digging."

"In case you forgot," James retorted, "Lee House controls the Ministry of Security, Punishment, and Corrections. I don't fancy them throwing me into their undersea oubliette if they uncover me sneaking into their secure data."

"I keep you around because you're better than everyone else at what you do. Am I not right about you after all?"

He grinned. "You're always right, Sun. I am, in fact, the very best at what I do."

And he was, which was exactly why she could not ask him to look into her father's secret project. Her mother did not threaten lightly. Sun couldn't take the chance that James's digging would alert Eirene's intelligence trip wires.

They had skirted the entrance to the queen-marshal's inner courtyard and entered the consorts' wing through a side passage rather than its gilded front gate. Startled attendants ceased their dusting and sweeping to stand back with hands pressed respectfully together as Sun passed.

Because she was unmarried Sun still lived in the consorts' wing. As heir she had her own secondary courtyard and suite of rooms for her Companions adjacent to the large courtyard suite reserved for Prince João. Its gate was guarded by twin statues of guardian lions. She relaxed as she crossed into her own territory at last.

The rooms were quiet, reflecting her recent absence. Dust motes swirled in streams of light angling through windows. A small janitor scrubbed the passage's marble floor with a cheerful whir. It was traditional for the queen-marshal to employ human attendants for mundane tasks like cleaning to display her wealth and her generosity. Sun had early on replaced the people assigned to her area with mechanicals that James made sure couldn't spy on her. Except for Octavian and her Companions' companions—cee-cees who like Isis combined the services of bodyguard, valet, and attendant—there was only a trusted cook, two factotums, a high secretary, and a clerk to round out her personal household.

As they broke out of shadow into the daylight gleam of the private courtyard, a crescendo of exuberant melody greeted her. Alika was standing in his favorite spot beneath the red gazebo. He didn't look up from his guitar because music was how he most comfortably communicated. The clack and shush of bladed fans opening and closing in time to the song's ecstatic rhythm traced Candace's martial practice around the gazebo. Isis and Octavian watched with approving nods. The cee-cee whirled to a halt, snapping the fans closed and hooking them on her belt in one smooth motion as Alika brought the piece to a close. He flashed a smile toward Sun.

"Perfect," she said.

"Your training scores have remained excellent, as expected, Honored Alika," said Octavian.

"Shoot me now," muttered James.

"And yours too, Candace," added Octavian.

"Your Highness." Candace bowed. "Sergeant Major. Welcome home."

Sun greeted the cee-cee with the appropriate words of reply but was already searching the courtyard's alcoves and shade-drenched benches for Hetty. Before she could ask, the sound of hurried footsteps brought her head around. The Honorable Perseus Lee barreled out of the service alley carrying a covered bowl.

"Sun! I was going to go with James to meet you, but it just happened." He jolted to a halt in front of her and with one of his radiant smiles tipped back the lid. "Look!"

Sun stared into the bowl's water, which bore a strange undulating quality but was apparently empty. "What am I looking at?"

"Medusas. Duke finally got them to reproduce in the lab."

Now she saw tiny translucent bell-shaped domes and dangling tentacles as sporadically visible fine lines washing back and forth in the water. Her eyes opened wide as she took it in. "Everyone told him it couldn't be done."

He slid the cover back on.

"Oi! I want to see," objected James.

Perseus started walking toward the alley. "I'd better take them back. I probably shouldn't have disturbed them, but I wanted to show you right away. I'm sure it's a good omen. They're said to be immortal."

James looked at Sun. She waved a hand, giving permission, and he raced off.

"Percy! Wait up."

The door to the kitchen area slid aside. Navah, Hetty's cee-cee, came out with a tray laden with a teapot, cups, and an artfully arranged platter of sweet bean cakes and deep-fried sesame balls, still warm. The pleasant aroma chased through the air.

"Your Highness! Welcome home! Cook has baked your favorite sweets."

Navah placed the tray on the table under the gazebo and began setting out the cups with her usual brisk efficiency and charming smile. Alika had started playing again, plucking out bits and pieces of melody as he did when composing. Candace gave Sun a skittish glance before going over to help Navah.

Sun frowned as it became clear Hetty wasn't here to greet her.

In a low voice, Isis said, "Your Highness, it's the anniversary of her father's death. She's at the shrine."

"Of course," Sun muttered, swept by a dark wave of shame. "I should have remembered."

"Hard to reckon time in any one system when you're traveling by beacon," said Isis kindly. "Octavian, I have a few things to discuss with you now you're returned. Shall we go to the office?"

Sun left her duffel in the courtyard for the factotums to deal with. After changing into slippers on the entry porch, she walked through the empty audience hall to the private reception room. Its balcony overlooked the palace's Memory Garden of the Celestial Empire. The pleasing arrangement of stone pavements and promontories, waterfalls and still pools, and flowering trees and scented bushes usually soothed her restless soul. Today she barely glanced toward the bright peonies and azaleas. Instead, she cautiously approached a small side room, off the balcony, which was set aside for the household shrine. Because Companions officially left behind their birth households to become part of hers, the shrine had a raw, fresh aesthetic unlike the well-worn traditional altars of long-established houses.

The Honorable Hestia Hope knelt on a pillow in front of an elaborately carved open cabinet arranged with a lamp, flowers, stones, and images of the deceased. Her long black hair was braided back in a casual fishtail adorned with a white ribbon to signify her mourning. Her posture was exact, hands pressed palm to palm and head bent just enough that her fingertips brushed her forehead. A pulse beat softly in her pale throat as she took in breaths after each long stream of prayer.

Standing in the entry, Sun let the flow of the beloved voice spill over her. By the slight lift of her chin and faintest blush on her cheek, Hetty had become aware of Sun's presence. But of course, being Hetty, she finished the full cycle of prayers at the prescribed tempo before she bent in a final bow toward her father's image. Only then did she rise in a rush of movement to face the princess.

"You're home, my dearest Sun. You have come home." Hetty's smile was a flower in full bloom.

Sun took a step toward her and grasped her hands tightly in her own. Only then, as if shocked awake by Hetty's cool skin, did she remember to glance over her shoulder. The shrine was in full view of the reception room and balcony, so she released her. Words failed her, as they often did when this stark, vulnerable emotion clamped her in its jaws.

"I know you're furious at the queen-marshal's command," Hetty said with her usual instinct for pushing straight to the heart of things, "but think, dear Sun, how well it benefits you."

"How does a six-month glad-handing tour of factories and training camps benefit me when I should be out on the front lines with the fleet?" She broke off. "Wait. I got a message from my father."

She blinked three times to activate the private link and its encrypted message, sharing it with Hetty via her ring network. Her father never used voice only. He always appeared in hologram, a gauzy ghost of a figure wearing spectacularly rich garments. This time he wore a long sleeveless embroidered coat that, hanging open, revealed a knee-length fitted gold tunic over loose trousers.

Hetty whistled appreciatively at the bold geometric patterns of the coat.

"Don't share this message with another soul, not even the sergeant major."

Hetty made a move to step away, but Sun grasped her elbow. "We are one soul with two bodies, are we not? You will always know all that I know."

"I have to go under the highest restriction of security for this project. That's Eirene's ears only, in case you are wondering how restricted it is. Not even Lee House is in this loop. So you won't hear from me for a while. This is the chance I've been waiting for, working for, all my life. We can break the hold of the Phene . . . I've said too much. Say nothing about what you heard. But be sure I'll be keeping an eye on your activities. Sun, your stubbornness about your Companions needs to end. You must pick Companions from Jīn, Bō, and Nazir to fill out a full complement. You should replace the Hope girl, too, with a Companion from the governor's line of Hope House instead of that disgraced Yele-tainted side branch."

"Not a chance," muttered Sun.

Hetty squeezed Sun's hand.

"You cannot needlessly antagonize the seven Core Houses. You need the support of all their ministries to rule effectively as queenmarshal, or to rule at all, given people's distrust of me. You should know better by now. I shouldn't have to be blunt. This goodwill tour can become a useful expedition to break in new Companions. Here are my suggestions—"

With a grimace of irritation Sun blinked off the sound, although she recognized the shape of the names on his lips. "Alika, James, and Percy are the only ones I trust. Besides you and Octavian, I mean."

"The prince—"

"Yes, I trust Father too, of course. I'm his most valuable resource. But I'm also a piece in whatever strange game he's playing, which I'll never fully understand because I'm only half Gatoi and wasn't born and raised on the wheelships as he was."

Hetty's smile had a laughing quality that always softened Sun, reminding her she could be wrong once a year. "I meant to say, the prince is right. Here's why."

She gently released Sun's hand and walked into the reception room and out onto the balcony. Leaning on the railing, she waited for Sun to come up beside her. Sunlight gilded the central pool, flashing on the backs of bright koi. Wind chimes sang. Fan-shaped gingko leaves flashed in the breeze as flower petals spun down to float on the water.

"You need all seven Core Houses. You know that. You need each ministry's support in full. Each of us Companions is your link that reassures each House you honor them."

"I'm not replacing you no matter what my father says."

"Hope House is well content that I am here. Prince João does not fully understand the politics inside each House or why Hope House would find it safer to stow me within the palace rather than their halls."

"Of course. But the other three just want to put more spies in my household."

As one, they glanced toward the open doors and the dim audience hall beyond. A rectangle of light marked the opening onto the courtyard where the other Companions and their cee-cees were, presumably, waiting for Sun and Hetty to return so they could enjoy a celebratory tea.

"James and I have done a little search," remarked Hetty with a mysterious smile.

"Are you saying you have some honorables in mind? Ones the Houses haven't already put forward? Or the ones I've already rejected?"

Hetty waggled her eyebrows.

Sun pressed a sudden kiss at the corner of Hetty's tender mouth, which tasted sweetly, sharply, of ginger. "How did I ever manage those years you were away from me on Yele Prime?"

Hetty pulled away and beckoned toward the garden's lovely expanse. It seemed uninhabited at the moment. But a stray gardener might be working behind a luxuriant shrub, or the personal attendants of the third consort could be taking an opportunity in the queen-marshal's absence to stroll amid the flowers and pavilions. Still, she allowed her left little finger to touch Sun's where their hands rested side by side on the railing.

"I've come back now and will not leave again."

"I know." Yet Sun shifted restlessly, rubbed her eyes, gave a sharp sigh.

"Dear Sun, you're agitated. What is wrong?"

"Would it be too much for my mother to offer me a scrap of praise? Tell me I've done well? Say she's proud of me?"

"That's not her way. To give you jobs to do? That's how she shows you that she thinks you're fit. She'd not have sent you to the front if she thought you incapable of a command. She placed you in position to allow for you to lead the crowning blow yourself. That is your praise. What higher can there be?"

"Then why send me on this ridiculous tour when there are more battles I could be sent to fight?"

"Logistics win campaigns. This will help you. People will be grateful that you care enough to visit where they live and work. They'll see you as they have not seen the queen-marshal for years except in news reports. You'll come alive to them. They'll take your part. And also you will learn while on the ground all the extent of our capacities. Our resource load, our freight, our training schemes. What we have in excess. What we lack. You'll need this knowledge later, mark my words. And one last thing."

"Campaigns are won and lost on supply," Sun murmured.

"That's right, and we have pushed both far and fast. Chaonia must rebuild—"

"—repair, and reinforce our lines. I know. I know." Sun frowned. "It's true we took a lot of damage at Na Iri. It's true we've gotten stretched thin all through the Hatti reaches. Imagine what might happen if the Phene knew how vulnerable we are and decide to attack while we're reeling from all our victories."

Hetty nudged her shoulder to shoulder. "Let's go have tea and speak of Duke's medusas."

"It's quite a feat," Sun agreed, accepting the change of subject.

In better humor she accompanied Hetty back to the courtyard where the others were seated, except Percy, who could never sit still. He was hanging from the gazebo roof's rim doing pull-ups but dropped gracefully to the ground as Sun and Hetty came up. Duke, his middle-aged cee-cee, hurried out of the service alley drying his hands on a cloth. Sun invited him to take the cushion beside her rather than serve with Navah and Candace so he could fill her in on the details of his research. Duke had been an unemployed marine biologist whose family had gone into debt to pay for his advanced courses. He had only applied for Vogue Academy's special course for "personal attendant" out of desperation when his clan's home had come within days of being sold to clear the loan. His serious but equable disposition matched well with Percy's impulsive, disorganized cheerfulness.

Thinking of the dismissive things Marduk and Moira Lee had said about Perseus annoyed her all over again. She sent the three cee-cees away and afterward cupped her hands around a bowl of tea. Her four Companions regarded her each with their own particular brand of patience or curiosity.

"You all know we're headed for Thesprotis and Molossia for six long months. So we are going to learn everything we can and make all the alliances and create all the goodwill possible. We will be ambassadors for the palace, but also for this great mission our republic is engaged in—"

James gave a choked sound and pitched forward at the waist, barely avoiding smashing the last bean cake with his face. "It hurts. It hurts. Can't you skip the deadly dull speeches with us?"

"I liked the sound of it," said Percy brightly.

Alika picked up the baritone ukulele he'd made famous on Idol Faire and tried out "This great mission our republic is engaged in" with several different melodies.

Hetty smiled, and when Hetty smiled, the universe smiled.

James popped back up, snatched the last bean cake, and stuck it in his mouth. "So good."

Sun glanced toward the doors that led into the kitchen area. No one was in sight. Through a half-recessed door to the right

she could see Octavian and Isis seated in comfortable chairs with
sake, talking over security and tutoring arrangements or perhaps
reminiscing about shared campaigns from the ancient days of
their youth.

She lowered her voice. "Percy, why would your aunt Moira be
visiting the queen-marshal at COSY?"

He shrugged. "She wouldn't. Governors never leave Chaonia
Prime when the queen-marshal is on campaign."

"Nevertheless, she was there. Was there ever any talk in Lee
House about her scandalous affair with Queen-Marshal Nézhā?"

"Queen-Marshal Nézhā?" Cheerful Percy drained away into a
frowning, uncomfortable visage. He picked up his teabowl but set
it down without drinking. "I never heard anything about that. But
I was only eleven when they sent me to you. Afterward I rarely saw
them once they realized I wasn't going to fill their ears with details
of your habits and secrets. They stopped talking to me. It's not that
they value loyalty. They require it."

"But Moira had to give up being one of my mother's original
and most trusted Companions because of the affair, didn't she?"

"Do we have to talk about this?"

"Yes, we do."

He sighed, shoulders slumping. Hetty cocked a critical eyebrow
toward Sun. James shook his head disapprovingly. Alika plucked
a single discordant chord. They all protected Percy, each in their
own way, but Sun had never underestimated Perseus Lee, not as
most people did.

"My gut is telling me this is important. I have to figure out why."

"Whenever my mother wanted to needle Aunt Moira, she
brought up how Moira had disgraced the family by getting ban-
ished from the Companions. She never said why, at least not in my
hearing. I guess they both knew perfectly well. It was just the nasty
way it always unfolded, like she was trying to goad Moira into
slapping her so then she could cry about being slapped."

James winced. Hetty settled a restful hand on Percy's forearm.
Alika watched in his usual silence.

"After your aunt Nona Lee died, and Lee House had to replace her as governor, is it possible Eirene was involved in having Moira named as Nona's successor?"

"Ha!" His laugh was like scorched earth. "As if Lee House would ever let any outsider poke grubby hands into its inner workings. Not even the queen-marshal."

"But Aisa Lee is the second child, isn't that right? Wouldn't it be expected that she would become governor after Nona?"

"Yes, but she was passed over in favor of Moira, who's youngest. Let me tell you that even after nine years I can still quote entire ranting speeches by my mother complaining about the Lee House council snubbing her unfairly."

"Wow," said James. "I've met Aisa Lee at court functions with your father, who's as handsome as he is scary. But she just seemed a little possessive and self-centered."

"You have no idea what a monster she is, and I hope you never find out. Do we have to keep talking about this, Sun?"

"Yes. Your mother's resentment doesn't explain why Moira was chosen as governor in place of her. There's something here I need to know, but I don't know what it is."

He ran a hand over his close-cropped black hair. "There was something funny about how Aunt Nona died."

James perked up abruptly. "Nona Lee torched a refugee camp in a retaliatory action that killed thousands of innocent people."

"That's not how she died!" Sun blinked on her net and did a quick search. "She died in a conflagration in Troia System after Phene sympathizers attacked one of our military bases. It's true a lot of refugees died in the neighboring camp. Collateral damage. But Nona Lee gave her life to salvage the situation."

"That's the Channel Idol story, the official story," said James. "That Phene operatives bombed the camp and Nona Lee died nobly during the rescue operations. Scuttlebutt whispers it was Nona Lee's operation from the get-go. It's said she accused the camp of being a front for Phene operatives and torched it on the principle of one guilty, all guilty."

"There are always conspiracy theories floating around deep in the twitch."

"I'll ping you the squib I found. I dug it up fifteen minutes ago while I was admiring the medusas. And I'm just getting started. For example, it's not clear if Nona Lee's body was actually found. If not, then whose remains took her place at her funeral?"

"Did you hear any rumors of *that* when you were little, Percy?" Sun asked.

Percy set both hands palm down on the tabletop, expression drawn and eyes weary. "You know why I don't talk about my family. Because they are awful. And as awful as my mother and Aunt Moira are, Nona was rumored to be the awfullest of all. The whisper even inside Lee House was that after she died they had to fill in one wing of the underground prison with concrete to hide her illegal experiments."

Sun exchanged a glance with James, and he nodded, fingers twitching as he started another dive. Percy kept talking, gaze fixed on his hands.

"The greatest fortune I ever received was when the House council picked me over my twin to come to you." He looked up at Sun, dark eyes brimming with unshed tears. "And you kept me on. I'm so grateful."

"They can't all have been awful," said Sun, turning over his comments in her mind. "What about the eight-times-worthy hero Ereshkigal Lee?"

Alika played the bravura opening run of his now-famous *Aspera Drift*, a musical tribute to the desperate battle fought almost six years ago at the edge of Aspera System, one quick beacon hop out from Troia.

"The adults are all awful, I mean. Not my cousins and siblings. They were still too young. My mother tried so hard to make Ereshkigal into a nasty little version of herself, but she couldn't ruin her because Resh was the best." Percy's smile ghosted back, tenuous and sad. "Resh used to drag Perse and me around, and sometimes when we had to our cousin Manea—"

"Purse?"

"Persephone. My twin sister. We were like the hooligan gang with Resh the ringleader."

"The eight-times-worthy Ereshkigal Lee was a hooligan?" James asked with a skeptical grimace.

Percy laughed. "You have no idea, and I pinkie swore not to tell. Well, Perse made me swear and threatened to bite off my right pinkie finger if I told."

"Bold! I like that!" said James.

Alika shook his head.

Hetty patted Percy's forearm with a sympathetic smile. The splay of her fingers against skin drew Sun's attention for a moment too long.

"It's weird, though," Percy went on in a musing tone. "Perse vanished after Resh's death. My mother told me Perse had a nervous breakdown, but that doesn't sound like her. She was always the bossy, conniving one. I missed her for so long."

"I remember," said Sun. "You cried every day for the first year you were here. It's the reason I didn't send you back like I did with the tedious rats the other Houses tried to foist on me."

His wry smile held regret, not self-pity. "Then I got accustomed to not having to deal with my mother and let it go. Sun, why does this matter to you so much?"

"I didn't like the way Moira Lee treated my father."

"What can Lee House do to him—or to you, for that matter? Sure, you're half Gatoi, and most of the Gatoi fight for the Phene, but the prince has always kept his side of the alliance with the queen-marshal. Anyway you're Eirene's heir. That gives your father a lot of clout. And a lot of protection."

Sun considered the table and its lack of bean cakes and deep-fried sesame balls, since they had eaten them all. As she pinged the kitchen for more, the door into Octavian's office slid fully open, and he and Isis walked out.

"Princess, the manifest of casualties has finally come in. You requested to be informed right away."

She jumped up. "I want to be involved in the funeral rites before we leave."

The others rose too, moving away, all but Perseus.

Sun studied his preoccupied expression, so different from his usual way of being present in each moment. "Percy, are you okay?"

"I can't ever forget I left Perse stuck in a pit of venomous centipedes."

"It wasn't your fault. Or your choice."

"I know. But what worries me is they kept her back, instead of me. They thought she was the one they could turn into them. It makes me sick to think of what she could be like now, stuck in their trap. Still, I guess it's out of my hands."

With an effort he took in a breath. The desperate, damaged boy who had come to her nine years ago was shucked away into the restively cheerful young man of twenty who could make almost anyone smile.

"We are going to have so much fun on this tour, Sun. I already have lots and lots of ideas to entertain our various hosts. It will be smooth sailing and an unending barrel of laughs."

7

Introducing the Wily Persephone and the Loyal Solomon with the Predictable Result of Their Foray into Battle

My best friend and I sit side by side on the intercontinental train. I've got my legs tucked up under me as I slump over the tablet that's resting on my thighs, fiercely studying for the final exam. Solomon sits with perfect straight posture and feet flat on the floor, eyes forward, on schedule and prepared like the star cadet he is. Around us, other travelers work, listen, read, and doze as the train speeds through a seemingly endless expanse of coniferous forest.

Solomon touches his chin and tips his hand at me in the sign for *good luck*. He stands and walks toward the back of the car, out of my sight because I don't turn to watch him go. I'm too busy with the tablet, which projects a three-dimensional model of the transportation system of the Republic of Chaonia. Interlocking threads create a shining network of transport hubs and lines across the surface of the planet and out into space, where they link up into the intersystem beacon routes.

A glitch burns through the model. It winks out, winks back in, then scatters in a fizz of bubbling sparks as the hum of the train stutters, kicks in briefly, and sputters away into an ominous quiet. I look up.

People start muttering as the train sighs to a stop like a huge creature letting out a death exhale. A man wearing the red-and-gold military uniform of the Republican Guard of Chaonia jumps up and presses both hands against a window.

"I saw something in the forest," he says loudly enough that everyone stops talking and turns to look out the window he's leaning against.

There's a lull of thick silence. Everyone, including me, is holding their breath.

An explosion booms, the sound tearing through my body like shrapnel. The car shakes and the windows ripple but don't shatter. The explosion is followed by another vibration with a pitch so low I can't hear it except as a jolt. My tablet fizzes to life, visuals flashing, then goes inert.

Dammit. A premonition of disaster whirls through my mind as my heart hammers, but I manage to hold on to just enough self-possession to roll up the thin tablet and stuff it into my sleeve pocket. No emergency lights are flashing. There aren't any lights at all.

The military man leans back from the window and glances around the carriage.

"Anyone here a transportation engineer?" he asks. "It looks like the explosion hit the power grid. Maybe if we go to the engine car we can figure out a workaround."

I raise my hand like I'm in class and unsure if I have the right answer. "I'm a cadet, studying transportation engineering. I'll go with you—"

A thunk interrupts my offer. The soldier recoils and flops onto his back with a slab of window sticking out of his chest. Just sticking there like a malignant sculpture.

My mind goes blank, and my skin goes cold. No one in Chaonia believes the war will ever come here, not after what Eirene has accomplished as queen-marshal. The Phene would have to slice through Troia's gate and Molossia's defenses to reach Chaonia Prime.

A packet of glowing ion fléchettes punches through the shattered window, slamming into the train wall and into several of the passengers too. Blood spatters onto my cadet's uniform before I can register the scope of the carnage. Screams and shouts break out as people scramble for cover. A blood-spotted child sitting in the opposite row starts to bawl as their parent tries frantically to shove them under a seat.

Finally, *finally*, my academy training kicks in, and I drop to the floor. The military man is lying on his back not two meters from me. He convulses, and the slab of window stuck into his body tilts crazily and with a terrible sucking sound tears out of his chest. Blood bubbles up from the shocking gash. My mouth has gone dry and my hands are shaking as I crawl to him and press hands to the gaping wound, trying to stop the blood.

Another soldier slips in beside me. "I'm a medic. Didn't you say you're an engineer? Can you get the train running?"

"I am. I can." Every citizen of Chaonia has a job to do, and I need to do mine.

Another spray of fléchettes hits the remaining windows. I twist onto my back, as if that would save me, but nothing hits me. According to the timer that's always running in the background of my network it's been 117 seconds since the glitch, even though it seems like an hour.

Focus. *Focus.* Check all parameters. Note all details. Find a way to the engine car and fix the power grid to get the train away from the attack.

Because I'm now on my back on the floor I see at an odd angle up through the banks of windows. Treetops seem to hang upside-down into the blue sky. Shade-striped gliders skim over the trees with an ease that strikes me as beautiful, until people drop down from the gliders' rigging onto the railway embankment and launch themselves at the train cars.

They aren't imperial Phene. That's easy to tell because these invaders have only two arms. They are something worse, the Phene's savage allies who seek honor through death in combat. We call them the Gatoi. These soldiers don't feel pain because their bodies are threaded with some kind of neuro enhancers.

The invaders climb the slick sides of the train cars. They pound energy axes against the heavy-duty clear windows, bolts sizzling out from each impact like webs of lightning. When panes crack the soldiers launch themselves through, heedless of the gouges the edges leave in their flesh.

I grab for my stun gun as a young man looms above me. He's no older than I am and yet already in the heart of the war, ready to die. The worst thing is his face, intensely focused and utterly impassive as he swings up the ax. I am nothing more than an object that's gotten in his way and has to be destroyed.

I trigger the stun gun. Its net of sparkling current coalesces around his body. He spasms as the charge jolts through him. Then, of course, his enhancers suck it up and turn it into energy, and the ax slams down onto my head.

There's More Going on Here than Even the Wily Persephone Can Know

I'm bounced out of the simulation so hard I'm momentarily stunned. We're using one of the academy simulation rooms, a large chamber that looks like a padded cell with gray surfaces that tilt and move so we can role-play and take practice performance tests.

Solomon points at me with a two-finger gesture. "You are so dead, Perse."

"Dammit!" I pull off my headset and throw it at him, but for a big guy he has incredible reflexes and dodges with a laugh. "Where in the Sixteen Courts of Hell did those Gatoi soldiers come from? I'm supposed to repair the train, not get my brains hacked out."

"Just adding a little extra color."

"The color of my brains is not going to be in the final exam. Why are you such a jerk to me when you play antagonist?"

He grins, all teeth and taunt. "How do you know a direct attack won't be part of the test? If you don't survive, you can't fix the train. If you don't fix the train, you don't pass and you don't graduate. I'm doing you a favor and watching your precious ass, just like I always have."

My heartbeat has slowed enough that I can laugh bitterly as I snag my headset off the floor. "Fine. You have a point. Shall we do it again? Only this time without the berserking Gatoi and their fucking axes."

"You'd rather face the Phene with their scary-ass four arms and their creepy Riders?"

"The power grid exam is to gauge my diagnostic and repair speed. Not survival."

"I'm just a squarehead, Perse. After graduation I'm going to get sent straight to the front lines. You need to know how to survive."

"Yeah. Yeah. I get it." Frustration thickens my voice. I flash to a horrible vision of failing and having nowhere to go. Nowhere but home.

"Hey, Perse. It's okay. You've got this."

He settles a heavy hand on my shoulder and squeezes. When we're standing side by side the top of my head only reaches his epaulets. Were he not the person I trust most in the academy I'd find his size and confidence intimidating. He comes from circumstances so opposite to mine that he understands needing to get away from a home that will kill you either in body or in spirit if you don't escape.

I clench a hand as I battle not to burst into tears. I'm not a calm person; I just fake it. "Shut up. Let's go."

Before we can tug on our headsets for another round a ping chimes through the air, followed by an expanding halo of orange light, which I perceive just beyond my right eye. It's the academy signal for an urgent incoming message.

A banner of coruscating words throbs in front of my eyes.

Stone Barracks cohort report to the Eyrie in 30 minutes

I groan, my pulse accelerating like I'm back in the simulation. "This can't be good."

He elbows me. "You worry too much. We're so close to graduation it's probably just an hour of Mandatory Fun. Maybe we'll get to pretend we're contestants on Idol Faire, performing the classics." He claps out a backbeat. "'It's like that, and that's the way it is.'"

I flip him a rude hand gesture as I blink at the exit. The seal slides open to reveal the equipment hall with its shelves and bins. We turn our headsets, gloves, boots, and coveralls over to the clerk, another academy student. Every cadet at the Central Defense

Cadet Academy works extra hours beyond their duty rota. It's how citizens pay for an education. Her black hair is pinned up in a bun, not cut short like mine, and she's neatly dressed in the brown fatigues that are our daily uniform. She offers the shy smile of a first year not sure if she can be friendly with fifth years. Solomon and I both smile back so brightly that she looks a little dizzied.

"Aren't you captain of the championship rugby team?" she asks with a worshipful gaze at Solomon.

"So I am. Cadet Solomon, at your service." He reads her name tag. "Do you play, Cadet Phan?"

Stricken to silence by his question, she shakes her head. Her flustered smile would be funnier if I wasn't sure some disaster is about to explode in our faces.

I tug on Solomon's beefy elbow, which my wholehearted yanking doesn't budge by a millimeter. "By my estimate it's going to take us twenty-two minutes to get there."

"See you again," he says with a sly wink that makes Cadet Phan blush.

As the equipment hall door slides closed behind us we head out at a jog across a grid of playing fields, taking the straightest course toward the Sun and Moon twin pagodas and the sky-tower that stand in the center of the academy's giant campus. We're well matched; he's faster and stronger, but I've got endurance.

"She's a baby first year, Solomon. Don't even think about it."

"Who said I was thinking about it? I was just being polite and giving her some social capital. She's probably already pinging members of her cohort."

"'Large, not-so-bright future marine can speak words of two syllables!'"

"'The dashing future marine was accompanied by a future engineer who was entirely unable to speak because she was contemplating the glorious career that awaits her. Someday when he's leading a phalanx of grunts on a rock-grabbing mission in a border system, her engineering unit will be assigned to dig latrines for him.'"

Even though we're running I have good enough aim—speed,

trajectory, and angle—to punch him on the upper arm, not that I stagger him. He's a massive packed bundle of muscle honed to its highest peak of performance.

"Weak ass, Perse."

"Fuck you, Solomon."

He starts a little dab of a victory dance while still running, stumbles, and barely avoids falling flat on his face. We both start laughing, then hush as we pass a corridor of classrooms in session. We jog down a walkway shaded by solar panels. The run has drained off almost all of my anxiety by the time we enter the central compound. Second-year cadets on gate duty salute us as we dash past.

We race around the edge of Heaven Lake, where bottom-feeding plow-headed cephalaspis cruise below surface-breathing lungfish and miniature long-snouted ichthyosaurs. By the time we pound up forty-five flights of stairs to the observation deck of the sky-tower my legs and lungs are burning. It's a climb we cadets do three times a week. The view is worth it.

The Eyrie is the top observation deck of the sky-tower, walled with transparent ceramic for a 360-degree panorama of the campus and its encircling forest. Thirty klicks to the north, and easily visible on a clear day, rises a sky-tower that's a clone of this one. It's part of an industrial park built for the war effort; twice a year we cadets get run through a seven-day training exercise on its avenues and blocks while the workers get their holidays.

Our Eyrie has an open floor plan, with classroom lattices in one quadrant, couches and comfortable chairs in another, and a cafeteria in a third. The fourth quadrant is a staging ground for various activities involving a sky pier that sticks out from the observation deck. Solomon, still breathing thunderously from the climb, gives me a thumbs-up because there's no rappelling or light-glider equipment being made ready for training off the sky pier. I whisper a prayer of thanks to the Celestial Immortals for this small mercy.

That doesn't mean we're out of danger. Our instructors have something evil planned. The question is what.

While they wait, the other Stone Barracks cadets are lounging in the couches and chairs. Our rack-mates, Minh, Ikenna, and Ay, wave us over to where they're sprawled on a big couch, sipping at lime soda and artichoke tea.

A huge virtual screen displays Chaonia's number-one entertainment and news stream, Channel Idol. It's a rare treat for us. Cadets are allowed no communications or news except monthly letters from home for those who have family who bother to write. The show on-screen is a retrospective of last year's Idol Faire, the biggest competition in the Republic of Chaonia, the one everybody watches. A segment on fourth-place finisher Bako, who crafted sculptures in free fall, dissolves into the smiling image of the third-place finisher, Ji-na, who was voted "the Face" of the season for her incandescent smile. Several of the cadets whoop enthusiastically as the screen replays one of her ethereal ribbon dances.

Behind us a bell rings. The doors close. Anyone who isn't here is out of luck. But I count all of Stone Barracks cohort as present. We all made it in time. Good for us.

My nemesis, Cadet Jade Kim, wears the coveted tiger emblem of cohort captain, an elected position in the final year. Naturally a horde of suck-ups surrounds the gloriously perfect cohort captain, although Kim's melting stare—as good as a kiss—is directed at a tall, elegant cadet standing nearby. Surely glamour girl Pon is too smart to succumb to that swaggering conceit.

Seeing me, Kim calls, "Oi! Asshole! You got here after all. I thought you would be late again."

"Speaking of bad dating choices," Solomon whispers in my ear as I ignore Kim.

"It seemed like a good idea at the time. I was a dewy-eyed and innocent first year."

He snorts. "I saved your butt from that disaster."

"So you did. I can't even joke about it."

"You have bad taste in crushes, Perse. And given how many crushes you get—"

"Shut up."

He laughs as he catches my glance toward Cadet Pon, who of course isn't looking at the likes of me.

We slide onto the couch, our buddies making room. Just as I'm about to ask if anyone knows what is going on, the sound on the screen goes silent. Ji-na's ribbons continue to weave flowing patterns in the air.

Senior Captain Ray strides out and places himself on a portable speaker's dais set in front of the screen.

We all jump to our feet and snap to a still and silent attention like a baby protoceratops sensing a hunting azhdarchid. Regular sessions of any kind are led by our drill instructors. The presence of the commander is unusual, and unusual means bad.

The senior captain is a small, wiry man with the sour face of a person stuck at a job he didn't want and couldn't refuse. I have a lot of sympathy for his situation. His gaze rakes us.

"Stone Barracks. You've survived five years at the Central Defense Cadet Academy. Out of 150 in your original cohort, you have a graduating class of 139. That's the best retention rate of the 20 cohorts that make up the year-five brigade. Combine that with your attendance record, your overall aggregated test score of 90.54, and of course your four-year streak winning the brigade hockey championship. I'm here to tell you that you've won the graduation prize. Through cooperation and support you beat the other 19 cohorts of your brigade. You're number one."

A wave of restless excitement pours through our assembled ranks, but we remain silent because we haven't been given permission to cheer.

"In honor of your triumph I'm here to tell you that you've already been passed through your final exams. You won't have to take them with the rest of the fifth years."

A shocked murmur runs through us.

"This makes you the best and brightest of the citizens of the Republic of Chaonia. You will become our first defense against the Phene aggressors."

His voice drops a tone, and we all lean forward like we're about to catch something he intends to throw.

"We here at CeDCA all know that Queen-Marshal Eirene and her marshals have been readying a bold plan to halt Phene depredations forever. That's why you'll all be shipping out early, next week instead of next month. And today you'll receive your placements. Dismissed."

He steps down from the dais and walks over to talk to our drill instructors Chief Bu and Chief Dara. The still-silent screen segues from smiling Ji-na to a montage of last year's second-place finishers, but the ping of an incoming message draws my attention away from the frivolous entertainment show.

Orange letters burn into the air, viewable only by me.

My heart stops. Metaphorically, of course.

Report to Naval Facilities Engineering Command, Beacon Division, Shield Fleet. Designator: Restricted Line Officer Beacon Engineer.

I dance around with my arms in the air. I can't stop grinning. Everyone else around me is just as ecstatic. We've probably all gotten our first choice, even Solomon, who wants to be posted straight to the thick of the action.

A second message flashes.

All cadets allowed a five-minute call to their official contact: all classified information interdicted. Loose lips sink ships.

The noise level drops from cheers to the buzz of conversation as everyone clicks through. They're excited to be given this chance to speak with their families and tell them whatever unclassified fraction of the news they can. I have no one to call. My "official contact" is a shell number that connects to an empty drop box nested inside the online menu of a nondescript ramen shop in the capital city. But I step toward one of the big windows, dip my head, and pretend to call, mouthing words to a listener who doesn't exist.

After ninety-three excruciating seconds of faked conversation I close down the false call. While waiting for my friends to finish I grab a celebratory glass of pink dragon fruit soda and drain it.

Cadet Kim starts sauntering in my direction, so I desperately look around for backup and finally spot Solomon. Given that Solomon is one of the most popular cadets in the academy, it's odd to see him standing off by himself, head tucked to one side, talking to the back of his hand at an angle so no one can read his lips.

Weaving through the crowd allows me to avoid Jade Kim while coming up behind Solomon.

"No, sir," Solomon is saying. "I don't have anything else for you."

He catches sight of my shadow on the floor. With a startled glance over his shoulder, he slaps the hand against his thigh to shut down the connection.

"Was that one of your uncles?" I ask. "Can't your family ever be glad for everything you're doing for them?"

He scratches his chin, mouth tight.

I'm ashamed of myself for having brought up such a painful subject, so I change my tune with a bright smile. "What posting did you get?"

"I got what I needed," he says with a rare frown. "My family will be okay now."

Around us, cadets link arms and start singing the traditional "Hymn to Victory." The big screen shifts to a close-up of last year's Idol Faire winner, a young musician popularly known as the Handsome Alika. He's a charming sight—any winner of Idol Faire has to be either genuinely good or visually enchanting, and he's both—but that's not what stops me dead and kills the joy in my heart.

The sound has come back on, but the in-room feed is drowned out by the cadets' singing. However, I can hear the unseen announcer's slyly teasing voice through my personal feed, a few milliseconds delayed from the in-room feed, the gap so small most people wouldn't notice.

Will the Handsome Alika return to compete again in this year's Idol Faire? What's he doing right now in preparation? Follow us for our daily check-in on where Princess Sun's goodwill tour has taken her and the stories of the citizens fortunate enough to have met her in person!

The view spins dizzily skyward from an overhead image of the republic's capital city of Argos, pulling out into space. The camera's eye twists past the triple wheels of Orbital Station Hesperus and falls into the bright prism of one of Chaonia System's five beacons.

A rainbow splinters across the screen. Experienced from outside, the passage through the beacon takes place in the blink of an eye. Viewers are dropped out of the beacon into Chaonia's sibling solar system of Molossia.

At first the image zooms out for us to see the system in its entirety. Channel Idol never loses a chance to remind its audience that we're at war. Molossia System is the main staging ground. Heavy cruisers and fast frigates spin a slow defensive patrol around the second planet, Yǎnshī, which anchors the crucial beacon to Troia. The fifth planet boasts the triple-wheeled Naval Command Orbital Station Pánlóngchéng and twin adjutant orbitals, as well as a constantly shifting array of ships like so many minnows flashing in the shallows of a vast ocean. The main munitions depot and military and civilian shipyards orbit the third planet. Here, ships freshly birthed from the yards undergo inspection and complete space trials while battered cruisers and frigates limp in from the front lines for repairs and refitting.

The camera's view narrows back to the beacon that's in high orbit above the fourth planet: Molossia Prime, with its famous marble-blue glamour shining against the black of space. The announcer's voice turns gaggingly chirpy.

"After five busy months building morale at factories and training camps, the princess and her Companions have been allowed a week off for a little fun in the sun."

A dizzying plummet drags the viewer's eye toward a balmy archipelago stretched along the equator. The focus narrows to a cluster of reef-ringed islets and at last zeroes in on a solitary yacht afloat amid the blue calm.

The Handsome Alika sits in the shade of an awning, plucking at the strings of his famous ukulele. But it's not him or the instrument

I care about. It's the group he's part of. He's no striving pipa player or impoverished scholar poet or risk-taking frontier adventurer, hoping to make it big and thus buy a permanent residence or access to education for a struggling family. He's really the Honorable Alika Vata. He already has it made.

It's the life I ran away from. For five years I've been cut off, out of contact, free from reminders of the way people live when they belong to one of the seven Core Houses that stand atop Chaonian society.

Don't feel sorry for me. I don't feel sorry for me. I left my noble family's island compound on a rainy day when I was sixteen, carrying a tote bag containing five items. One of the items was enough credit to get my chip—every Chaonian has a chip implanted in their skull when they're seven—wiped and replaced with a new identity. The Honorable Persephone Lee became humble and dirt-poor citizen Persephone Lǐ Alargos, born and raised in the teeming metropolis of Argos. My excellent test scores high enough to qualify for CeDCA were the real thing.

I ran away from home after my parents and aunt informed me I would never be allowed to fight in the war. I was the spare, being held in reserve in case something happened to my twin brother the way something terrible happened to our beloved elder sister.

And there my twin is on-screen, bigger than life, looking trim and sleek. Perseus is laughing in a way he never did at home as he dives into the glassy water to go after a wink of light on the seafloor. He was sent at age eleven to become one of Princess Sun's Companions. I still miss him, but it's not at all clear he mourns me. His life of congratulatory excess, cutthroat court intrigue, and the best connections money and status can buy agrees with him.

In ten days I ship out to train as a beacon engineer, starting as a lowly ensign apprentice. I will become one of the heroes who fight the Phene and their vicious Gatoi allies. In this way I will honor the memory of my dead sister, and I'll do something useful with my life. I'll have comrades-in-arms instead of servants and rivals.

"But what we're all asking is, once this goodwill tour is done, what's next for the heir to the throne of the Republic of Chaonia?"

The camera zooms in for a close-up of Princess Sun's self-important glower. I've never personally met the infamously competitive and overachieving princess nor any of her privileged Companions, with the exception of my twin.

Fortunately, now I'll never, ever have to.

"Stay tuned to Channel Idol."

Royal Wedding Updates!

In a balmy archipelago stretched along the equator of Molossia Prime, a yacht named the *Glorious Halcyon* floated amid the calm of a cluster of reef-ringed islets. Sun sat cross-legged on the deck blinking through a virtual sheaf of classified intel she'd already read. Her temper had not been improved by five months of glad-handing in this infuriating exile. Worse, she'd run out of targets to focus on in this enforced ten-day week of idleness that she was cursedly sure had been requested by Channel Idol. The more they could stream Alika practicing while shirtless aboard a luxury yacht, the more they could entice their audience with the possibility he would compete again in this year's Idol Faire.

Seated on a cushion in the shade, the Handsome—and currently shirtless—Alika tried out various embellishments for a ukulele accompaniment of the ancient travelers' classic "I Am a Vagabond." Candace was asleep in a bunk, awaiting the night watch. Octavian stood watch at the prow while Isis held the wheel with her pteranodon perched on a shoulder. Percy and Duke leaned at the starboard rail, excitedly pointing at a vibrant coral formation about a quarter klick away.

Her gaze slid past them to the person closest to her. Hetty reclined in a lounger examining the same intel, which Sun had passed to her via the ring network. The rise and fall of Hetty's breathing distracted Sun, making her think of night and cur-tained alcoves and two bodies pressed belly to belly to become one. A breeze rustled the fabric of Hetty's pareo, curling it up over the curve of her knees. Her skin was effortlessly golden beneath the strong light, finally getting color after the four years she had spent living in a dome on Yele Prime's Congress moon with her Chaonian diplomat father and her Yele-born scholar father.

Hetty glanced up to find Sun staring at her legs. She arched a playful eyebrow and punctuated it with a teasing smile. Eirene's words to João from almost six months ago flared into Sun's thoughts: *It's bad enough you've given me a half-Gatoi daughter. Chaonians will never stand for a half-Yele child becoming queen-marshal.*

Sun yanked off her hat so she could lie flat on her back. With hands linked behind her head and ankles crossed, she glowered up at the blisteringly blue sky.

Hetty broke the silence. "What do you think, dear Sun, about this first report?"

"The one about Admiral Manu possibly being spotted at Hellion Terminus, of all places? It is curious. He's never made a public speech for or against my mother. He doesn't seem to be linked to a faction at all, as unlikely as that seems of any Yele. So why would the only living Yele admiral worthy of that title turn up at a dead-end backwater of the Phene Empire? What if it's a false-flag operation by the Phene to try to break my mother's alliance with the League?"

"Rumors are distraction. Sun, look here. This is the report you need to note. There's shortages of armor coming soon if factories can't meet increased demand. You should be advocating for—"

"Hold on."

Sunlight caught briefly on a tiny object hovering above the mast, a flash Sun would have missed if she hadn't been looking directly at the tip of the mast swaying above her. She slowly stretched out an arm as if reaching for the brimmed hat she had just cast aside.

"Slide your stinger over here."

Hetty gave no outward sign of having heard the whisper. Instead, she languidly dropped a foot to the deck as if stretching her leg and nudged the weapon as if accidentally toward the princess's fingers.

Sun tilted her head to get another angle on the object: small, probably no bigger than a thumb, and coated with a nonreflective surface to make it hard to see. She inhaled and exhaled fully, inhaled again as her fingers wrapped around the rifle and exhaled until her shoulders relaxed. On a held breath she sat bolt upright as she swung the rifle up to sight level and released a pulse.

With a snap and a burst of light, the object tumbled out of the sky to vanish into the water. Everyone on deck swiveled their heads to look.

She jumped to her feet. "Did anyone see where it went in?"

"I'll get it for you!" Percy dove off the side of the boat, barely making a splash.

Hetty glanced skyward. "Why fetch the wasp when Channel Idol will just send more to sting our every step?"

As if in answer, Alika strummed a cadence to take him out of the song he was playing and into another. "'. . . every game you stake, I'll be watching you.'"

With an impatient shake of her head the princess got up to lean on the railing and scan the sea. Hetty closed the sheaf and got up to stand at Sun's side. The water was so clear they could see an object resting on the sand. Percy dove straight and true for the seafloor, where he scooped it up and kicked for the surface. He breached, took a breath, and threw it toward them. Sun caught it one-handed and displayed it on her palm.

Hetty examined the tiny drone. "No Channel Idol logo. It's just blank."

Sun walked to the prow, where Octavian stood making sweeps of the horizon with his enhanced vision. He reflexively tapped the rifle hanging along his back before glancing at Sun's open hand.

"It looks like a standard-issue media wasp, Princess, but you never know. Channel Idol's wasps *are* required by law to display their logo. They're also not allowed to coat them with cloaking materials. So it could be a rogue outfit selling to pirate channels. It could be the usual Lee House security overkill."

"It could be a spy-bot," she said with a glance toward the stairs that led down to the cabin.

"Sure. And it could be military grade, the queen-marshal's intelligence team keeping an eye on you."

"Things *have* been suspiciously quiet. It's odd how little news we're hearing even on the inner court network. It should have occurred to me our communications stream might be being deliberately censored."

He nodded. "See if the Honorable James can do a trace on the signal. Also, that was a good shot."

She responded with a curt nod of acknowledgment, but behind her straight expression burned a blaze of satisfaction at Octavian's praise.

"Oi! Duke!" Percy had taken advantage of being in the water to swim over to the coral. "There's trilobites here! We can get images and a census."

Duke released the tender from its garage and motored the little boat over.

"Do you want Wing to scout for any more suspicious wasps, Your Highness?" Isis called, raising a hand to allow the little animal to rub its beak along her fingers.

"Not until I have more information," said Sun.

She went to the open hatch that led down into the saloon, where James was staying out of the sun after his spectacular sunburn of two days ago. He'd heard everything that had been said up top. His voice rose out of the open hatch as her shadow fell across it.

"It's actually 'every step you take,' not 'every game you stake.'"

"What is?" Sun asked.

"The lyrics Alika messed up because victory has gone to his head. Come look at this. Bring whatever you shot out of the sky. I just got an anomalous reaction, and I think they might be related."

She jumped down the ladder into the saloon. Navah looked up from the galley where she was arranging cups and saucers on a tray. She nodded to acknowledge Sun's presence before collecting the teapot from its warmer.

James was using the dinner table as a platform. He'd pulled up various data streams to create virtual towers of glowing numbers piled up into the air like a holographic three-dimensional image of crowded skyscrapers in miniature.

"What do you have?" Sun asked.

He tugged his flatcap over to the right, a sign of triumph. She could always tell his mood by the cap's tilt and angle. "You know how little news we've been receiving through our net connections?"

"Yes. Octavian and I were just talking about that."

He waved a hand through the pulsating towers of numbers. The gleaming numerals shuddered, faded to gray, and popped back to a brilliant yellow as his hand moved on. "These are data stacks. The instant you shot down that object, this happened."

He pushed aside the towers to show what appeared to be a small green sapling unfurling at their base.

"What's that?"

"My way of representing a suppressed network. Look at these tendrils." He snagged a stylus from behind his ear and tapped the table's surface, peeling back a layer of code to show a dark network like roots glowing beneath the sapling. "I think what you shot down isn't a wasp filming our every laugh and fart. I think it's a suppressor."

"You mean someone has been deliberately cutting off our access to the net? So we're only receiving the feeds they want us to receive?"

"That's right. If I'm correct, it's been going on the entire five months we've been traveling. There should be three other suppressor drones up there, using a triangulation effect around the central seed—"

"The central seed being the one I shot down."

"—to fully excise our contact to the net. Look what happens if I tug on this new thread."

He poked with his stylus at the shining green sapling and with a gentle stroke encouraged its single baby leaf to unfurl. A tower of data climbed in a tight upward spiral out of the leaf. Images and sounds flashed in the air. Ads had the strongest signal, smashing like bricks through a window.

Vogue Academy readies Chaonia for our republic-wide graduation season! Are you graduating or know someone who is? Be the vanguard, not the laggard. See all the latest fabric trends from the premier style and innovation institute and its top design vogues and fashion companions. And don't sweat your exams! You've got this!

"Turn it down!" said Sun with a surprised laugh. "No. Wait!"

A new image appeared depicting a box of small rectangular cakes, each cake baked with the Double Happiness character for good fortune and happiness in marriage. The sunburst representing the royal house shimmered into view, superimposed over the cakes, and exploded as fireworks. A spritely soprano sang out the good news.

Royal wedding updates! Color schemes for your block party! Bake these Double Happiness cakes!

"Royal wedding updates!" exclaimed Sun as the full import of the words hit her. "Is my mother getting married again?"

A loud crash came from the galley.

Sun had barely drawn breath before Octavian dropped feetfirst down through the hatch, rifle raised. He lowered the weapon as they all looked toward the galley.

Navah had dropped the tea tray. Shattered porcelain and puddles of steaming liquid lay in a scatter pattern around her beaded slippers.

"You startled me, Your Highness," she said. "It won't happen again."

Sun immediately looked at Octavian, but he gave the swift slight downward dip of the chin that meant to leave things as they were.

A shape appeared at the top of the hatch. Hetty called down, quite out of breath from the shock of hearing the unexpected crash. "Sun? Are you all right?"

"It's all right," said Sun without looking away from Navah.

"I'll clean up." The cee-cee turned away to open the galley locker.

"We *are* being censored," Sun whispered to Octavian, still keeping her gaze on Navah. "But by whom?"

"It's got to be military intelligence under the command of the palace," said James. "Look here."

He had faded the data towers into barely visible ghost images and superimposed a three-dimensional and color-coded route map of their long trip through the provincial cities, industrial parks, and military sites in Thesprotis and Molossia Systems.

"See these brownout zones?" He traced lines with his stylus. "These are all areas where for various reasons—interference, topography, isolation, military security—it is easiest to censor net access. Note how all of our tour has stayed within brown zones."

"A trip whose every stop the palace arranged," said Hetty, who had knelt at the top of the hatch so she could peer down into the galley.

"Including this particularly isolated week in the middle of nowhere with no satellite link. And all done according to protocol, so nothing to make us suspicious." Sun studied James's map.

"Not until you spotted that drone," said Octavian. Rifle set casually at his hip, he was still watching Navah as she stepped back from the locker with a vac and started its quiet suction.

James pulled the brim of his flatcap down until it was almost over his eyes. He squinted as he poked at the data. "Until we bring down the other suppressors I won't be able to access anything except ads because they override everything else."

The recipe and a demonstration of how to bake the cakes shimmered in the air, accompanied by flashes of festive fireworks.

James looked at Sun. He pulled off his cap and set it on his knee. "Do you think the queen-marshal made an arrangement for you to get married without telling you?"

"That would be just like her," agreed Sun, "but no. She needs my father's permission to make legal arrangements regarding me. He'd never let her get away with it, and anyway he would tell me first."

The princess bent her gaze to the sapling's data stack, which was still growing. Images flashed in the air and scraps of phrases whispered past her ear as the new connection tried to fully open. The three remaining suppressors were still acting as a baffle. A bright announcement burbled at the edge of Sun's vision, splashed with red-and-gold highlights for a military flair.

See this fresh interview with a patriot soldier you'd love to bring home to your family! All quiet on the front lines because of the brave service of our troops and the industrious labor of our workers and farmers. Send a message of support through Channel Idol's registry, approved by the Ministry of Defense.

"What if she sent me on this trip to keep us so far away we can't be on the guest list? Who could she be marrying that she would want to hide it from me? It would have to be someone whose elevation to consort wouldn't insult Baron Voy and the Yele League after all the work she did to get them under her control. We have to find out. Octavian, you and Isis plot a course to the space elevator. We're ending the goodwill tour and making our own plans from here on out."

James twisted his cap in both hands. "Ending it, as in, cutting it off before it's meant to be over without the queen-marshal's permission?"

"That's right," said Sun.

"If you do this, do you have any idea of the harangue about duty and respect for elders I'm going to get from my father? And then Anas will feel free to give me the elder-brother lecture he so delights in. Are you going to make me endure that?"

"You knew what you signed up for when you stayed with me."

She reached up to touch Hetty's bare foot where it rested on the top step. Hetty's skin was warm from the sun, like balm to a person whose spirit could never find tranquility. Sun let her hand linger there, savoring the contact, then realized she was doing so in the sight of the others and pulled it back.

"You'll come with me, Hetty. We'll take out the tender and track down the other three suppressors."

Navah shut off the vac and, kneeling beside it, picked up a last broken shard of cup. "Now, Your Highness? Should I open the garage and release the tender?"

"No need. I've got it in hand. James, if I can get you all four suppressors, can we get a full comms feed or are we still in a brownout zone?"

When he didn't reply she turned. He'd bunched the cap's fabric into clenched fingers as his lips parted in alarm at something he was seeing in the data.

"Wait! That's not right—"

Whatever else he meant to say was cut off by an explosion.

10

In Which the Wily Persephone's Hopes and Dreams Are Shot Through the Lungs and Turned to Greasy Ash

At 0521, nine minutes before the barracks bell, I wake up. What I remember of my fading dreamscape gives me the same feeling I get at New Year's when I can eat all the red bean–filled rice balls I can stuff in my mouth: a little sick to my stomach with satisfaction.

Restricted Line Officer Beacon Engineer.

This is what I dreamed of and worked for.

I climb down from the top tier of the triple rack I was assigned on my first day and have slept in for almost five years. Cadet quarters are facing triple racks with three-centimeter-thick foam mattresses to sleep on, curtains for privacy, and lockers to hang our uniforms. Still in my skivvies, I trot down the length of the barracks to the head. I do my business, wash my hands and face, and give a victory five to those of my cohort who, like me, have risen before the bell. The bell clangs just as I return to my rack and pull on my coveralls. Minh hops down from the middle tier and slaps me on the back with her prosthetic hand.

"Whoo! Whoo!" She shimmies a few dance steps as she snaps out a rhythm with her flesh hand. Ten days after Senior Captain Ray's announcement we're still in victory mode.

In the facing triple, Ikenna and Ay groan like they do every morning, but as they climb out of their berths they're grinning too. Complaints are just for show now that we've gotten prime assignments. The top tier facing mine is empty; that cadet washed out in month two of our first year, and we five have been tight ever since we rescued the poor kid before he strangled in a wire-pit trap in the Thousand Hectare Woods obstacle course.

They change into their coveralls as I poke the still-closed curtain of the bottom-tier rack.

"Hey! Solomon Solomon. Cadet Solomon." I blink to open my net access and check the virtual watch I use to organize my time. "You have twenty-six minutes to rise, shine, and eat before muster and PT."

A monstrous bulk shifts ponderously behind the curtain as it makes a low, threatening grumble. "Unhhhn. Leave me alone. I thought we didn't have to run laps this morning because we're getting fitted for flight suits."

"You wish. Get up."

"Rise and shine, Cadet Li," says the silky voice I once mistook for sincerity. I turn to see Cadet Jade Kim leaning against our lockers with arms crossed and a smug half smile. "I think you want to talk to me and not to that junkyard hatchling."

Solomon is out of his bunk and up in Kim's face so fast I don't have time to think up a retort.

"You want to repeat that?" Solomon asks in his softest tone. He's half a head taller than Cadet Kim and maybe twice as broad across the shoulders, not that Jade Kim isn't also a well-built specimen of youth, which is how I foolishly leaped into the pit of that relationship in the first place.

Minh, Ay, and Ikenna step up beside Solomon, Ikenna with arms crossed and barracks light glinting on his weaponized glasses, Ay ostentatiously adjusting her leg brace, which is heavy enough to do damage to soft flesh, and Minh flicking the razor blade on her multi-tool hand in and out to a brisk beat.

"Nobody insults my family," Solomon adds without moving. His fist hovers one punch away from the most gorgeous face in the academy.

I slide between them, careful not to touch Kim's heat-seekingly attractive body lest the piece of trash think I still harbor lustful thoughts. "Solomon, I don't care if you break that perfect nose, but I do care if you get disciplined for aggravated battery and lose your posting five days before we ship out."

He lowers his fist. "I'm not letting it go, Kim. I'm just saving it. You'll know when."

He grabs his coveralls out of his locker and stalks away toward the showers.

I nod at the others, and they take the hint and leave the two of us alone.

"That was charming," I say to Kim. "Just like always."

Kim shrugs it off. Knowing you're the top-ranking cadet of the entire academy, and that you've lived up to your family having given you the auspicious name of Jade, can give a person a certain strut. "I got a fast-track posting to a Tulpar-class cruiser, the very one made famous in the battle at Na Iri because the heir was on board."

"The *Boukephalas*?"

"That's right. Top of the line. I'm going straight to the Eighth Fleet in Molossia, ready for the big push into Karnos that we all know is coming. It's the exact posting I requested."

"Of course it is," I say with a fake smile. "Why should I care since fortunately I'll be too low class to ever run across you on your fancy ship once we're out with the fleet?"

"Because I had to get top-level security clearance even to apply for that posting. Since the communications room is short of bodies due to the war, I was called in last night for an emergency watch at 0300. Which means I saw the most interesting message flash up twenty minutes ago just as I was being released for muster. But instead of being for Persephone Earth-Field Lï it was for Persephone Wood-Child Lee. Which is odd, considering the only Wood-Child Lees in the Republic of Chaonia are the Lees of Lee House and its branch lineages."

Every nerve in my body blasts into red alert. No one here at the academy knows except Solomon, not even Minh, Ay, and Ikenna.

Kim smirks. "People at home are not going to believe when I tell them who my girlfriend was."

"I was never your girlfriend."

"All right then, my—"

"Shut your mouth!"

Before I can punch that smug face and get my own charge of aggravated battery, a ping lights up just beyond my right eye. The chime is followed by a steadily expanding halo of orange light. A banner of coruscating words throbs as if on a virtual screen hanging in the air.

DISCHARGE NOTICE

    Cadet status at Central Defense Cadet Academy for the person enrolled as Persephone Lǐ Alargos has been terminated at the command of the governor of Lee House.

    Report to Senior Captain Ray for final orders and dismissal.

"Fuck! Fuck! Fuck! Fuck! Fuck!"

Suddenly Solomon is beside me, resting a hand on my shoulder, his voice gentle. All around us cadets hurrying to get ready have stopped to stare.

"Hey. Perse. Hey."

I start sobbing as my hopes and dreams die right there, shot through the lungs and turned to greasy ash. I should have known better than to think my family would let me go.

Solomon and I sit side by side on a bench in CeDCA's depot. Windows give us a view over the landing strip that runs parallel to the final five thousand meters of the train line that ends at the academy. It's a pretty view of runway and forest rising beyond, but all I can do is stare at my hands.

"Don't go quiet on me, Perse."

I laugh shakily because I want to cry again. "Percy used to say that to me. I never told you that, did I? It's why I trusted you that first time, do you remember?"

"Which time?" Solomon's always been a good listener. He can move fast, but he can also sit with the unshakable patience of a rock.

"When we got assigned as lab partners in first year. It was that stupid reactive titration lab. When I got stuck."

He chuckles. "Oh, right. I'd gotten used to you taking the lead, and all of a sudden on that one you shut down. We had a stopwatch on that lab."

"Yeah. I was sure I was going to fail and be kicked out. I froze. But you got it done."

"It was close, but close doesn't matter as long as you beat the bell."

I punch him on the arm like a victory slug, but my heart isn't in it.

He shakes his head. "It's always bad when you go quiet. It eats you up and burns you out. You're better off letting it out."

"Crying and swearing?"

"Why not? I go to the gym and punch things. It's all right to not be able to handle everything."

Sagging forward, I press my hands to my face. "What am I going to do? I don't want to go back. I can't go back."

I think of Minh, Ikenna, and Ay helping me pack my duffel and walking with me until they were called back for muster. Of Chief Dara, one of our cohort's instructors, kindly allowing Solomon release from muster in order to accompany me to the depot so I didn't have to go alone. Because alone is the way I arrived here, on a seat on a train knowing no one, not sure if my gambit would work and my disguise would hold up.

"I thought I could get away from them by changing my implant and coming here, I really did, but I was just fooling myself."

He rests a hand on my shoulder. I appreciate it, I do, but there's no comfort to be had. Then he stiffens, shades his eyes as his gaze shifts to the sky, and whistles softly.

"Will you look at that."

The two bored MPs on security duty step outside their guard booth to get a better look at the aircar dropping in for a smooth landing. Of course my family sent an expensive Swallow-class vessel, with its sleek frame and pretentious exterior detailing in soft purples. It's humiliating to have their wealth thrown in my face, knowing everyone will be talking about the cadet who lied.

I don't know what else to do, so I get up and walk outside. Solomon keeps pace beside me. The MPs don't even ask us to identify ourselves because by now everyone knows. As we approach, the hatch lowers soundlessly to make a ramp.

"Peace be upon you, welcome, and please be seated." The aircar's machine-bright voice sounds fresh out of a factory. This is not one of my family's old aircars, whose years of service have given them a sheen of personality.

"Thank you," I say politely. "Do you have a designation?"

"S W 4 11 O W. I am not authorized to share my serial number or registry designation."

Definitely straight off the assembly line.

I tuck my duffel in one of the aircar's flight lockers. Solomon looks over the embroidered seats, the control panel and display sphere, and the glass-fronted mahogany galley cupboard loaded with food and drink.

"I've never flown in a private car. Or flown at all except for training."

"Please allow me to inform you that I am only authorized to take one individual at this time," says the Swallow.

He steps back. "When my aunties start talking like that I know I've really messed up. Do you get to pilot this, Perse?"

"It'll be set on an automated course so I can't run away again."

He retreats down the ramp. I follow, as if one last touch of boots to the ground will give me the strength to get through this. It turns out he wants to whisper in my ear away from instruments in the aircar that might be recording our voices.

"I know people, Perse. We junkyard hatchlings have ways around that stuff."

"Let it go, Solomon. Don't let Jade Kim be the jerk who rules your life." He gives me his hundred-kiloton stare so I quickly go on. "Your family gets away with off-grid sidelines only because my family's not looking for yours."

To my surprise, Senior Captain Ray emerges from the depot and hurries toward us. Solomon gives me a hug as cover to slip a thin rectangular object into my left hand. "If you need help, send a message on this. It's keyed to your retinal signature."

"How'd you get my retinal signature?"

"I set this up so people will think it's a study aid. It won't work for anyone but you." He releases me as the academy commander approaches with a brisk step.

"What won't work for anyone else, Cadet Solomon?" the senior captain asks.

"Giving me a hug to try to get my recipe for malasadas."

The commander's weary gaze lightens as he licks his lips. "You gave Cadet Li the recipe and you won't give it to my cook?"

"Cadet Lee needs it more since she's no longer a cadet," says Solomon, and Senior Captain Ray remembers who my family are. I wonder if he's always known or if it came as an ugly surprise and he's waiting for the ax to fall on his career when Lee House decides to punish him for not figuring it out. With a sigh he taps the back of his hand.

"Departure time is now." He seems about to speak a few more words, then changes his mind. It's never, ever wise to say anything about the family who run the secret police in the Republic of Chaonia.

I give him a salute, possibly the last salute I'll ever make.

He salutes in response, the final piece of respect he can offer. "You were a good cadet, never asked for special treatment or gave anyone any trouble. You kept your eyes on your goal with commendable discipline."

"Thank you, sir."

Solomon gives me an encouraging nod. I step into the Swallow, and the door whisks shut on its own, cutting me off.

"Please allow me to inform you that this vessel is under automated control. In order to depart, you must take a seat."

The moment I'm strapped into the pilot's chair the Swallow shudders to life and rises straight up. I stare out the window as the buildings, the garden and orchard, the training range and gymnasium and pool, and the high-security fence dwindle into the distance. Only when I can no longer see the twin pagodas and sky-tower in the wild landscape do I check to see if my parents or Aunt Moira have left a message. I can't call up anything current: no communication, no news, no trade reports, no shipping schedules, not even the weather report.

"Please allow me to inform you that all connections to the global net are restricted. However, I have been given permission to share several of the most popular Channel Idol retrospectives and dramas. Would you like to see the previews?"

Without waiting for my response a virtual scenario pops up around me, fading into a slow pan of a Chaonian fleet poised in space with a giant orange planet and two blue moons hanging in the background. My breathing tightens as the view slides past a massive beacon and onto an opposing fleet recognizable as an imperial Phene task force by the twin helixes on its dreadnoughts. The audio pops on like a demolition blast targeted to my heart.

Replay the communications surge from the battle of Aspera Drift. Thrill to the courageous exploits and tactical brilliance of the eighttimes-worthy hero Captain the Honorable Ereshkigal Lee. Newly released ops will give you insight into her stunning sacrifice.

Cursing, I painfully bite my tongue before I mash enough buttons to mute the sound. The previews start flipping through an automatic countdown: the rehash of last year's Idol Faire; a hugely popular horror-drama from my childhood called *Plague of Clones*; a commentary on a commentary on the official republic-wide Year Ten history course covering the rise and fall of the Apsaras Convergence; the early episodes of the long-running historical serial *Journey to Landfall*.

I shut down the program to blessed nothingness. The windows offer a spectacular view of the rising foothills and the mountains beyond, snow glittering on the highest peaks and the sky threaded with clouds, but it all looks smeared with funeral ashes.

Probably they've been planning this all along, to pull me out right when it will hurt the most. It would be just like them.

I spin the object Solomon gave me through my fingers, examining it from every angle. It's a slick black rectangle about the size of a playing card, made of ceramic. In its glossy surface I see the ghost of my face staring back at me like a long-vanished duplicate caught in an unknown prison.

"Malasadas," I say.

A tracery of blue lines chases a tight circle against the surface, then irises to a bigger circle within the card's luster like a secret gate to a hidden universe. I start laughing as a spinning visual takes shape in the air, projected from the card: Solomon in the cavernous galley with the academy's chief cook, walking Virgil through the process of frying batches of dough in a pot of hot oil.

Fine. Let them call me home. Let them do their worst.

I'm not beaten yet.

11

The Gatoi Prisoner

He wakes up in a cage. Bright lights shine down on him from an overhead so white it is nothing but glare. He shades his eyes with the back of a hand, trying to understand where he is. The compartment is large and rectangular with gray bulkheads. A secured hatch is just visible from where he lies on his back. A faint *drip . . . drip* whispers at his ear like a message trying to flower into life on his comm-link, but he can't hear the rest of his squad. No comm. No voices. Nothing but that drip.

What if they're all dead except him?

It would be better to be dead than to face the disgrace of being taken prisoner.

The sting of a mood stabilizer courses through his body, folding up the spurt of agitation until it is confined into a neat mental box. He can still find a way to fight and thus to die with honor. He's sure of it.

Pushing at the corners of his mind, he tries to remember what happened.

His squad was on a routine operation in the outer reaches of Hellion Terminus, boarding a suspected smuggling vessel through a secured airlock. He was midway back along their arrow formation when the captain of the suspect vessel stepped into view holding a clipboard manifest. Nothing odd in that; she was showing it to the squad leader when she'd glanced up and he'd seen her face full-on.

The memory blurs into a burst of static.

He touches a forefinger to each eye to reboot his network but it's not ruptured, just interrupted at the flash. The next thing he remembers is waking up here.

He trawls a diagnostic through his body. A cut on his right thigh is healing; he can sense the tissues stitching together in the unhurried and confident way his grandmother knits socks. There's a gel wrap hissing into a second-degree burn on his left hip as it cools the skin. Bruises along his right side feel tender, but no bones are broken. All systems go except for the glitch in his memory. He can't recall how he got the injuries.

He eases up, bracing for an attack, but nothing moves.

The cage is mesh, its strands pulsating in visual bursts that hit his body as a steady hammer: *wham wham wham.* It's a suppressor, meant to dull the neurosystem that gives him enhanced strength, agility, and stamina. He already has a headache, and it is only going to get worse.

His eyes adapt now that a spotlight isn't shining straight down onto his face.

There are seven mesh cages, including his own, set on stout legs up off the deck, as well as six insulated body bags lined up to the right of the hatch. Since the bags are sealed up he can't see if the corpses are part of his squad. He counts three other prisoners, all banner soldiers like him.

The closest one lies sprawled facedown, network gone dark. He wonders if the soldier is dead, if their family will ever get the body back or even know of their loved one's fate, so he whispers a prayer for the lost dead who vanish into the heart of Lady Chaos.

The drip is coming from a soldier twisted in an awkward sideways contortion, face turned away from him. By the thunderbolt design of the cuff he can tell it's not one of his squad. Blood pools at the edge of the cage. When enough pressure builds up, a drop separates and falls to splatter on the chrome-colored deck.

"Recruit."

He meets the gaze of the third soldier, two cages away. She's an experienced-looking officer, tough and capable, with a gleaming artificial jaw and rank markings glowing down her right arm. She wears the cuffs of the Thunderbolt Banner.

"Colonel." His right hand comes up reflexively before he remembers he's indoors and not required to salute.

Her smile is weary but real, like a glimpse of home. "This your first tour, Recruit?"

"Yes, Colonel."

"Where were you taken prisoner?"

"I'm not allowed to give out that information, Colonel."

"Very good, Recruit. That's exactly what you're supposed to say."

He misses his family, and even the crass joking of his squad. So he risks a lighthearted comeback. "I never actually knew where we were. They just put me in the belly of the snake and gave me my orders."

Her gaze flashes down to his cuff, a snake's body twisted around itself with a fanged head at each end. "Typical of snakes," she retorts. "All that wisdom but too reticent to share it."

He grins. It's like he's opened a little door in the cage, given them room to breathe and be resolute.

"Blessed Lady," the colonel murmurs under her breath, "must they send them out so young?"

She coughs with a wet, sticky sound. Blood slicks her hand. Suddenly he's afraid that whoever injured and tortured her is going to do the same to him. She meets his gaze as if she can parse his thoughts. He stiffens his shoulders. He'll be ready. He won't shame his family. His destiny will unfold according to the fractals of Lady Chaos.

He speaks the ritual words known only to the banners. "I am bound by the ancient covenant and by the crown of light."

"So are we all. Listen carefully, Recruit. We're in a research facility on Chaonia Prime."

"Chaonia Prime?" He struggles to orient himself. He grew up in a nomadic fleet that stayed in frontier territories and never, ever probed into the inner systems of any of the great confederacies. But like all children raised in the banners he learned about the many enemies lurking beyond the safety of the banner fleets, the people he would one day hire on with, or fight against. "The Republic of Chaonia is governed by a queen-marshal in cooperation with a citizens assembly. But my teachers all said it is just a tyrannical military dictatorship."

The colonel scratches at an eyebrow, smiling wryly. "The universe is a complicated place. What matters to us is that fifty-three hours ago there was a hostile takeover at this facility. I was one of the people in charge of the work being done here, until I was shot and put in this cage."

She touches a hand to her chest, which is encased in what looks like a sleek ceramic vest. The vest is tethered by an IV line that threads through the mesh into a small box fixed against the base of the cage.

There are a lot of questions to harvest from her words, so he starts with what seems most immediately puzzling.

"What work would banner soldiers be in charge of inside the Republic of Chaonia? The Chaonians are the treacherous enemies of our Phene allies. They fight us. They don't work with us."

"Didn't you learn that Queen-Marshal Eirene married a Royal of the Gatoi as her second consort? About twenty years ago. Right around when you would have been born."

He shakes his head. "I never learned that. Can it be true? The Gatoi have always been allies of the Phene Empire. The Phene have always had our backs. No Gatoi would ever go against such a venerable and honorable trust."

The colonel sighs. "This isn't the first time I've had this conversation with fresh young banner soldiers brought in from the front. What distorted garbage are they teaching you kids these days? Listen, Recruit. This project is being jointly run by a Royal working with sympathetic Chaonian scientists, under protection from very high up in the Chaonian command chain. Those body bags? Four of my banner soldiers and two Chaonian marines who were helping us defend the project."

It seems insubordinate to openly doubt an officer, so he redirects his skepticism to another question. "Then who was the hostile doing the taking over?"

"I don't know, not yet, because I was put out of commission early on and the assailants weren't wearing identity badges. But I do know they are Chaonians."

He whistles. "Factional infighting. I thought Chaonians were all united under the rule of their queen-marshal."

"No government is all united."

"Except the Phene."

The colonel flinches, then makes the hand gesture to avert evil spirits. "Speak not of their power. Fortunately for us there aren't any Phene here. For the moment, the question is who our captors are and if they intend to keep us alive."

"Who are the other two soldiers?" He knows she won't tell him their names, if she even knows them. Names are a private matter among the banners, reserved for family. Rank, a chosen battle name, and honorable service are the public face a soldier wears.

She indicates the unconscious bleeding one. "A sergeant under my command. He got wounded in the attack, like me. And this one"—she points to the one whose network has gone dark—"a private from Arsenal Banner. Sleeping off a drug the researchers have been using to slow his reflexes by shutting down the neural enhancers."

"Why are you working with people trying to cripple us?"

"The only people who are hurting us are the Phene."

He frowns, unable to hide his distaste for the words, but says nothing.

She sighs again. "If the work here can be brought to fruition it will benefit all banners. On my honor, it's true. I wouldn't be involved in this project otherwise."

Gatoi do not swear lightly by their honor. He wants to trust her. But the situation lies so far outside of anything he's ever been told or experienced that he's not sure. "Are there more here? More prisoners like me, I mean?"

"There are, but where they are now I do not know. I've been confined in this compartment since the attack."

"Was there anyone else with me when I was brought in?"

"Your arrow, do you mean? No. You were brought into this compartment alone, under heavy sedation." She gives a glance to the right, reading information from her internals. "You arrived nine hours and twenty-eight minutes ago. I have an ally still moving freely within the area. So I'm certain you were placed here in this compartment, with me, on purpose. With you here we have a chance to retake the facility."

"You and I aren't children of the same banner," he objects. "I'd need permission from my clan council to work with you."

"Normally, yes. But there's a Royal here."

"How did they capture a Royal?"

"They didn't. As I told you, the Royal was running this facility before the takeover." His surprise must be evident on his face because she lifts a hand to forestall any questions. "I don't have the time nor do you have the security clearance for me to explain more than that. He's hidden for now. We need to get him out before they find him. Can we work together, Recruit?"

He's never actually seen a Royal and doesn't have much interest in seeing one now. As his grandmother likes to say, *"They bleed and eat and pee just like we do, no matter what the old stories say."* But every banner soldier is required by oath and honor to protect the Royals. So he signs obedience.

Satisfied, she goes on. "You're mobile in a way I'm not. I have an idea that might work. The mesh works by a device called *percussion echo.* I will explain how to disrupt it, and then—"

A clank sounds from the hatch. As its wheel cranks around he rolls up into a crouch. To get to him the Chaonians will have to bring down the mesh. The moment it comes down he'll spring. He's faster and stronger, and his ability to change direction at speed is what won him his battle name. He'll die fighting, as honor demands.

"I need you to stay alive for the sake of all the banners, Recruit," the colonel says in a low voice as the hatch grinds open. "Do you understand me? There's more at stake here than you know."

Five Chaonian marines in helmeted battlesuits come through, weapons ready. They are followed by an individual wearing a white lab coat, eyes obscured by goggles, hands nervously clutching a tablet. The lab coat is accompanied by a woman wearing a calf-length gold tunic whose fabric shimmers.

The colonel hisses softly, seeing something in this woman that makes her angry. He has no idea what it is. He's only a recruit, barely out of boot camp, vat-grown, as his squad-mates joked, which just means he was born and grew up on an Ouroboros-class wheelship surrounded by the many escort vessels of the Wrathful Snakes banner fleet. But the colonel is studying the woman in the gold tunic with cold intensity, so he studies her too.

The woman is of medium height, with pale skin that's weathered in a way never seen in the fleet, where there is no damaging planet exposure. She keeps her black hair up in a bun and wears a distinctive emerald tree brooch.

"This is the prisoner who was just brought in?" the woman asks the lab coat, pointing at him while ignoring the colonel the way she would ignore a lamp.

"Yes. According to the report he was an unexpected capture at Hellion Terminus. He broke formation during a routine boarding mission and without provocation charged the captain of one of Chaonia's undercover surveillance vessels."

"Yes, I know which vessel and which captain. How do you think we figured out this place existed?"

The lab coat flashes a look toward the colonel, who gives an infinitesimal shake of the head. The prisoner can't figure out who is fighting whom, and what tangled web is being woven, so he just observes.

"He's perfect." The woman looks him over in the obtrusive way non-clans-people do, half-admiring and half-repelled. "Young. Fit. The striking looks of a savage innocent. And a fortunate history of impulsive violence and lack of discipline. He'll do very well to shock the audience and discredit the heir. Get him ready to travel."

The colonel says, "Removing a prisoner of war from a safe prison facility is in violation of the rights of prisoners of war."

"Tell that to your Phene masters," says the woman. The colonel opens her mouth to reply but closes it abruptly as the lab coat gives her a swift negative dip of the chin. The woman doesn't notice because she isn't looking at the lab coat as she goes on in a tone oozing disgust and condescension. "You Gatoi had a chance to ally with us, but you chose to sell yourselves to the Phene instead."

She goes out the hatch. The lab coat casts a frustrated glance toward the colonel before following the woman out.

Two of the marines come forward, unlock the wheels on his cage, and push it toward the hatch, leaving the mesh intact. This world is so far out of the frame of reference of a youth still wearing the socks his grandmother knitted for him that it's dizzying. Whatever happens, he has to be courageous and dignified, to represent his banner and his people so no shame comes to them. Honor and service must guide him. There's more at stake here than he knows.

The colonel switches back to the ritual speech used among the banners, which outsiders never learn. "Don't forget what I said, Recruit. My battle name is Evans."

"It is an honorable name among the people, endurance without flagging," he replies in the proper way. "My battle name is Zizou—"

The mesh pulses with a fierce pressure that knocks him onto his back and leaves his bones and flesh numb. He lies there, too stunned to move, as they open the mesh and pull off his uniform jacket and his socks.

When they push him into a much larger chamber he can't move to see anything except the thick mesh above his head and a catwalk above that, running along the ceiling. But he can hear the woman in gold and the lab coat speaking, their voices tinny as if heard through a tube.

"We must destroy this entire operation," the woman is saying.

"The queen-marshal herself funded this project," objects the lab coat in a desperate tone. "We're not supposed to tell anyone. But she authorized it."

"She funded it in total secrecy, hiding it from the Core Houses *and* the high command. That's because she knows we would never approve it. She should know better than to listen to that barbarian and his cunning intrigue. He's untrustworthy and likely a traitor too. It's a pity he's been too clever to leave incriminating evidence. You're sure he's not here? You know the consequences if you're lying to me."

"Governor, please listen. There's nothing treacherous about this operation. It will benefit Chaonia."

"The only good Gatoi is a dead Gatoi."

"We are taking every precaution. Percussion echo keeps the subjects under control. Just give me another month, I beg you. We're so close to a breakthrough."

"You can't change the essential nature of savages who believe their greatest destiny is to die fighting for their bloodthirsty goddess."

"That's not what's going on. We have collected compelling evidence that the Phene are conditioning and controlling the Gatoi through their neurosystems."

"The Phene did not implant those neurosystems in them. The Gatoi are born with those neurosystems. It's who they are. What they are. It's how they survive."

"That's not what I mean, Governor. What the Phene do is an encoding, if you will. When young soldiers are sent to become auxiliaries with the Phene imperial army, the Phene have figured out a way to engineer the already existing neurosystem to compel them to obey Phene commands."

"This is a wild theory. Unproven. Ridiculous."

"But what if it's true? If it's true, it means the auxiliaries have been fighting to the death against us only because the Phene force them to do it. If it's true, if we can find a way to short-circuit the programming without the Phene finding out we've done so until it's too late to alter their conditioning protocols, it will change the course of our conflict with the Phene."

The lab coat breaks off and glances at the prisoner in alarm.

The woman says, "It doesn't matter that he heard. He'll be dead by tomorrow night."

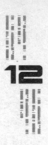

12

Their Laughter and Careless Smiles

The first outpost built on Molossia Prime was a temple named Dodona, sited amid scenic lakes as a foothold for a new colony. During the reign of Queen-Marshal Yǔ, when the Republic of Chaonia became a vassal state of the Phene Empire, the Phene had conscripted the temple and turned its grounds into a massive military base and administrative center. After the Phene retreat in the wake of their disastrous attempt to invade the Yele League, Queen-Marshal Metis, Yǔ's daughter, had left the district under military control and with restricted access for civilians. So when they reached the mainland, Sun and the survivors in her party had the famous temple to themselves.

Octavian stood twelve paces behind her as she burned offerings of incense and spirit money in honor of the deceased. The sharp blend of scents helped her tears flow. Unlike Hetty she could not concentrate on prayers. Her mind kept cycling through the moments after the explosion.

They'd rushed up onto the deck to see smoke and flames rising from the tender. Security 'birds had swept in within the hour. Investigators had proclaimed it a terrible accident. But she knew better. She just needed proof before she could act.

"Princess? We're ready to go." Octavian pinged a file into her network. "The queen-marshal's office has sent its condolences and requests you take a ten-day mourning retreat at the Uncorrupted Land sanctuary on Merciful Island. They've attached a revised schedule that will allow you to finish out the last month of visits—"

"No."

The others were waiting on the temple's portico, having already made their offerings and said their prayers. James held his cap against his chest. Alika played a quiet dirge. Hetty touched Sun's arm fleetingly, for comfort. Their cee-cees stood in the shadows, heads bowed.

"Let's go." She marched her group to the secondary comms center, an old Quonset hut left over from the weeks when Metis's corps of engineers had had to bring the base back on line quickly. The new primary comms center built by one of her uncles was three klicks away, and Sun wasn't about to make the trek.

The ensign on duty jumped to attention as Sun strode in. Her network access was still compromised by a deeper layer of suppression technology, doubtless controlled by the queen-marshal's staff.

She said to the fresh-faced ensign, "Give me secure access into the manifest of the military shipyards."

The ensign gulped but stayed stiff, chin up. "Your Highness. You'll need clearance from Captain Mirza at primary comms."

"The manifest," repeated Sun, temper sliding toward its sharpest edge.

A stern-faced chief popped out of a cubicle, took one "oh shit" look at the princess, and hastily said, "Ensign, with respect, wartime regulations dictate that the queen-marshal, her Companions, and the heir supersede chain of command."

Sun gave the chief a curt nod. As soon as the ensign linked her into the military node, she blinked straight into the manifest. The *Boukephalas* had two days earlier cleared inspection and was in orbit waiting to join up with the Eighth Fleet.

She patched through to Captain the Honorable Charles Tan. "I'm coming aboard. Consider your orders countermanded."

Alika plucked a discordant note.

"Sun, are you sure—" began James.

Hetty said, "I do not think—"

"Follow me or stay behind."

They dropped through the beacon into Chaonia System with all comms dark except for the secure military transponder. Leaving the *Boukephalas* on lockdown to keep her presence secret from Channel Idol, Sun took a Kestrel lander to the palace. She and her party disembarked wearing the dress uniforms standard at court for everyone who had military training, which was every adult who could serve in any capacity.

The princess chose an unobtrusive side passage to make her way to the queen-marshal's inner courtyard, a square garden surrounded by intimate audience chambers where the queen-marshal took supper with her own Companions and inner circle. This nexus of court activity was eerily deserted, as if a plague had stripped it of human existence.

Where was everyone?

Even Sun could not just walk into her mother's private suite. By the silence and the lazy *tick, tick* of a shutter knocking in the breeze there was no one to be found. She headed for the public wing of the palace, with its audience halls and temple square.

"Let me enter first." Octavian stepped in front of her as they reached Victory Hall. Sun gave him a questioning look. "Empty rooms may be a sign of civic unrest."

"There hasn't been civic unrest since the reign of my great-aunt."

"Even so, Your Highness."

She allowed the bodyguard to go through the door first, though the precaution felt like cowardice.

A glare of sunlight through open gates struck deep into Victory Hall. Any citizen could cross Petitioners Bridge to enter the hall, a common stop for tourists and locals alike. Yet on such a pleasant afternoon not one sightseer strolled through the exhibition's shifting narratives and images. Each of its shimmering augmented-reality pillars of calligraphy described one of the crucial battles of Chaonia's history and, most prominently, those of Eirene's reign.

They passed a stirring account of the sixth battle of Kanesh, where Queen-Marshal Nézhā had sacrificed his flagship and thus himself so the bulk of the fleet could escape a massive Hesjan ambush. The young Eirene had succeeded her brother as queen-marshal in place of his infant child. It was ever thus: a competent adult heir was preferable and even necessary given the incessant state of emergency.

There was, as yet, no pillar commemorating Na Iri.

James doffed his cap and pretended to shade his vision as they made their way around the pillar commemorating the battle of Aspera Drift. "Look, they've put a brighter halo around the image of Ereshkigal Lee. My eyes hurt."

"Don't mock," said Sun. "She died courageously."

"Whsst." Five paces ahead, Octavian halted. "Princess, to your right."

A familiar figure bustled toward them from the massive entry gates that led into the Temple of Celestial Peace.

Crane Marshal Zàofù wore a gratifyingly startled expression. "Sun! You are on Molossia."

"If I were on Molossia, I would not be here."

"And yet here you are," he reproved in a tone that reminded Sun of Zàofù's many complaints about her father's unsuitability to be consort. He swept his gaze over her retinue and offered a tiny dip of the chin in the direction of James before returning his full attention to the princess. "Had the queen-marshal wished you to break off in the middle of the assignment she gave you, she would have sent for you."

"Have you not heard the news, Marshal? My itinerary was cut short by the deaths of the Honorable Perseus Lee and Duke Guī Alargos when our yacht's tender exploded." She studied his face as she spoke, seeking any pinch of shame or surprise, but he merely furrowed his brows.

"A sudden and unexpected calamity—"

"I suppose it was unexpected."

"What do you mean, Your Highness?"

"A Lee House security detail arrived within the hour to assist us in collecting the remains, not that there was much left of the tender or the two men. They came so quickly that either they knew of the explosion in advance—"

He blustered, wringing his hands. "What are you saying?"

"Assassinations are not unknown in Chaonia's history. An

explosion of such intensity is certainly suspicious. But I struggle to find a reason why Percy would be targeted. He had less ambition than a bucket of rocks. And Duke had no connections that would offer benefit to anyone in the case of his death. So either this security detail knew about the attack in advance, which is unlikely unless my mother wants me dead—"

"You are her heir!" The marshal regarded Sun with a troubled gaze.

"—or a security detail had been shadowing me the entire time without me ever being informed I was under observation. Does the queen-marshal not trust me?"

His mouth popped open, but he controlled himself and found a calming tone. "Such a shock must be debilitating, and—"

"It may be debilitating for you, but it energizes me to seek answers."

She spied a group of splendidly dressed people emerging from the gates that led to the temple: the queen-marshal attended by her Companions and other notables, including her most recent consort, Baron Voy. The festive clothing they wore revealed the happy occasion they were celebrating.

Thinking of how disrespectful their laughter and careless smiles were to dead Perseus, Sun was too furious to speak. Fortunately Hetty always knew what to say.

"With such a cloud of grief Her Highness Sun was sure her mother's wedding had been postponed."

Zàofù shook his head. "The dates for the festivities were set in motion months ago."

"Oh, were they now? Set in motion when Moira Lee visited the queen-marshal at COSY, perhaps?" Sun snapped.

He blinked, but recovered with the speed of an experienced soldier. "It's not possible to halt such proceedings without inviting bad fortune."

Sun stepped around the marshal and headed for her mother.

Seeing her, the queen-marshal stopped dead. "Sun! What means this? I did not have you recalled from Molossia."

"Death recalled me. Or have you forgotten about the news already, engrossed and diverted by your latest conquest?"

"We all regret young Perseus's death, so don't try to shame me in such a public fashion. I have no idea what your goal is." Eirene's brow furrowed into its thunderous aspect, all storm and threat. "I suppose your father put you up to it."

"What do you mean by that?" Sun stiffened.

"He's jealous of what he does not possess."

"You fancied him well enough once upon a time. You still use him when it benefits you, even if you try to hide it from your own court."

The queen-marshal raised her right hand, stabbing with two fingers toward her daughter. Although she did not touch her daughter, the gesture was remarkably aggressive, always Eirene's style. "Your inability to see past your own pride and your blind loyalty to that impossible man is exactly why I arranged matters to keep you out of the way for the wedding."

Baron Voy glided forward, interposing himself between mother and daughter. Aloysius had the grace of a dancer and the speed of a fencer, and he deployed his diplomat's smile to powerful effect.

"Now, here, Eirene. Let no clouds mar this auspicious day. Let me speak to Sun. I will meet you there."

The queen-marshal cast a final glare toward her daughter and, with her household, crossed out of the hall toward the landing deck.

"I know what you're thinking," said the baron in his pleasant voice with its rich Yele timbre, the accent every Chaonian strove to emulate.

"Do you? What exactly is that?"

"You're concerned at the impropriety with regard to Perseus Lee. But he's officially part of your household, not the queen-marshal's household and not his birth household, not anymore."

"We have observed the fitting rites." She bristled defensively.

"That wasn't the point I intended, Your Highness, for of course I do not doubt you have done everything correctly." He offered a gracious nod of acknowledgment. "As for the wedding, this really is the most auspicious possible day for such a glorious union. We all know better than to go against the ancient traditions of the Celestial Empire, which sustain us in rightful harmony with the universe."

"You seemed remarkably unconcerned at being supplanted by a new consort," said Sun, knowing the words to be rude and yet driven by the raw wound of Percy's death.

He chuckled. "Eirene and I contracted a marriage of alliance, a seal of peace. Queen-marshals marry as they must to secure the stability of their realms. Not just for personal satisfaction."

When Sun did not answer, Baron Voy gestured toward the open gates that led into the temple. "The marriage has already been solemnized. The feast will be held at Lee House as soon as everyone assembles. You have clearly come a distance, in haste, and with grim news as your shadow. The queen-marshal will understand you are too tired to attend. Rest in your chambers to collect yourself after the trouble we are all so sorry to hear about. May I have some of my household serve you with food and drink after your journey?"

"I'm not going to my chambers, Baron."

With a wry smile he gave her the appropriate half bow, for although she outranked him by being heir to the queen-marshal, he was nevertheless a reigning consort with influence over both the queen-marshal's council and the Yele League, whom he represented. "Then I shall see you there."

13

In Which the Wily Persephone Is Reminded That White Is the Color of Death

A proximity chime wakes me, followed by the Swallow's voice.

"Please allow me to inform you that we will be landing shortly."

The sun's rim breaches the eastern horizon. Below, the grand city of Argos has woven itself along the spiny coastline with the persistence of mold. The great henge where the popularly elected Citizen Assembly meets is built from massive ceramic stones as glossy a black as the card Solomon gave me. Facing it, the queen-marshal's palace rises out of the shallow bay like a half-sunken ship with seven mirrored sails, wind and sun glittering in its vanes. The light-studded arches of Petitioners Bridge link the palace to the land.

I dig into my duffel for the tuning fork Resh gave me before she left for the fleet; it's one of the five items I took with me when I made what I thought was my great escape to CeDCA. Clutching it like a talisman against harm, I squint into the rising sun to try to catch a glimpse of home, an island out on the waters. So I'm surprised when the Swallow signals me to strap in, then drops down toward the huge spoked transportation hub everyone calls the Wheelhouse, right in the middle of the city. With its eight arms reaching all the way around the world, you can get on a train and never get off until you step back out onto the Wheelhouse concourse.

People with access to private aircars never land on the secure tarmac by the Wheelhouse; they don't need to because they don't use public transportation. But the Swallow sets down on the landing pad next to a reinforced security hangar just as its exterior floodlights snap off for the day. Gendarmes emerge from the guardhouse. Adrenaline spikes through me. I am the worst of children, for I have defied my parents and abandoned my obligations. Perhaps my family honestly intends to kill me, since death is just another form of running away.

Then I see a young woman walking between the guards. She's wearing a fitted mid-thigh-length tunic of shiny gold damask over sheer leggings that sparkle like miniature stars have gotten caught in the fabric. In stark contrast to her fashionable clothes she's carrying a camo duffel that could have been distributed from the same factory-issue commissary as mine. The closer she gets the more beautiful I see she is: tight black curls colored with blue and silver highlights, curves in perfect proportion, and an amazing face. Instead of being perfect like they've been poured from a mold, her features have a striking aesthetic that makes you stare to try to figure out what makes it so alluring: nose a little too big but not really, eyes that look sleepy and alert at the same time, a strong chin that gives weight to her face. The guards are sneaking looks at her, trying to be polite about it, like they can't believe they've stumbled so close to a treasure they may never see again in their lives.

The door irises open. I step away from the window, self-consciously straighten my rumpled tunic, and turn to face the entrance.

The Swallow says, "Please allow me to inform you that I am here to pick up a passenger, according to my instructions."

The young woman appears, walking with a stride I admire because it feels purposeful and confident. The sight of her makes me miss my friends, wishing I had someone beside me to share this with. Solomon would die from sheer awestruckness.

She pauses at the ramp.

The Swallow speaks. "Peace be upon you, welcome, and please be seated."

She climbs the steps into the interior and offers me a poised smile as the door shuts behind her, sealing us in and the guards out. She's wearing a scent of sandalwood as if she's come from a temple. Her dark brown complexion is flawless.

"Peace be upon you," she says.

I reflexively answer, "And upon you peace."

She nods, acknowledging the formal reply. "I have the name Tiana Yáo Alaksu, although I go by Ti. Are you also bound for Lee House?" Her voice is melodic, perfectly modulated to be neither too distant nor too familiar.

"I am," I say, because now I am incredibly curious. "I'm Perse."

"My apologies. I am not familiar with the name."

"Short for *Persephone*. Uh. Persephone Li Alargos. But call me Perse. Everyone I like does."

Her eyes wrinkle up like she's restraining a laugh, and she drops a bit of the formality. "What do people you don't like call you?"

"Asshole."

She laughs, and I let myself grin just a little.

The warning bell chimes. As she indicates her duffel, a softer accent starts to flatten her formal diction. "Where do I stow this? I've never traveled in a Swallow. I remember watching guests arrive in private aircars for the wedding of Queen-Marshal Eirene to Baron Voy. I thought he was so handsome! I guess not attractive in the ways that count, though, what with the queen-marshal getting married again. In a love match this time, so they say."

"The queen-marshal is marrying again?"

"How can you not know? Such big news! It's everywhere on Channel Idol!"

The warning chime pings twice. "Please allow me to inform you that it is necessary to take your seats."

"Hold on." I show her how to strap in for the ascent. "The administrators at CeDCA limit our access to the system-wide net."

"Why wouldn't they want you to know about the queen-marshal's upcoming marriage?"

"News distracts from our studies."

As I strap into the flight chair next to her, Ti keeps talking in a bubbly way that makes me think she's nervous and trying not to show it. Maybe she left behind friends too and wishes they had her back.

"The royal wedding is certainly the main topic these days. Red banners hanging over the main avenues. Double Happiness cakes in the markets. A drink called 'the Lovers' Knot' made with pomegranate and chocolate—which, if you ask me, is nasty."

The Swallow vibrates as it rises. She giggles, slaps a hand over her mouth, exchanges a glance with me, and giggles again. Her polished accent is sliding away like an avalanche gaining speed. I find her citizen's bluntness exhilarating.

"Sorry, I'm not usually this goofy. It's just . . . I'm the grand-daughter of kalo farmers from Abundant Wine Province. I never dreamed of traveling like this."

"Why are you headed to Lee House?" I ask cautiously, hoping my speech has picked up enough rough edges from my classmates to not give me away.

She lowers the hand, which, I note, is perfectly manicured, her nails painted with tiny white roses, symbolizing devotion.

"Work. I'm a graduate of Vogue Academy. I'm to be a cee-cee."

It's all clear now. She's for my twin brother, Perseus. I wonder what happened to his cee-cee, Duke. I hope nothing bad. He was my first crush, the true unattainable because he was only hired when Percy was sent to the palace, and at eleven I definitely never let anyone know about my secret longing, certainly not Duke.

"I signed up for a seven-year term, not a lifetime contract," Ti adds. "What are you here for?"

"This whole trip came as a complete surprise. To be honest, I have no idea why I've been summoned or what the Lee family wants from me."

"Bodyguard, maybe? I mean, if you've been training at the Central Defense Cadet Academy."

I glance down at the CeDCA badge stamped into the fabric of my tunic. "I'm specializing in transportation engineering. You know about the academy?"

"Doesn't everyone? A boy from Aksu—that's my people's hometown—got into CeDCA seven years ago. He was the first person from our local district to pass the entry exam. The celebration in his honor lasted a week. Maybe you know him? Anders Rèn Alaksu."

I trawl my memory back through the waters of my first year but come up with no fish on that hook. "No. Sorry. The academy has fifteen thousand cadets."

She's wearing a set of cheap brass bangles around her left wrist, and she toys with them as she muses, much more comfortable now she has me pegged as a citizen like her.

"He told me a rumor went around that one of the cadets was a kid from one of the Core Houses. Imagine! Someone who could have gone anywhere they wanted—to the royal academy even—but they had to steal a place from a worthy citizen's child who didn't have those options. How selfish is that!"

She pauses, catching my wince. "Is something wrong?"

"Light in my eyes. Look." I raise a hand to shade against the sun.

She shades her own eyes to follow my gaze. "Wow."

Wind feathers the waves. Now and again the gold-frilled spine of one of the huge leviathans we call a *wave-swallowing charybdis* pokes above the surface. Generator towers stand in clusters, water churning around them. We are speeding toward one of the seven atolls dropped like spores into a half circle across the vast bay: the islands owned by the Core Houses who provide the ministers for the ruler's council, the marshals for the Fleet and the Guard, and the Royal Companions for the rulers themselves. It's an old tradition borrowed from the lost Celestial Empire: eight noble houses rule the lives and destinies of everything in the heavens.

Especially that of a wayward, rebellious child.

My bravado is starting to wear thin. Words die in my throat as Lee House's island compound comes into view and the aircar banks toward the landing field. The island forms an irregular oval encircled by a wide reef. Its buildings and gardens in their turn encircle a large central lagoon—public pavilions like the audience hall, the banquet hall, the receiving halls, and the tribunal cluster at the southern, narrower end of the island, built three meters above sea level along a boardwalk that looks over the lagoon. Extensive residences and service buildings crowd the broader, rockier northern end. Everything faces inward. For all its wealth and glamour, Lee House is a fortress ringed with a cliff-like exterior wall, glowering spotlights, and stun cannons. Once you've walked in and the gates have closed behind you, they won't let you out.

"Wow, that's imposing. You nervous too?" The sympathy in the twist of Ti's lips chokes me up.

"Yeah. I'm nervous."

As we skim low I notice both the visitor and family hangars are full. We put down at the service entrance amid tight ranks of delivery aircars and a double column of armored military vans marked with the sunburst of the royal house.

The presence of royal vehicles worries me so much I don't at first respond when the door whirs open. "Please allow me to inform you that we have successfully arrived at our destination."

Ti grabs her duffel and heads out ahead of me. Protocol dictates I go first, as an honorable of the house, but of course she thinks I'm a newly hired bodyguard. As citizens in the republic we are equal under the law, while within the umbra of the royal administration a cee-cee outranks a bodyguard.

I grab my duffel and hurry down the steps to the pristine ceramic pavement. Out of sight, around the curve of the car, a familiar voice speaks.

"Peace be upon you. I am Abdul-Lee Kadmos Rèn Aljiu, your chatelaine and supervisor—that is, if you are Citizen Tiana Yáo Alaksu?"

"And upon you peace, Citizen. I am she. I am reporting to fulfill the terms of my contract."

"Very good. I thought . . . but never mind. If you will come this way . . ."

I step into view. His politely bland expression cracks into a grin. As quickly as I see it, the smile vanishes and he becomes the outwardly solemn teacher who was my tutor for nine years. He raises a hand, fore- and middle finger pointed toward the heavens, our old signal for silence.

"Citizen Tiana, I see you have met the Honorable Persephone Lee. You both will come with me. The schedule has been moved up, and there isn't much time."

As Kadmos heads toward the hexagonal gate that leads into the service wing, Ti's gaze fixes on me with narrow-eyed accusation. Her lips pinch together as she gives me a wrinkled-up scrunchy face. Then she recalls herself as she truly takes in who I am.

"Honored Persephone, please allow me to apologize for any discourtesy I showed you in the depths of my ignorance," she murmurs, sarcasm a layer of sickly sweet syrup coating her tone.

"It's Perse. Please. I meant what I said." I start after Kadmos.

Ti lengthens her stride to catch up. "You're the girl in Anders's story, aren't you?"

"His complaint is fair. After my sister died my family made it clear I wouldn't be allowed to join the military and would have to take my place in the business of Lee House. Let's just say I'm not interested in being groomed to join a family tradition of spying, torture, and extrajudicial murder. The blind admissions process for CeDCA was my way out."

"Yet here you are." She gives me a side-eye glance worthy of a master, and it makes me smile because in a funny way it feels like a peace offering.

"Yeah. Here I am. And here you are. One girl's disaster is another girl's delight."

"Wah! I am just here for work, no delight intended." She glances around, then grabs my wrist and pulls me to a stop, leans close, whispers, "Extrajudicial murder? Is that really true?"

In that instant I know in the depths of my stony, untrusting heart that I hope we can become friends, and I couldn't even tell you why. So I kiss her on the cheek like kinfolk greeting.

"Cameras and listening ears everywhere," I murmur into her ear.

She releases my wrist and steps back with a nudge against my hip to alert me.

Over to our right, the hatch of a military van pops open. A file of guards push out a display cage with glass walls as if they're transporting a valuable piece of art. Equipped with a hoverboard base, the cage glides a handbreadth above the ground.

A young man stands in the cage, arms akimbo, elbows brushing either side and face a handbreadth from the glass because there's no room for him to turn around. He's wearing dark green trousers and nothing else except a metal sheen of circuitry drawing patterns like elaborate tattoos over his honed chest and arms and his tawny, beardless face. He looks like energy held on a leash. Heat on legs. Let's be real. If he were a cadet in one of the other fifth-year cohorts, I'd have been hanging out at his playing field every night.

But he isn't a cadet. He isn't even Chaonian. I can't help but hiss a little, as an audience in a theater will do when a villain walks onto the stage.

Ti slaps a hand to her chest. "Is that a banner soldier? I thought they couldn't be captured alive. You must never look them in the eye because they are programmed to be predators and will imprint on you as prey."

He sees us. Sees *me*. His whole body shudders like he's trying to break out of a thousand ropes binding him taut. He slams a shoulder so hard to the right that the hover platform rocks. Immediately one of the guards jabs a prod through a small hole in the cage and presses it into the prisoner's back. Both Ti and I flinch and then swallow as a cascading pressure change disturbs our ears. The prisoner sags, although he doesn't drop. Percussion echo is the only known counter to a Gatoi soldier in full flood—it's a means of disrupting the neural flow—but it has a low rate of success in battle because it has to be applied to bare flesh.

Now rendered unable to move or gesture he nevertheless keeps his gaze fixed on me as the cage hovers toward the security hangar with its escort of eight guards. His eyes gleam; they actually gleam a sullen, oily amber like they are conducting energy. His stare challenges me, and of course I don't back down or look away. I couldn't even if I wanted to, and I don't want to.

Only when the cage, and the man, vanish can I tear my eyes away. My heart is pounding and my cheeks are flushed. *"You have bad taste in crushes, Perse,"* Solomon would mock, and then I'd have to punch his arm and hurt my hand as I'd feebly retort that looking isn't crushing.

Ti interrupts my scattered thoughts in a voice rough with anger. "My father fought in the campaign at Kanesh. He came back with an arm missing. Said a Gatoi fighter tore it off. Literally tore it off."

"I'm sorry." I swallow, shaking off the intensity of the moment as I recover my voice. "That's rough. I adored my sister Resh. I used to follow her around when she was home on leave. She was the best thing in my life when I was a kid."

"The eight-times-worthy hero Captain the Honorable Ereshkigal Lee, savior of the Second Fleet," Ti murmurs. "When I was younger and played War Against the Phene we all used to fight over who got to be her."

She squeezes my hand, and I squeeze back in solidarity and in thanks.

"Girls! Hurry!"

Ahead of us Kadmos uses his retinal signature to key open a hexagonal gate. It's a relief to leave behind the courtyard with its unexpected glimpse of a captured Gatoi berserker. We follow my old tutor down a lane flanked by carpentry and repair shops and warehouses. He halts in front of a round gate and waits for us to catch up.

Addressing Ti, he says, "Round gates indicate egress into the private residential areas. Hexagonal gates are present in all the service areas. Square gates are for Lee House security only. The audience hall and temple have octagonal gates. That's your first lesson. Now come along. We have only one hour before we have to be in the main hall."

"Kadmos, we saw a Gatoi prisoner. Is he here to be interrogated? How was he captured?"

He steps through the gate without answering me. His back is stiff, the way he would stand when his teaching was being observed by my father or aunt. His posture gives me a message, but it's the unexpected appearance of his schoolroom avatar that surprises me: a shiny gold ★ blinking in my field of vision. Lee House students are given a private comm-link to their tutors to keep study chatter out of the main Lee network. I'd thought my family would have closed mine down, but evidently my departure four years and nine months ago was so abrupt they didn't bother, or else they knew they would drag me back eventually.

On the comm-link a three-finger signal for silence appears in a flash of alarm red before winking out. Kadmos doesn't look back, but I've gotten the message. Instead of impatiently repeating my questions I follow in silence.

As we walk down the old familiar lane with two-story residential buildings on each side I notice the usual décor of red lanterns and potted dwarf elm and pine trees has been embellished with troughs of white carnations and wreaths of white irises on every door. White streamers hang from all the upstairs balconies.

I exchange a worried glance with Ti. The crowded hangars, the Gatoi prisoner, and the mourning embellishments all point to a blend of victory and disaster, news my family hasn't bothered to let me know beforehand and has, in fact, taken some pains to conceal from me.

Kadmos takes us not to the children's wing but to an apartment door along the lane given over to living quarters of the unmarried adults of the family, anyone twenty or older. He ushers us into a small reception room so precisely furnished with three chairs, a couch, and a side table for refreshments that it feels like a stage set. The back sitting room looks over an interior garden. We don't have time to glimpse more than magnolia in bloom before we are herded up a flight of stairs to a bedroom suite. A white-haired woman wearing the high-collared uniform of my father's interrogation division awaits us. She's accompanied by two racks of clothing in various styles, the fabrics in shades from white to ivory to pearl.

White is the color of death.

A sick fear boils up in my belly, burning at the back of my throat.

"Who's dead, Kadmos?" I demand.

The woman taps her ear as a signal to someone who isn't here, someone she is communicating with.

Kadmos presses his palms together, gives a curt bow, and withdraws.

"Who died?" I ask again, shaking because I realize the woman is not going to tell me. Maybe her tongue is frozen so she can't talk, or maybe everyone is under orders not to converse with me like the way my mother got tired of me beating her at chess so she made me play blindfolded while claiming she was doing it to help me improve.

All the torqued-up anger and resentment uncoils in a burst.

"Tell me who died!"

The agent blinks. That's all.

Ti glides forward like a doll brought to life, her movements fluid and graceful as she flips through the rack of clothing, assaying each outfit and then assaying me.

"Honored Persephone, give me a moment . . . Let's find a decent outfit. No, too busy, whoever thought of you in bows and ribbons? *Zut!* No one wears scalloped sleeves! Oh, dear, this has a sallow tinge that will look awful on any complexion—what were they thinking? Here, this classic uniform jacket style will suit you best."

"Bland like me," I mutter.

Her eyelids flicker with a suppressed emotion, but instead of replying she indicates double doors that lead into a spacious dressing room. "Citizen, I will assist the Honorable Persephone into her garments in the privacy of the other room."

The agent raises a hand, and the doors into the dressing room slide closed and click shut so we can't leave. Footfalls scuff the stairs, a tread like the ascent of doom. My hands clench. With the outfit draped over her arm, Ti turns to face the entry. A twitch of apprehension flattens her lips before she controls it and fixes an unobjectionable smile on her beautiful face.

The man who walks in wears a formal mourning robe, the splendor of his dress matched only by its elegance. Each accessory is a subtly gradated shade of white: his belt, the braided trim at the hem and sleeves, even his tassels. The fabric shines like light, so blinding that Ti flinches, averting her eyes. I deploy the nictating membrane built into my eyes to cut the glare.

Of course I bow. He's my father.

But as I straighten up, anger takes hold of my tongue.

"Who is dead?" I demand.

"No greeting, beloved daughter? No affectionate words for your father after our long separation?"

My father is a seer of Iros. Born with eyes blind to the visible spectrum, he sees heat and lies.

"Respected Sir." I bow again, even though it's not necessary. "I'm not glad to be home, or to see you, if that's what you mean."

He nods gravely, acknowledging the truth of my words and not offended because unlike my mother he is no hypocrite. His seer's gaze examines Ti. What he seeks I don't know, except that her physical beauty can mean nothing to him.

"You are Persephone's new companion?"

"I am, Your Honor." She gives the exact forty-five degrees of bow proper to a citizen meeting a foreign dignitary who is also a high government official because of his marriage into a Chaonian Core House.

I interrupt. "I thought she was for Perseus."

His attention returns to me. I take an involuntary step back.

"Your brother is dead."

Dead. The word makes no sense. "Percy . . ."

"Is dead," he repeats.

"But I just saw him ten days ago . . . he was on Channel Idol. He was just on Channel Idol swimming on Molossia Prime. The ocean looked really beautiful . . ." My voice fails.

"That's where it happened," he says. "Ten days ago."

Ti stares at the tableau made by me and my father as at a speech being given in a language she doesn't understand.

"Did you know?" I ask her. "It would be all over the news."

She shakes her head, thrown off-balance for once. "No news of this tragic death has been announced on Channel Idol. No wonder my hiring and departure happened so fast."

"Why hasn't it been on the news?" I say to my father. My hands have started to sweat. He doesn't answer, which means he won't answer or thinks I ought to already have figured it out. I add, "Duke was there too."

"Duke too," he says without a flicker of emotion. "It was an unfortunate accident. Of course legally Perseus no longer belongs to our household. Thus we are not legally responsible for the mourning rites. But naturally we mourn. Your mother asked for you."

"For me?" I can think of few things that would please me less, nor do I have any reason to think my mother wants me except as a passive receptacle into which she can pour her manifold complaints.

"She insists that she, I, and you observe the old Chaonian tradition of one hundred days of austerity. The altar room has been set up with a memorial for—"

He blinks, breaking off, and steps to one side to listen to an incoming message. By the twist of his mouth the news displeases him. But he is a seer, trained in a rigorous discipline, and cools any spark of anger as he turns his attention back to me.

I take another step back, reach out, and find Tiana's hand. When her fingers close around mine it surprises me how much comfort I take from her grasp.

"A change of plans," he says. "As soon as you garb yourself in appropriate clothing you will be escorted to your new duty station in Scylla Hall."

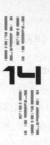

Rule of Sun, Rule One

Sun lay on her back on a bench, hands linked behind her head, ankles crossed. Her body was resting, but her mind was ablaze as she stared at the blue sky through the transparent dome of Scylla Hall. Upon arrival at Lee House she and her Companions had not been escorted to the banquet hall as she had expected. Instead they had been shown into this hall furnished with a huge sculpture of a five-necked scylla wrapped around a large circular bench carved from staggeringly expensive cherrywood.

There, for two hours, they waited.

"Still locked," announced Isis as she and Wing finished yet another circuit of the five entry passages, all sealed shut.

"I was completely taken by surprise," the princess murmured to Hetty, who sat cross-legged on the floor beside her. "That must never happen again."

"You must not mumble in these halls, dear Sun." Hetty tapped the princess's forearm, then let her fingers linger on skin, luxuriating in the contact. "Lee House will be listening. You know that."

"There's plenty of covering noise." She tipped her chin to indicate the others.

Alika had seated himself on one of the wedge-shaped scylla heads, using the astonishing sculpture as a stage on which to play. He was working his way through chord progressions, scales, and arpeggios on the koa ukulele he used on Idol Faire. The clack and shush of bladed fans opening and closing traced Candace's martial practice around the circular hall. With his cap perched precariously at the back of his head, James hunched over a tablet, his fingers tapping much more noisily than they needed to. Navah crouched over a portable burner preparing a fresh pot of tea. The gurgle of boiling water rose to a whistle.

Percy would have been barging around making jokes and getting in the way. He had been the best at distracting observers with his antics to give Sun a measure of privacy.

Percy. Dead.

Her cheeks got hot and her throat choked on the rage she could not reveal beneath the eye of surveillance.

Keep your temper in check.

She had to move. A roll brought her up to her feet. She called up the encrypted text-only message she had received from her father. It had come in exactly five hours after she'd left a ping in his safe box telling him the news about Perseus and Duke, a message James had managed to get out three hours after the explosion. She'd read the words twenty or thirty times already.

"This business with Perseus can't have been an accident. Be alert for more trouble. Your enemies will use his death as an excuse to plant yet another spy into your inner circle."

"Maybe my mother genuinely believes in his project, but it's no coincidence she got both me and Father out of the way before the wedding festivities," she muttered to Hetty. "Some faction within the court is finally moving against us. I'm sure of it."

A shift of air whispered a change of pressure in the lofty hall. One of the passages opened.

As Sun turned to face the passage she closed her hand into a fist to banish the message. "Here comes the spy. Greet them as they deserve."

James rolled up his tablet. Navah stood over by the wall holding the teapot. Candace spun into an en garde position while Alika kept his seat on the sculpture and with a clever cadence shifted into an ancient song from the long-abandoned palaces of the Celestial Empire. His voice was sweet and true, and his singing as sharp a weapon as Candace's razor-edged battle fans.

Your cheating heart
Will tell on you

A short young woman strode into view. Seeing them, she halted so abruptly the taller person walking behind almost ran into her because the tall one was staring with a glassy expression at Alika.

Hetty whistled under her breath. "I'd draw her in a heartbeat. What a face!"

Sun frowned, studying the Lee girl, who was dressed in a severe military-cut jacket buttoned over trousers of off-white damask silk adorned by dangling strings of pearls. "Could James's wild dive into the twitch have caught the truth? She really does look like her war-hero sister, taking into account the difference in height and weight. I didn't think the eight-times-worthy and very dead Captain the Honorable Ereshkigal Lee was your style of unobtainable crush."

"It's not the Lee girl that I'm speaking of."

"Oh, you mean the cee-cee." Sun allowed herself to look away from the enemy at the glorious vision standing one step behind and to the right. "Effulgent Heaven! She's put us all in the shade."

"Tread with care. I sense a cunning trap."

The passage behind them sealed off, leaving the Lee girl and her cee-cee confined in the hall with them. The intruder finally collected herself enough to speak.

"I thought you were on Molossia—" The Lee girl broke off as her voice echoed too loudly beneath the roof.

"You have to be careful when thinking," remarked James in his laziest drawl, tugging his cap forward for emphasis. "You don't want to hurt yourself."

"Well, *that* was certainly an original insult," retorted the Lee girl with a crass lack of manners. She fixed her glare on Sun. "So *you* are Princess Sun. Is there anything I need to know about serving in your retinue, which it seems I'm now required to do?"

Sun raised a hand, palm out in the gesture that meant *do not fear.* "Rule of Sun, Rule One. Never show weakness because the moment we show weakness, we will die."

"Does Her Highness speak with the collective 'we' or in a royal first-person 'we'?" The Lee girl quirked up one eyebrow.

Sun's jaw tightened. "What do you think?"

The eyebrow lowered as she ventured a falsely sympathetic smile. "I think the plural royal you—that's you—shouldn't trust anyone in Lee House."

"Does that advice include the singular individual you—that's you—standing in front of me as my newest Companion?"

The smile faded into a hard stare. "Believe me, I wouldn't be here, forced to become one of your Companions, if I'd had any choice in the matter. What is Rule Two?"

"There is no Rule Two. There is only survival."

"You need to intone that with more of a *mwahaha* villain voice. Maybe lean closer as if you intend to loom ominously over me." She tapped the top of her own head with a mocking gesture. "Not that you're quite tall enough to loom, I mean. Not even over me, and as you may have noticed, I'm short."

The memory of blood in water was never far from Sun's thoughts. "We can trade insults all day, but I don't care about your cheap shots. Your brother and his cee-cee were *murdered*."

The Lee girl swayed. Her cee-cee placed a hand on her back in a show of support. "I was told it was an accident."

"It's true the judiciary ruled the incident a mishap with a malfunctioning motor. But consider this." She glanced toward Hetty, who looked over to where Navah was setting out the tea tray. Sun whispered so only the Lee girl could hear, "If the tender had been stowed in its storage hatch inside the yacht when it exploded, we all would have died. It's pure chance Percy and Duke had taken it out when they did. It wasn't an accident, no matter what the judiciary ruled. It was an assassination attempt."

The Lee girl sucked in a breath, but she didn't give ground. "That's a serious charge. If it were true, Lee House would know. My father is a seer of Iros, obliged by his oath to the god to tell the truth. He told me it was an accident."

"So your father always tells you the truth?"

"Of course he does. Doesn't yours?"

"Nice try, but you obviously don't know my father. So let's get back to your honest dad. Did he ever tell you all the Lee House daughters, including you, are clones of your aunt?"

"What? *What?*"

"What, are they clones? Or, what aunt are they clones of? To answer both questions, clones of the aunt who was implicated in the destruction of an entire refugee camp."

"First of all, clones have been illegal since the plagues that hit during the collapse of the Apsaras Convergence. Eight hundred years ago."

"Yes, thank you. I know history too."

"Second of all, my aunt Nona died before I was born. And your so-called *history* about her is just plain wrong. She did everything she could to save the camp."

"Of course that's what Lee House would say. They're the ones who covered it up. She bombed the camp into shards for the crime of being inhabited by refugees who dared to seek a safe harbor away from the fighting on Kanesh. She claimed the refugees were harboring Phene spies. She said there wasn't time to sort out the innocent from the guilty before the guilty betrayed the republic." She tilted her head to the left as she measured the Lee girl from top to toe before looking her in the eye with a shake of the head meant to convey disappointment. "Your father never saw fit to tell you the truth about her?"

"You're making that up to rattle me. You weren't alive then either."

"I'm the heir. I know a lot of things that involve the highest level of security clearance as well as particular information the official histories keep secret." She glanced at James. He tipped his cap. "For example, your aunt's grotesque legacy of illegal bio-experimentation is why all the Lee House daughters of your generation are named after death goddesses from the Celestial Empire. Unless they really did not tell you. I suppose they might not have wanted you to know."

Hetty squeezed Sun's hand. "Enough. That is enough. You can stop now."

The Lee girl was shock-faced and pallid. "You *b*—"

"Perse," interrupted her cee-cee, gliding forward like trouble on glorious wings. She wore a glistening dress, a crown of hair woven with tiny lights, and a smile so polished it was a threat. Her bow was gracious, her hand gestures like flowing silk. "Peace be upon you, Your Illustrious Highness."

"And upon you peace." Sun crossed her arms as a shield against an ambush.

"As her humble cee-cee, please allow me the honor of introducing to you the Honorable Persephone Lee, your new Companion. She comes to you today in obedience to the covenant pledged between the seven Core Houses and the constitutional throne, the eighth House, that each House shall always provide one of its own children as a Companion to the heir. As hostage, as guardian, and as loyal friend. I myself have the name Tiana Yáo Alaksu. For myself I have sealed a seven-year contract to serve the Honorable Persephone. We had expected a more formal introduction and perhaps even a briefing." She caught the Lee girl's eye and gave her a nod before turning back to Sun. "You may find us unprepared for the transition into your esteemed company. If there is anything we need to know before we proceed with today's expectedly joyous celebration, I pray you humbly, let me serve as I am trained to do."

Hetty laughed with delight.

Alika plucked a wrong note and, startled by the dissonance, stopped playing.

"Alika," said James with a smirk, "you look like you've been pole-axed and left for dead. Your mouth is open."

Alika closed his mouth. When Tiana smiled sympathetically at him in her most decorous manner, he began fiddling with the tuning knobs.

"Dearest Alika," James continued, "sometimes I forget you're the most rustic of country cousins, plucked from impoverished obscurity. And then I remember all over again."

Alika flushed. "Could you be more of a jerk, James?"

"Yes, I could, but I won't be out of respect for our new comrades." James pulled off his cap and offered a sweeping bow in

Tiana's direction. "To beauty and accomplishment, I offer all my admiration."

"Enough games," Sun went on, flooded with manic cheer now that the Lee girl had been put in her place and gutted. "We loved your brother, Persephone, and we don't want you. That's the collective we, for me and my companions. But it seems we are stuck with you despite—"

"What joyous celebration?" the Lee girl interrupted. "Lee House is in mourning for my brother."

"Fake innocence doesn't work on me any better than mockery does," retorted Sun. "Furthermore both tactics annoy me, as I hope you've learned with our last exchange. If you haven't, our time together is going to be very rough. So back off."

A bell rang once, twice, and three times. Isis appeared from a passage behind them, checking her harness of weapons. Wing landed on her shoulder and, with a chirp of satisfaction, folded its leathery wings.

"What bell is that? What signal do we hear?" asked Hetty.

"It's the official summons," said the Lee girl. "You do know that Scylla Hall is where supplicants and criminals are made to wait before they are brought before the Lee House tribunal, don't you?"

"So your family is deliberately insulting me by making me wait here, is that what you're saying?"

The Lee girl's expression shaded from hostility to something more like puzzlement. "Yes, but why would they want to insult you? They are loyal Chaonians, and you're the heir."

Sun muttered in a voice that only Hetty was close enough to hear, "I am as good a Chaonian as any of them are, as I've proven ten times over. What do I lack that my mother the queen-marshal allows me to be slighted in this way?"

Hetty rested a hand on Sun's forearm with the softest touch. "In my eyes you lack nothing. That's the truth. Well, patience, maybe, and a tuneful voice."

The gentle humor slid right off Sun's armored nerves. She stood in rigid silence as her Companions and their cee-cees efficiently readied themselves.

Then she beckoned to the newcomer. "Persephone, you may stand beside me as your twin used to do, and murmur secret messages in my ear. Percy knew everything and everyone and all their business too, just as a child of Lee House is meant to do. I rely on you for the same service."

The Lee girl's look of alarm surprised her. Tiana whispered in her ear and evidently reassured her enough that her expression relaxed marginally.

"Of course, Princess Sun." With her cee-cee as close as a shadow behind her, she stepped in and took her place.

Sun hooked her fingers around the girl's elbow, just as if they were the best of friends. "Call me Sun. All my Companions do. It's a mark of our familiarity and equality. I'll call you Persephone."

"I prefer Perse."

"I am sure you do, Persephone."

The girl had a dead-flat stare like she'd tamped down the steam trying to boil out of her ears. Unlike Percy she had the ability to remain silent.

"We go," said Sun.

Octavian had all this time been standing in camouflaged silence against the wall. Shock staff in hand, he stepped out of the shadows. His booming voice startled the newcomers.

"Princess. Stay on full alert."

A passage opened. Beyond the open seal a rectangular, glass-walled transport pod awaited them. They hung on to overhead bars as the pod shot out on tracks over the clear water of the central lagoon. Iridescent fish flashed within alternating patches of white sand and feathery coral speckled with brilliant anemones. A right curve took them to a long boardwalk lined with walled pavilions, each large enough to accommodate big crowds. They disembarked in front of a pavilion draped in festive red. A swarm of media wasps zoomed in on their group and especially on Alika.

The pavilion's massive archways were carved to resemble the

intertwining necks of scyllas. They opened into a huge hall packed with round tables decorated in red tablecloths and gold place settings. Notables from every branch of the republic and the court were already seated, chattering noisily. All wore festival clothing.

"This looks nothing like a funeral meal." Persephone's lips pressed together as her gaze dropped to compare her clothing, then lifted to examine how Hetty had softened the brightness of her yellow dress with a cream-colored crocheted overskirt wrapped in a decorative netting over the skirt of the gown. "Why is everyone dressed for a wedding?"

Sun tightened her fingers on Persephone's arm harder than she needed to, but all the girl did was tense her muscles against Sun's grip. "You do know who my mother the queen-marshal is marrying, don't you?"

"No."

No.

"How would I know?" Persephone went on. "We receive a censored feed at the academy. I haven't spoken to my family for almost five years."

A pinprick of suspicion shivered in Sun's mind. "Is that true?"

"With your stratospheric level of security clearance you can easily find out where I've been." Under her breath she added, "Asshole."

Tiana whispered, "She really doesn't know, Your Resplendent Highness."

"Princess Sun!" An attendant wearing the emerald tree badge of Lee House pressed palms together for a bow. "Your Highness! I'm afraid all the seats are filled, but we can set up an extra table in the overflow pavilion. If you'll follow me I'll take you—"

"Oh no, don't agree," said Persephone. "They're setting you up to place you in the cheap seats with the lesser dignitaries."

"Or you're setting me up to discourteously reject your powerful relatives' hospitality and be seen to make a scene out in the public eye." Sun gestured toward the watching wasps.

The Lee girl rolled her eyes. "Fine, then. Have it your way. Lead on."

The pinprick in Sun's head sharpened.

"Your Highness," said the attendant, "come now or be left out-side."

From inside a fanfare of horns announced the imminent entrance of the queen-marshal. Sun wanted to distrust the Lee girl. But that pinprick burned.

With a click, the doors began to slide closed as a second fanfare blared.

15

A Feast for Weary Souls

Sun tugged Persephone forward through the narrowing archway into the cavernous hall. A quick scan gave her the lay of the land.

A head table was set up on a platform at one end. A wing of auxiliary head tables flared out to either side of the head table. Here the governors and notables of the seven Core Houses sat in places of honor, raised above the rest. Perseus's mother, Aisa, was not in attendance. Even if legally the duty of arranging proper funeral and mourning rituals for Perseus had fallen on Sun, it wasn't surprising his womb mother was avoiding the banquet, twisted with misfortune as the Honored Aisa must surely feel, having now lost two of her three children. Her spouse, Kiran, was also absent.

As the governors turned to look at Sun, the buzz of conversation quieted. People craned their necks to see who had arrived in the nick of time.

By casual measures Sun did not stand out when among her Companions—not as tall as Perseus or Hestia, nothing like as striking as Alika, and lacking James's affectations of dress and posture. But no one could ever mistake hers for a placid, tranquil soul. Her heart was an inferno and her will an adamantine blade.

She caught the eye of Crane Marshal Qìngzhī Bō of the Seventh Fleet, seated with his staff at one of the front tables.

The marshal stood. "Let the hero of Na Iri take this honored place."

His staff vacated their seats.

Hetty sat to Sun's right as Sun gestured Persephone to the seat on her left. Alika, James, and the cee-cees took other seats at the table.

The fanfare gave its third and final call. Everyone rose.

Queen-Marshal Eirene strode in with confidence. By the ruddy color in her cheeks she'd already partaken of a few cups of wine.

As host, Moira Lee entered last of all. The governor of Lee House was dressed in an outfit of an unimpeachable shade of rose pink. Her daughter, the Honorable Manea, walked beside her, dressed in a consort's elaborate red robes embroidered with golden phoenix feathers. The way Persephone's mouth dropped open in astonishment at the sight of her cousin garbed and painted as a bride turned the pinprick in Sun's mind to a warning that seared.

"You really didn't know," whispered Sun.

"Is this some kind of a joke?" Persephone hissed.

"The queen-marshal lacks a sense of humor. My father is the only person ever known to have made her laugh."

The Honorable Manea's dyed-blond hair was short and spiky, streaked with pink highlights, and her eyes shone a sparklingly artificial blue. The right side of her face was painted in an elaborate bridal bouquet of pink lilies and red orchids. Their dazzling green-glitter stems wrapped down her neck into the gold-weighted neckline of her gown, as into a vase.

People's eyes got caught on superficial things so it was easy to look at blond, blue-eyed, curvy Manea with her painted embellishments and not see the bone-deep truth beneath: that she and her black-haired, brown-eyed, leaner cousin Persephone had the same facial structure.

The queen-marshal raised a hand for silence but did not speak. It was not her place to greet the guests, as she was a guest herself in Lee House. Yet her swift gaze found Sun, and her brow creased as at an unsolved problem. Eirene hated unsolved problems. If only Prince João was there to interpret the subtle twists and turns of her quicksilver moods. He had that gift, as Sun did not.

Moira Lee's smile was practiced and generous, shaded with the correct leavening of regretful sadness. Her gaze paused on Sun with an unreadable squint. Then she opened her arms in greeting to the assembly.

"Peace be upon you, and welcome to all of you who have entered Lee House as our guests at this banquet. Today we ask you to enjoy our hospitality as we celebrate the union contracted ninety days ago, sealed last month, and observed throughout Chaonia as a festival."

Ninety days ago! Sun had been touring the deepest levels of the Myrmidon gold mine on Thesprotis Terce, cut off from the net.

"After the years of conflict on our borders, we need—and I believe we *deserve*—a feast for our weary souls. For I give you today this unexpected romantic story, my treasured daughter Manea and our most beloved queen-marshal, Eirene. They have found in each other that rarest of gems, a love match between deserving hearts."

Sun stiffened, her right hand closing into a fist. "As if my father isn't deserving?"

Hetty pressed her fingers in between Sun's, prying them apart and easing the fist into openness. "Hush, hush," she said softly. "Let harsh words pass unheard. Sit still."

"It's meant as an insult to my father," Sun whispered. "I should walk out."

"I know. You know. They know you know. So *no*."

Cups were raised and the health of the handsome couple toasted to hearty cheers throughout the hall. Sun could not bring herself to touch the full cup at her plate. It would be like drinking poison. Yet when Hetty elbowed her in the ribs, she gritted her teeth and knocked it back in a single gulp. Her Companions drank with proper gusto, except Persephone, who still wore a blindsided expression that made Sun feel they were sitting on unexploded ordnance, waiting for a switch to click over into a blast.

The orchestra in the loft played "The Moon Represents My Heart." Many gazes skewed toward Alika, who had adapted the traditional and beloved classic as part of his Idol Faire repertoire last year. He had his dreamy smile on, swaying to the languid beat. Sun wrenched her thoughts away from her own anger for long enough to glance at Tiana. The cee-cee was again staring starstruck at Alika, revealing a fascinating glimpse of naïveté at odds with her adroit manners. Interesting.

Moira proceeded with a round of introductions of the most honored guests, each toasted with another cup of wine. Eirene drank heartily, as always. Sun clutched her cup, forgetting to drink until, each time, Hetty elbowed her. Of course Moira made no toast to the heir to the throne and did not again look her way, as if she did not exist.

"We at Lee House have a special gift to present to the queen-marshal, now our precious in-law," said Moira. "A reminder of our unflagging loyalty to the republic."

Persephone sucked in a breath, as if she'd been slugged. Pressing hands to the table, she rose.

"Sit," murmured Sun, abruptly realizing how out of place Persephone's stark-white mourning clothes appeared in this assembly. How disrespectful it would look that she, the heir, allowed unlucky garb into a wedding feast in her train.

Persephone sat, then rubbed her forehead as she made the aggrieved grimace that seemed to be her preferred expression. "You don't understand. I've figured out my aunt's game. Why they brought the prisoner here."

"What prisoner? Lee House didn't know I was coming."

"Of course they knew. They know everything. They intend to humiliate you in front of all the people in this hall and with the entire republic watching on Channel Idol."

The urgency in the Lee girl's voice braced Sun. So when a procession of security guards entered and the guests began to talk with a rising crescendo of excitement and alarm, she was prepared for some manner of slap.

But she wasn't prepared for the sight of a banner soldier trapped in a glass display cage, quivering with prideful rage at being treated like an animal. The angle of the cage placed him full front to the hall with his back to the queen-marshal and the head tables. Everyone—and all of the citizens watching on Channel Idol—could drink in the sight of an enemy Gatoi looking ready to kill them all if only he could break free. Some of the guests booed. Others hissed.

Many turned to look at her. At Princess Sun, the daughter of a Gatoi Royal who had been Eirene's most egregious and outrageous indiscretion.

Moira pressed a hand to her heart and intoned, "This gift we give to you today, Eirene. A rare captured Gatoi. He will stand as reminder of your valiant deeds and noble leadership. He will stand as a reminder of the dire threat that faces our republic in the person of these *savages* whose long alliance with the Phene threatens the integrity of the republic itself. I am sure all of us here will drink a toast to the hope that you and our beautiful daughter Manea will produce a suitable heir for Chaonia with true Chaonian blood."

Sun was on her feet in an instant. "And what is Sun, then? Do I not have true Chaonian blood? Am I not suitable?"

Moira smiled with blissful ease. She raised her cup in a challenge to the entire hall, and indeed to the wasps and a republic-wide audience across multiple systems eager to drink up any intoxicating drama.

"Ask your father, Your Highness. Why is he not here to celebrate today, as Baron Voy is? Why would he feel obliged to leave the palace in disgrace if he were a man innocent of treasonous thoughts? Why should we trust the child he left behind to infiltrate the court?"

"Sun, no!" said Hetty.

Sun flung her cup at the high table.

Moira ducked aside too late. The cup hit her in the head before clattering to the ground. She yelped and staggered back with a hand pressed to her cheek.

Into the stunned silence the queen-marshal's famous bellow rose, piercing to every corner of the vast hall.

"Shame! Shame on you, Sun! And shame on me for your dishonorable behavior toward our hosts. I knew you wouldn't be able to control your temper and your petty jealousy. Which is why I didn't invite you!" She gestured toward her daughter.

In the glass cage, the prisoner followed the gesture's line of sight. Seeing Sun, he also saw Persephone seated beside her.

As furious as she was, Sun recognized the lightning flare of his neural network on and across and within his body. His mouth opened in a silent scream as he slammed his shoulders first to his left and then to his right and then again in a rebound so hard to the left that with a sizzling crackle the corner seam popped. The side of the cage gave way with a grinding tear and a crashing thud onto the ground.

He jumped down as people scrambled away from the nearest tables in a clatter of noise, but he didn't even look at them before leaping high and fast over an entire table scating eight people. With a second leap he landed smack in the middle of Sun's table. The tabletop shuddered but did not break.

Candace was already on her feet, chair tipping backward, snapping out her battle fans. Hetty grabbed Sun's arm to pull her away, but Octavian broke Hetty's grip to interpose his own body between the princess and the prisoner.

"It's not me he's after!" Sun shouted.

Too late.

The banner soldier dove for Persephone. Driving her to the floor with the full force of his attack, he fixed his hands around the Lee girl's throat and began choking her.

16

The Wily Persephone Realizes This Is Going to End Badly

I'm slammed back onto the ground so hard that pain from the impact obliterates all sound. For the first eternity of shock, it's impossible even to react. The world collapses until all I can see is *him*.

His expression is flat, a soulless and lifeless machine singing with lightning stabs of energy beneath his skin. The fingers that close around my throat are anything but lifeless. His pulse throbs into my flesh. His amber stare bores into my head, but I see no personality or emotion behind the eyes, only a void. As black spots blur my vision, Solomon's face flashes into my thoughts. All those extra hours of hand-to-hand training.

"You're small, so avoid grappling. But if you're forced to, then fight dirty. For example, if your opponent has balls, then kick them in the balls."

I jam my knee up between his legs, but the Gatoi doesn't react. Blood thunders in my ears as I try to twist my body to get an elbow into his ribs, anything to dislodge him. His fingers dig agony into my throat. He's barely breathing, like killing doesn't even wind him.

Sun's emphatic voice penetrates the eerie silence. "Don't hit him. Be ready to drag him off."

The black spots turn into a haze that brushes my face with spidery threads. It's not haze. It's Hestia's white silk scarf. Abruptly the cloth is twisted across his eyes to blind him.

The moment he can't see me his hands release my throat.

Air.

I fade out.

"Perse?"

My head is being cradled on a lap. Two fingers rest lightly on the pulse at my throat. The scent of sandalwood encourages me to open my eyes.

Too tired to sit up, I croak, "What happened?"

Ti unbuttons the top two buttons on my collar to ease the pressure on my throat. "You're going to have a bruise."

Sound rushes back in a roar of shouting. An alarm bell clangs with a *wrang wrang wrang* that drowns out everything. All at once I remember we are in the hall at a wedding banquet in honor of Manea.

Manea. My cousin has become consort to the queen-marshal of the republic. *What is my family plotting?*

"Silence!" Eirene's shout breaks through the chaos.

With Ti's help I stand. Adrenaline screams through my body, scorching out the last traces of dizziness.

Ti whispers, "Are you sure you're all right? I was afraid he was going to crush your windpipe."

Reflexively I swallow. The movement hurts so badly I wince and hope I never have to swallow again. Nervously I look around for the Gatoi. The prisoner stands passively with the scarf bound over his eyes as Sun's bodyguard wraps some kind of wire around his legs.

"You are no better than your father," Eirene declares in a ringing voice whose words will carry across the many solar systems that make up the Republic of Chaonia. Wasps hover close to catch them all. "Reckless. Self-obsessed. Unrestrained."

"Untrustworthy," a voice calls from somewhere in the hall, the speaker untraceable. Yet the word hangs there, heard by all.

"You have so little self-control you have insulted our hosts with this petty display."

"Ask yourself what Lee House's purpose is in concocting this marriage," Sun retorts, for she hasn't backed down at all.

The queen-marshal stands with the toes of her black boots over the edge of the dais, on the brink of plunging off. By the fury washing her flushed face and the flashes of ire shimmering in her obsidian eye she is certainly thinking about taking the leap.

"Now you insult me, your own mother! As if you think I am so easily led."

"That's what they said about your romance with my father, isn't it? Easily led. Unrestrained. Self-obsessed. Reckless." Sun's voice rings forcefully into the shocked silence. "But he's the only person in this court who is honest with you. Lee House certainly isn't being honest."

"How dare you!" Eirene is frozen with fury, her color high, gripping a wine cup in one hand, but I sense the ice cracking. In a moment she'll shake off the wine and the rage, and she'll act.

Sun turns the prisoner as if he's a puppet, to face the high table.

"Ready?" says Sun to her bodyguard.

"Ready."

She yanks off the scarf. At first the Gatoi just stands there. His back is sweat-streaked and sculpted with muscle and made strangely beautiful by the luminescence of neural enhancers tracing ghostly patterns beneath his skin. By the angle of his head he's glaring at Queen-Marshal Eirene as one does at an enemy's ruler and commander in chief. Then his head shifts as he surveys the rest of the people at the high table. When it happens it's like getting hit by a sledgehammer, an impact so powerful it stops your whole world. His body tenses to rigidity. The map on his back flares so brightly I have to deploy my nictitating membrane to cut the glare.

The Gatoi has forgotten about me. Like a thrown spear he launches himself toward the chair where Manea is seated.

The bodyguard yanks on the wires. It doesn't stop him—nothing can stop a Gatoi gone berserk—but it trips him. He falls on his face with a satisfying smack. Even so, he starts scrambling up with no awareness of the blood flowing out of his nose. Yet the fall stalls him, giving the girl with the fans time to club him on the head. This blow staggers him for just long enough for the body-guard to apply a massive percussion echo charge to his bare torso.

He collapses as heavily and completely as my plans for my future did when my family yanked me out of CeDCA.

Eirene drops her wine cup. It clatters to the dais and rolls to the edge, catching on the lip. A fierce red glow sparks deep in the queen-marshal's obsidian eye.

"You put my consort at risk! You insult me! You—!"

Her foot catches on the cup, and she slips sideways as the beam of weaponized particles slices drunkenly toward the ceiling and cuts through a chandelier. Fragments of crystal hail down over a table of startled celebrants.

In a tone of self-congratulatory arrogance that couldn't possibly be more annoying, Sun says, "I present to all of you the woman who is preparing to attack Karnos System and accost the Phene Empire! She can't even keep to her feet."

The way everyone in the hall turns to stare doesn't make her blink, but it's not like she craves the attention. I'm not sure she notices how everything and everyone now seems to revolve around her as the sun to our busy, scattered, outraged planets.

"I can't take my eyes off her," murmurs Ti in my ear.

I can't take my eyes off her either.

Eirene climbs to her feet, flushed and furious. A trembling Manea grasps at her sleeve, but the queen-marshal shoves her back. A pinpoint of red light targets Sun's right cheek. I grab for the princess, but she bats my hand away without taking her gaze from her mother.

When Octavian moves to place his body between her and the queen-marshal, Sun lifts her chin and says, "Get out of the way. If she wants to shoot me, let her shoot me with premeditation in front of the entire hall."

Pride will not bow or retreat. The two women—mother and daughter, queen-marshal and princess—look a great deal alike at that moment. This is going to end badly. Aunt Moira's anticipatory expression tells me everything I need to know. She's set Sun up to bring her down in public, for everyone in the Republic of Chaonia to see. If Eirene kills her in a fit of rage, so much the better.

What my family wants harmed, I will protect. Even if Sun is a bitch.

I jump up on a chair and then to the tabletop with a thump. The queen-marshal and everyone glances toward me in surprise, jarred by the movement more than the noise.

"An excellent experiment, would you not agree!" I shout in what Solomon calls my "intimidate-the-first-years" voice. I add a formal bow at the precise thirty-six degrees appropriate to the queen-marshal. "Apologies for the interruption, Your Majestic Highness. Recently a researcher gave a guest lecture at the academy in which he suggested the Phene are using engineered hallucination to compel the Gatoi to fight. None of the higher-ups believed it. I'm not sure I believe it. But could this incident be proof the Phene are manipulating Gatoi soldiers? We mustn't let the Phene know we suspect."

Eirene shifts her murderous gaze from Sun to the Gatoi soldier lying prone and last to me, the hapless messenger. Her brow creases, the red-hot edge of rage blunting as she considers my provocative words. She's startled but not as surprised as she ought to be.

"Where did you get a Gatoi prisoner, Moira?" she demands.

My aunt grits her teeth, then with an effort relaxes her jaw so she doesn't look so obviously thwarted or guilty. "Return the prisoner to custody," she calls to her chief security officer.

"I'll take charge of him," says Sun. Iris and Candace drape the prisoner's arms over their shoulders. "And with all respect due to Lee House, I will retire from a celebration at which I am clearly not welcome."

I leap down from the table to join her Companions as they march toward the doors. We move at a collective walk that's brisk enough to get us out fast but not so hurried it seems like we're running. Even though that's exactly what we're doing.

"I did not give you leave to depart!" thunders Eirene as she no doubt recalls that Sun has shamed her in public. "You will wait in detention until I am ready to deal with your savage manners and your disrespectful—"

We spill onto the boardwalk as the doors close behind us, sealing off the hall and the queen-marshal's booming voice. All the pods are gone, leaving us caught on a five-meter-wide boardwalk three meters above the water.

A trio of clicks vibrates through the air. Hundreds of wasps clatter to the boardwalk in a patter like hail. Tiny splashes pepper the lagoon as more of the miniature cameras sink underwater.

"What's happening?" Ti asks. She's on my left, Sun on my right.

I unload the truth. "Lee House's spy killers have wiped out all electronics. Channel Idol will be required to scrub the entire incident from its official broadcast, although Lee House will retain the incident in its files. Whatever happens to us out here right now will be seen by no one except Lee House's security team and maybe the queen-marshal."

A detachment of eight Lee House sentinels emerges at the south end of the boardwalk. They're escorting a windowless pod.

I add, "That is a security-enhanced and watertight pod used to convey dangerous prisoners to the high-security cells carved into the seabed beneath the atoll. Eirene is healthy enough to live a long time, barring death in battle. So if Lee House can discredit you, or make you disappear, they have a path to putting Eirene's child by Manea on the throne."

The sentinels ease closer. A second detachment hurries down the stairs that lead up to the outer ring wall's guard walk and parapet.

"Is there another way out?" Sun asks in a low voice.

If Lee House is that ambitious—and of course they are—I've been deployed as a pawn in my family's schemes, a spare to be used and discarded. Not me. Not now. Not ever.

"I know all the entrances and exits in Lee House. Then it's a matter of where we go afterward."

Her gaze goes distant as she checks her link. Her eyes narrow. "They've locked me out of the military grid. That didn't take long!"

"I can get us out of Argos. But leaving will set you at odds with the queen-marshal."

"So be it. She'll regret our public dispute once her anger and pride cool."

What about your pride? I want to ask, but now is not the time.

I blink open the schoolroom link to Kadmos using my personal icon.

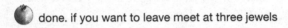

emergency unlock maintenance door at boardwalk

recommend three jewels gambit

I smile even though I have nothing to smile about. Kadmos has known all along there is something fishy about my recall. If I can't trust him then I might as well get in the security pod.

done. if you want to leave meet at three jewels

The ⭐ blinks three times, then vanishes.

"Start walking toward the other end of the boardwalk," I say to Sun.

She starts walking with her Companions and their cee-cees in train.

At the security pod the attendant's false smile turns to the frown of an interrogator whose time is up without having gotten the information their superiors demand. "Princess Sun! There's no exit that way. I must insist you come with me."

"This is your last chance to surrender," I murmur as we stride along.

Sun snorts. "I don't surrender."

We head straight toward the first detachment of sentinels. The Companions shift position, turning their formation into a spear with Sun as the tip. Because she strides without slowing down, the sentinels naturally hesitate. They're used to people giving way.

To Sun's left, the girl with the fans flips them out from under her arms. The *thap* of battle fans snapping open is enough to cause half the sentinels to stop dead rather than move into range of razor-sharp leaves.

Octavian lengthens his stride to surge out ahead of Sun. "Move aside for Her Heaven-Sent Highness, Princess Sun."

The sentinels step aside. House sentinels wearing identical uniforms and carrying shock staffs are no match for a former marine who walks like a jackhammer ready to break you down. We sweep past as a fast-moving storm.

At the end of the boardwalk a service door slides open to reveal a ramp.

"The ramp goes down to the service dock," I say.

Ti enters first as a sign of trust. The door whooshes shut behind us, cutting off the shouts from outside as the sentinels finally figure out what I'm up to. I invested a lot of time at CeDCA learning how to jam and unjam systems, so it's easy for me to drop a short-term loop into the door that will keep it locked for ten minutes. Even better, my global net is still CeDCA-locked, so they can't penetrate my communications feed. Because I'm working everything through the Lee House school net, they won't be able to figure out what happened in here until they break the loop.

"This way," I say.

The others glance at Sun, who nods. I hustle down the ramp to a dim chamber with a floating dock. Ten boats bump against moorings. They have open decks with utility lockers on either side of the helm and extendible platforms at the stern.

"These are the maintenance boats for the atoll and reef," I explain. "I need them all turned on and their shades, their retractable awnings, pulled out."

Sun gestures. Her people run for the boats, leaving the Gatoi on the ground. He's so limp I might mistake him for a dead man if not for the slow rise and fall of his gleaming chest. I tear my gaze away. No time for distractions.

Instead I slip my tuning fork from where I've strapped it under my jacket sleeve. It's adjustable, perfect for a beacon technician.

"Alika, how good is your ear?" I ask.

"My ear is good." The timbre of his voice is light, nothing like his powerful singing voice, but by the tightening of his jaw I can guess I've annoyed him.

"That's what I figured," I say placatingly. I beckon him to the stern of the closest boat and indicate a tube, positioned at the stern of the boat, that submerges into the water. "This is what we call a *screamer.* Tune it to oscillate through the E-flat minor tonic triad."

"Okay." He looks at Sun for permission. She nods. Of course he has a 440 Hz tuning fork tucked into his ukulele case. He taps it on his knee, presses it to the tube, and starts fiddling with the resonance.

I clamber into the adjoining boat. Music is part of my study cluster not because I play an instrument but because for a lot of systems work I rely on my ear. Sound can give subtle information about the health of interlocking systems whether a body or any environment.

Unexpectedly Hestia's cee-cee speaks up from the boat moored next to mine. The cee-cee is petite and pretty, wearing her hair in braids beneath a decorative beaded cap. She looks more suited to administration than fighting, but you can never tell with a cee-cee because they are specifically trained to multitask.

Her voice is strained. "I don't understand why we're doing this. We're just causing more trouble. The queen-marshal's anger always blows over. We should retire quietly with the sentinels, like they asked us to, and wait it out."

"Nah, what fun is there in that?" I pull back my lips in what my mother always disapprovingly called my *snarl-grin.* "Overreacting gets their attention. The bigger the tantrum, the better. Anyway, in case you didn't notice, all electronic eyes went dead on the boardwalk, so everything that happened and will happen to us has become invisible. We could have been shot and our blood scrubbed off the ground and no one the wiser. Official story will become 'retirement to the country' with 'an unfortunate accident hang gliding' to follow in a month. Don't you know how this works?"

I'm shouting by now. How can people who live so close to power be so stubbornly ignorant about how it functions?

"Princess Sun has been the queen-marshal's understood heir for years." Navah's mirror-bright bracelets jangle as she flings an arm wide in a gesture that begs the others to support her objection.

"No one wants to hurt her, especially not now with an assault on Karnos in the offing. We must all stand united against the enemy."

"That's enough, Navah," says Sun. "We're going."

"Who can pilot a boat?" I call.

Hestia, the cee-cee with the battle fans, and the jerk who wears the ridiculous flatcap all raise their hands. So does the jerk's cee-cee, a woman of at least fifty who has the hard-core look of a fighter you never, ever want to mess with, complete with a wicked scar under her left eye, a prosthetic multi-tool arm seamed on just below her left elbow, and a bright-eyed miniature pteranodon perched on her shoulder.

"You four each take a boat and follow. I'll remotely pilot the others."

"Wait," Sun cuts in. "I'll go with you, Persephone. Candace, James, and Hetty, you each take a boat. Isis, go with Hetty to guard the prisoner. Alika, with Candace. Navah and Octavian stay with me. Tiana . . ." For the first time she hesitates.

"Sun, you can't be so hard-hearted as to leave me alone," says the jerk, sweeping his cap off his head and pressing it to his chest. "I will escort the beauty."

Ti looks at me and rolls her eyes. I'd laugh, but there isn't time.

"Go on," I say to her.

Sun doesn't contradict me.

Alika calls, "Done with the tuning."

As I finish tuning my screamer and tuck the tuning fork back under my sleeve, I can't help but remember how Resh would goad us younger ones into following her into risky adventures like scylla screaming. She always claimed it was to prepare herself for the military command path she was in training for, the career that killed her, but in hindsight I understand she was preparing us to develop the skills needed to navigate war and politics.

I link up the unpiloted vessels on a tight loop that chains back to my ● icon. My loop will only work as long as we're within two hundred meters of the island, but that's all the distance I need. Octavian stands right behind me like he expects me to betray Sun and intends to smash my head in the second I do.

The water door lifts out of the way, revealing a sky with scattered clouds and a sea whipped by wind. We look like kids in fancy party outfits going for a drunken joyride, and I should know. Swiping my hands across a virtual screen I pilot our boats in a tight group out of the dock. As we enter the calm atoll waters that the reef encircles, I open up the motors so we race parallel to the island's ring wall in a neat line like beads on a string. Our destination is Three Jewels pavilion, almost halfway around the island from where we are now.

Light winks in my peripheral vision. Glancing back I see Navah, in the second boat, tipping an arm up against the glare of the sun. Its reflection scatters against her bracelets. For an instant my floating virtual screen sheers to white as it adjusts to the new light levels. An answering signal winks from the security walk on the ring wall.

Something splashes hard in the water just off the port side of our boat.

They're shooting at us.

Octavian shoves Sun down, shouting, "Get under the shade. *Under the shade!*"

Sentinels are running atop the perimeter wall to keep pace. A shot pings hard off the metal strut that holds up the shade awning, and a hot hissing odor burns past my nose and makes my eyes water. Tear gas.

Weapons pop out from beneath the sleeves and skirts of the Companions and cee-cees. They all have safety latches wreathed like vines around their retina-triggers; such latches are required to enter Lee House. The vines wither as if singed. A hum of charged weapons sings in my ears.

"Hold your fire!" cries Navah. "They're only using stun guns and beanbag projectiles. If you open fire, they'll say you were the aggressors."

A second round of plops spatters the water around us. A projectile pings off the hull, spraying pellets into the water. Octavian drops like an invisible fist has slammed down out of the sky and nailed him.

17

There Is Nothing the Wily Persephone Can Do
That Sun's Companions Can't Do Better

Sun drops down beside Octavian, checking his pulse. There's a red mark where his neck meets his shoulder, the impact site.

"Do the beanbag projectiles used by Lee House contain invisible pellets?" she demands angrily. "He's knocked out cold, but I can't find the missile that hit him."

Fuck.

We have to get out of here.

"Get under the shade," I snap as I increase our speed. "We have to take the risk of skimming the edge of the open ocean and hoping no big ones are feeding close to shore this morning."

"Make it so," says Sun.

"I wasn't asking your permission. I was just informing you. *Hold on!*"

I turn a sharp right by an underwater boulder painted orange. It marks a channel cut through the reef. Hestia follows. The rest of the flotilla alter course like a gaggle of ducklings. Waves slop against our hull. An incoming swell rocks us hard as we meet the open water. We skip over the big swells, prow crashing down over each wave. Someone shrieks in terror in one of the other boats, but I laugh.

Octavian groans. Sun sticks her head out from under the shade and, scanning the sky, says, "Two aircars rising from the far end of the island."

"That's the service landing area. Might be routine, might be coming after us. We're almost there."

"Where are we going?" Sun asks as we bank left to continue parallel to the edge of the outer reef.

"There."

The hexagonal pavilion called Three Jewels is a three-tiered golden pagoda. It sits atop three monstrously huge jade menhirs embedded into a submerged mound built atop the seafloor just beyond the edge of the reef. A red-roofed pedestrian bridge spans the wide reef, connecting the island to the pavilion. Sea churns around and between the bases of the gigantic standing gems. The gaps between the menhirs are big enough for a boat to pass through, but only thrill-seekers or the truly desperate would ever aim to thread such a needle in this kind of crazy wave action. Shouts of protest rise from the other boats as I cut control to their wheels and chain them to me. The boats slam across the choppy water, sending so much spray in our wake that we're like a long fountain of celebration as I bring us in.

As soon as we cross out of day and into the shadow of the pavilion's floor—which is now our ceiling—I kick my boat around, back it up to a narrow dock, and secure us with a line. The dock provides an entry space to an elevator door and a service staircase built into one of the menhirs.

Octavian sits up. "I can't see," he says, rubbing his eyes.

"Because it's dark or because your eyes aren't working?" I ask.

He grunts, shifts his neck as if making sure his spinal cord hasn't been compromised, and blinks enough times I think he must be piecing through his net's sub routines to make sure they're online. "That was a good shot. Where are we?"

"Escaping. Sun, open a stopwatch. Tell me when sixty-seven seconds are up."

The elevator door opens. Sun whirls into a crouch, a stinger steadied in both hands.

Kadmos steps out, carrying two camo duffels. He looks haggard and he's breathing hard, like he ran here, which he must have done. The elevator doors close behind him.

"This is my tutor, Kadmos," I say.

Sun doesn't lower the gun as I wave him forward.

Octavian mutters a curse under his breath as he pushes up to his feet and blocks Kadmos's entry onto our boat. The bodyguard is still trembling, but I don't think it's because he's mad at Kadmos. I think he's in incredible pain.

Kadmos halts. "Honored Persephone, I brought your bag and that of Tiana. We don't have much time."

Sun keeps the pistol aimed at Kadmos, but she speaks to me. "Explain."

I gesture to the other boats now bobbing on the pool beneath the pavilion. Ti waves at me to show she's all right.

"Here's the plan. This elevator leads down to a service tunnel used to bring food and drink to this pavilion for festivals and parties. There's an access stairwell from that tunnel to the supply train. The trains run in an undersea tunnel from the island to the mainland. You don't think Lee House flies everything in, do you?"

"We're going by undersea train?"

"No, we're going to make them think we're escaping in a cargo train. It's the best I can do on short notice. Sort everyone into this boat and the boat Alika tuned. The other boats remain empty. But keep the shades out to their full extension so aircars can't easily see who is where or if the other boats are empty."

"Stand down, but search the bags," Sun says to Octavian.

He steps back, bracing himself on one of the awning struts. Kadmos swings the two bags onto the boat. I extend an arm for him so he can hold on and climb in, but he steps back instead.

"I am still employed here, Honored Persephone."

"What if they notice the missing bags? Find our exchange on the school net and arrest you?"

"I have my means of staying invisible. Is there anything else you need from me?"

I glance at Octavian, who is running a sensor over each duffel. Even though it didn't seem like he'd gotten hit that hard, he's blinking too frequently, and his face twitches in quicksilver grimaces. He pauses twice to catch his breath.

"Your sixty-seven seconds are up," Sun says to me, then calls to the other boats. "Hetty, you take command of the second boat."

"Alika needs to stay with her in case he has to retune the screamer," I say.

"All right. Alika, Isis, Tiana, you stay with Hetty. You'll also guard the prisoner."

"Hey!" I object. "Ti comes with me."

"Your cee-cee is hostage for your good behavior. James and Navah, with me. Candace too. I want you to check out Octavian."

Candace is the fan girl. James tips his chapeau at me with a cheeky grin that makes me want to pull the cap off his head and slap him with it.

Navah clambers in last, nervously leaning away from where Octavian is braced against the railing. "Shouldn't I be with the Honorable Hestia? Where are we going? Why are we still running? This isn't a game."

"Gosh, seriously? You could have fooled me!" I retort.

Sun catches my eye and shakes her head in such an odd way that I shut up.

Kadmos steps back to the staircase. "Ready, Honored Persephone."

"Ready," I answer. "Release the krakens."

He vanishes down the stairs before I remember that I should say goodbye.

A rumble shivers deep in the ground, followed by a second roll like thunder and then a third and fourth, as a force in the earth beneath us starts moving.

Sun asks. "*What* did you release?"

"The four undersea cargo trains. One runs to each major cargo depot in Argos. The trains terminate at this end at a junction beneath this pavilion. My family will think we took one of the trains because I can't steal an aircar and the sea isn't safe."

I call to Hestia, who stands at the controls of the other boat. "Stick close to me!"

We nose out through the entrance. Water slops over the prow as we hit the mess of a windy bay. I power out, leaving Hestia to follow under her own steering. With a blink I trigger the screamers in the two boats carrying passengers. Then I send the other boats, in pairs, into a scatter pattern toward the ocean. We take a long curve that will make it look like we're headed out to sea with the other boats but which will actually bring us to land on the outskirts of Argos at a park called Point Panic.

"Three new aircars," says Sun, peeking out from under the shade. "They're making for the mainland. Looks like they took the bait."

"Princess! Get back under the shade." Octavian yanks her back into concealment. He's sweating, runnels streaming down his face. His complexion looks gray.

I open the throttle gradually, skipping over the waves as I pick a route. The swells are bigger than I'd first realized, with the incoming wave patterns dictated by where and how high reefs and rocks lie under the surface. We Lee children grew up out here on the island, which meant we were in the water before we could walk. I can't pilot an aircar, but I know the sea.

"Why won't they guess we're on the boats?" Sun asks.

"Holy fire, what's that?" cries Candace. She's kneeling, braced against the constant slamming bounce. For a bold young person with such great martial-arts moves she looks slack-jawed with fear now.

A feathery gold crest breaches the water about one hundred meters away, the curl of a wave-swallowing charybdis coming close to the surface and then rolling back beneath without a glimpse of its head. The crest itself towers a good five meters over the water, a knife slicing through the swells. Its barnacle-streaked neck is wider than our boats.

"That's why they won't guess we're on the boats. Sea monsters. Wave swallowers aren't carnivores, but their size threatens us. If you have a private comm-link to your Companions, Princess, now would be the right time to warn Hestia that she's about to get hit with a cross swell."

The gold crest vanishes beneath the waves as the charybdis dives. The first side swells hit and now we're pitching and yawing in all directions. Octavian groans like he's nauseated, but there's nothing I can do for seasickness.

"Surely you've seen a charybdis before," I say to Candace. "Didn't you grow up here in Argos?"

"No. I grew up on military ships."

A big swell rises ahead of us, the water growing into an intimidating gray wall. I run up it diagonally along the front and slide over to the back face, the boat slamming down and rolling side to side. James laughs with his face turned to catch the full force of the spray. Candace shrieks, and Sun says to her, "You've got this."

I glance back, convinced I'm going to see an overturned boat in our wake, but the second boat dances over the swell and into the trough between waves with more grace than I'd managed. Sun catches my eye, and even in the midst of all this she raises her brows challengingly as if to remind me there's nothing I can do that any of her *real* Companions can't do better.

Ti is seated cross-legged on the deck of the other boat, wind and spray tearing apart her perfectly styled hair. Somehow she still looks as if she's posing for a photo shoot.

I catch Sun watching her with a strange intensity that bothers me, and I say, "Oi, Princess. Cee-cees are protected by their contracts. She's off-limits to her employer, and that means you too."

That's my second mistake, getting so distracted by my annoyance that I take too steep an angle on the next big swell. The boat pitches hard to port, way, way up, and everyone but me and James slide down, scrambling for purchase on the water-soaked decking. As annoying as James is I have to give him credit for having good sea legs.

I shout, "Candace! Navah! Back to the other side for counterbalance."

Octavian loses his balance entirely and smacks flat onto the deck. He lies inert, which is a good thing as I steer a better path over the next two incoming swells and finally get out to deeper water. Hestia keeps pace, and now we can open up our throttles and steer toward Point Panic. We've drifted too close to the nearest pair of decoy boats. I study the water, an anxious flutter in my chest. Is there a shadow beneath? Is that huff of distant whitecap the first hint of a scylla's venom?

Octavian's whole body heaves, shoulders jerking as he flails. Sun and Candace together aren't strong enough to hold him down. With a roar of agony he throws back his head, and blood erupts from his mouth like a creature spitting poison. Red droplets spray over the white bulwark.

He slumps forward. The red mark on his neck has turned into an ugly scabrous hole that starts pumping out blood like it's a machine draining him.

James hasn't seen yet. He's scanning the sky, one hand holding his cap onto his head as he leans out to get a better look toward the island receding behind us. "More aircars."

Candace looks up from beside Octavian. "Is there an aid kit?"

I kick a latch to show where it is stored because I can't pause. The aircars aren't my biggest problem. I'm seeing whitecaps over by the decoy boats, more disturbance than the wind can be kicking up. We have to get out of here.

Sun hooks up the cover and snatches the square kit with its red cross and crescent. She shifts over beside Candace, who has pressed a palm against the wound to stem the bleeding.

"Hold your hand here to stop the blood flow. Let me see that . . ." Candace paws through the kit and pulls out an implement. "Yes! Hold him down. I've got to seal the wound."

"We must surrender!" cries Navah. She hasn't shifted from the other side of the boat, even though we could use her help. "Blessed Heaven! We'll all die if we don't—"

"Shut up." Candace sounds scared as she looks at Sun. "This is dark tech. It's called a *late bloomer*. This kind of weapon isn't even allowed in the military."

Sun's scowl is blistering as she twists the three brass rings on her left hand. Helplessness doesn't agree with her.

"*Scylla!*" James yells.

It rises out of the sea like the huge cables of a giant suspension bridge have gotten loose and are lashing this way and that, cutting through wind and waves. Each cable is a living neck, bronze and glossy, and each neck ends in a vast horned head. Their jaws aren't quite big enough to bite our boats in half, but if even one of the necks slams down full force onto our boat it will crush and sink us.

I see only two heads. The other three are still underwater, listening for the yammer of the screamers or humming their own call. They sing in a tonality that tunes to our understanding of E-flat minor, for reasons no one knows. This is what Resh taught us; they'll go after the other boats and leave ours alone because they hear our tuners as one of them. She got in terrible trouble once when a scylla caught a decoy boat. It wasn't the risk to us children my mother minded. It was the cost of replacing the boat, which came out of her expense account.

Every gaze, except that of the unconscious Octavian, shifts to stare at the hypnotic movements of the sea monster and its gleaming maws. So many teeth. Scyllas are the ocean gleaners, the razors that clean the dying organic debris from the ocean. They play no favorites. They just do what they are born to do.

One of the visible necks twists to look toward the nearest decoy boats, but the other sways closer to us. The bulk of its body pours along like a monstrous cloud beneath the surface. I hold to my course, and Hestia stays on my tail, but I'm watching the scene as it unfolds. One set of whirling gold eyes hooks its gaze on the wake our little boats leave and tracks it back to its source.

To us.

A third neck curls up out of the water to begin tracking us with its shining gaze. The huge body begins to shift course. Hestia moves her boat up alongside ours like we're racing, and maybe we are. Maybe one of us can make Point Panic if the scylla attacks the other one.

Sun says, "Can we outrace it?"

"We're loaded to capacity and can't go as fast as the decoys."

Candace speaks in a flat, angry tone. "His heart's stopped beating. They killed him."

"None of this would have happened if you'd obeyed orders and let them detain us briefly." Navah twists her bracelets round and round her wrist. She's breathless and keeps glancing at Octavian's body.

I give a curt laugh. "You don't fire tech like that at people you only intend to *detain briefly.*"

"We've got to surrender before worse happens," Navah says.

"Enough!" snaps Sun. "We've let this game go on for too long."

Across the gap Sun and Hestia exchange a look. I don't know if they have a private comm-link or if they just understand each other that well, but Hestia nods.

Sun raises her pistol.

And shoots Navah twice in the chest, pops I barely hear over the E-flat minor thrum of the engine, the slap of waves, and the ceaseless rumble of the wind.

James catches Navah's falling body. Nothing can disguise her look of shock as blood spreads a stain down the silk of her blouse.

"You think we haven't known all along you were attached to Hetty in order to spy on me?" Sun asks in a calm voice. "Do you think we weren't feeding you false information to pass on to whoever your masters are? That I don't suspect you killed Percy and Duke, thinking you were going to kill me and yourself in the bargain?"

Navah's lips open. No sound comes out.

"Who hired you? Who do you owe that much loyalty to?"

"No," she croaks. "I say nothing."

"Throw her overboard, into our wake."

James dumps her over the side. She flails because she's not dead yet. As soon as the scylla scents her blood in the water it will come after her. And the instinctive scylla ritual of circling before it snaps up its prey will give us the extra minutes of time we so desperately need.

I'd feel sick, but I don't have time to think.

We race on, bouncing over the swells. I can finally turn into the arc of our curve to put the wind at our backs so we rock less.

Sun kneels beside Octavian's body, thumb and forefinger framing the suppurating wound, a hole into glistening tissue, a glimpse of bone beneath. "I'll start CPR."

Candace stops her with an arm on her shoulder. "Your Highness, don't put your mouth on his. If that was a late bloomer, and I don't know what else it could have been, his lungs and heart have been pulverized and infected. So it could propagate into you if enough of it gets into your bloodstream."

Sun glares at Octavian's body like her will alone should be able to bring him back to life.

"You just can't take the chance," Candace adds. "I'm sorry."

"Do we throw him overboard for the scylla too?" I ask. "Blood or singing are the only things that draw them off."

"No. I will never allow Lee House to know they killed him. We take him with us. Do you have a plan, Persephone Lee, or do I need to take it from here?"

Her gaze drills into mine. It irks me to have to look away as we reach the long surf break offshore of Point Panic, but I can't play at a stare-down. The shoreline is a hive of channels amid stretches of reef. It's a twisty route in to where surfers can paddle out to a break along the back reef, where it's safe to surf because it's too shallow for both the swallowing charybdis and the carnivorous scyllas.

"I plan to avoid getting shot and discarded, whether by you or by my family. To that end, I'm taking this escape in stages. And . . . *Hold on*. This will be rough."

We slam-slam-slam across a choppy set of waves, skipping through the troughs as spray soaks us and the windshield streaks with streaming water. Then we're inside and skimming too fast across smoother water. My skills are rusty as I cut our speed abruptly, throwing the boat into a fishtail stop. In the other boat Hestia slows gracefully to a halt.

The sandy seafloor glimmers as the sun comes out. A rocky beach awaits us, but I can only nose in so far.

"If you extend the back platform it's easier to get into the water. Swim in." As they start disembarking, hauling the body, I call over to the other boat, "Alika. Let it revert to the default frequency."

He's staring at the water in horror, clutching his precious ukulele that will no doubt be ruined in the swim.

For some reason I start laughing. Maybe it's just pure adrenaline, but he looks so lost and, as they say, *at sea* that I take pity on him. "There should be a waterproof dry bag in one of the lockers. The dry bags all are flotation-enabled, so they won't sink. Grab the first aid kit too. And the emergency gear. Hurry. I can't disembark until everyone's off."

I hand my boat's emergency gear bag to Candace and stuff Tiana's duffel into a dry bag. The crew of the other boat figures out how to use the life ring to float the unconscious Gatoi toward the beach. Last off, Ti strips off her beautiful yellow gauze overdress and wraps it around the shift she's wearing beneath. She waves to me before she makes a perfect dive and starts stroking like a competitive swimmer. When she reaches my boat she pulls herself up.

"Why did your tutor bring our duffels?" she asks. "Not that I'm complaining!"

"I guess he figured we'd need them. Do you need help getting to land?"

"I'm a superb swimmer," she says with an unflustered smile that reminds me how much I don't know about her, that we just met *today*. She slides into the water and, dragging the big dry bag after her, heads for shore with the others.

Once the second boat is also abandoned I chain the two boats together and give them a course, oceanward, through the reef. Then I toss my duffel over the side and leap off after it. The water closes over my head, and for three seconds I relish the seawater's welcoming embrace. Then I kick up to the surface and swim for shore, hauling my duffel behind. CeDCA thinks of everything; our duffels are sealed and waterproof and—like the dry bags— have auto-activated flotation bulbs.

In the distance aircars whine like angry bugs. The fierce keening of a feeding scylla slices through the air with painful intensity. As I splash up onto the rocky beach I'm glad of my boots. The others have assembled beneath the shade of a tile-roofed shelter built over a sightseeing bench. Even though they are all bedraggled and wet there is still something stirring and even sensational in the way the princess and her loyal companions have arranged themselves around the bench, with the dead man flat on his back, arms crossed respectfully on his chest, and the shirtless prisoner on his stomach, bare back gleaming. Ti's sitting with a bare right foot propped up on her left knee, blood dripping from her foot.

"You're hurt!" As I take a step toward Ti, Sun raises her pistol. And aims it at me.

Sun Is Forced to Admit She Hadn't Seen This Coming

Somehow it always came down to blood in the water.

Sun stared down at the Lee girl as she emerged like a soaking-wet and thoroughly disgruntled sea goddess. Strands of black hair were plastered to her face, and she clawed them aside impatiently. Only when the significantly more perceptive Tiana gave a sideways nod to warn her did the Lee girl see the pistol.

"How do I know you're not in on it?" Sun was too angry to shout, what with Octavian dead at her feet and Navah's blood on her hands.

"In on what?" That reply wasn't innocence. It was a challenge.

"The attack that killed Percy. The plot to discredit me at the banquet."

"Whatever's between your mother and you is not on me."

"I knew you would make excuses," said Sun, crossing her arms so she didn't lunge forward and fasten her hands around the Lee girl's throat. *Keep your temper in check.*

The Lee girl moved in under the shelter's roof to get out of sight of visual surveillance. She set down her duffel with a thump.

"Listen, Princess, maybe the queen-marshal is already sorry she got angry and wishes you would come home, all insults forgiven, poor misunderstood Sun. Maybe my family is even now convincing her you deliberately plotted an attempt on Manea's life at the feast using a Gatoi soldier. Or maybe there's another faction at work. Hiring Navah to assassinate you doesn't feel like Lee House's mode of operation. Lots of people hate Chaonia generally and Eirene specifically."

"Then who was Navah working for? Why try to kill me and not my mother?"

"Besides your humble charm? It's true this could all be a complicated scheme to completely discredit you and elevate Manea's future child to heir. In which case I am playing my role as reluctant but helpful Companion only to betray you in the end. So fine. Go it alone. However, I can get us out of Argos. I'm betting no one else here can. Not even you."

"Why should I trust you?"

"I don't care if you trust me."

"You'd care if you were dead."

"Actually, if I were actually dead, I wouldn't care because I'd be dead."

James snorted, tipping his cap toward the Lee girl with his irritating inability to take anything seriously. He should have been weeping for Octavian. They all should have been, except there wasn't time. They had to escape first, and if Persephone Lee had a workable plan, then Sun had to figure out if she could trust her.

"How did you know about the research into engineered hallucination?" she asked.

"That's an unexpected change of subject." The Lee girl glanced nervously at the prone banner soldier as she touched her bruised throat. "There was a researcher who showed up at a weapons conference six months ago. A speculative conference, nothing top secret. There were only seven of us in the room for his talk because the higher-ups thought it was pie-in-the-sky twitch diving. He received such a cold reception he didn't bother to attend the final banquet, which I know because I looked for him."

"Why did you go to his talk? Why did you care?"

"I like networks. The subdermal patterns the Gatoi have remind me of networks. Do you think there's something to the idea they're being controlled by the Phene? I was just playing for time when I said all that at the banquet."

Sun lowered the pistol. "All right, Persephone. Get us out of Argos. Then we'll talk."

Persephone had a decisive manner that Perseus had lacked.

"Once they've searched the cargo trains and tunnel they'll guess we escaped on the boats. So here's the plan."

Sun raised a hand. "Stop. First, I must address the cee-cees."

Persephone's brow wrinkled. "We don't have time."

"It's necessary." Sun turned to the others. "According to your contracts you have the right to refuse service that precipitates an imminent threat to your life. This turn of events falls beyond what any of you can have expected when you signed up as employees. Go if you wish, with no shame attached. Furthermore I don't want anyone to stay who would rather leave. Tiana?"

The cee-cee had just pulled a handheld dryer from her duffle. "I'm staying. I need my paycheck."

She threw in a reassuring nod to Persephone, and the Lee girl let out a breath in relief and nodded back as the cee-cee began pulling moisture from dripping clothes.

"What about you, Isis?"

James's cee-cee was from a minor branch of Samtarras House, one downward step from losing House status and becoming citizens. She'd been with him since he was made a Companion. James didn't even look her way; he was watching the boats reach the open water.

"I stay," Isis said.

"Candace?"

Alika went through cee-cees about as fast as he broke strings. That Candace had been with him almost a year was testament to the fact she hadn't had to survive an Idol Faire season with him yet, but she fit in well, and her military background was impeccable. Yet Sun was jolted when Candace pulled off her cee-cee's ring.

"I'm out, Your Highness. Apologies. This isn't what I signed up for."

"No harm, no foul." Taking the ring, Sun squashed an urge to call her a coward. "Candace Jiāng Alyǎnshī, we are quit of obligation."

Alika had taken his ukulele out of its case and was examining it minutely for any sign of damage. He looked up now with a surprised flare of the eyes. "Are you leaving, Candace?"

"I am. That late bloomer . . . I didn't sign up to get shot at with outlawed dark tech."

The look she gave Sun betrayed a bloom of fear, an emotion Sun had never before seen in her face. The pistol shot. Navah's startled expression as blood soaked her shirt. The splash she'd made when she hit the water. Her flailing arms as the sea swallowed her, bait for the scyllas. Sun could practically hear Candace's thoughts: *What if she decides she doesn't trust me?*

The cee-cee tried to arrange her expression into something steady, but the words came out shakily. "Honored Alika, we are quit of obligation."

"Right. Well. Toss me that pack of strings I gave you to carry, will you?"

Candace winced at his toneless reply but fished into a pocket and threw a green packet, which Alika caught.

"We are quit of obligation. Your contract also binds you to silence about all our activities. You can get a train at the station. Go!" Sun liked Candace, but done was done. She saw no need for inconsequential farewells.

Wiping tears from her cheeks, Candace hurried away.

No one called goodbye because Persephone was already talking.

"There are three train stations within walking distance. I'm hoping that will confuse search parties. Point Panic Sports Garden is closest to us. I need two volunteers to take a short-haul van from Panic Harbor Station out toward the Heffalump Trunk Escarpment. There's a rental service at every end-of-the-line station. I've got a route plotted through the warehouse and manufacturing district that should allow you to avoid notice. You'll take the logging road toward Auspicious Forests Province, but you'll double back at Sublime Point lookout and make your way through the Autumn Peace residential zone to Orange Line Station at Autumn West."

Sun considered the possible ramifications of this elaborate movement. "Why don't we all just take the van?"

"The van is a decoy."

"Very well. Who'll take it?"

Gaze flashing to Candace's receding figure and then back to

Sun, James spoke in his usual drawl. "Isis and I will do the aunt-and-nephew ploy. That always works. We'll rent two vans to confuse matters and drop one at random along the way. Do we all meet up at Autumn West Station, then?"

"That depends on what happens next," said Persephone. "We'll have to let you know later. Princess Sun, you do have a secure channel to your Companions, right?"

"I'll pretend you didn't ask that stupid question. By the way, I'd suggest you pull a bag over your head. I'm releasing the banner soldier."

The Lee girl went from cool and composed to jumping backward like a frightened squib. "What? *What?*"

Alika forgot himself enough to smirk, entertained at this display of ignorance about banner protocol.

The Lee girl dug frantically into her duffel and yanked out a scarf printed with the CeDCA logo. As she wrapped it hastily around her head, leaving only a slit for her eyes, James laughed. Hetty looked away, frowning. Tiana stepped nobly up beside her employer, still clutching the sandal as if it could possibly be an effective weapon. Although given everything Sun had seen of the cee-cee so far, she had to wonder if it could.

Sun triggered the cutoff on the wires that, wrapped around the Gatoi prisoner's legs, had been pumping a steady dose of percussion echo into his neuro-enhancers. Released from its dampening effect the prisoner reared up like a cobra sensing a threat, then leaped to a crouch, ready to spring. Persephone pressed a hand over the scarf to hold it in place as its coils loosened and started to sag, exposing bits of skin.

"That's right, if he doesn't see your face he won't attack you," Sun added as the damped-down anger tightened in her chest.

The banner soldier's gleaming amber gaze fixed on Sun because she was speaking. She could almost see the grid of his thoughts as his homing system analyzed her presence for threat. In an instant more he would attack.

She extended her right hand, palm up. Being the daughter of a Royal caused her no end of trouble and suspicion in the Republic of Chaonia, but her father had made sure she understood her obligations within the banners as well. She knew the ritual words.

"Where the heavens above did not exist, and the earth beneath had not come into being, there dwelled the cosmic waters, which are the substance of all. Out of this ocean rose Lady Chaos, who gave birth to the eleven exiles."

His chin came up like he'd been slapped, all the surprise he allowed himself before he tipped forward onto his knees and rested his hands, palms down, on hers.

His voice was low, scarcely more than a whisper, with a smoky timbre. "Thus Lady Chaos said to her twelfth child, the last born, the Royal: protect my offspring, and in exchange they will serve you when you call."

"I call you now, according to the ancient covenant," said Sun. "I am born beneath the banner of Royal, child of João, child of Nanshe, child of Ashur to the tenth generation. By the binding of the crown of light I assert my right to demand your service until I release you."

He touched his forehead to her hands. "I am born beneath the banner of Wrathful Snakes. I am bound by the ancient covenant and by the crown of light."

She placed her left hand atop his buzzed-short hair, thus cupping his head and therefore his loyalty between her hands. "You know my name. What do I call you?"

"My battle name is Zizou."

"It is an honorable name among the people. Elegance with precision. You will act as my bodyguard. My safety and security, and that of my companions, is yours to defend to the death."

"So will it be."

She released him, knelt beside Octavian's body, and touched her ring to the ring the dead man wore. The rings had a kind of microscopic burr to them, sealing to the skin of the one who wore them; only the touch of another ring could unseal the connection unless the person wearing the ring took it off themselves.

At her touch Octavian's ring loosened. She pulled it off his lifeless hand. Zizou put it on, eyes flaring as he felt the bite of the burrs.

"He might want to cover his torso." Tiana pulled a baggy hooded sweatshirt from her duffel. She tossed it to the Gatoi, then shook out a square of folded fabric to reveal a striped surfboard bag. "The body will fit in here. It's a hover-bag and can lift up to 120 kilos."

There was a pause as everyone stared at her.

She shrugged. "I just thought a corpse would draw notice."

"I'll do it," said Sun. This wasn't the time to ask if Vogue Academy had a class in "hiding the evidence."

Octavian was a deadweight as she and Tiana rolled him into the hover-bag. She paused before she sealed it closed, wondering if this was the last time she would ever see his face, and then she was furious that the ashen cast of skin and the blank stare of his once-keen brown eyes was the last glimpse of him she would take with her.

"James and Isis can take the hover-bag," said Persephone. She was kneeling, back to the rest, as she dug through her own duffel.

Hearing her voice, Zizou began to turn to see who was there, and Sun snapped, "Eyes forward, Recruit. Don't ever look toward that voice, on my order."

James extended a hand. "Here's Navah's ring. I slipped it off before she went into the water."

He spoke in an unexpectedly harsh voice, with a glance at Hetty's grim expression. Hetty had not spoken since Navah's death, and Hetty not speaking was like the sun not shining.

But Sun had done what was necessary, so she sealed the fabric over Octavian's head and took the ring without comment. James and Isis hurried away with the hover-bag in tow.

Sun pulled two rings off her hand and held them out. "These are the rings Perseus and Duke wore, so I give them to you, Persephone and Tiana. They'll feed you into my secure network. Persephone, you'll go separately with Hetty. The other three will come with me."

Hetty gave Sun a nod, but it was stiff and disapproving. Sun could not shake a sick feeling rising in her gut at Hetty's continued silence. Yet there was nothing to be done. They had to go.

"Which station?" she asked the Lee girl.

"Sports Garden. A royal wedding means a republic-wide holiday, so there will be a lot of people out and about. And our fancy clothes won't look out of place."

Sun slipped Navah's and Candace's rings onto her fingers as she started walking. The sting of their connection reminded her of the consequences of disloyalty.

Zizou strode a few steps ahead like he were expecting to absorb a spray of shrapnel on her behalf. With the hood pulled up he was eminently ignorable except for the crisp power of his stride. Tiana walked alongside with her duffel slung over a shoulder. Alika cradled his ukulele case protectively against his chest.

Persephone had pulled on a black peacoat to hide her mourning clothes. She twisted her brother's ring onto her middle finger. As she and Hetty hurried away down a different path she rewrapped the scarf in a more practical fashion.

Sun's network blinked as a 🌀 appeared with a message:

OUCH. WHAT WAS THAT?

CONNECTION, Sun replied.

FUNNY HAHA. MAKE SURE ALL PERSONAL LOCATION TRACKERS ARE OFF. TAKE THE RED LINE TO THE WHEELHOUSE. MEET ON THE 1435 GREEN LINE FOR DRUM TOWER. SECOND TO LAST CARRIAGE, SIT IN THE DOWNSTREAM END SEATS.

A code pinged in. Sun forwarded it to James, almost lost to view as he and Isis shepherded the hover-bag toward the Point Panic industrial harbor. She telescoped her vision in on his receding figure. After a moment he raised a hand with two fingers up to show that the code looked legit to him. She forwarded it to the rest of the party.

Hetty was almost out of sight beyond rocks and towering shore bushes and hadn't glanced back once. Had killing Navah been a mistake? No. Absolutely not. They had proof Navah was a spy, so they'd have had to jettison her anyway. Octavian was dead because Navah had drawn attention to their boat with her flashing bracelets.

Octavian. Percy. Duke. Their deaths would not go unanswered. She swore it.

They reached a windbreak of cypress trees. Beyond lay an expansive public park with playing fields and picnic facilities. Alika had been here before—it had been a competition stop on Idol Faire—so she let him guide them through the garden with its changing rooms for swimmers and surfers, the badminton, volleyball, and basketball courts, and a profusion of table tennis pavilions and handball cubes.

The sports garden was crowded today. No one celebrated alone in Chaonia, and every citizen was required to celebrate on royal occasions. Local citizens were out in their best clothes, playing chess or mah-jongg or Go, singing along to Channel Idol's streaming karaoke, or crowding up to one of the food carts where free food and drink, nothing too expensive, were being disbursed courtesy of the Ministry of Rites and Culture. Wide banners draped every available surface, big messages painted by the local schoolchildren: "Let happiness bloom" and "At last the skies above are blue."

Several projections showed a band and dancers in full performance, ostensibly from the hall where the wedding feast was taking place, although Sun had her doubts since she'd seen no stage in the hall. Their party clothes did indeed make it easy to slide through the crowd. Every public festival was an opportunity to dress up. They passed masked monkey kings and mermaid warriors in towering crowns, silver-gowned elves and Asgardians encased in augmented-reality armor, children wearing myco-facture mecha suits and elders in kaiju headdresses pretending to steal their candy with mock roars.

Poor Zizou gave a classic double take when a group of people painted with Gatoi-style tattoos shimmied through the crowd.

Their pretended dance moves broke the spell. No banners ever danced in that jerky "savage" style.

He glanced back at her, and for the first time she saw a glimpse of personality behind the obedient banner soldier—his brow wrinkled in puzzlement.

"What was that, Royal?" he asked in a low voice. "Those are not our cousins. They are just painted to look like them."

"Ignore it for now. I'll explain later."

He plunged on, scanning the crowd for whatever a recruit raised within the banners would consider a threat.

Everyone in the crowd was wearing at the very least a ribbon or headband or sash of red in honor of the wedding. Sun grabbed a bunch of ribbons from a pillar festooned with the red and gold of the military, thinking of Octavian. She could barely recall life without him nearby. It was unfathomable that he was dead even though that had been his job: to save her life, even at the cost of his own.

Those responsible would pay for this. They would pay dearly, and they would pay over and over and over again. Every time a glimpse of the feasting hall flashed into view on a pillar or screen her fury flared anew, blue-fire hot.

Tiana was opening a path by letting her duffel "accidentally" bump into people hard enough that they stepped aside. Alika kept his head down, using the case to conceal his face. At last they reached the pillars and rainbow awnings that marked the transit forecourt. All trains and trams in the Republic of Chaonia were free as part of the war effort, so no fee barriers blocked their way. The Red Line platform was glowing with a fading pink; a train had just left.

Down at the far end of the platform Candace was stalking the edge like she meant to jump onto the rails. Sun prided herself on her ability to suss out people's weak spots, but she was forced to admit she hadn't seen this coming. Raised on shipboard and later on orbital stations by a string of relatives in the shadow of the dead parents who had given their lives fighting for the republic, Candace feared abandonment. Sun had thought that would make her loyal through the thick and thin of dealing with the Honorable Alika.

"Tiana, how long have you worked for the Honorable Persephone?" Sun asked.

"I just met her today." Tiana was also looking toward Candace as she turned the ring that had belonged to Duke around and around on her left forefinger. She had amazing control over her expression. Her face revealed nothing but a pleasant mask.

"Then why are you sticking with us, under these circumstances?"

"You have no idea what it means to be poor, do you, Your Munificent Highness?" Her smile was a scorpion: perfectly designed and with a sting at the end. "Begging your pardon, but people do all kinds of dangerous work because they have no choice."

"You could have taken less-fraught cee-cee work."

"Not anything as well paid. If I'm injured or killed in the line of duty my family gets a big payout in compensation." She gestured back toward the park they'd left behind. "Do you think everyone celebrating cares about the royal wedding? Some have come so their children can have sweets and festival foods they can't otherwise afford."

"A fair perspective." Sun looked back toward Candace.

It really chewed at her to be proven wrong. Which strand of Candace had she misread? How had she miscalculated? She watched the young woman pause at the platform's far railing and scan the view beyond the station's awning, which looked toward the central city. From where she stood Sun could not see whatever Candace saw, a sight that made the young woman stiffen, take a step back, then whirl and with an expression of grim determination stride back down the platform toward Sun and her group. She unclipped her fans from her belt but didn't open them.

Sun waited for Candace's 🏮 icon to ping into view, but of course it didn't. The ring was also a sophisticated scrambler that kept Sun's personal communications network private.

Seeing Candace's approach as a potential threat, Zizou placed himself between them.

"It's all right," said Sun as Candace stopped at a prudent distance and clipped the fans back to her belt.

In a low voice she said, "There's a security Hummingbird incoming."

There it was. The faint *chutter chutter chutter* blended into the festive beat of a bhangra tune and the buzz of conversation and laughter from the sports garden. A schedule board flashed: 5 minutes to next inbound train.

"Alika, check security comms traffic," said Sun, and to Candace, "Estimate for set-down?"

"Five to eight minutes, going by visual cues."

Sun pried a ring from her finger and held it out. "In or out?"

"Dammit." Candace's lips pinched together. She huffed out a big breath, grabbed the ring, and slipped it on.

Sun looked up and down the platform, but Hetty and Persephone were nowhere to be seen as the schedule board flashed: 4 minutes to next inbound train.

Alika said, "I'm not hearing any emergency security chatter."

"With Navah gone it can't be her calling them in. They might be conducting a standard search pattern. We're going to chance we can get on the train before our pursuit spots us."

Hetty and Persephone walked onto the platform at the terminus end. Sun flashed them the go-ahead command, two fingers gesturing toward the tracks. Hetty nodded in reply.

Would the Hummingbird land before the train arrived? Candace wiped sweat from her forehead, fingers tapping on her fans.

The tiles on the floor glowed to signal an incoming train. The *chutter* of the descending Hummingbird rose over the noise of the revelers. People on the platform turned to look as the wind off the machine's blurred wing-blades bent the tips of the cypress. The security vehicle settled into a landing beyond the sports garden, out of sight behind the trees.

A gust of air heralded the incoming train.

Its exterior gleamed, the usual projected advertisements tuned for the day to characters for *Heart to Heart* and *Good Fortune*. Doors sighed open and passengers trickled out, few enough that Sun and the others could board without waiting for the outward rush to cease. But the sparse crowd also made them more visible. The hearty roar of conversation and celebration from the garden dampened, a sure sign the security forces had left the Hummingbird and were now pushing through the crowd. Looking for Sun.

"Close, close, damn you," Tiana muttered under her breath, twisting the strap of her duffel.

Down the open gangway of the long interior Sun spotted Hetty and Persephone at the rear of the train.

Candace's 🦪 pinged: INCOMING.

A person wearing the sleek black helmet and spruce-green uniform of the gendarmes trotted into view, helmet camera blinking as it scanned the passengers leaving the platform. Sun stepped behind Zizou, letting his body hide her, as the others turned their faces away. The door-closing alarm buzzed.

"That's them!" Just as the gendarme began running toward the train, the doors closed with a whoosh.

The train jolted forward.

Sun grabbed for a strap. Through the windows she saw the gendarme give the hand signal for *target acquired* to comrades reaching the platform. She laughed.

"How can you laugh?" How quickly Tiana dropped the proper honorific. No flattering titles now!

"Why not laugh?" Sun retorted. "The doors closed. We're here. They're there."

"They'll signal ahead and trap us at the next station or at the Wheelhouse."

"They'll try. That doesn't mean they'll succeed. I have a move no one will expect."

19

In Which the Wily Persephone Experiences Turbulence

The Honorable Hestia Hope and I take a parallel track through the festivities in the sports garden. We walk far enough away from the others that we don't seem to be together but near enough that we can keep Sun in view.

She says, "Your father is of Yele, is he not? A seer of Iros—"

"Yeah. What's it to you?"

My brusque interruption does not disturb her equanimity. Her voice is of the timbre people call *musical.* "I also have a father who's a seer. A scholar of linguistics who can trace his academic genealogy to Mavva Varc-Gallia."

"Who is that?"

"The foremother of linguistics! Anyway. My scholar father met and fell in love with a Chaonian House–born diplomat."

"I'm not sure I'd describe my parents' bond as a romantic one, and it's damn sure my mother's not a diplomat," I reply ungraciously. But I pause before I say anything worse and instead give her a glance. She gives me a nod like she wants me to know that she gets me, and maybe she does get me about this one thing. So I add, "It sucks to be half Yele in a Chaonian town. I try to keep it secret."

"There is no shame in love, or shouldn't be."

"Which only means there all too often is."

She smiles appreciatively before pulling back into her own thoughts. We make our way onward in silence, although it's no longer as awkward. She looks weary, and why wouldn't she be? They lost Percy and Duke already. The two deaths today came so fast and so shockingly that I can only keep my head in the game by pretending this is a VR scenario, not real. I try to think like Solomon would, keeping my eyes on Sun's group and the churn of the crowd around her.

Even though he's wearing a nondescript gray hoodie I can't stop noticing the Gatoi soldier. He moves like a sated carnosaur through a herd of oblivious herbivores, deftly weaving in and out to keep his body between Sun and anyone he identifies as a potential threat. Every masked monkey king gets a sharp look, and yet he gives an almost imperceptible flinch each time a person passes capped by one of the snake-haired wigs worn to mock the Gatoi deity known as Lady Chaos.

Sun's party passes out of view onto the transit platform. Hestia breaks away from me. For an instant I think she's dashing after Sun, dumping me while keeping Ti as a hostage . . .

Instead she snags a basket of steamed buns from a food cart and hustles back. "Someone has to keep the party fed. Or at the very least, to think of food."

We hurry onto the glowing platform. A hot wind whips over our heads as a Hummingbird lands with a loud *chutter chutter* behind the wall of cypress.

"The train should reach the platform before the gendarmes do." I check the train number listed on the arrivals screen. "Oh, good, it's a Diamondback."

"Why does that matter?"

"It's an older-model train with more manual overrides."

From halfway down the platform Sun gives a two-finger gesture toward the tracks, and Hestia dips her chin in reply.

"It'll be close," I add, since Sun's gesture is clearly an order to go for the train. "Can you tell me why Sun shot your cee-cee? I'm just asking because I want to know if I'm likely to be next."

Hestia—Hetty—has a calm gaze and steady hands. I'm guessing she doesn't rile easily even if she looks miserable right now. "We knew there was a spy within our ranks. We guessed it might be her, but needed proof. When proof we got, we kept her on. You see?"

"Keep your friends close, and your enemies closer."

Her eyes crinkle, but whether she's amused because she approves of me or is angry at what she takes for a jest I honestly can't tell. "You understand the game—"

"It's no game. Four people are dead."

"Death takes us all," she retorts.

The platform flashes as the train slides in. The doors open. About twenty people push out, and we slide in against the flow. The doors close behind us just as a detail of gendarmes hits the platform.

"They've seen us," I say.

The train glides out of the station, back toward the center of Argos. The bay glimmers to the east. The sails of the palace wink and shine under the sun. Assembly Square sits like a black blot in the middle of densely built neighborhoods roofed with white clay tiles. Solar collectors decorate roofs in elaborate designs.

Hestia starts walking forward along the open gangway toward Sun. There aren't many other passengers, and they give her a cursory glance. Me, they look at twice, trying to figure where they've seen me before. I've pretended for the last two years as I shed my baby fat that the uncanny resemblance between Resh and me is just family genetics, but Sun's accusation echoes in my head. I know she said it to trip me up. But the question resonates through every part of me: Are Resh and I both clones of our aunt? How nuts is that?

Sun has noticed us coming, although she's got her head bent as she speaks to Alika.

He heaves a dramatic sigh, then rolls his gorgeously lashed brown eyes. "Oh, very well, if there's no other way," he says in a resigned tone.

As Hestia and I reach them Candace adds, "I'll do it. A flash-invite will make more sense coming from me."

Her gaze goes distant as she taps into the global net. I have no idea what she's doing, although I wonder why she's back with our group after she quit. Since I am *still* locked out of the net I have no idea why Ti giggles, a hand pressed over her lips.

"That's brilliant," she says to Sun through her fingers.

Sun gives a one-shoulder shrug like she doesn't care about praise, but I'm pretty sure the princess is secretly eyeing Ti to study the effect her "brilliance" is having on my cee-cee. Mine.

Ti looks at me desperately, although I have no idea why. "Isn't it a brilliant idea, Honored Persephone?"

"Sure," I temporize, not wanting to give away how limited my net access is.

Alika pulls his ukulele out of its case, sits, and starts tuning. Up and down the train, heads turn and whispers rise.

Hestia takes the lid off the basket. "You have to eat. I knew you would forget."

Sun glares at the steamed buns but takes one. Hestia offers the basket to each of us in turn, although Alika ignores her. I grab a bun more out of habit than hunger. With the first bite the rich sweetness of custard melts so deliciously in my mouth that I gulp down the rest of mine before the others have even taken a second bite.

"What is this?" asks Zizou in a low voice. His back is to me so I can't see his face, but he's holding the bun between his thumb and middle finger like he expects it to explode. His apprehension is kind of cute, if the confusion of violent, dangerous, predatory automatons can ever be termed *cute*.

"*Bāozi*," says Tiana patiently. "Maybe you have a different word for it. *Manapua. Bun.*"

"It's purple," he says in a tone that suggests purple is a mark of poison.

"It's all right, it's a kind of yam," continues Tiana in a soothing voice. With a gesture of thoughtless reassurance, she rests fingers on his forearm.

He jerks away as if her perfectly manicured and flower-painted fingernails are razors in disguise. The movement so startles her that she, too, steps back, bumps into the seat, and sits down hard beside Alika.

Taking her impact as his cue, Alika strums what my network identifies as a G7 suspended fourth chord. It's the distinctive opening to one of the ancient songs he revived as part of his Idol Faire competition last year.

A girl halfway down the train shrieks as she tugs so hard on her friends' arms that her mermaid crown falls off.

"Aaaaaaa! It's Alika! It's really *ALIKA*!"

She surges forward. Her friends grab her arms and haul her to a stop with embarrassed titters.

"It's all right," calls Candace. "You can come closer. Gather round."

Not everyone in the Republic of Chaonia follows Idol Faire, but it's hard to ignore Alika. Everyone knows his story: a minor cousin in a minor branch of Vata House. He and his impoverished relatives were struggling to survive on a frontier post where the House had exiled a disliked ancestor who lost a long-ago battle over control of the family ministry. Only after Vata House's first ten candidates to be Companion to the princess were humiliatingly rejected by Sun did the family trawl the depths of the lineage database. They finally found what they thought would be an insulting and mocking choice: a painfully shy and hopelessly unfashionable boy immersed in music studies. He even lived in the industrial dome of an isolated terminus system on a planet with an unbreathable atmosphere. Although only fourteen at the time, Sun had the acuity to measure his potential. Maybe she also had the gift of seeing how the growth spurt of adolescence would remold his features, or maybe she plotted his Idol Faire rise from the beginning of their relationship and forced him to undergo cosmetic surgery to get that face.

But the face Alika shows to the people on the train isn't the face of a pushover or a pretty mediocrity. When he sings, he shines. When he plays, he's incandescent. As a few of the other passengers timidly venture closer he catches a gaze here, and a shy smile there, and nods to include them in his orbit. The girl with the mermaid crown is sobbing with worshipful tears as he segues from "A Hard Day's Night" into a virtuosic piece of astounding finger-work. It's one of his own compositions, "Turbulence," a soundscape tribute to the poisonous winds of his home world.

Even I am so caught up in the music that it isn't until pillars and signs flash past that I realize we have reached the next station. All along the platform people stare at our incoming train, wondering if the flash-invitation that's just been bombed across the Chaonian network is true. I can't see the flash-bomb, of course. My network is still in cadet lockdown. But I can guess what it says.

The train slows to a stop. As the doors slide open I prod Alika forward to the front of the train, right next to the closed door that leads to the operator's cab. Alika jumps up to stand on the last seat. Tiana slings our bags onto the bench and floor next to him to create some breathing room. We're fortunate the platform isn't that crowded, because almost everyone waiting pushes onto our train. People abandon the other side of the platform and their trip to some other destination to grab this unbelievable chance to hear the winning Idol play live and unfiltered. The platform conductor, who makes sure everyone is standing behind the line before the train enters and leaves the station, gapes through the window at Alika, forgetting to do his job as the train pulls away.

"'I'm all alone here, without any hope but you,'" Alika confides melodically as if to each new individual who pushes onto the train. At the next stop, his "'Hurry, get on now, it's coming,'" gets people clapping along to the beat.

At the third stop I see a squad of gendarmes trying to push through to the train, but the desperate crowd, hoping for a glimpse of the Handsome Alika, shoves back at the gendarmes.

The doors open. The way people elbow and jostle to get inside would give anyone pause, but Sun observes it with the calm of a tactician measuring her battlefield. The girl who first screamed is now pressed against me, her purse digging into my hip. She's glassy-eyed, so close to her idol she could reach out and touch him. So far everyone in the train has behaved respectfully, but this heat of anticipation could break into boiling chaos between a breath and a scream.

I lock arms with Sun, who locks arms with Zizou, who locks arms with Hestia, who locks arms with Candace, who braces herself against the seat to the right of where Tiana sits.

"That's enough, my dear friends," Alika calls over the melody he's playing. "Be kind to each other. Don't push."

Those fortunate enough to get on stand crushed together and yet eerily silent as he breaks off to wave at the people on the platform who weren't so lucky. Their screams of excitement drown out the warning horn that alerts people the doors are about to close and the train to depart.

There follows a moment of terrifying confusion as people are pressed past the safety line into doors sliding shut, only to be frantically tugged back by their companions as the train jolts forward. As we leave the station I see a gendarme speaking into a wristcom. The tunnel cuts off my view as we race onward through the dark into central Argos.

We pass through the next two stations without stopping, which means security has over-ridden the controls. I'm betting they plan to trap us at the Wheelhouse. Once we arrive there, they can deploy an entire division of gendarmes as well as manipulate barriers and gates in the concourse and corridors. Alika's speed-drenched rendition of "Battle at Aspera Drift" keeps people focused on him, not that anyone cares about a missed stop at this point. My left hip is really starting to hurt where it's being pinched painfully against the latch of the door into the cab.

He's clever in his choice of tunes, pitching a sense of solidarity among the people as he lights it up.

"'We'll start the day tomorrow,'" the crowd sings along to the ancient classic with fevered enthusiasm. They would ride with him all the way around the world if they could.

But we don't have that far to go on this leg of the journey.

By the time we approach the Wheelhouse I'm drenched in sweat and starting to ache from the strain of pushing back against the press of bodies. Sun, Zizou, Hestia, Candace, and I keep holding our tight semicircle of space around Alika. He's standing on the seat with Tiana sitting beside him on top of her duffel. As he starts in on a plaintive ballad about lost love she plays along, turning to look out the windows, so he ends up singing to her proud back while the rest of us see her perfect profile and stern, regretful expression. Not a voice murmurs or body shifts, as if the audience fears to interrupt his heartbreak.

"I know you'll be a star in somebody else's sky, but why, why, why can't it be, can't it be mine?"

Together he and Ti make a stunning image, him pleading, her refusing. Half the audience is crying and the other half trembling with adulation. Even I have tears on my cheeks, and I know it is all an act.

Republic law prohibits personal broadcasting. Anyone wishing to upload live feeds onto the net must have a license for a wasp. But even the government can't control the twitch. I am certain this is being illicitly broadcast by everyone here. Candace will be streaming it via Alika's dedicated sub-channel, courtesy of Channel Idol. Three-quarters of the realtime audience on Chaonia Prime is probably bolting from the coverage of the royal wedding to tune into us.

The cavernous interior of the Wheelhouse opens around us as we glide in under the vast concourse roof. Gendarmes are out in force but separated from our platform by the sheer monstrous size of the crowd that has mobbed the Wheelhouse in response to Candace's flash-invite. Any spark will set off a stampede. I glance at Sun, wondering if she will sacrifice citizen lives to protect her own.

She catches my eye and says, "Your turn, Persephone. The gendarmes won't use lethal fire for fear of hitting citizens on the queen-marshal's wedding day."

I cup hands around my mouth so no camera can read my lips. "Our target is still the 1435 Green Line to Drum Tower. There are surveillance cameras covering 83.7 percent of the Wheelhouse concourse and corridors. The best dead zones lie in the corridors between levels. Best chance we have to confuse the cameras is to change clothes in dead zones and then reverse direction and split up. In smaller groups we'll make our way in a roundabout manner to the correct platform for our train."

"How do you know all this?"

"When I was fifteen I spent months plotting an escape route from my family. With the war on, there are not enough resources to fix minor things like broken surveillance cameras in the transportation system."

"Ah. All right. Alika, we need outerwear and masks."

I'm struck by how she's pulled in her fire, letting Alika hog all the attention. She's not that different in appearance from the girl who'd first screamed, the one still pushed up against me, who also has chin-length straight black hair and wears a red-and-gold festival tunic like Sun's. No one around us is looking at Sun, but I know the cameras at either end of the open-gang train are without question fixed on the heir specifically. People who work for my family know Alika is a distraction even if it might be hard for these observers to look away. He's wearing an embroidered gold sherwani, the knee-length formal wear traditional at Vata House. It's wrinkled and still a bit damp but nevertheless magnificent. His long black hair is pulled back into a now disheveled bun that somehow makes him look even more appealing, as if he needs a little tender loving care from you, yes, random *you* there in the audience.

He segues into a strumming refrain and speaks over it in his concert voice. "Peace be upon you, my friends! Welcome to the Wheelhouse. The city of Argos is celebrating. I am here to help you find your joy! But look what happened! I lost my festival ornaments on the way."

Amid shrieks and cheers we get hit by a shower of masks and myco-facture helmets and the long embroidered jackets that are Chaonia's most common festival wear. I grab several jackets and a kaiju mask as the train reaches a platform and sighs to a stop. Seeing Alika, the people outside start pounding on the windows and shouting his name. The doors don't open.

"We split up." I speak into Sun's ear. She's holding a mermaid crown in one hand and a Lady Chaos mask in the other. "You take the Gatoi and Ti and a change of festival gear . . ."

The doors still haven't opened.

"You trapped us." Sun grabs my arm, her grip so tight it hurts.

I don't try to shake off her hand. In a way, her consternation makes me cocky. "I'm way ahead of you, Princess."

"Because they'll lock down the doors for as long as it takes to evacuate the concourse? We're fish in a barrel—"

"That's what they're supposed to think. But this is an old Diamondback model with specific structural quirks. I know my trains. Watch, listen, and learn."

The people packed inside with us start murmuring impatiently as they realize the doors should have opened already. I pitch my voice to carry above their talk.

"Oi! I just got word from the conductor. The automatic door opener broke. You need to pull out the emergency windows. Those who can must crawl out. Make space inside so no one gets crushed while we wait for rescue. Just don't *panic.*"

Right on cue, Alika starts shouting for people to remain calm, which of course only agitates them more. As emergency windows get opened and people start to climb out I start hammering on the locked cab door.

"Oi! You in there!" The door is a thin sheet of metal and not soundproof. "A passenger is caught in one of the doors. Press the manual release! Open the doors before their leg is crushed!"

"Turn your face to the wall."

When Sun gives an order it's impossible to resist. I pull my scarf tighter around my face. Because we've kept a corner of space here at the front of the train, there's room for Zizou to kick. The latch breaks. He wrenches the door open. I dash inside to find the terrified operator holding down the emergency lock button as a voice speaking from central control blasts through the speaker: *"Do not open the doors. I repeat, do not open the doors."*

"Sorry," I say as I slam the operator to one side and pound my fist down on the manual door release.

The doors open with a gasp. Everyone starts shouting as people tumble out of the packed train. I can't tell if they're frightened by the stunt with the emergency windows or thrilled that they have an astounding tale to tell of their encounter with the Handsome Alika. Just days before the new season of Idol Faire begins! What a publicity coup!

What matters is that we grab our bags and as many masks and

jackets as we can handle and shove out with all the others. The concourse is a roar of gendarme whistles, sobbing youth, a voice crying for a doctor, and the squeal and hiss of brakes along other platforms. It's perfect cover for a bold escape.

The girl who'd screamed and her two friends have joined a seething circle of fans outside the door, waiting for Alika to emerge. As Sun, Ti, and Zizou break away from us, swirling away into the crowd, I tap the girl on the shoulder.

"Oi! What's your name?"

She stares uncomprehendingly at me until one of her friends nudges her. Then she says, "Hana. This is Chūnhuá and Luciana."

"You want to be in the adventure? It's part of the previews for Idol Faire."

Their eyes get wide as Alika, with Candace on one side and a somber Hestia on the other, steps off the train. The people who swarmed the concourse haven't forgotten him. They crowd close, shouting and crying in excitement.

Candace and I take point and jab a path through the throng, Candace brandishing her furled fans and I bumping my duffel ahead of me like a ram. Alika follows in our wake, strumming in the troubadour-as-vagabond-strolling-about-town style he made famous in Idol Faire. I can't hear what he's playing. His trio of acolytes hangs on him. Hestia holds the rear guard with an emergency bag slung over her shoulder.

No one can miss our progress, and there are seven of us now, including Hana with her hair cut like Sun's and her long red-and-gold silk tunic, which from a distance looks enough like Sun's that it will be easy to believe she is the princess.

Of course I'm risking innocent people's lives. I'm a Lee House child, after all. It's what we do. But I'm gambling that on the queen-marshal's wedding day they will try to avoid causing injury or death to bystanders. If I'm wrong, we're about to find out.

20

The Masks That People Wear

Zizou's gaze sweeps the crowd's minefield of threat. People shove as they try to reach the train from which the Royal, whom the others call Princess Sun, just disembarked. His job is to keep her alive. But never in his life has he moved amid such a burn of heat and moisture and reeking air with so many loud voices clamoring like a relentless hail of blows to his head.

"This mob is going to make me late for my—"

"It's really ALIKA!"

"No, it's just a lookalike doing a Channel Idol promo—"

"Aaaaaaaaaaaaaaaaaaa!"

The Royal speaks. "Zizou, put on this jacket."

He drags on a garment whose loose, long sleeves fall to his knees. It flaps open as they keep moving away from the train. Before he can demand clothing that won't hamper his movement if he has to fight, the young woman who touched him without asking permission hands him an embroidered sash. He wraps the sash twice around his waist to keep the jacket closed.

The Royal vanishes from her place at his shoulder.

He whips around to attack, but she's merely knelt, hiding herself within the crowd as she tugs on a jacket like his except hers is gold instead of green. She hands him a random mask from among the four she's holding by their straps.

A mockery of the face and hair of Lady Chaos leers up at him. He flinches away from the crude blasphemy of the mask's goggling eyes and a purple tongue made of slimy rubber stuck out between obscenely parted lips.

The Royal's gaze sharpens. "Drop it," she says.

He can't move his fingers. Nothing in his training prepared him to fight against the contempt represented by the mask.

The Royal snatches the mask away and hands him a new one, a heavenly dog with a happy face and perky ears.

She tugs on a stylized demon mask painted red. "Tiana, have you plotted the best route?"

"I know how to get to the Green Line." Accomplished Tiana has disguised herself behind a handsome red-and-white fox mask and a cape fringed with fluffy tails.

"Ping me the map."

"I don't have a map, Your Excellence. But I've been through here a thousand times like everyone else in Argos who doesn't have an aircar. We'll go roundabout. Like Perse said."

Seen through the opening of the mask the Royal's eyes flicker with a narrowing he interprets as anger, but immediately afterward the Royal chuckles.

"Point for her. Lead on, cee-cee."

Tiana elbows her way through the throbbing press of the crowd. The Royal falls in behind, and he takes up a rearguard defensive position.

"Zizou! Put on the mask."

"It blocks my full field of vision."

"Put on the mask."

He puts on the mask, although he hates it.

Over her shoulder Ti calls back to him, "If you twist up the cloth of the sleeves you can tie them up so they don't get in your way."

It's a practical suggestion that works surprisingly well. He's sweating already; the atmosphere is kept much cooler on wheelships, and he's not sure why they turn it up so high here. Then he recalls a fact from school about planets and climate zones.

An erratic movement to his right grabs his attention. He swings around to confront.

A youth has fainted. Friends are trying to haul the limp body out of the press before they're trampled. No one notices. The crowd's attention has fixed on a clot of gendarmes headed their way. The Royal elbows her way through to the frantic group. She grabs the fallen youth. The friends are too fearful and shaky to react efficiently, so Zizou cuts in behind and shepherds them like a ball in play toward a trellis alcove where they might find shelter. Whistles blast as gendarmes close in. He braces for impact, hands into fists, muscles charged with adrenaline.

But the enforcement officers blaze past, headed toward the train, not noticing the Royal because she looks like just another masked celebrant assisting a hapless companion out of danger. Smart thinking on her part.

The alcove contains benches and a statue of a local deity wearing a beatific expression and holding a hand in the sign for *fear not*. Sim screens float at the entrance, gleaming with the characters for *Respectful Happiness* and *May You Always See Heart to Heart*. A bigger screen broadcasts images of the food being eaten at the wedding feast. Platters of sizzling beef and displays of red, orange, and green melons carved into the shapes of flowers glisten celestially. The whistles of the gendarmes get drowned out by the crowd's thousands-tongued voice lifting in a song even he knows: "I have left my home behind me, and I seek what lies ahead."

"Can you manage from here?" the Royal asks the friends of the unconscious youth as they huddle within the alcove's shelter in disheveled shock.

"Yes, yes, please accept our gratitude."

"Don't mention it."

The Royal gives the rescued people a curt nod before gesturing to Ti to head onward. She doesn't look at him because she knows he cannot shirk his duty to protect her. The expectation steadies him. By fulfilling this duty maybe he can erase a fraction of the taint of capture that stains him. Maybe. It would have been better to die with his squad.

As they push outward from the center of the concourse the press lessens and they see no more gendarmes. Breaking their original party into two groups has worked to give the Royal space to escape; good tactics on the part of the one who suggested it, the Persephone whose name is tribute to a goddess of death and rebirth. The name nags at his thoughts. He worries he did something terrible at the feast that he can't recall.

"This way, Your Magnificence," says practical Tiana in her harmonious voice. Then: "Zizou?"

He snaps back into focus and pads down a wide stairway in their wake. The Royal has a brisk stride and confident posture that her mask and new jacket can't disguise, while Tiana gives herself a stoop and slight limping roll to confuse anyone scanning the passageways via camera. He slouches, and shortens his steps, shifts of gait that won't hinder his ability to respond to an attack.

They head down an underground corridor that, like any enclosed passageway, has a unique pattern of vibrations and echoes. Groups of people rush and wheel past in the opposite direction, murmuring about train delays and the threat of a riot and ridiculous Channel Idol stunts and will we really see him, is he really truly here in the Wheelhouse giving a concert?

The Royal hesitates at the first intersection, trying to read signage, some of which is painted on the walls and some of which must be visible in augmented reality in the Chaonian state network he doesn't have access to. But he's used to navigating passageways marked with symbols, so he spots the Green Line symbol before the Royal figures it out.

"No, this way." Tiana waves them down a different passage.

"That's to the Red Line," says the Royal.

"Exactly, Your Munificence. We don't want to take the most direct route."

The Royal nods permission. The farther they get down the echoing tiled passageways, the more the traffic clears out. People stride past with heads lowered, no one offering an acknowledgment as they would at home. It's as if everyone is invisible to everyone else.

They come to an intersection. Tiana takes the direction marked prominently with Red and Blue Lines rather than the one listing Green and Purple. After counting to ten steps under her breath she halts against the faded pink tiles of the wall, strips off the fox mask and the cape, and adds, "According to Perse's directions we're in a pocket of surveillance opacity right here."

The Royal pulls off her mask, then shucks the jacket and turns it inside out. The lining is a nondescript brown. She examines the two masks left to her before glancing up at him as he pulls off the dog mask. The people walking past barely glance at them as Tiana says, a little too loudly and in a voice pitched higher and more nasal than her normal tone, "Whew! That mask is so hot. Glad to get it off."

The Royal holds out a cheap-looking elephant mask with crumpled tusks and a gold token affixed to the forehead as a sign of good fortune. "Zizou, I was wrong to hand you that first mask. I should have paid better attention. It was disrespectful."

"No problem," he says, because he doesn't know what else to say and he's startled by her words. It is easier to pull on the elephant mask and take a gray jacket to tug it on over the green one, obedient to the plan. Tiana stuffs the discarded masks into her duffel.

The Royal fixes the final mask over her face; it's a white hockey mask striped with red, the universal symbol for sudden, violent death. Tiana has already transformed herself with a mermaid crown whose half mask covers her eyes and nose with sea-green sparkles. She swings on a cape of fluttering ribbons that hangs to her hips, disguising her distinctive clothing.

"We go back—" she says, taking a first step back the way they came.

The Royal wiggles her fingers to say, *Wait.*

A group of three masked revelers rushes past toward the Red Line. Only then, when the cameras will see three people moving on, do they walk back to the intersection as if they are coming from the Red Line. The long, curving passageway they take now might almost be one of the main rings on a wheelship, the infinite circle that gives the ships their Ouroboros-class designation. He starts to feel more comfortable, not that home ever has this much grime on its surfaces or stink to its scrubbed air, but the sense of containment settles him.

In a low voice Tiana says, "Your Auspiciousness, I just got a ping from Perse, on our private duo-net. She says she's starting phase two."

"Phase two? Does she always talk like that?"

"I couldn't say, Your Benevolence. She wants us to take the 1435 to Drum Tower as with the previous directions but instead get off at Thunderous Surf Station. With all the attention on Alika she's got to split up their group. She can't do that and also make the 1435."

"Did she say all that in one ping?"

With or without a mask, Tiana is an Ishtar come to life. But it's her quirk of a teasing smile—he would never dare tease a Royal—that makes him decide to forgive her for the unasked-for touch.

"No, Your Beneficence. But it's my job as her companion's companion to be able to comprehend the whole from the least."

"You're slipping up," says the Royal, deadpan. "Benevolence and beneficence are a bit too alike."

"Apologies, Your Perspicaciousness. It's the press of activity and the risk of arrest and death that puts me off my game."

The Royal laughs. The echoing sound causes an elderly passerby to look their way with the smile the grands get when they see the young ones enjoying life. He remembers how the socks his grandmother knit for him were callously yanked off his feet. A spike of hot anger scalds him.

The Royal's gaze snaps to Zizou. "You notice something, soldier? Anything to report?"

He dials down the anger with a spurt of calm-alert psychotropics. "People talk more here than at home."

She gives a half laugh that could be amusement or contempt. "On-planet we have plenty of air for useless words. Anything else?"

"The ruse to split up worked."

"I'm sorry to say it was the Honorable Persephone's idea. She's the one you tried to kill, so it's a good job you didn't manage it." She starts walking.

He's so taken by surprise by this revelation that the two women get six steps ahead before he hustles after.

"When did that happen? At the feast?"

Tiana glances back in unfeigned surprise. "You don't remember?"

"All I remember is a flash that blinded me. Just like . . ." He breaks off.

The Royal says, "What does it remind you of? Tell me."

He has to obey any lawful order when a Royal commands. This question is not unlawful.

"It happened to me before. A flash of blinding light that interrupts my memory. The first time I don't recall anything afterward until I woke up a prisoner on this planet."

"Where were you being held prisoner?"

"I don't know. I never saw anything but a large room and a hangar. I was transported by airship to the place where you and I met."

"Where did the flash happen the first time?"

"When my squad was on patrol."

"Where was that?"

"I'm not allowed to give out that information."

Tiana glances back as if expecting the Royal to angrily demand answers, but the Royal knows that no one who is bound into the banners will break the code.

"Without revealing any classified information, can you speculate on what might have triggered the flash that first time?"

"I don't know what caused the flash any of the times."

"It happened to you twice at the Lee compound, right?"

He squints, trying to knit together the shards that are all he can recollect after the airship landed. "Maybe three times."

"That's right," says Tiana. "Perse and I saw you being offloaded at the service dock."

"I don't remember seeing you," he says apologetically. "I remember seeing a face, and then a flash."

The Royal nods. "On patrol, that first time, did you see a person right before the flash?"

"Yes. The captain of the ship we were boarding to clear its manifest and make sure they weren't smuggling—"

He breaks off. Now he's said too much, revealed a part of their orders and purpose that might give a hint as to where they were patrolling.

"I won't ask where you were or what orders you had. But tell me this: Did the captain of that ship resemble the Consort Manea or the Honorable Persephone?"

He blinks, wanting to remember if remembering will help him solve the glitch.

He was midway back along their arrow formation when the captain of the suspect vessel stepped into view holding a clipboard manifest. She was showing it to the squad leader when she'd glanced up and he'd seen her face full-on.

"She was old."

"Old," she says with a triumphant lilt to her tone.

They continue in silence as Tiana picks up the pace. After turning a corner they emerge onto a long underground platform serving the Green Line. Clusters of people await the train. Some wear festival masks while others have the flat affect of people who have already thrown their minds ahead to their destinations. A pair of maintenance workers wearing gray coveralls are chatting at an open network box built into the wall. A flash winks in his peripheral vision. One of the maintenance workers is holding a hand mirror to surreptitiously surveil the crowd. A gust of wind signals an incoming train. The workers close the hatch on the network box.

"We have to get on the right car," says Tiana. "It's got a broken camera on one end."

"How did Persephone have the patience to dig out all these tiny details?" the Royal demands with another of those odd laughs.

Tiana smiles with a sphinx's knowing. "We all have our obsessive qualities, don't we, Your Gloriousness?"

"You're good."

"It's how I graduated first in my class and got offered such a plum assignment."

The train pulls in, and the doors open. He waits until the last instant to get on. Ignoring the train, the maintenance workers each pick up a black toolbox and walk away.

The door slides shut behind him. Tiana settles into a plush bench seat at the back of the last car. She takes the window side, her duffel crammed under the seat, and he takes the aisle side, fixing the Royal between them. There are twenty-nine other people in the car, half the seats unfilled.

"It's just five stops to Thunderous Surf Station," says Tiana in a low voice as the train moves onward.

He says, "Are we clear? May I take off the mask? It stinks."

"You may," says the Royal.

He strips off the wrinkled elephant face and, keeping the hood pulled low, takes in breaths of fresh air tinged with salt and humming with the motion of the train.

From halfway down the car a voice exclaims, "Look at the feed! I told you we should have tried to stay for the concert! How can anyone be so adorable?"

Virtual cubes have popped up in the aisles, playing visuals from the wedding feast side by side with the commotion in the Wheelhouse. Wasps zoom in on a tableau of the Handsome Alika handing bracelets made from ukulele string to the three girls they met on the train. He has the grandeur of a Royal gifting battle treasure to a common banner soldier. The girls are weeping and shining.

Tiana murmurs hoarsely, "How does he do it?"

The Royal stiffens. "Where's Hetty?"

Tiana leans forward to scan the virtual tableau. Besides the three girls, only the soldier with battle fans is now in attendance on the celebrity. "Ha! Perse and the Honorable Hestia have both skipped out while the attention stayed on him. She's so clever, isn't she, Your Appreciativeness?"

"How far are you going to bait me?" asks the Royal with a glower.

Zizou's caution breaks because he misses the bantering jocularity of his kinfolk. He says to the Royal, "You like that she's not afraid of you."

Both of the women shoot up eyebrows, as if surprised he can speak or annoyed that he's stuck his foot into their byplay. Before either figures out a reply the people in the live feed start walking.

Alika pulls on a monkey king mask as his soldier escort glances back toward the watching eye. From a flick of her wrist a fan shoots out from under her arm to smash into the wasp. The image tumbles, cracks on the ground, and goes dead.

The Royal leans forward a fraction. The train pulls into the next station, and the cube feed stalls as the doors open and then close. When the cube snaps back on it's to see a monkey king dressed in Alika's still-wrinkled sherwani striding down a passageway amid a crowd of laughing celebrants. Zizou can see by height and posture that the monkey king isn't Alika.

"It won't take them long to figure that out," says the Royal.

"It only needs to be long enough," says Tiana.

The train glides onward. The Royal taps a foot restlessly as blank walls and nondescript stations slide past, then braces as the train emerges into the light. The view astonishes him. Waves roll in from a deep-blue horizon, build amplitude, and crash over unseen obstacles into white foamy lines. It's mesmerizing, each new wave rising and breaking in a different variation from the one before. A cloudless sky darkens at the horizon until he can't distinguish any line between sky and ocean, and he wonders if they are inside a vast blue sphere.

The train pulls into a seaside station. The doors open. Two people lugging duffels embark and take the seats opposite, bags crammed between the seats. The Royal jerks forward to grasp the hand of the person wearing a half mask rimmed with flames.

"You're here and safe," she says in a tight voice.

The person named Hestia nods, her fingers tightening over Sun's hands.

In a murmur he can only hear because of his enhanced hearing, the Royal whispers, "I had to kill Navah. You see that, don't you?"

"D'you fear it's you I'm mad at? It's myself. I should have been more careful. I just chose the first kind, pleasant face with any skill and did not vet her as I should have done."

"You returned to me grief-stricken by your father's death. Of course you hadn't the energy to realize an unknown agent was being attached to you as a spy. It's not your fault, and I won't let you say it is."

Hetty's color changes, darkening with a blush.

These two love each other.

"It's nice to see you, too, and get out all these deep feelings, but we're not safe yet, Princess," says the one who must be the strategist, Persephone. She has the voice of an angry queen, molasses sweet at first brush and then stinging with slow acid. Her features are entirely concealed by a gauze mask painted with the features of a skeleton.

"I see you found a bag to cover your face," remarks the Royal. She nudges him with an elbow. "No voice trigger?"

He's figuring out what she means. "Are you Persephone? Did I attack you?"

The skeletal face fixes on him. Disks like pearls screen her eyes. "You don't remember?"

"We can discuss that later," says the Royal. "As long as you keep your face hidden so he doesn't choke you to death. Where do we meet Alika?"

A whistle blasts, but it's the wrong key, not the warning chime for departure. Gendarmes rush onto the platform. The doors begin to close, stutter to a halt, then whoosh back open.

"Stay seated! Nobody move!"

The gendarmes rush into the car like heat-seeking missiles to a target.

He gathers himself, reading their scatter pattern and positions, ready to move. Waiting for a command. The Royal says nothing as her lips press into a thin line.

A gendarme with blazing captain's stripes blocks the aisle. "Princess Sun, you are under arrest on the charge of sedition and attempt to assassinate Queen-Marshal Eirene. If you resist, we have orders to shoot to kill."

She stands, pulling the mask from her face. Her words ring out clearly. "Let the other riders disembark at once so no one is hurt."

"If you don't resist, no one will be hurt."

She isn't looking at the captain. She's watching people leap up and shove their way out of the car, desperate to get out of the line of fire if it comes to that.

Zizou can feel in every fiber of his neuro-enhanced being that it is going to come to that. He can sense it in the way shining Tiana rests a foot alongside a long clear tube looped along the length of her duffel to give it some external rigidity; in the way flame-capped Hestia has drawn her hands to her belly; in the way gaunt-masked Persephone leans forward just enough that she doesn't startle the gendarmes but so her duffel is within easy striking distance.

The Royal's proclamation falls with the force of ancient truth. "I am heir to the throne of the Chaonian Republic. You have no authority to arrest me. Stand down, so you and your squad won't be hurt."

One of the gendarmes guffaws. "Aren't we supposed to just take 'em out?"

Their captain says, "Shut it, you jenkins! Princess Sun, you are under arrest by order and authority of the Minister of Security."

"Lee House," says the Royal with a glance at the skeleton's face who is Persephone. "The order comes from Lee House, not from the palace."

"In the name of the queen-marshal," adds the captain hastily and without conviction.

A flash catches in Zizou's peripheral vision. Out on the platform that same pair of maintenance workers push against the flow of people fleeing the stopped train. The pair are headed in their direction, each carrying a black toolbox. Behind them, the platform lights flicker and begin to go out one by one.

Tiana whispers, "Your Highness, these gendarmes aren't even wearing the emerald tree badge of official Lee House security. These are just facsimiles of gendarme uniforms."

Sun turns to him and speaks the ritual words that command the banners. "Let your actions not shame you and your banner. *Strike.*"

21

In Which the Wily Persephone Wonders If Treachery Has Sunk Her Beneath Notice

The Gatoi erupts out of his seat so fast that by the time I register where he is four gendarmes, including the captain, are down. Sun calmly sights down the length of the car and pulses three quick shots from a stinger I didn't know she was carrying. Three gendarmes collapse like they've been punched.

I've grabbed the standard-issue combat knife tucked inside my duffel. Using the confusion to cover my action, I sweep up the duffel and heave it at a gendarme somehow still on his feet between the seats behind me. Its weight knocks the man backward over into the next set of benches. His head hits with a horrible thunk.

"Surrender into my custody now and I'll see you are not charged with insubordination," says Sun. "Kneel to acknowledge my authority."

The jenkins who had laughed now shouts, "Let's do this!" and leaps forward. The others, swearing, trigger their weapons.

"Duck!" Ti holds a tube she's detached from her duffel. With a flick of her wrist it fans open into a rigid parasol, which she shoves in front of the princess. A staccato rattle shakes the clear shield as riot bullets and ion fléchettes bounce off its hard surface.

They really are aiming to kill. This has gone far beyond a drunken mother-daughter spat.

Hetty is bent double, keeping herself out of the line of fire, which is all focused on Sun. She rips the decorative netting overskirt off her dress and rises in a whirl, flinging the fabric toward the nearest gendarme. The netting spreads like wings to tangle in his arms and legs. He pitches forward and falls face-first onto the captain.

We're not in the clear yet. Fléchettes ricochet from the parasol. Some hit the windows, which, instead of breaking them, bounce them back toward us. There's a thunderous hail against the parasol, and then silence. I don't see the Gatoi.

"Four left." Sun's on one knee, not even breathing hard, left forearm braced on her right as she again takes aim with the stinger. "Ti, on my word, shift the shield to the left. Strike!"

Of course the remaining gendarmes all sight on her and fire. Zizou rolls up from between the facing benches four down from us—how did he get that far that fast?—and in a blur of kicks and strikes hammers blows along their backs. The one I hit with my duffel lies crumpled between seats. I can't tell if he is dead or just unconscious.

My mind goes blank, and my skin goes cold.

Zizou races down to the other end of the car and back up, making a sweep. The graceful way he moves shakes me out of my stupor; his confidence; the eerie and troubling beauty of the neural patterns that shine on his face.

"The captain is dead, but the rest are still breathing. Do I kill them?" he asks Sun in a tone so ordinary it's as if I'm hearing a different language, one I hope never to comprehend.

"No. I don't kill messengers." Sun kneels beside the nearest, touching the uniform in the spot where there should be a badge. "You're right, Tiana. They are counterfeit gendarmes."

"Ah!" Ti winces as she sets down the parasol and rubs a shoulder, her fingers coming away reddened with blood.

"You're injured!" I cry. "Let me see."

Sun grabs me by the collar. Reflexively I bring up the knife. Hetty pins my arm to the floor with both hands and her full weight. Sun tightens her grip until I start choking.

"Who sent them? How did they track us?" I'm lucky Sun's stare hasn't killed me already.

Ti's pained gaze hardens with a horrible flash of suspicion, but then she shakes her head as if brushing away a disloyal thought. "There are wasps and cameras everywhere. There was no guarantee the plan would work—"

"Incoming," says the Gatoi. "Two squads, one from each end of the platform."

Sun releases me with a shove that slams my back into the seat, the pain of impact a red-hot blast along my spine. My eyes water. I gasp, "I don't know. I swear it."

It's too late. People are screaming and running toward the exits, while the gendarmes let them pass like so much chaff. Twenty-four are closing in on our car, a wall of death armed with stingers and fléchette rifles. I snap a quick set of images.

The neural patterns on his face flare with a harsh gleam as he says, "Go out the emergency window to the track side, Royal. I will hold them off while you escape."

His little speech is so noble that momentarily I think I'm in a VR sim and this will end with Solomon laughing his head off when my body is punched through with a hundred ugly bleeding fléchette holes.

Solomon.

I grope in my pocket for the malasadas disc. It's a wild chance. I tug off the skeleton mask and hold the disc up. I can see my eye reflected in the glossy surface. A tremor buzzes through the disc as if I've woken a sleeping creature.

"Malasadas," I say stupidly to the disc as if it can hear me.

Sun slaps the disc out of my hand. "Curse you and your conniving relatives. To think I almost fell for your discarded daughter story."

The slap of running feet grows louder as the gendarmes close in.

"Royal," says the Gatoi urgently. "If you do not escape out the track side, then they will kill you."

My hand hurts, my back throbs, and my bruised throat has started to stiffen up so it's painful even to turn my head. But turn my head I do, gritting my teeth, because when I look out the window I see a pair of maintenance workers in coveralls walking briskly toward us along a parallel track. One is a tall and generously built woman who looks vaguely familiar. She is staring at her left hand and glances up directly at our end of the car. Directly at me.

Are these Lee House agents? My family will not use me for

their schemes. I would rather die than have them extract me safely while Sun dies. I would rather die honorably than live with the disgrace. Just like Resh.

So I say, "Princess, I have an idea—"

A sizzle of heat blasts in off the platform and through the open doors, accompanied by clatters and thumps. The heat slams into us in a cloud of toxins. My vision darkens. Sun keels over, barely catching herself on her hands. Ti sags backward, eyes fluttering as she coughs raggedly. Hetty holds a hand over her mouth and nose as she pulls a breather-gill from the emergency kit and presses it on before digging back into the bag to find another. The Gatoi flares so brightly I can't help but look straight at him. He turns and sees my face.

It happens like a switch flipped over. One moment he's making ready to fling himself into the fray to protect the princess with his life, all brilliant nobility that is the stuff of great tales. The next his eyes glaze with a sullen, oily amber gleam. His features congeal into a rigid inhumanity more frightening than any mask as he targets me.

Me.

I yank the skeleton cloth down to conceal my face. His shoulders droop, his chest heaves, his eyes roll up in his head, and he collapses atop one of the fallen gendarmes.

Hetty presses a second gill over Sun's nose, then rises.

I pull the cloth mask back up, leaving it tucked atop my head. My vision hasn't clouded as I'd thought. All the lights have gone out. I can breathe perfectly well, but Ti struggles to suck in air, and she's clearly about to pass out.

I lunge for the emergency kit, but Hetty is there before I am, efficiently adjusting a third gill over Ti's face. The smart fabric molds itself to her skin, providing a filter. Her breathing steadies. My panic settles. That's when I see that Hetty has used the commotion to get hold of my knife.

Sun steps over the bodies to kneel beside the still-unconscious Zizou. Night has overtaken us, and all the lights on the platform have gone out. A pair of beams advance on the car and pause by one of the open doors.

"To the fortune of the queen-marshal we swear our service," says a robust female voice.

Sun stands, stinger raised, as the maintenance worker takes one step into the car. She sweeps a light beam up and down the car to illuminate the limp gendarmes. Beyond the open doors gendarmes sprawl on the platform. The light's intensity dims while widening the lens to create an aura that surrounds Sun like a halo.

"Who are you?" Sun asks.

"My name is Naomi Solomon. I'm accompanied by my nephew Hekekia." She displays both hands to show herself unarmed. "You'll find a small black disc over by that window. I wonder if one of your people would pick it up for me."

Sun nods. "Not you, Hetty. Tiana, you do it."

"I'll get it," I say, because Naomi Solomon's broad shoulders, square-shaped face, and thick black hair look very like those of my good friend Solomon.

"You don't touch it, Persephone Lee," the woman says sharply. Her beam stabs into my eyes, forcing me to deploy the nictating membranes.

Ti looks at me for permission. I'm so grateful she trusts me.

"Give it to her. I've got nothing to hide," I say, though I hear how defensive I sound. Ti hunts around until she finds the disc where it's slid beneath a seat into the corner. With the deliberate movements of a person painstakingly trained not to make any sudden moves that might trigger a violent reaction, she steps around Hetty, negotiates a path through the fallen gendarmes, and extends her arm.

The woman takes the disc.

I say, "My barracks-mate Solomon gave that to me so I could call for help if I needed it. Are you part of his family? Is that why you came when I activated it?"

Another worker steps into the car, a burly young man about Solomon's age. Sun twitches but doesn't otherwise react as he opens the black toolbox he's carrying and the woman drops the disc into it. He snaps it closed, and they both exhale with obvious relief.

"That will kill the tracker," says the woman.

"The tracker?" Sun holds the stinger calmly, ready to use it. Not a flicker of doubt or fear disturbs her expression. The intensity of her focus is a second presence hovering around her.

"The disc is ours. An unknown party embedded a foreign tracker into one of our emergency alerts. You can understand why we would be quick to investigate when we discover our gear has been tampered with." The woman points at me.

I'm stunned. I kept the disc with me the entire time at Lee House. It was never out of my sight, and no one touched it except me.

"The toolbox blocks the signal so they can't track us now, but they have your last point of contact, right here," the woman adds as a final thrust to my heart. She turns to Sun. "More will be on their way."

"I have two other people in the Wheelhouse, and I won't leave without them," says Sun. She's not looking at me, as if my treachery has sunk me beneath her notice. Marked me as the outsider I am.

"We can get them out. Meanwhile, there are three Humming-birds—"

"Five," says the young man.

"—five Hummingbirds incoming. These gendarmes will wake up in about seven minutes. Come with us if you want to live."

Leave No Companion Behind

Emotion will impair your reason if you let anger or pleasure control you, Octavian had taught them.

Sun watched as Persephone Lee allowed herself to be blindfolded alongside Tiana. Was Persephone lying? Naomi Solomon thought she was.

They transferred to an underground maintenance shunt. Encased in an equipment hauler their group rolled along deep underground beneath the passenger and freight tiers. Dull red lights flashed past at intervals. The air that puffed through the vents had a musty stink. When Naomi Solomon approached them with leather bands to bind eyes, Sun raised a hand, palm out.

"I go with my eyes open, or not at all. If that's not acceptable, then drop me and the Honorable Hestia and my bodyguard off wherever you wish, with our thanks. You may do as you wish with those two."

"I'll wear the blindfold if it's needed. Sun!" Hetty gave a warning shake of her head. "Consider mine an act of trust. That's fair."

"I will take offense to any treatment of the Honorable Hestia that suggests she can be treated in any way different from me," added Sun.

Naomi Solomon did not bow or scrape, nor did she look intimidated. She merely nodded at Hekekia, who passed a wand over all five of them to make sure no other illicit tracking devices clung to their persons.

"It's not protocol," objected the young man. "Can I at least bind the arms of the Gatoi while he's still unconscious?"

"No," said Sun. "He will obey me in all that I ask. Do you not trust me?"

"Hekekia, Princess Sun will be queen-marshal, through her mother's womb, and owes us the same respect we show her." Naomi's tone caused her nephew to shuffle his feet and heave his shoulders but say nothing.

Not everyone knew when to keep quiet. The Lee girl sat cross-legged in the corner, gauze skeleton mask still pulled down over her face and a leather blindfold hiding the pearls that gave her eyes. The near disaster had not chastened her.

"Princess, I should warn you that however polite our captors may seem, they make their living as thieves and criminals."

Sun smiled at this unexpected attack. "Is that true?" she asked Naomi.

"We work outside the restrictions the law places on the poor and dispossessed, Your Highness. Some call it thievery. We call it survival."

"How are you dispossessed?" Sun asked.

"We can talk story later," said Naomi as the hauler slowed.

The vehicle lurched to a halt. A rusted door that looked as if it hadn't been opened in a hundred years was set into the tunnel wall. A beam of light lanced out from a virulent patch of rust and scanned Hekekia's face. With a pneumatic cough, the door popped open into a vault of darkness.

"No way am I touching that beast, Auntie," Hekekia said, indicating Zizou's limp body. "They have snake poison in their skin, for real."

"I do not fear what is not poisonous," said Hetty. She knelt and slung unconscious Zizou over her shoulders through the open door. Octavian had trained them all to be able to carry a heavier person in time of need. *Leave no companion behind.*

As Naomi sent the hauler on its way and sealed the door, Hekekia guided the still-blindfolded Persephone and Tiana up concrete steps in a darkness alleviated only by the two beams of light, his at the front and Naomi's at the rear. It was a long way up, but Hetty did not flag even with the weight of Zizou pressing her down. Sun carried with her a hundred questions, but Naomi's silence was all the hint she needed. Even Sun could be patient when it suited her.

The stairwell ended in a broken ladder that did not reach the ceiling hatch, rendering the exit useless. Naomi tilted the remaining lower rungs to create a horizontal platform. The hatch above slid open on a hiss of icy air.

Balanced on the rungs Naomi rose, elevator fashion, vanishing through the hatch like a celestial messenger transported into the court of heaven. The air in the tomb-like space had a musty, metallic scent that made her eyes itch. The young man's gaze darted from Sun to the unconscious Zizou, whom Hetty had settled on the ground.

Zizou's foot twitched. Sun nudged him with the toe of her silk shoe. He subsided although his breathing shifted.

Hekekia was no fool. "He's faking it."

He unlatched the bottom of the black toolbox to reveal a secret compartment. He raised a snub-nosed stinger, his gaze never leaving the banner soldier.

"It's illegal for anyone not in the military to possess stingers," remarked Sun. "Usually they're traceable. How is it you have one?"

"You'll have to ask the aunts," he said. "Or Grandmother, if you dare."

"Are you Solomon's cousin?" the Lee girl asked.

"That curdled egg! Always acting like he's better than the rest of us. But he's the one who cheated to get into CeDCA."

Persephone jerked around, homing in on his voice. "Cheated! He never cheated. He's a star cadet! You're just envious he got out and you didn't have enough ambition and discipline to do so."

"That sounds like his kind of stink talk." He spat noisily to the floor near her feet.

"Like scrap, you asshole?" Persephone curled up to a crouch and raised her hands to show herself ready to spar.

He snorted. "You can't even see me."

"My hearing is exceptional," she retorted.

He poked lazily at her, and she batted away his arm as if she had sensed it, or made a lucky sweep.

"Stand down, you two." Although Sun was beginning to find the dispute instructive she didn't have time for it. "Are you sure that blindfold works, Hekekia?"

"Not even a prosthetic can see through leather."

"We'll discuss it later. Let me see the stinger."

He hesitated, as well he might.

She extended a hand. "Give it here, soldier."

He handed it over. She ran her hands along its smooth length and examined the angle of the sawed-off barrel.

"Interesting," she said, handing it back. He received it with a startled expression. "Does that angle skew its aim?"

"Yes. If anyone who hasn't trained with it tries to use it, they won't hit what they're aiming for. Makes people leery of stealing our gear."

"You can't just insult Solomon like that," broke in Persephone.

"Let it go," snapped Sun. "We'll discuss your friend Solomon after you've pleaded your traitorous case."

"I didn't betray you."

"I'm sure she didn't, Your Highness," said Tiana, "and I can prove it."

"Thank you," Persephone whispered, shoulders sagging in relief. "At least someone believes me."

A whistle from above interrupted them. Naomi's face appeared, haloed by a backlit mist. "Send up the two prisoners and then Her Highness and the Companion. The Gatoi can stay down there until we decide—"

"That's not acceptable," said Sun.

"I wasn't negotiating, Your Highness. I'm up here, and you're down there."

"Zizou, can you jump that high?"

He opened his eyes to measure the distance, about ten feet. "Yes."

Naomi's face dropped closer as she knelt to get a better look. A frown gave her broad face the look of an incoming storm. "Was he just faking being unconscious?"

"No," said Sun, who had timed the break in his consciousness and filed the information away for future reference. "But he's conscious now, and as dangerous as you think he is. We're allies, not enemies, Auntie. If I may call you that."

"Clever girl, you are. All right, then. But if he bites, we kill him."

"As long as we're allies, he won't bite you."

They ascended one at a time into a refrigerated compartment that proved to be attached to the smoky, steamy kitchen of a cheap ramen shop. Naomi handed them grubby cooks' aprons out of a bin marked for laundry. Cooks and waiters glanced their way with casual interest before being whistled back to work. It seemed people came in from the cold with regularity. In the eating area beyond swinging doors, music trumpeted above the rumble of customers talking, laughing, and eating. It was a brass-and-drum court hymn that marked a queen-marshal's recessional. Channel Idol must have given up on Alika and returned to the wedding feast. Had so much time passed already? What was her mother thinking as she walked off the public stage into the arms of her bride? Was she sorry for losing her temper with her only heir? Was Lee House using the queen-marshal's infatuation for a young woman half her age as cover for their own deadly plotting? Or was Eirene playing a complex political game to reinforce her power at the expense of her half-Gatoi heir as well as her Argosy child and the nephew no one talked about?

"This way, Your Highness." Naomi's words cracked into Sun's straying thoughts.

The woman indicated a passage that led farther into the building. Sun's attention turned to Hetty, who grasped one of the doors before it could swing fully closed and peeked into the room beyond as onto a forbidden paradise. The food hall was packed with customers wearing the work-worn faces and inexpensive garments of provisional citizens who eke out a living with piecework, salvage, and various forms of off-net hustling and gig labor. Hetty's scholar father had written an economic treatise on the dangers of a provisional class left to churn in a mire of poverty and fenced-off opportunities. But what struck Sun most was the lively roar of conversation and how they ignored the official feed of the royal wedding. They knew it wasn't intended to offer any real benefit or change for them.

Hetty inhaled, licking her rosy lips as if the scents of ginger, shoyu, and fried rice made the air edible. She had the ability to relax and enjoy the pleasures of the world, a gift Sun found dangerous and always alluring.

"My people haven't eaten for some time," Sun said to Naomi.

"They will be fed, as guests of our house."

She'd come this far and still lived. So she followed Naomi down a passage. A door had been propped open into an alley. A bulky old mechanical of the kind usually only seen in historical shows was half blocking the route to the street as it scrubbed the wall of a neighboring warehouse, whistling merrily. At the open door a small woman in a splattered apron was holding out a bucket. Two customers plucked wriggling strands of spongy pinkish flesh out of it with tongs and deposited them in ceramic jars.

Sun was startled into a double take as she remembered all the marine biology lessons she'd sat through with Perseus and Duke. "Those are the throat cilia of a charybdis. It's illegal to possess or sell them."

"Yes," agreed Naomi calmly, beckoning her on. "If you will."

She led them up a lightwell fitted with steps. Everything was clean but worn, with faded paint and burnished scuff marks. The metal steps reminded Sun of ships' stairs inside the mothballed fleet tethered to Naval Command Orbital Harbor Zhēnzhū in Thesprotis System. Footfalls echoing, they climbed past a second and a third floor. At times like this the world grew sharp, each detail amplified: tiny letters carved into the railing by some long-forgotten person; motes of dust swirling in sunlight shining through a round window; the buried rumble of a train passing underground.

Naomi ushered them into an unexpectedly spacious attic room whose stuffy heat was being tepidly pushed around by wheezing fans. A shabby sofa had been positioned beneath a paned skylight cut in the shape of a Titan-class ship. Iced drinks rested on a tray placed on a low table.

Four women sat on the sofa. The family resemblance to Naomi was strong; they were big-boned with brown eyes. At the far end of the attic a table seating at least thirty was being laid by young people.

The women on the couch sized them up. No receiving line of governors or visiting notables had looked as intimidating as this frowning assembly. Most imperious was the tall, stout, gray-haired old woman who sat at the farthest end of the sofa with a straight back and hands folded on her lap.

Sun opened her hands, presenting them palms out. "Warmest greetings, Grandmother and Aunts, to you and to all who live under the sun of Chaonia and within the net of the beacons. I am Sun. I am born beneath the banner Royal, child of João, child of Nanshe, child of Ashur to the tenth generation. I am the daughter of Eirene, queen-marshal of the Republic of Chaonia and descendent of the argonauts who founded this realm. These are my companions, my bodyguard Zizou and the Honorable Hestia Hope. The two prisoners also fall under my orbit and thus my protection. They are the Honorable Persephone Lee and her cee-cee, Tiana Yáo Alaksu. We thank you for opening your home to us in these dire and unexpected circumstances."

The old woman dipped her chin, a gesture Sun chose to interpret as permission. Coming forward, she offered her hands to each aunt in turn, and they each briefly clasped her fingers. Naomi shadowed her to make introductions.

"My sister Hana. My cousin Lea. My cousin Mikala. Our aunt and commander, Rahaba."

The old woman held Sun's hands firmly between her own and examined her closely without speaking.

Sun let her instincts guide her. "Commander Rahaba. Are you not of the knnu lineage?"

"You have a clear eye," said the old woman in a raspy voice. "We are of that lineage. We trace our line back to the Celestial Empire and its voyaging fleets."

"How come you dwell on Chaonian soil if you were once one of the space-faring lineage who guided our ancestors long since across the vast expanse?"

"Our ships were stolen from us by Hesjan pirates twenty-five years ago," she said without the slightest change of expression, "with the connivance and assistance of the Yele League who were then stirring up trouble between Chaonia and the other unaligned systems."

"That's right. Before my mother brought the Yele League to heel."

"That's right. Like many others dislodged by that trouble, we came adrift to this place, where we have made our way ever since."

"Are you citizens of the Republic, Commander?"

"To the fortune of the queen-marshal we swear our service."

"So must all provisionals swear, if they wish to live in the republic."

"Yes. All who are required to live in this district are provisional, the floating people, unmoored and unanchored. When the government wants something from us, they take it by claiming we owe it to them. When we ask for aid, they reject it by reminding us we are due nothing."

"Yet you aid me and mine now."

"We keep our promise to the queen-marshal. Also, your companion had an object in her possession that compels our attention."

From the door Hekekia burst out, "That girl is a Lee House spy. The gendarmes followed her. But we have the corrupted disc."

He held out the black toolbox.

"Take it into the safe room and open it," said Commander Rahaba. "I want a diagnostic immediately."

"Yes, Grandmother." He went out.

Sun beckoned to her companions that they should greet the elders. Zizou made his way down the line with a quaintly formal bow for each one. Hetty ventured with a hitch in her step that made Sun think she had never met provisional citizens before and wasn't quite sure how to address them.

"Until the prisoners are absolved or accused, they must remain blindfolded," said Rahaba. "You may now eat."

"This way." Naomi led them down the long attic room to the table.

"Who else is to meet us here?" Sun asked, counting eight places.

"Two more of your companions have been extricated from the Wheelhouse and will join you as soon as they get here."

"To fortune we give thanks," Hetty murmured and dabbed at her eyes.

Sun absorbed the news with a relief she would not show because it would be like showing weakness. "When will they arrive?"

"Please do not wait to eat, for it could be some time," Naomi added. "There's a washroom through that door."

Sun let the others go ahead and made sure they were settled before she washed her hands and face and took a seat between Zizou and Hetty. Naomi sat on a chair facing Sun. A pair of young people brought bowls of thick noodles luxuriating in a salty broth and a platter laden with scallions, corn, grated garlic, and raw mushroom. They ate with intensity, slurping their broth—all but Zizou, who considered the soup with misgiving before finally cautiously sipping at it.

"You have to eat," said Sun. "I command it."

"It's not what I'm used to, begging your pardon, Royal."

Persephone had pulled up the gauze mask enough to expose her mouth. She said, "What are you used to?"

Was her tone hostile, or curious? Sun couldn't tell.

Zizou set down the bowl, opened his mouth as if to speak, then closed it again as the stairwell door opened. The women on the couch, iced drinks in hand, all looked up as Candace entered the room, scanned it for threat, and stepped aside.

Alika knew how to make an entrance.

Holding his ukulele and looking miscast in a cheap festival jacket, he paused at the threshold and in an instant took in the scene. His attention swung like a spotlight to the women on the sofa. Then he looked toward Sun.

She gave a nod of command. His jaw tightened fractionally, but he knew what he had to do. He strummed the familiar opening chords of the popular song "Our Haven" from the traditional opera *These Long Voyages* before breaking off and offering a little bow.

"My thanks for this haven, gracious aunts."

The stern expressions melted. The iced drinks were hastily set down on the table. It took barely any time at all before Alika was seated on the sofa giving an impromptu concert to their hosts, playing all their favorite songs. People appeared from other doors to listen. Sun waved Candace over to the dining table. Once the cee-cee was seated, Sun went back to her own meal, distracted only when Hetty leaned into her to whisper in her usual way, as if forgetting that the warmth of her shoulder pressing against Sun's fired down her every nerve.

"He is your best weapon. They don't know who cannot see the power of art and charm to lure the eye and sway both hearts and minds."

"He's worked hard," said Sun more curtly than she'd meant. She tipped away just enough so they were no longer touching.

Hetty's lashes fluttered with her usual mischief. In retaliation she pressed her leg against Sun's under the concealment of the table.

Sun perfectly recalled the first time they had touched in a way no longer childlike. Assigned at the age of eleven as one of Sun's seven Companions, Hetty had left with her fathers at the age of thirteen to live on Yele Prime. For five years, one living on Chaonia and one on Yele, the two girls had communicated with long encrypted letters into which they had poured their tenderest and most explosive secrets, or at least Sun had. Hetty had no particular secrets. She was deep waters but clear and unclouded all the way down. In the wake of the unfortunate death of Hetty's diplomat father, she'd been returned precipitously to the palace after her scholar father in his overwhelming grief had retired to a hermitage.

Which meant that one random day a door had opened and, unannounced and unexpected, Hetty had walked in, smiling through a wash of tears. In a rush of unfamiliar and defenseless feeling Sun had cast free all moorings and embraced her. One soul in two bodies.

So she didn't move her leg. She allowed the warmth of Hetty's flesh as a balm against her own although in general she never liked revealing her vulnerabilities and especially never in public. But Hetty's presence was a comfort always.

She addressed Naomi. "We are grateful for your aid but must go soon."

"As soon as— Ah! That was fast."

Hekekia appeared from the stairwell, gave a startled look at Alika on the sofa, and made his way to Naomi. He handed her a black disc, which she held up to her eye.

Naomi addressed Persephone, who was sipping a last bit of broth. "Where did you get this disc?"

Persephone set down the bowl.

"It was given to me by Solomon Iosefa Solomon. He knew I didn't want to go back to Lee House. They recalled me when I hoped I was shed of my family forever. He said if there was trouble I could say the code word and someone from his clan would rescue me. That's what I did when we were trapped by the gendarmes."

Naomi's frown held a lash of fear. "We've scorched the tracker embedded inside this. It's tuned to a private security channel used by Lee House's enforcement wing."

Alika's playing faltered and stopped.

Everyone turned to look toward the table, toward blindfolded Persephone.

Hands curling into fists, she said hoarsely, "But that means . . . that means . . ."

"Don't try to deny it," snapped Naomi. "You know what you did."

Sun knew the decision was upon her, so she made it.

She pushed back her chair and stood. "I believe Persephone

Lee was given the disc and did not know it contained a tracker. I believe someone gave it to her knowing she would not suspect."

From the sofa, Commander Rahaba spoke up. "What proof have you, Princess Sun? The likeliest explanation is that her own people employed her to help them destroy you."

"What benefit to Lee House to send a daughter under an assumed name to CeDCA for so many years, when they have better uses for her? I knew her brother well, so I believe she is telling the truth, that she ran away from a home she hated and took an assumed identity to escape her family. If she's guilty of anything it is naïveté. Lee House would never let her escape. They would keep her departure secret, and find a way to surveil her without her knowing. I'm right, aren't I, Persephone?"

"But that means . . ." She slumped forward, hands bearing the weight of her head. "But Solomon gave it to me. Solomon. My best friend."

"If it were me," said Sun, "I would want to have a talk with Solomon Iosefa Solomon. Didn't I overhear Hekekia saying that he didn't have good enough scores to get into CeDCA? And yet got a place anyway. Is that true?"

Persephone lifted her head with desperate hope. "The day when we got our assignments and were allowed to call home he was talking to one of his uncles. There must be a record of that conversation. That will prove his innocence."

"He has no uncles on-planet he could talk to," said Naomi in a hard voice. "They all joined the Guard, as Solomon was meant to do before he got admitted to CeDCA."

Sun crossed the room to stand before Rahaba. "Commander, it seems I can do a favor for you in exchange for the help you've given me today. You must wish to know who has compromised one of your devices."

"Lee House has always been the enemy of provisionals and the floating population," said the commander. "There's no news in that, Princess Sun. You are quick to accuse a son of ours rather than the obvious candidate from among your own people."

"I'm right about this."

"Enough to risk your life? We can take care of Persephone Lee easily enough."

"I have accepted her as one of my Companions. If she has betrayed me, then she will pay. But that is my prerogative, no one else's. With all respect, Commander, not even yours."

Rahaba considered Sun in silence, then spoke. "The ministry now knows we have these objects, and they've learned how to tap into them. The welfare of my people rests on my leadership and my responsibility to guide and protect them."

Sun trusted the instinct that gave her warning, and goaded her into action.

"Your people are my people. Their welfare is my business and my responsibility." Only now did Sun realize the woman wore braces on her lower limbs, a means to help her walk; perhaps an artifact of growing up on the deep-space voyaging ships that were calibrated to an artificial gravity less than that on Chaonia. "If it pleases you to accept this arrangement, Commander. There's a ship in it for you."

"Ah. Such an offer is an intriguing move on your part, Princess Sun. But your position is weak."

"It only seems weak because Lee House has overreached. The queen-marshal's anger will blow over. It always does. She can't afford to lose me."

"You don't lack confidence."

"I know who I am."

"Very well. We fell to Chaonia through no fault of our own. You are the first to offer us acknowledgment, much less dangle the possibility of a return to our ancient home among the stars. Let it be known that I agree to this alliance. I cannot get you all the way to the academy, but I can provide secure transportation to any port of call within greater Argos and its neighboring districts. I ask you to take Naomi with you to deal with the son of our house in our own way."

"I will treat Naomi as I treat my own. This I promise you.

We'll go right away. We have more people to meet up with who are waiting for us. And one vow I must fulfill before anything else."

"Sun," said Alika, "I'm so hungry. Can I eat something before we go?"

When the aunts' remonstrating gazes turned upon her, she could not refuse.

The Pyres of Autumn West

They descended from the Heffalump Trunk Escarpment onto the coastal plain north of the main bay. The sprawling industrial districts were interspersed with residential cores and fields of greenhouses, but it was the hundreds of small fires burning along the rocky shoreline that drew the eye.

Hekekia had driven them all the way from the south of greater Argos, exchanging vans three times with unnamed associates to confuse pursuit. When he pulled up across the street from Orange Line Station, Sun sat staring at the people emerging from the station headed toward the flickering red flames. Some carried their deceased wrapped in a sheet on a traditional stretcher while others conveyed them in a hover-bag or on a wheeled death-wagon pulled by mourners.

She turned to look back into the van rear, which had buckles and straps to fasten cargo. Persephone was seated right behind her, head tipped back to rest against the seats as if she were trying to sleep, not that anyone else in the group looked at all sleepy. It was obviously impossible to tell with her because she had to wear the gauze mask over her face.

"Is it accident you suggested we meet at Autumn West?" Sun asked her. "Some way the train lines work that made it safest or most efficient to avoid notice?"

"No. When you said you wouldn't allow Lee House to know they'd killed your bodyguard, I took that information into account when I plotted our escape. Maybe you have other plans for his body, but there wasn't time to ask. Any Chaonian is honored by the funeral rites available here."

Streetlights flashed on to illuminate the wide white path that led to the sea and its nightly pyres. A steady stream of people flowed past, a tide dragging her into bittersweet memory. She did not really remember a time when Octavian wasn't beside her, patient as a tutor, relentless in weapons training, unshakable in watching her back. How could anyone understand what he meant to her who had not walked that road alongside her all these years?

"You've surprised me, Persephone Lee."

"You surprised me when you refused to give me up to the Solomon family."

Sun leaned toward the other woman, lowering her voice enough to force the Lee girl to pay closer attention. "Let me make this clear if you didn't believe me before. You're one of my Companions now. If you betray me, it's for me to punish you, not anyone else. Anyway, you didn't do it."

Persephone raised her head off the seat back, her tone caustic. "How can you be sure?"

"Because you're an asshole. You pretend you aren't, and people doubtless mistake you for a consensus builder or a group problem solver. But you are not so different from the family that raised you. You'll do what's best for you, whether out of principle or desire. That's why they gave me Perseus instead of you. They recognized he didn't have the character to be what they are. That's why you left home for the academy, because you didn't want to do their dirty work, but that's not to say that you won't do dirty work, just on your own terms. That's why your family is willing to sacrifice you in this scheme of theirs: they don't trust you."

"That's harsh," said Persephone, yet Sun was sure she heard a smile in her voice.

"I've got a ping," said Hetty from the back of the van. "Two hundred meters to the south."

"Got it," said Sun.

A nondescript rental van pulled up behind theirs. At the Solomon compound they had exchanged their expensive banquet garments for plain workday gear and paper mourning jackets. So when they got out to meet James and Isis they looked like any other ramshackle group.

James strode forward with a grin and grasped Sun's arm. "You had me worried. Smart strategy to come here, Sun."

"We can thank Persephone for that. Can you do a trawl of our three secured drop points to see if my father left a message packet for me? He never goes more than seventy-two hours without pinging me an all-safe."

He tugged his cap low over his eyes to signal he was working.

Isis guided the hover-bag forward. The pteranodon was perched at the front of the bag. In the dark it might be mistaken for an icon brought to accompany the corpse into death. Sun rested a hand on the hover-bag, staring at the seal with a glare that no one dared interrupt.

Eventually she spoke. "He once told me he prayed for only one thing: an honorable passage. We'll give him one."

"We have to turn the van in or it'll be reported stolen," said Isis.

"I'll make sure it's returned in an untraceable way," said Hekekia. He turned to Naomi. "Aunt, are you sure I can't come with you? I really want to punch Solomon in his lying face."

"That's why you still run errands," said Naomi. "Get the other van sorted, then return here and wait for us."

They worked their way in among the groups of people. The pavement gave off a gleam, making it easy to follow even in darkness. Ash filtered down from a breeze wafting inland off the sea. People walked in silence, so they did too—no chatter, no songs, but as they got closer to the shore they heard voices and music. The path ended in a plaza. Merchants sold wood, oil, disposable lighters, paper mourning jackets, winding sheets, powdered incense, and tiny funeral bells.

Naomi was the only one who possessed untraceable coinage. Tiana volunteered to shop. At length she returned bearing everything they needed and a token with a pit location stamped on it. They walked the hover-bag about a klick north along a boardwalk that ran parallel to the sea. Smoke and stinging-hot ash from the nightly pyres made their eyes stream. Mourners wailed. Bells tinkled as they burned up. The smell of sandalwood drifted on the air like grief.

Their pit was one of many crematory slots set into the rocks and with an open view to the sea. Water slushed and slapped three meters away against a revetment. A pair of attendants had arrived before they had to leave a wagonload of wood. Tiana helped Sun detach the bag from its hover mechanism and carefully bundle the corpse out of the fireproof bag into a sheet without ever touching it flesh to flesh. The rest stacked the logs inside the open jaws, laid flat, of their slot. Zizou kept watch, crouched in the shadows so he could see up and down the boardwalk. Wing glided in circles above, her vision tracked through Isis.

After they'd weighed the body down beneath a few more logs to keep it pinned as it burned, Sun sprinkled powdered incense over the wrapped body.

"When he was a boy Octavian Yíng Alhesperus lost his family in the siege of Troia Terce. He told me he joined the Chaonian military so no other child's family would meet the same fate. It's also why he quit, when he realized he had become the very monster that had made him into a soldier. He was a hard man, and he never tried to make me feel better when things were rotten. People thought he wasn't friendly, that he didn't like them, and he didn't like most people, it's true. I trusted him with my life, and he gave his life to save mine."

She held out the bag.

Hetty took it, and sprinkled incense in her turn. "He sat beside me all night at my father's pyre, when my other father was too broken by grief even to attend. He didn't say one word. Just being there was the only word he needed to say."

James doffed his cap and slapped it against his chest. "I'm a good shot because of that bastard and how he would not let up on our training. I swear his name for me was 'You lazy son of a bitch, stop talking and start shooting.'"

Sun cracked a smile as she wiped her eyes.

Alika sang a lament.

"I served with him," said Isis. "He never left anyone behind."

Candace whispered, "When I came to the palace he told me he'd met my parents once, and that my mother was a wicked poker player and my father ate too many beans."

Persephone sprinkled incense to be polite.

Naomi said, "May his soul watch over you and his spirit aid you in your time of need."

Tiana added, "May he sail the ocean of stars and make his way to the Celestial Empire and an abode of peace."

"Zizou?" Sun asked.

Without moving from his vantage point he said, "Are you really going to burn him up? That seems a waste. We recycle everything."

Everyone looked at Sun, tense with anticipation.

She merely nodded. "So must it be among the banner fleets. We observe different customs here."

She emptied the oil over the wood and the wrapped corpse, then set the fire. The flames took quickly, leaping and crackling. She began to sing the Hymn of Leaving in a trembling soprano. They let her finish the first verse before they joined in to finish the full sequence. Heat blasted in their faces.

When she was ready, Sun pushed the mechanism that closed the jaws over the pyre. This closing created a sealed container which was drawn down into a crematory chamber hidden below. They remained standing for a long time, some still praying, some in silence. At length a chime announced completion. The slot opened and the container rose into the air. Though it was no longer at its greatest temperature, heat pulsed off the surface. The jaws opened to reveal the coarse remains and the pale wood ash. Sun took off the paper mourning jacket and tossed it on the pyre. The paper blackened, then flared up, utterly consumed.

"Thus I fulfill my vow to you, that you be given the honorable rite of passage."

The others followed suit.

Sun gathered some of the ashes into a small steel cylinder Tiana had purchased. The first streaks of dawn had barely begun

238 · KATE ELLIOTT

to lighten the sky when the attendants appeared to collect the remains, which would be flown by drone out over the water and consigned to the waves.

She looked questioningly at James.

"Nothing from your father. No contact. No packets."

"That's not like him."

As they headed back to the station, hurrying to get there before full light, Sun said to Persephone, "Can you get us to CeDCA undetected? I know the only way to get there is by train."

"Why go there?" Persephone's voice was muffled by the mask. "Don't you have some secret refuge where you can hole up?"

"I don't retreat. I attack. If your friend Solomon is working with Lee House, James can find a way to trace those conversations you say he was having with an 'uncle.' That will give me proof to convince my mother she's being used. I am heir to Chaonia and the destiny that awaits us. No one will take that from me. No one. Do you understand?"

24

A DISPATCH FROM THE ENEMY

Dear Mom,

I don't know how the pre-beacon voyagers survived with their sanity intact on journeys that took months or years. And that's nothing compared to the flight of the refugee fleets from the Celestial Empire who spent generations in transit. How did they stand the forced confinement? The commanders keep us busy with routine, but by now the most even-tempered people are restless and the impatient ones are stir-crazy. Writing letters to you about the minutiae of my tedious days is how I cope, I guess, even knowing you won't read this letter because I shall have to void it. But I wanted to tell you

---

Apama stopped typing as the bugle for assembly piped through the ship. Since there was no way to turn down the volume in the cramped cabin, she let the sound reverberate through her body. Maybe this was the clarion call they were all hoping for, action at last.

I wanted to tell you how much I love you and appreciate everything you've sacrificed for me.

Rising, she closed the tablet and stowed it in her locker with her lefts while with her rights she unhooked her pilot's dress uniform jacket and pulled out her boots. She tugged on the jacket over her gray tee and sealed her boots.

Assembly for lancer pilots was on the flight deck with the sixty-four lancers racked up and everyone lining up according to rank. She joined Ana and Renay in the last row.

"What's up?" she asked.

"Rumor is they're finally going to tell us the mission," said Ana.

"At five months out from Hellion Terminus there can't be any risk of a leak," added Renay.

"You think there's infiltrators on this ship?" Apama asked.

"Don't be naïve, Ice," said a pilot in the row ahead of them, looking over his shoulder. "There's always someone willing to take money to do any slimy, sli-i-imy thing."

"Shut up," said her rack-mates together.

"It's all right, I know what they say about me." She busied herself straightening her jacket, not wanting to give Lieutenant Anu "Buster" Fe Smith the satisfaction of thinking his snide comments hurt her.

Fe Smith seemed ready to make another jab when, fortunately, the colonel entered with her adjutants. There came Gail, silent for once as another adjutant set down a crate. Colonel Ir Charpentier stepped up on it.

Just then Delfina slipped through one of the cargo doors, buttoning up her jacket. She sidled up beside Apama with a grin like sugar.

"Did I miss anything?" she mouthed.

"Where were you?" Apama mouthed back.

Delfina winked at her.

When Delfina got bored she got sloppy. Probably she'd never had to take military discipline with proper seriousness because she didn't have as much on the line as people like Apama, Renay, and Ana did.

"Attention!" A master chief's voice silenced any last whispering.

The colonel cleared her throat.

"You've long since figured out why we installed knnu drives alongside the beacon drives and torch drives in these ships. You've been disciplined in accepting the strict rations needed to sustain the extra weight and energy. You've been patient as we've taken the long road from Hellion Terminus, the way our ancestors once always had to do before the engineers of the Convergence built the beacon network. You've been diligent in playing and replaying the simulations that are preparing you for the mission. Now your discipline, patience, and diligence will be rewarded."

Because of the silence Apama noticed the constant background thrum of the knnu drive under its baffles and the steady whir of the ventilation system, which usually faded into the ambient noise of ship life.

"We will enter Molossia System from deep space at a trajectory that allows us to immediately hit the naval command orbital station in orbit around the fifth planet Pánlóngchéng."

"Whoa," someone whispered in a row ahead.

"Knnu drives are difficult to track regardless. Additionally, we'll be using baffles to disguise our life-support heat signatures. Our plan and our expectation is that because no one expects an attack from deep space they won't see us until it is too late."

"Our weapons are surprise and ruthless efficiency," murmured Delfina.

The colonel glanced their way. Apama pressed her boot over the other pilot's foot in warning, but Delfina merely fluttered innocent eyes.

"Once in-system we toggle to torch drives. We will smash and run, taking out whatever ships are at the command station. We will proceed to the third planet and its munitions depot. There we expect to meet more concerted resistance since they'll have had warning. Our goal is to damage the depot and nearby shipyards. We will again smash and run, slingshotting around the third planet for a final cross-system sprint to the second planet, Yǎnshī. We will do as much damage as possible to the naval command orbital station there before we exit Molossia System through the Troia beacon."

The colonel waited as the pilots took in this astoundingly bold plan with gasps and excited whispering. Once they'd quieted she triggered a halo-screen, a 3-D rendering of Molossia System, showing its six planets and where they would be in relation to each other when the fleet reached its destination. The fleet appeared as a hazy cluster of pinprick lights that moved in a swarm to each target in turn. The path of attack allowed them to avoid Molossia

Prime, the major population center, which anchored the beacon that led to Chaonia.

"Any questions before I proceed?"

"Are we going to attack Chaonia System?" asked someone in the front row.

"No. It's too well defended, and our position isn't strong enough yet. I know you all want to. The Chaonian menace has been fierce and brutal. It hasn't helped that they've ground the Yele League under their bootheels and forced them into an alliance. But not everyone in the Yele League is happy about that alliance."

She glanced toward the shadowed threshold of an open hatch where two figures stood side by side. One was a Yele admiral people had been gossiping about; though he had only two arms he was said to be a crack shot and an expert pilot as well as having defeated two imperial Phene fleets in battle twenty years ago. But time and tide, as the old saying went, can turn an enemy into a friend.

The other wore a clear helmet molded to fit the individual's head, as did every officer of colonel's rank or higher when they were in battle. Apama firmly shifted her gaze away, not wanting to be caught staring. She knew what the other person was. Everyone did since there was only one way to coordinate plans across the vastness of space with the kind of immediacy necessary to synchronize fleet movements in separate star systems.

The colonel coughed into a hand, a flicker of nervousness crossing her usually confident features as she tore her gaze away from the two individuals at the threshold.

"Our intelligence operatives working in Chaonian space have recently confirmed that Queen-Marshal Eirene and her high command are plotting a major offensive to take Karnos System. We've received advance notice that three Chaonian fleets have been deployed to Troia in preparation for a coming offensive through the Hatti region. They've been building up to it since they grabbed a toehold in Aspera System five years ago. Our models didn't predict the speed with which they have ramped up their industrial output. By damaging their military and industrial capability in

Molossia we should set back their plans by several years at least. But that's not all. Because we have a second battle to fight as part of this mission."

She gave them a moment to process this new information, then went on.

"This is where you lancers will do your part. In Molossia System you'll be scouts and skirmishers. You will stay away from the main confrontation, which will be undertaken by the cruisers and dreadnoughts. We're going to hit and run, and we're not going to slow down. But the Molossia attack is being run in coordination with a second major assault."

The halo-screen shifted to a wider view, reaching from Molossia to Karnos. Star systems floated like islands in an oceanic void, some connected by the glowing silver lines representing beacon routes while others hung alone.

"A second assault fleet under High Admiral Sula Si Tanarctus will leave Karnos just before we reach the heliopause of Molossia System. They will cross by beacon into Aspera System. Once there, they will attack the Chaonian emplacements beyond Aspera Drift with so much power the Chaonian forward fleet will be forced to retreat via beacon to Troia to regroup. I promise you, we will wrest *all* of Aspera back from the Chaonians and the ghost of Ereshkigal Lee."

Many of the pilots hissed, as had become the custom when the infamous name was mentioned. Apama remained silent. She had no love for the very dead Ereshkigal Lee, but if Lee had been doing her duty, then how was that any different from everyone here?

The colonel went on as the hisses faded.

"So as you can see, we will hit the enemy from two sides. The Tanarctus Fleet will chase the Chaonians as they retreat from Aspera and follow them into Troia System. Our fleet will crash through Molossia and afterward drop into Troia by beacon. We will also hit the Chaonian ships in Troia. Once we've done as much damage as we can, both our fleets will withdraw through the beacon back to Aspera System. There, we will set up a new and stronger perimeter."

Apama found herself on her toes, leaning into the words. With a careful exhalation she rocked back to her heels. Succumbing to an emotional reaction never made life easier.

"You'll get full briefings in your pod groups, at fifth bell. But for now, I have one more thing to say to you. I want you to listen with all your heart and all your might. Many of you are too young to remember we once controlled all of the Karnos hinterlands, the Hatti reach, Kanesh, and Troia System itself. These places belong to the Phene Empire, not to belligerent upstarts. This mission will put a stop to Queen-Marshal Eirene's grasping ambitions. She'll have overreached for the last time. We will hold Aspera. And when we are ready, we will take back Na Iri, we will take back Tarsa, we will take back Kanesh. We will take back Troia! Are you ready to do your part, lancers? *Are you ready?*"

Cheers reverberated off the bulkheads. For an instant the thrum of the knnu drive seemed a distant memory rather than a daily reminder of how long it took to cross space at the slow speed of their antediluvian ancestors fleeing the wreck of the Celestial Empire.

Delfina elbowed her. "Why no cheering, partner?"

"We just need to do our jobs, not use artificial stimulation techniques to wind up people's limbic systems."

"You are Ice for real, Ap. Ice like Saint Aveline."

"I pray to Saint Arthas."

"I know, but I guess I'd have a poker face too if I'd grown up with what you had to deal with—"

Apama signed *stop,* and Delfina shut up and signed *peace* in response.

Dismissed, the pilots milled around, buzzing over the news and what it would mean for them. Lancers sometimes took the brunt of an attack, expecting death, and sometimes they were the bothersome gnats who kept the enemy distracted but stayed mostly out of their way. It looked like this time they'd get both jobs.

She didn't feel like pointlessly speculating over details they were going to get soon anyway, so she headed for the cafeteria to get a snack to tide her over until dinner. But she wasn't the only one with that idea, or maybe he followed her on purpose.

Footsteps padded up behind her. Buster shoved past with his toadies Lieutenants Peroz "Croak" Ru Nemeth and Veto "Skinny" Sb Flores hopping in his sleazy wake.

"Ei, Apama, how about that drink you promised me five months ago? I'm all in for getting better acquainted—"

"If you're not going to use my call sign, then it's At Sabao," she said in the cool tone she'd had a lot of practice producing when she'd have preferred to snap into a white heat of anger.

"Shellbao, you mean," he said with a derisive smile, reaching out in a move meant to squeeze her upper arm to insultingly test whether she was soft- or hard-skinned.

She stepped back fast enough that he missed and looked clumsy as his hand thunked into the bulkhead.

"It's not against the law for her mama to be a shell." Croak blinked with all the wit of a daxter. "But Buster says he heard your mama is a sex grifter with a bastard child."

Her rack-mates hurried up right then.

Delfina drawled, "Say, Croak, I hear your mama's a stunt."

With a screech of rage, Ru Nemeth swung at Delfina, clipping her chin. Ana and Renay had already set legs out to sweep him down. He fell with a yelp.

"I guess you have to defend her since you've got her slime all over you from racking with her," sneered Fe Smith.

Apama had heard the slur a hundred times during her training, but her rack-mates hadn't. They hissed in displeasure, pushing forward to confront the other pilot.

"What is *wrong* with you?" Ana demanded.

"Mind your own business, you toad," Renay snapped.

"Lancers! Attention!" Gail came striding up. His usually cordial expression bore no friendly glint now. "I don't want to know what's going on, but it's clear the long voyage has worn down everyone's nerves. Buster, report to medical for your retinal clearance."

"But I cleared all my retinals—!"

"What did I say?"

"Yes, ma'am."

"Croak. Skinny. There's a backup in the mechanics' head. I need two volunteers to clean it up."

The look Fe Smith shot at Apama had a javelin's prick. "Some shiny pretty shell's caught the commander's eye," he muttered.

"And after medical you'll report to skunk duty in the pipes, Buster." Gail paused long enough to set everyone off-balance before adding, "Do you hear me, Lieutenant? If I hear any more of this matter, you'll be pulled from the cockpit."

Fe Smith's lower left hand twitched but he did not gesture an obscenity, although Apama could tell he wanted to. Gail gave Apama a brisk nod before heading back the way he'd come. He knew the pilots would obey. The consequences if they did not weren't worth risking.

Ru Nemeth shot a whisper toward his friend. "Are you a complete jenkins? I thought you were yanking her chain because she turned you down for a bang. You got us in trouble, you dumb shit."

"But you are a shell, and more importantly you are a bastard, aren't you, At Sabao?" Fe Smith growled as a parting shot. "Your mama cut off your caul when no sire wanted to claim you, and now you just ooze. Or else your grifter mama stole seed that wasn't rightfully hers and covered her ass and didn't file the proper lineage report. What I'm asking is, why is Command covering *your* ass? Why did the whole fleet wait three days for you to get dumped on us?"

Renay and Ana crossed their uppers and set their lowers akimbo, a stance of such mockery that Fe Smith flushed with anger and humiliation.

Delfina said, "Let it go, lobster face."

Apama kept her words in her mouth, just as she'd been taught, and an icy gaze fixed on the bulkhead, although she kept Fe Smith in her peripheral vision. But the trio slunk away, headed for their temporary assignments. The toadies had already started in on their companion, insulting his character and his ancestors as their voices faded down the passage.

She could see the question in her rack-mates' eyes and braced herself. Every Phene child was born with a record of ancestry. This legal requirement had nothing to do with family or marriage and everything to do with tracking genetic lines across populations. So it had always been from the earliest foundation of the triple capital systems, Anchor, Auger, and Axiom, when the Phene consortium of scientists and laborers had broken away from the stifling customs of the motherland of Mishirru and set off in ninety-four fleets to found their own homeland.

Ana asked, "Has he hassled you before?"

"Nothing I can't handle."

"Tell us next time."

Renay chimed in, "We've got your back."

Delfina added, "Is everything okay, Ap?"

"Sure," she said, grateful she wouldn't have to tear open her mother's past to gratify people's curiosity. Not that her mother ever discussed her early life or how she'd come to get pregnant with Apama. "Everything is fine. We're about to launch the most audacious attack of the war, and our unit will take heavy casualties. I'm going to get a sorbet. You coming?"

In Which the Wily Persephone Twists and Turns

Three hours after dawn we hop a high-speed cross-continent Mamba freight liner that will stop at the industrial park near CeDCA. While there, the final eight cars will break off for a spur run to the academy. Although cadets grow all of our own food as partial tuition, the academy houses fifteen thousand cadets as well as support staff and families, which means the academy isn't fully self-sufficient.

Today one of the freight cars is half-filled with jute bags of spices destined for CeDCA's kitchens. James disables the car's security bot, replacing its live feed with a loop he cobbles together from previous footage. As we settle, Zizou takes in an appreciative breath and smiles with unexpected sweetness, as at a fond memory. When I realize I'm staring at his tempting mouth I look for a place to sit where he's out of my line of sight. After the rush of our escape and standing awake all night over the pyre, I'm exhausted. Stretched across two of the bags I sleep hard, drenched in the scents of cumin and nutmeg.

When I wake, my body can instantly tell we've slowed down. A strange vibration buzzes within the ring Sun gave me. A sixteen-rayed sunburst flowers in my vision, nine points gleaming and seven in stasis. James crouches beside me, cap pulled jauntily to one side.

"Got it. I've finally connected your ring past that universal block on your network. Now you're fully in Sun's private ring. No matter how far away you are she can track you and communicate with you. That means outside Chaonia's net and outside the security web."

"No one is outside the security web," I retort.

"That's what they think." He doffs his cap with a flourish.

I rub my eyes, not sure I believe him even though I want to believe I am shed of tracking discs and parents who suborn my best friend into spying on me.

The boxcar door has been cracked open to let in air. Sun is seated there beside Zizou, her head cocked to one side, sucking in his words as if she is a black hole's gravitational field.

"Then they wheeled me into a much larger chamber with a catwalk," he is saying. He has a quiet voice at odds with the way he transforms into a killing machine.

The landscape beyond is grass and scrub. A herd of styracosaurus graze in the distance, mixed in with a herd of dwarf diplodocus and several handsome nodosaur of the kind ridden by bold knights in the days of the Celestial Empire. The scene is peaceful, a tiny piece of the long-lost homeland re-created here.

Alika tunes his ukulele. Aunt Naomi sits beside him like a starstruck fangirl. I think she's blushing. Tiana is asleep, curled up against her duffel with an arm thrown across it like it's a stand-in for a lover she misses. Candace and Isis are pacing through a warm-up exercise on a bit of open floor they've created by pushing aside sacks marked with the characters for black and red pepper.

Hetty offers me a tasteless, high-calorie ration bar and a wedge of salty cheese whose sourness makes my eyes water. I gulp down cider, burp because I drink too fast, and, after peeing in a waste bucket someone was smart enough to grab, lie down again. I've lost track of how long it's been since that terrible meeting with my father in Lee House, before he threw me to the wolves. Of course he has every right to do so; he's my father. That I am an undutiful daughter just makes it worse.

Everyone goes back to sleep in the manner of soldiers who rest when they can. Zizou remains seated cross-legged at the half-open cargo door, brown hands resting on his thighs. His posture is easy but alert as he scans fields of maize, beans, and squash. I know exactly where we are. The train will take forty-three minutes to traverse this populated farming district before it speeds back up. Lips parting in soft wonderment, he leans forward to look at the sky. A flock of archaeopteryx flies past. My gaze drifts from their colorful feathers to where his black hair is trimmed short in a neat line along his neck. I remember the perfect sculpted musculature of his back and wonder what it would be like to run my hands over his skin.

He glances over his shoulder as if he's heard the shift in my breathing. I close my eyes even though he can't see my face; I don't know why I pretend I haven't been staring at him.

You have bad taste in crushes, Solomon would say.

Solomon.

A sick feeling of dread kicks up into my heart. It can't be true. I won't let it be true. I twist and turn my thoughts down every possible path that can exonerate him until at last the soothing rhythm of the train's motion overtakes my agitation. With the musty smell of jute in my nostrils, I slide back into a sleep as dead as my family wanted to make me because they know I'm not a dutiful daughter and thus I am expendable.

When I wake I've slept through the long night. We've reached the barracks district built north of the industrial park. Sun lies on her stomach at the half-open cargo door as we slowly pass blocky buildings in a cool predawn light. Ti is seated next to the princess, in the elegant posture of one of the demigoddesses worshipped in the realm of Mishirru: right arm outstretched and propped up on a raised knee, with her other leg crossed under her. The rising light pours its homage across her glorious face.

"Why do those residential blocks have barbed-wire fence around them?" Sun asks.

Ti replies in a melodious voice, although her words aren't as kind as her pleasing expression. "I'd guess those are barracks for workers hired in from Troia System refugee camps."

"I suppose the fence is necessary to control the inevitable troublemakers."

"The trouble doesn't usually come from the workers, Your Diligence. Floaters are required to sign three-year contracts and aren't allowed to leave the work site until their contracts are up. They're charged exorbitant prices for rent, food, and maintenance. So in the end they are as likely to end up in debt as to be able to return home with money."

Sun gives her an incredulous look. "That can't be. Citizens have rights to prevent such exploitation."

"Floaters aren't citizens, Your Sanguinity. The laws don't apply to them."

"It shouldn't be like that, not if they're serving the republic."

"Of all the people in this train car, surely you are the one with the most power to do something about it."

Sun measures her for a long time. I'm not sure whether the princess is annoyed at Ti's plain speaking or if she's wondering how even in common workday garb Ti can look so glamorous and beautiful and, if I'm being honest, sexually attractive.

I slide over to wedge myself rudely between them. "Can I help, Princess?"

"Zizou's asleep. You can take off that death's head."

"Like I'm taking that chance. I don't think so." But I pull the cloth up off my face anyway and take in a breath of the air rushing along our faces as we roll past rows of greenhouses. "We must have decoupled from the main train."

"We did. I'm just sitting here wondering about your cee-cee."

"What about her?" I pause, then add, "The contract a cee-cee signs specifically prohibits any romantic or sexual exchange between the cee-cee and their employer. Or their employer's employer, which means you."

Sun shoots me a look that would slay a person who hadn't already burned her bridges, as I have. "I am not now nor have I ever been a person who exploits my power for that kind of self-satisfaction. Maybe you are. I wouldn't know."

"Ouch," says Ti. "You walked into that one, Perse. And I know my rights, with you, with Her Fastidiousness, with the rest of the Companions, and with the palace."

"So proclaims the simple country girl from Abundant Wine Province," I say with a laugh.

"A simple country girl," Sun points out, "who has felt free to address me about the economic and legal situation of provisional workers and impoverished citizens in the Republic of Chaonia. I don't think that's part of the curriculum at Vogue Academy. I'm surprised you confront me, knowing I can have you terminated."

"But you won't," Ti retorts. "What honor would you have, if you ignored the tradition that allows any and every citizen to petition the palace when they have a righteous grievance? That's not you, is it, Your Honorableness?"

Sun examines Ti a little too long, then regally inclines her head. "There's more to you than meets the eye. And you and I both know there's a lot of you that meets the eye. I'll leave you to my Companion."

"We'll be to the academy in twenty-six minutes," I say to Sun before she moves away. "There's a curve a half a klick before the depot where we can jump off unseen. Our best bet is to cut through the back paths to the gymnasium behind the fifth-year brigade field. After muster I can grab Solomon."

Sun nods. "I'll wake everyone up."

She goes to where Hetty is curled up against a bag of salt. The look that softens her face as she studies the Honorable Hestia makes me sorry I said anything about Ti.

An elbow digs into my ribs. "Ow," I protest. "What was that for?"

Ti crosses her arms in a way that makes me wish she would hit me instead.

In a low voice the others can't hear she says, "Listen. Let's clear the air so there aren't any lingering questions. I felt a connection the instant we met. I think you felt it too. We can be friends, and I hope trusted companions, but we can't be lovers."

I raise both hands, palms out. Heat warms my cheeks, but I'm not going to ruin this by letting embarrassment choose my words. "I won't lie and say I don't find you attractive. But I value our friendship and our professional relationship more than the random circumstance that I find you sexy. Is that good enough?"

She grins, preening with a chuckle like she's laughing at herself. "Trust me, I'm always a little disappointed when any individual doesn't find me attractive. I've worked hard to hone skills I can use."

She sticks out a hand and we grasp hands to elbows, the unshakeable grip. Her skin is soft and her clasp is firm.

I release her elbow, feeling we've crossed an important bridge. "Why did you believe me about the disc?"

"I can't live being suspicious of people who I feel a connection to. I'd rather get burned. Anyway, nothing you've said or done since I met you fits the profile of a liar and a sneak and an assassin. I could be wrong."

"Have you been wrong before?"

She considers the question seriously, rubbing at her chin. "Not really. Like your father. At first glance he is cursedly good-looking. Surely a seer of Iros who can see heat and lies would know exactly where and if you are getting hot and bothered."

I wince, and she cracks a wicked grin.

"He dresses exceedingly well, a consideration I particularly admire. But people like me have to be a good judge of nuance."

"What kind of 'people like me' are you? I've been slow to realize the simple kalo farmer act isn't your real story. Heaven knows I haven't had time to look over your record, not that I have access to it, since my family hired you."

"There's not much to tell. I grew up in a refugee camp in Troia System."

"But you're a citizen. You said so. Only citizens are admitted to Vogue Academy."

"My grandparents *are* kalo farmers. My father grew up in the lo'i fields in Abundant Wine Province. A lot of people there join the military in the hope of qualifying for better schooling. After he lost his arm in the Kanesh offensive he didn't have a high enough rank to qualify for anything except a low-end mechanical prosthetic."

"How did he end up in a Troia refugee camp? Every citizen who's mustered out is guaranteed transport home."

"He didn't want to leave behind the people who depend on him."

"You're saying your mother isn't a citizen."

"My womb parent was a citizen, and a soldier. She died a long time ago. The only mother I know is the mother who raised me. She's the refugee. There's nothing hidden in my record. I graduated top of my class, which is why I was allowed to apply for this position. I didn't realize it also meant my employers were willing to see me killed. Maybe exactly because Lee House looked over my record and realized I am the expendable kind of person whose family can't make a fuss if I vanish, as long as the death tithe is paid out."

"You can leave. I won't ask this of you."

"I know my contract allows me to leave under these circumstances. But I meant it about needing the money. It's astoundingly good money, and it's all going to my family." She yawns, belatedly concealing her mouth behind those perfectly manicured nails, then lowers the hand to offer me a lazy, bright smile. "Sorry. It's not you, it's me."

I tap my fist on her arm. "Take a nap. I'll keep watch."

She gets up, takes a few steps away, then says over her shoulder, teasingly, "Is it permitted for you to keep watch? I mean, what with you being under suspicion, and us arriving at a government facility."

From behind us a soft male voice says, "I'll sit the last bit of watch with Persephone Wood-Child Lee."

I yank the mask down over my face, trembling. Just then, as my adrenaline spikes, a message packet pings into my 🜨 mailbox. It's anonymous, sent via some long workaround through my school network that probably just wormed its way through a loophole in the industrial park's net shield. Sure it must be Kadmos, I unthinkingly open it.

My father appears in hologram. For an instant I see him through Ti's eyes: a handsome, impeccably groomed older man who stands with the effortless posture of a Yele native who has never had his humanity or conduct called into question. A seer of Iros is unimpeachable. Everyone knows that.

Channeled through the shield's slowed-down bandwidth, the hologram fizzes, crawling forward until it's all loaded. Finally the recorded message speaks as I stare in frozen horror. I know how receiving a message from my father will look to the others, not that anyone can see my private feed, but I can't stop now it's started. I have to know what he has to say.

"Yes, how can Perseus be dead?" my father muses, as if continuing a conversation he and I started a moment ago. "A question I'm delighted you have asked, since for you not to have asked would suggest you feel no sense of obligation to your parents. Perseus deflected an assassination attempt on Sun, saving the princess's life at the cost of his own. But perhaps she hasn't explained that to you."

He knows I'm with Sun. He's seeding doubt, just as he always does.

"As long as Perseus lived you were free to do as you wished, as unfilial as your desires may have been. But all that's changed. You are a smart girl, Persephone. You can comprehend the importance of Manea's wedding and what it portends for Lee House's place in Chaonia. Do not dishonor your ancestors. Not this time."

His image glances up at a sound approaching from out of my view, although I will always recognize that particular staccato clip of footsteps. He touches a hand to the top button of his jacket, the one nervous tic he has. I can almost taste his disdain across the gap of hours and distance between us.

"I asked not to be disturbed, Aisa."

"I know you're talking to *her*."

My mother steps into view, wringing her hands. Her heavy mascara has streaked as if she's been crying, but it's more likely she splashed water on her face so it would appear she's been crying.

"Heaven correct you, Persephone. How can you continue to shame me with these rebellious actions? I can't believe you go on making me endure this pain. Even after I lost your darling brother."

Darling brother. I want to puke on her lying face.

My father turns a smile on my mother, an expression that anyone except my mother can see is grotesquely artificial. I loathe the two of them together: my mother's endless litany of complaints and his unctuous smoothing down of her ruffled, spiky emotions that do nothing but mirror her back to herself.

"Dearest Aisa, you must not allow yourself to become perplexed and discomposed by your daughter's antics. You know how easily you sicken."

"It's far too late for that, Kiran! No one ever has any respect or concern for my nerves. Moira certainly doesn't."

"No, indeed, my love. But let us keep our focus on the goal." He keeps his face turned toward her, since she never likes to think anyone is getting attention that she deserves, but in switching tones makes clear he's speaking again to me. "You perceive the necessity of continuing this communication later. Expect me to be in touch."

He snaps his fingers. The image collapses into a spark of light.

I sag forward, catching my weight on my hands.

Behind me, Zizou says quietly, "Are you all right, Persephone Lee?"

My skin is beginning to itch from the constant rub of the mask's cheap synthetic fabric, but I'll die if I remove this irritation from my face.

"If the mask is troublesome for you, you could blindfold me instead," he says, sliding in to sit beside me.

My heartbeat accelerates as if I'm sprinting. *Blindfold me.* There's a thought. He doesn't touch me, but I feel the heat of him, the way he's holding himself carefully away from me, respecting my space.

"If you're blindfolded you can't keep watch," I say.

"I have enhanced sensory feeds. Your elevated heart rate shames me. You fear me because I tried to harm you."

My reaction is a bit more complex than that, but I'm so surprised at his simple, sincere words that I don't know how to answer. I glance back into the car. Fortunately the others are too busy waking up and making ready to go to pay attention to us.

"I don't have any recall of what I did to you. I don't know why I attacked you, just that everyone says I did. But on the honor of my banner I tell you now, Persephone Lee, I am sorry for it."

I grew up with a mother who fakes extreme emotions to coerce people to do her bidding, a father whose cold rationality makes him good company at dinner while his insincerity makes him dangerous the rest of the time, and an aunt who efficiently runs an effective and thus feared security apparatus. We must be kept safe against the Phene menace and their spies and collaborators, like the Gatoi.

Maybe Zizou is making some convoluted ploy to win my trust and then murder me. But I don't think so. I think he's as confused as I am. Also, if I'm being honest, I'd really like to touch him, to see if I can feel the coils of energy beneath his skin.

"It's a fair offer," I say, hoping my suddenly dry mouth doesn't give away my uncomfortably explicit thoughts. "I don't want to give up my mask, just in case. I don't have anything else to bind your eyes with."

"I grabbed one of those leather blindfolds before we left that one place with the council elders," he says.

"You did?" I'm blushing, and truth to tell, I'm a little aroused thinking about it. Which I pray to all the gods and all the hells that he cannot tell.

"I thought it might be useful if you and I ever had a chance to talk."

"You thought about talking to me?" I've turned into a pitiable echo.

"Doesn't honor matter to Chaonians? What I did was dishonorable. And not of my own choice, which makes it an assault against my will as well as against you. Do you understand what I am saying? If we can figure out why it happens, maybe we can stop it."

"All right," I say, rising to the challenge because my poor judgment can't resist, and anyway I do want to figure out what's going on. "Turn your head."

He has in fact tucked a wide leather belt into the sash of the jacket he was given to wear. I venture boldly to slip it out, which means I have to slide my fingers beneath the sash to get ahold of it.

His body is all honed muscle. I would swear he smells of silk and magic. He inhales sharply. My fingers are still resting against his torso.

Then I realize he's craned his head to look outside and his reaction has nothing to do with me.

"That!" He points toward the industrial park's sky-tower, which has just come into view. "I saw it for an instant before the aircar hatch closed. With those three tall cylinders behind it."

"Whoa." I beckon to Sun. "Princess, Zizou says he saw the sky-tower and three smokestacks when he was being loaded into the aircar that took him to Lee House."

Sun studies the sky-tower rising amid refinery smokestacks and factory blocks. By her intent expression, her mind is churning at a million klicks a second. "If you had something you really wanted to hide, you'd hide it amid ordinary activity in the middle of nowhere. Like using an industrial park to hide a secret laboratory studying neural enhancements in banner soldiers that allow the Phene to control their behavior."

I remember how my sister died. I think of Ti's father's arm. "The idea about Phene compulsion channeled into Gatoi neurosystems is just a theory. The Gatoi can't be changed. They fight to the death. That's just who they are."

"That's not who we are." Zizou's frown is sharp.

I've offended him, and probably Sun too. I look at her. "They're weapons the Phene use to fight us. You can't argue with that."

"Of course I can argue with that," she replies. "Not all banners fight for the Phene, no matter what people say. Each of the eleven banner fleets makes its own decision on whether to hire out soldiers to the empire. Do you think a Royal like my father hasn't noticed that banner soldiers who fight for the Phene take exponentially higher casualties than ones who've hired out at other times and in other conflicts? What if they *are* fighting to the death because they're being coerced? For example, in a way that would make Zizou attack you even though he doesn't want to and has no memory of doing it?"

Zizou shakes his head. "Our behavior is our own. We are not creatures on a leash."

Sun grasps the base of my mask, fingers bunched around the gauze pooling at my neck. "Do you want to see what happens if I pull this off her head?"

"No!" His flash of anger makes Sun smile with a dangerous edge of triumph.

In the recesses of the boxcar everyone stops what they're doing to look toward us. She releases me. "Lee House thinks they discredited me. But they're the ones who've made a mistake."

"Wait, Princess." My breathing finally settles, my distracted mental capacity coming back on line. "You know what's going on with the facility Zizou described, where he was being held, don't you?"

"It's the most parsimonious explanation and the only reason my father's adjutant Colonel Evans would have been there as Zizou describes. The queen-marshal agreed to the project with the proviso that my father would leave court as if in disgrace to hide both the project *and* her cooperation. Now I can guess she also saw the agreement as a means to get him and me out of the way so she could marry Manea Lee without any interference from us."

The train picks up speed as we reach the forest's verge and leave the industrial park's buildings behind. Sun's fierce glare is directed back the way we came. I'm strangely grateful she considers me on her side rather than her enemy.

"But that doesn't mean she isn't also genuinely interested in controversial research that could benefit Chaonia."

"All of Chaonia wants to defeat the Phene," I say.

"Most Chaonians think of the Gatoi as savages whose essential nature can't be changed, as you yourself just said. They'll consider the project a shameful waste of funds. Another reason for her to keep the project and her participation secret. So how did Lee House find out?"

"Not through me! I had no idea—"

"I know it wasn't through you," says Sun impatiently. "I need to find out why my father has stopped sending me an all-safe ping. There must be a way to track down the lab's location. Persephone, is there a way we can get from the academy to the industrial park without alerting CeDCA command?"

"Before or after I punch Solomon and break my hand?"

Her brow wrinkles in annoyed puzzlement.

"You'll understand when you meet him. We can wait for the train to be unloaded, sneak back on, and bail out when we pass back this way. That would be easiest, but it's a twelve-hour turn-around."

"Faster options?"

"Every brigade field has an armory stocked with weapons, equipment, and vehicles for field exercises, four-wheeled Bears, three-wheeled Wolverines, and two-wheeled Foxes. Some are stealth fitted. It's final exams week, so no one will be out in the field. If we can borrow two Bears without being noticed they might not be missed for a while. But it's a risk."

"Moira Lee deliberately reminded everyone watching Channel Idol that I'm half savage Gatoi. She forced me to become a fugitive. If the lab hasn't already been destroyed and if we can find it, we can dig out proof of what Lee House did. I'm betting Moira didn't get the queen-marshal's permission to assault the project even though they're supposedly the tightest of old friends. That will infuriate my mother, and turn her anger from me to Lee House."

Trees glide past. The scent of pine grows strong, a scent I've come to love in my years at the academy because it smells like freedom. Sun chokes down a sneeze.

"Persephone, get us to an armory after we track down your friend Solomon."

Not my friend anymore, I think with a rush of ill feeling that twists my chest into knots. I can't get my head around the fact he betrayed me and played me while I poured out all my secrets to him. But this isn't the time to say that.

We get the bags sorted and everyone in line to jump off, starting with me and ending with James and Isis, which tells me how much Sun trusts and relies on them.

We crest a modest ridge to see the academy laid out in the wide valley below. From up here it looks like a huge square grid dropped onto the landscape with the perfect blue circle of Heaven Lake and its attendant Sun and Moon pagodas and sky-tower a jewel at the center. The eastern half of the town is the civilian residential zone and the western half is the academy, with cultivated fields and orchards woven through the grid. With the mechanicals we call *night janitors* already back in their docking stations, it's all quiet, the empty walkways and service roads awaiting the flood of movement that is about to start.

It feels like coming home, a warm sense of rightness in my chest.

I set my face against obligation and obedience, and in that way my parents are right to chide me. But for all its isolation and restrictions the academy has nurtured me in a way my family never did. I won't be Lee House's pawn, not like Resh, the most dutiful of daughters. She will be the hero sung about in songs and remembered in gauzy memorials and fictionalized tales. I'll tell my own story, in my own way, even if it makes me ungrateful.

In four minutes and thirty seconds we'll reach the depot that anchors the northern edge of the grid. I scan the view as the train traces a slow curve toward the long airstrip and the arrivals depot with its sidings and hangars. Twelve gulls are sitting on the tarmac with camouflage tarps pulled over them. An orbit-capable shuttle sits in the open, absorbing sunlight for its batteries.

The tinny whistle of the regular morning-assembly alert blares. Cadets will be leaving the barracks and headed to muster on one of the brigade fields according to their year. I should be down there right now giving my coveralls one last check to make sure the legs are properly tucked into my boots.

Zizou says, "What's that? In the sky?"

Sun raises a hand to block the glint of the rising sun. "I see it."

Four ships are racing down out of the heavens. When I telescope in I get a visual of blocky silhouettes. "Those are merchant freighters."

But merchant freighters don't hurtle planet-ward like attacking warships. They attach themselves to big Remora barges and get hauled through beacons to their next destination. The high-pitched whine builds in volume as the ships close in, the sound underlaid with an odd cycling resonance I've never heard before. Or maybe I have heard it, but only in the simulation room.

Sun snaps, "Alika, what's that frequency?"

Alika blinks three times, seeking info. "Chaonian merchant freighters don't cycle at that frequency. Give me a sec." He sucks in a shocked breath. "I get a match to Phene gunships."

"Those are not Phene gunships," I object.

A series of loud pops cracks through the air. The train car shakes. Exclaiming, everyone staggers, bracing on a wall or sitting down hard on sacks. An explosion booms so loud the sound tears through my body. A churning cloud of dust and sparks billows out from the Moon pagoda where a missile has just punched through it.

26

In Which the Wily Persephone Is Hyped on Adrenaline

A memory of that last academy VR session scorches into my mind—the ax falling on my head.

"This train is a moving target. We should jump off now, before drop troops hit."

"Wait!" commands Sun.

Flames are shooting out from beneath the eaves of the topmost roof of the Moon pagoda. But that's not what Sun is looking at.

A streak of light slams into the sky-tower just below the Eyrie. The shock of impact rolls over us, rattling the train. We all duck instinctively even though we're too far away to be hit.

With a fearful shriek of metal grinding and torquing, the top of the spire lists in a slow-motion bend that makes me hold my breath. Shards of deadly debris rain toward the ground as the metal superstructure screams with a noise that stabs into my ears. Unbelievably it doesn't break off but jolts to a stop and hangs there crookedly. Pieces of the spire and comms dishes and antenna and probably the tables and couches from the Eyrie shower the ground in an erratic rhythm like a hailstorm.

The night-duty staff is still up there, if they've even survived impact, if they aren't part of the debris.

I must only think about what's right in front of me.

The train jolts to a halt as another explosive crash rolls over us. Ahead, part of the depot's roof collapses. Clouds of smoke turn incandescent in a boil of flame.

"Fuck," says Isis with a lift of an eyebrow. Wing cheeps as if in response. The rest of us brace ourselves, awaiting Sun's command.

The emergency siren engages with a howl. Three of the enemy ships dip down to just above the treetops and speed out of sight westward over the forest. I'm sure they're headed toward the industrial park. The fourth ship curves in a high arc up into the sky like it's coming around for another pass on the academy.

Sun tilts her hand to signal *go*. I bolt across the train to the other cargo door, slide it open, and jump. Everyone leaps out after me as I sprint for the tree line about forty yards up a slope. Smoke and ash sting our faces, although it's not as bad for me with my death's-head mask giving me some protection. James snatches his cap as a gust of acrid air picks it up off his head, and he stuffs it down the front of his jacket. The screeches of tortured metal in the sky-tower reverberate like the cries of a wounded behemoth.

We race in under the trees and, once there, turn back to take in the carnage. Heat roils up from the burning depot as a hot wind slamming into the trees, causing them to sway and rustle. Sun and Zizou aren't with us. She's racing forward along the cars toward the locomotive and its crew car. Four people wearing train-crew gray scramble out and, seeing her, run toward her. She directs them toward the trees. Only when they are headed to safety does she follow in their wake. Zizou brings up the rear, seeming unaware of the shocked glances the train crew are giving him because his hoodie has fallen back to expose his face and its gleaming threads.

"They're not landing, they're headed for another target," says Sun as she trots up. "Change of plans. Perse, I need you to—"

She breaks off as Zizou whistles an alert.

Far up in the sky shine two lengthening streaks of light: our alert fighters in ballistic re-entry. The two ships are coming in at such speed I can already distinguish their wings.

A flash catches my eye, like the sun rising only I'm looking south with smoke in my eyes and ash on my tongue.

Sun tenses.

"Fuck me," I say, spotting an enemy ship spinning back into view above the Chaonian fighters. The hostiles know at what elevation the fighters will have to start braking to get a targeting solution.

The lead Chaonian fighter shatters into a cascade of debris and flames. Ti covers her face. One of the train crew starts sobbing. The rest of us watch with a choking sense of futility and helplessness.

The trailing pilot manages to get a lock. Two streaks fly through the air and impact the enemy ship. Fire blossoms from the hull, but although pieces of the hull break off and plummet toward the ground the hostile doesn't slow. We never even see the return fire.

The second Chaonian fighter is slammed sideways so hard the momentum of the kill turns into a long, slow, inexorable tumble. Somehow the pilot manages to hold the tumble aloft long enough that the craft doesn't hit buildings. Instead it disintegrates in a violent flaming furrow across a wheat field, the pilot's funeral pyre. The enemy ship races away on the same westward path as its brethren, trailing a line of smoke.

I try to speak, but I'm too numb for words.

A second set of alarms blares in the drill for battle stations, an alert I can barely distinguish beneath all the other noise. The cadets will scatter to armories and rail gun emplacements.

James says, "That hit took down communications. I've got no global net access."

"Mine is dead." Sun grabs my arm. "There must be a local academy network."

I blink my CeDCA net open. "Yes, an online shell. It doesn't work outside a twenty-klick radius. The sky-tower is our link to the global net. You're the heir. Don't you have top military access? Satellite access?"

"Not at the moment. James, get us into the academy shell." She waits.

After a moment he says, "Got it."

"Senior Captain Ray is in charge," I add.

She nods. "James, patch a priority in my name direct to him and his adjutant."

"The command center is going to be swamped with messages," I say.

"Contact your cohort. Tell them to gather live-fire weapons and overland vehicles. Set a meet point. If anyone makes visual contact with Ray tell him Princess Sun is here and I'm taking command."

A day ago I would have demanded what and why and how, but instead I flood the entire fifth year with pings. The academy network flashes a *Service overloaded, please be patient* message in reply while a virtual wheel spins.

The conductor is an older man, pale and sweating. He gives a creditable salute. "Sergeant Brysyn Song Alargos, Your Highness. I served twelve years in the Twelfth Battalion. We have two raptor guns on board."

"I need the train readied for immediate transport."

He salutes. "Yes, Your Highness."

"Aunt, will you stay here and set up an aid station?" she says to Naomi Solomon.

"I will. What's your plan?" Naomi wears the same stunned look we all must have, but she's ready to act.

"I'm still figuring it out. Hetty, get the cars cleared enough to load up cadets. Leave anything not in the way. Be ready to move in twenty."

"Got it," says Hetty.

"Leave the bags."

Alika clutches his ukulele case against his chest.

"Leave it," she says.

I honestly think he's going to protest. Instead he mouths inaudible words—swear words—as he seals the case inside a dry bag and sets it atop the gear.

Sun addresses my cee-cee. "Tiana, if you're not battle-rated, then stay with Naomi."

Ti looks a question at me because it's my order to give, not Sun's.

It's an easy choice. "Stay with Naomi."

She nods. I unseal my duffel, pull out one of the five things I brought with me from home—an illegal stinger disguised as a pair of antique tonfa—then give the bag into her keeping.

Last of all Sun addresses Zizou. "You have served honorably, soldier. I can't take you to the assembly because I need the people here to see me as Chaonian first and only. Do you understand? It's no reflection on you but rather on their prejudices."

"Are you releasing me from your service?"

"No. Head into the forest. Move at speed but under concealment toward the industrial park. I'll pick you up later. Guard the ring. That's how I track you."

He meets her gaze, as he cannot meet mine. I envy her for being able to address him face-to-face. His expression has the honest intelligence of a person who holds to a code of conduct that does not shame him, no matter what anyone else may think about it. He is not cowed by her, not subservient, and he looks utterly sincere. He's nothing like I've ever thought a Gatoi would be.

"I am bound by the ancient covenant and by the crown of light," he says.

He jogs into the forest. We run southwest into the academy section of town. Firefighting mechanicals come clanging past us to the smoking depot and start spraying it with suppressant. Alarms have gone off all over campus. The top floor of the Moon pagoda is still burning. A spiderlike fire mech crawling up the exterior of the pagoda darts in through a broken window. The top of the sky-tower jolts down another degree of arc with a screech. We all flinch but pick up our pace. This time surely the sky-tower's spire is going to break off and crash into the plaza below, but it holds like a horribly broken limb barely attached by straining ligaments. Debris is still falling. I can't see what's going on at the base of the tower and pagodas, if there are any people left alive to evacuate.

As we clear the train tracks, running at a good clip, I stake out a route that will take us aslant through a stretch of cultivated land to my brigade's armory, close to the forest's edge.

Eighty-seven reply pings come piling in from my cohort as the academy network connects through its emergency workaround. Out of habit, before I realize I've done it, I open a line to Solomon.

"Perse?" His voice rings tinny in my ear. "Where are you? Is this really you?"

If it were me before everything that's happened, I'd have said he sounded relieved to hear me. But I'm so hyped I explode with bursts of rage-filled speech when I should be using all my air for running.

"Yes. Me. The person you betrayed. You fucking spy. I thought we were friends. But no. I'm just your cheap ticket. To a career. You couldn't earn. Any other way. Also. CeDCA under attack. Do this." I ping him a long list, then click off and suck in air as I realize I didn't wait for his response because I'd known I could rely on him utterly.

He pings me back: Done. At the armory in 10.

Nothing from Senior Captain Ray.

I send a ping back to Minh, Ikenna, and Ay to tell them to stick with Solomon. Then, jaw tensed, I open a channel to Jade Kim.

"Oi, handsome. I'm here with Princess Sun. I need Senior Captain Ray. You're his best cadet. So. His adjutant will answer your ping."

"You must be joking," says Kim in a laconic beyond-fucks-to-give voice. "Don't be an asshole, not that there's any chance you couldn't be."

"I am with Princess Sun."

"Where in the hells are you? The senior captain is probably dead. I was on duty in the comms center until twenty minutes ago. He'd just come on to take a classified secure call from the queen-marshal as I was leaving for muster."

The news strikes me mute. The senior captain: dead. Jade Kim: avoiding death by minutes. How can anyone process that? I blink my net off before I realize I've cut out all the active pings. I'm ashamed that despite all my emergency training I keep making elementary, novice mistakes. I freeze up, and forget what I'm supposed to do.

Sun easily keeps pace with me, the others at our heels and James lagging behind as we pound past gardens of beets, parsnips, and peanuts spattered with burning oil and an orchard of 'ulu festooned with bits of debris. Around us the alarms break off one by one until all that's left is the eerie groan of the dangling spire, the crackling of flames at the depot, and the steady movement of cadets, academy staff, and mechs headed to duty stations while civilians flee to designated shelters.

With a wrench of will, I refocus. Sun blinks through files I can't see. She must be trawling deep into the cadet archive.

"What're you looking for?" I ask, puffing air.

Her reply is clipped but steady, timed to her exhales. "After-action reports on cadet training exercises."

"What about when hostiles come back?"

"They won't come back here. They knocked out the tower and depot to buy time."

"Time for what?"

"You should have figured this out already. We're going after them."

"If you're wrong they'll circle back and destroy CeDCA—" A blast of ash in my face makes me cough. I can't get my breath back, but Sun's already answering.

"I'm not wrong."

Most of a brigade has gathered inside the armory where fifth years muster for field exercises. The big doors gape open as stragglers stream in. The armory stands partway up a slope on the edge of the forest at the westernmost edge of the grid. We have a clear view into the center of town toward the appalling sight of the broken sky-tower and smoke-wreathed pagoda. Our brigade commanders, jovial Chief Bu and serious Chief Dara, stand on the riding platform of a six-wheeled Bear with Jade Kim and Solomon at attention behind them.

Chief Bu speaks into an amplifier cuff to boom words over the crowd. "Fifth Brigade will create a perimeter guard. Form up by—"

The chief breaks off as the background rumble spikes in volume. The ground trembles. I stagger to a halt. The topmost roof of the Moon pagoda shudders. Flames shoot out of its eaves. With a fearful rolling grumble it pancakes onto the roof below. The massive whump sends hammering shock waves through the air, cadets swaying, my ears throbbing. Incredibly the lower floors hold, but it's just a matter of time.

Sun shoves up to the vehicle and leaps up onto the hood. The chiefs do a double take as they recognize her. When she indicates the amplifier cuff, Chief Bu hesitates for a breath because Sun is not in the academy's chain of command. But she is who she is, so he peels it off and hands it over.

The princess speaks into the cuff, her voice as sharp a call to arms as any siren.

"Stand to attention, Fifth Brigade! I am Princess Sun, daughter of Eirene, the queen-marshal of the republic you are sworn to serve. Like you, I just witnessed a craven attack by Phene raiders on a peaceful town."

There's a stunned silence as the cadets take in her accusation.

In a low voice meant only for her and Dara, Chief Bu says, "Do you have classified intel on those freighters, Your Highness?"

"I have the same sound signatures you have analyzed by now."

Chief Dara says, "Like I said, Bu, disguised exteriors, gunships underneath."

"What does an attack on the academy accomplish?" Bu shakes his head. "No strategic or tactical benefit."

"It's not an attack on the academy," Sun says. "You've heard the theory the Phene are controlling Gatoi soldiers with engineered hallucination."

"Wild speculation." Again Bu shakes his head.

"Except it's true. There's a classified lab hidden in the industrial park. Chaonian scientists are working to break Phene control of the banner soldiers. It will change the course of the war. Do you understand?"

Chief Dara whistles.

Bu says, "Yes. That's big."

Facing the assembly, Sun speaks into the cuff. "The Phene are headed for the industrial park. A second wave of our high-atmosphere alert fighters will take at least thirty more minutes. They might be held back in favor of ground-based fighters who have to be prepped, fueled, and armed. Even a quick reaction force will take an hour. But *we* can get to the park in twenty minutes.

And you cadets have done training exercises in its avenues and blocks. You know the ground, and the tactics that work."

She turns to Solomon, who for once is all out of killing ripostes. "Cadet Solomon, do you stand against the Phene?"

"Of course I do!" He catches sight of me, his brow furrowing as I realize I've still got that stupid mask pulled over my face.

"Good! Because I need soldiers who honor Chaonia and our ancestors. I need soldiers who will take the attack to the Phene. I need soldiers who will not allow the enemy to brag of how they slapped us in the face and escaped unharmed. *Are there soldiers here?*"

"Yes! Yes!" The cadets surge forward.

"We'll go in two ground waves. Half on the train. Half to accompany me overland. I need twelve volunteers to fly the gulls."

"With all respect, Your Highness, the gulls are unarmed," says Chief Bu.

"The Phene don't know that. Unarmed gulls can harry gunships to distract them. Who is bold enough to draw their fire away from our ground attack?"

Since the training vehicles are older-model alert fighters with no ammunition, flying the gulls is as close to a death sentence as any action that will be taken today.

To my shock Candace springs up beside Sun. "I will go, Your Highness. My parents died fighting for Chaonia. If that is to be my fate, then I embrace it."

Jade Kim's beautiful eyes have narrowed speculatively, taking in Sun, Candace, the chiefs from whom the princess has wrested control of the situation. Taking in me, in my skeleton mask. I yank it off, not wanting to seem like I'm hiding.

A sardonic smile lights that handsome face. Kim calls down to me, "The death's head suits you, asshole." Then turns to the princess. "I have my pilot's qual, Your Highness. I'll go."

A new rumble rises from the Moon pagoda. My chest constricts with anticipation. The structure implodes. The fourth floor slams down onto the third, and the whole thing collapses and tips over sideways, roof tiles avalanching into the churned-up waters of

Heaven Lake. A horrific rumbling shattering noise piles in until I cover my ears, head bowed. Grit and heat gusts into my face, stinging up into my nose, coating the inside of my already dry mouth.

As the worst of the deafening sound dies down, every gaze turns back to Sun.

Chief Bu steps forward. "I'll take command of the gulls."

She nods as at an answer she'd expected. "Hold your approach until the rest of us have had time to get there. Mob the Phene ships as the train arrives. The train troops will grab the attention of any Phene ground troops while the overland group strikes from the flank. It seems the big cargo barges are a good bet to provide cover along the avenues, if that's needed."

"Your Highness, that's a lot to coordinate. If we wait for the quick reaction force—"

"No. The Phene will be in and out before the QRF can get here. We act now."

The ping of an incoming message from the executive officer hits my academy net. Orange letters flicker into view: All hands, this is Captain Vata. Evacuate all personnel to bunkers and await orders at

The letters fizz out in a burst of static as a flash lights up the horizon. Thunder booms across us so deep and resounding that it is like the rake of claws. Windows shake. Something massive just happened in the industrial park.

Everyone starts talking, but Sun flicks up a hand for silence.

"We are headed for a secret lab at the industrial park. The lab contains captured Gatoi soldiers. Do not, I repeat, do not attack subdued prisoners. There will also be Gatoi working for us as guards at the lab. They are our allies."

Everyone is staring at her in mingled disbelief and determination.

"The Phene use Gatoi drop troops," says Solomon. "How will we tell the difference between enemy troops, subdued captives, and supposed allies?"

She stares him down. Although he's much bigger, her presence envelops him. "You know how to tell an ally from an enemy, don't you, Cadet Solomon?"

She deliberately looks at me and then back at him. He blanches, as well he might.

She says to me, "You and Solomon will work together."

I hate her in that moment. But it's a brilliant piece of maneuvering, so I nod.

"Chief Dara, you're in command of the train, with Lee and Solomon as adjutants. The Honorable Hestia Hope will remain at the depot to secure all cargo. Let's go."

27

In Which the Wily Persephone Is Stabbed by a Splinter of Rebellion

Solomon and I gather up the cadets of Stone Barracks and another three cohorts. There's a weapon for each cadet, but most fire only webbing or tracker spray.

Solomon says to Chief Dara, "There's only live-fire weapons for a quarter of us. What if we collect janitors and program them to be a first wave? Mechs will draw fire."

My right hand clenches into a fist just hearing the sound of his lying voice.

The chief says, "Do it." Then he turns to me. "Cadet, last we heard, Queen-Marshal Eirene called for her heir's arrest."

"That's right." I make up a story on the spot even though it makes no sense if you think for two seconds. "It's a decoy story. They have to keep this operation secret from the Phene."

He gives the go-ahead. We set out at a run northeast across the academy grounds, back toward the depot in its haze of smoke. By the time we reach the train, mechanical janitors are rolling up to join us, their sweeper and scrubber arms furled and sensor stalks swiveling toward the chief. Boxes and crates litter the ground. Cadets clamber into the empty boxcars, loading the mechs. Solomon sees his aunt and stops dead exactly like a small child caught eating the entire malasada he'd been told to share with his siblings.

Naomi gives him a shake of the head that makes me hope I get to be there when she drags him. If we survive this.

A splinter of rebellion stabs me. *Why are we doing this? We should just keep running.*

A gust of wind blows stinging ash into my face. I don't know how many dead there are or if their bodies will be recoverable. The Phene can't attack without us answering. Anyway, people are trapped, or dead, in the lab, people we need to help. People like Zizou.

I scan the forest but see no sign of him. On the western horizon, in the direction of the industrial park, dark smoke rises with an ominous message.

As I jump into the crew car Tiana emerges from the haze around the depot. She's smeared with ash and soot. Her gaze looks a little wild above an emergency filter mask fitted over her mouth and nose. She raises a hand with the sign for good fortune. The train lugs once and glides away.

Hetty comes running from behind a pile of cargo, making ready to hop aboard.

Chief Dara calls down, "If you are the Honorable Hestia Hope, you're tasked with remaining behind to secure the cargo."

She staggers to a stop with an expression of disbelief on her face. Setting her hands on her hips she watches us go with a stare that ought to be able to drill a hole through the locomotive.

We pick up speed, leaving CeDCA behind as the trees close around us. The door between the crew car and the locomotive remains open so we can see Conductor Song and his engineer at the controls.

"Hey." Solomon offers me a weak-ass spider rifle that shoots webbing.

I ignore him as I twist my tonfa together to engage the stinger.

He looms over me. In a soft voice he says, "I had no choice, Perse."

"You always have a choice."

"Solomon. Lì." It takes me a moment to realize Chief Dara is using my academy name. He has a bag of nine battered old walkie-talkies, used for exercises where we're simulating ground fighting on worlds with no net. Solomon and I each get two, while the chief keeps the others for his unit. "We'll lose the academy network before we reach the park," he says.

"Don't you have military-grade satellite access imbedded, Chief?" I ask.

He shakes his head. "Only the CO and XO. Faculty links in via the sky-tower."

"Doesn't the industrial park have its own regional local shell, like the academy does?"

"Sure, but getting everyone clearance will take time. We'll communicate with the walkie-talkies. Just remember, the Phene will probably be able to overhear you."

"The radios aren't encrypted?" I ask.

"They're Phene-made. Recovered and refurbished from the storage cellars here. They date from the occupation."

Solomon whistles softly. "I didn't realize they were that old."

"For now they're all we've got."

"Your Highness?" the chief speaks to the air as he projects a map on the crew car table, an aerial view of the academy township. It's not a real-time map; it's an exercise image for classwork. "Are you seeing this?"

The royal sunburst appears in my left eye view, showing Sun has dropped into the academy loop.

"Go on," she says, the sound of her voice accompanied by the grumble of engines and the grinding thump of vehicles racing at speed across uneven ground.

By closing his hand Chief Dara zooms the map scale outward. Then he slides the view westward until CeDCA gleams at one side of the table with the industrial park appearing at the opposite edge, sited on a flat plain. An expanse of forest fills in the gently hilly space between. This is the land Sun is currently crossing with the rest of the cadets, twenty-five to twenty-seven klicks depending on what route she takes.

"You'll reach the industrial park along its eastern edge," he says. "The rail line and its depot connect at the northern edge."

The chief centers the map on the industrial park. Its grid is an exact square, five klicks by five klicks. I briefly admire the complete lack of imagination displayed by the original zone planners. With a road around the outer edge to separate it from the forest and four north-south avenues crossed by four east-west avenues, the park looks from above like a five-by-five-sided tic-tac-toe board. The sky-tower rises from the centermost square, surrounded by administrative buildings and citizen housing. Each square kilometer is a walled block whose buildings orient inward, to control access. Except for an extension to the north for the floater barracks and greenhouses, everything else lies within one of the twenty-five smaller squares: train depot, warehouses, and factories as well as the big ore refinery and its smokestacks taking up most of the southwest quadrant.

"Do you have any idea where the secret lab is?" he asks.

Static blurs her answer. She repeats. "No. We have wasps hunting to try to find where the Phene have set down."

"You're sure they'll set down? They might just bomb the zone into rubble."

"They'd have done it already if they meant to. They'll land as close as possible to an entry zone. We have to follow them in. Hold on. Hold—"

Static interrupts. All background chop cuts to silence.

"We're out of range." Lips pressed tight, Dara scans the orderly layout of the industrial park. "You remember from our field exercises how the avenues intersect at big plazas. If the lab is in the park, they'll have to land a gunship in the closest plaza. Any approach up one of the main avenues is a killer line of sight, simple to negotiate but hells to attack."

With a thoughtful frown, Solomon says, "It was almost impossible to dislodge a defensive force set up with sufficient cover in the plazas if they also had control of the immediate surrounding buildings. Not without a massive assault wave willing to endure massive casualties."

"Sun said she'd use Whales to screen her advance," I remind him.

"We might be able to get the barges started since we disembark here." The chief taps the depot and its rail sidings, situated at the northeast corner of the grid. The big cargo barges known as *Whales* rest beside long loading docks. "I'll send a team in to the depot comms center to see about getting control of the Whales. The rest will split into three groups. Li, your people will not have live-fire weapons. Take mechs as your vanguard. Under cover of their advance, go block by block and sweep for civilians. Get them to safety in the forest. The Phene may decide to destroy the park as they depart."

If I were a different person I'd wish I had a more bellicose assignment, but I'm aware of my limitations.

"Solomon, your people will share spider rifles and live-fire weapons. Your mission is to divert and distract so my group can take out as many of the enemy as possible and leave an open path for the overland group to enter here along the eastern edge." He taps the four east-west avenue terminuses at the eastern edge, then adds, musingly, "Princess Sun fought well at Na Iri. She didn't lose her nerve."

We spend seven minutes marking out lines of sight, tagging entry gates into the factory blocks, and identifying places squads can retreat to take cover, just as we would in any training exercise. The familiar cadence keeps us focused.

"Take control of your units. Countdown commences now. Eight minutes."

I clip the stinger to my back and pull down the mesh telemetry helmets we've all grabbed. Then I climb up an interior ladder through a hatch onto the train's roof.

All transcontinental trains have horizontal ladders secured along the top for raptor shooting. Cadets are already up top as visual spotters, recording through the camera on their telemetry gear and relaying the view to the chief. The air tears at me as I swing up and over, grabbing hold of the nearest set of rungs. The park's sky-tower should be visible from here, but it's enveloped in a churning cylinder of black smoke.

Part of my mind is careening with the realization I could be responsible for walking people to their deaths. The other part is so calm it's flatlined.

Solomon clambers up beside me. To get away from his double-dealing justifications I crawl forward along the ladder. He's right on my tail, and he grabs my ankle and shouts over the rush of air.

"I did my best to just report in rubbish and trivial nuisance stuff. I didn't—"

"You shivved me in exchange for a place you hadn't earned."

"I didn't approach them. They approached me. They threatened my family. They blackmailed me."

I want to believe him. Part of me does believe him.

I shake my foot out of his grip. He doesn't try to hold on. There's no time for anything else, and we shouldn't have said this much. Yet I can't walk away with my back turned to him, not like this.

"Stay alive. You can make your pathetic excuses afterward."

"Keep your head down, Perse."

He drops off midway down the twelve-car line. I smell spices, and recognize the boxcar we rode in to get here. I guess Hetty decided not to bother to unload the sacks.

I crawl along to the last car, sure I'm about to be flung off into the trees. There must be a way for me to visually situate everyone in Sun's ring network, but I don't know what it is and this isn't the time for me to figure it out. Where is Zizou? What will happen to him?

What if we die and I never get to hear Solomon's voice again?

I reach the last car and drop down among the cadets waiting in nervous silence. I have charge of three boxcars of cadets, including Ay and Minh. I give the other walkie-talkie to Ay. Using a close-range platoon circuit I flash out a map of the industrial park as well as withdrawal points in the forest.

"Squad leaders, this is platoon leader. We're about to reach the limit of the CeDCA network. Go to hand signals. Our mission is defense and rescue of civilians."

The train's brakes squeal as we start a slowdown on a slope descending toward the plain. The trees thin, giving way to cleared ground. I lean out the open boxcar doors to get a better view. My gaze is drawn inexorably to the pillar of smoke spearing up into the sky. I can't see the spire; it's consumed inside a living, breathing, writhing creature made out of dense, dark ash.

Beyond it undamaged smokestacks stand as placidly as if it were any ordinary day. The plain here is as flat as an unfolded pancake, and since none of the buildings in the factory blocks are more than three stories high it's possible to get a sense of what's going on. Nothing moves. Several Whales sit motionless on the avenues. There's not even a district-wide alarm blasting, just the rumble of flames and erratic pops as objects inside the sky-tower break off or explode from the heat, which slams as pressure into my face. Are the civilians hiding in their domiciles or locked down in their work blocks? How many are already dead?

The sky spreads blue and bright beyond the smoke, no sign of enemy ships. Did Sun jump to the wrong conclusion? Did Zizou lie about seeing the sky-tower? What if this is a feint meant to knock down the continental sky-towers in preparation for a Phene invasion over Argos?

A new sound whines at a pitch higher than the wind roaring in my ears and the death rumble of the burning sky-tower. For an instant I want to cheer, thinking a new flight of alert fighters has reached us already. Then I realize it's six gulls flying in a V wedge. They've come in too soon. We're not boots on the actual ground yet.

The Phene react before I even spot their gunships. A thunk chases through the air. A gull spins a full circle and drops crazily toward the ground. A second gull explodes in a sickening burst of flame.

A third gull gets clipped and, tipping sideways, veers wildly as the pilot struggles to stay in control. A wing tip clips the side of a smoke stack, tearing off. As the bulk of the vessel crashes through a field of greenhouses and sparkling glass, the detached wing flies straight toward us.

We all duck. An impact smashes into the train, which lurches horribly. I stumble, grabbing on to the person next to me, and we both slam into the boxcar wall. A painful squeal pierces the air. The train jolts to a grinding halt.

I stare with horror toward the other end of the train. The wing has sliced right through a crew car, severing the locomotive, and gone on to dig a gouge through the trees. The derailed locomotive has cranked around to an acute angle, blocking the tracks. The three boxcars nearest the devastated crew car are also off the rails, one pitched over onto its side.

Cadets stream from the middle cars, Solomon waving them on.

"Get the janitors out!" Ay calls. Her words electrify me.

"Move! Move!" I shout, jumping to the ground.

My squads scramble out as they would in any field exercise where we are judged on speed and effectiveness, as if this monstrous conflagration is merely an augmented-reality obstacle arranged by our instructors.

My walkie-talkie squawks. "Li. Over." It's Solomon.

"You're senior cadet. What orders? Over." I'm shamefully relieved to pass the responsibility to him.

"Sending Ikenna to you. Get to the depot comms center. Patch us in. Get a real-time map view. May have a bead on hostiles on north-south one at plaza two. I'm taking all mechs. Over."

"Affirmative. Over."

"Out," he says.

I turn to Minh, on my right. "Take one squad for recovery. You're in charge of medical. There will be more casualties. Ay, take a squad with Minh. Strip every live-fire weapon from any cadet who's dead or too injured to fight."

Ay winces. "That's cold, Perse."

"This is not a drill. Follow me when you've got the weapons."

She knows. It's just that it's so ugly. They hurry toward the wrecked train cars.

High overhead a fourth gull gets hit, screaming sideways in a trail of smoke. A puff of white blooms in the sky. As I lead my group at a run across a siding toward a nondescript building identified on the map as the depot comms center, I pray the pilot has ejected safely. Maybe Candace. Maybe Jade. Have they bought us time with their own lives? I don't have leisure to feel anything as the last two gulls from the first V make tight turns and fly east back toward CeDCA. Where are the other six gulls?

The doors of the depot's comms center aren't even on lockdown. They slide open as Ikenna and I and our accompanying squad use close-quarters tactics to secure the space. The single-room building is fitted with a transparent wall placed to overlook the most easterly north-south avenue, which must be the "one" Solomon mentioned. On the side walls, multiple screens cycle through various camera views of the industrial park's plazas, avenues, and factory blocks. A pair of shock-faced techs gasp with relief as they identify our uniforms.

"What's going on?" demands one with long hair and tear-streaked cheeks. He's breathing as hard as if he's been running. "Admin is gone. Blown away."

"This is not a drill. We need access to your local network shell."

"We barely had time to send a shelter-in-place to the barracks before workday start. Then everything went down. Even the fire and rescue mechs. Everything."

"Fuck," I observe wisely.

Ikenna moves to the control board. "You must have an emergency workaround."

"Everything went down," rasps Long Hair again, a broken loop.

Even inside the comms center we can hear the rumble of the burning sky-tower, see the greasy smoke and black ash swirling heavenward. The clear wall gives me a view straight down an avenue, but the haze means I can't see the full five kilometers to the southern edge. Below the comms center, Solomon has already massed our mechs into rows and started them rolling on the wide avenue in a staggered phalanx. He's stacked a second wave of janitors with big sacks of spices and salt, a smart move since the sacks can be piled to form protective walls. Cadets advance behind them. The civilians are going to have to help themselves, keep their heads down. We don't have enough resources for both assault and recovery.

Two of the mechs in the front row of Solomon's assault line jolt to a halt as they're hit by hostile fire. I telescope my vision back along the trajectory. One point eight klicks south, a Whale has been abandoned in one of the big intersections. This intersection must be Solomon's "plaza two," the second plaza on this avenue counting from the north. The glint of a barrel peeps out from behind the cargo barge.

"Hostiles ahead!" I shout into the walkie-talkie, then realize I forgot to push the Talk button.

The air ripples. Another janitor lurches backward on its treads, sensor stalk peeled right off. The broom attachment of a second janitor goes flying. Every cadet advancing behind the phalanx of mechs drops to the ground.

"There!" says the short-haired tech, pointing at one of the screens.

Seen in close-camera view, two enemy soldiers are using the grounded barge for cover as they scan north, south, east, and west along two intersecting avenues. They're tall, more like Solomon than like the average stocky Chaonian. They look and move like us. They are us, the same us, descendants of the Celestial Empire, but I can't restrain a shudder when I see their four arms, one pair cradling a spare weapon and the other pair aiming with a main weapon. It just seems wrong.

Before I can warn Solomon again, before I can ask Ikenna if he's figured out a workaround to at least get the general alarm to sound, the sky-tower falls. It appears at a slow sideways lean out of its pillar of smoke and fire. Then gravity drags it crashing across the southern half of the park. Our glass observation wall rumbles amid the deafening roar, and we all flinch.

Behind us, the comms center doors whisk open. Too late I whirl with stinger raised. Three cadets appear, weapons ready. One shouts over a shoulder, "All clear!"

Two Bears and three Wolverines rev on the siding as a handsome figure gracefully hops off the nearest Bear. The mouths of both techs drop open as the Handsome Alika strides into the room carrying a glorious max-model stinger and an attitude to match, no Channel Idol smiles for this audience.

"Put down that junk stinger, Lee," he says with a harsh curl of the lips. "I'm taking over the Whales operation."

"You got here fast," I say stupidly.

"As you would have known had you checked your pings."

"What pings? We're out of range."

"Unbelievable." He jerks his perfect chin toward Solomon's

284 · KATE ELLIOTT

formation. "Go with that group. They look like they know what they're doing. I'll keep the techs." His gesture includes Ikenna.

I turn away to hide my hot flush, in case he's the kind who would be glad to know he got under my skin. My eyes catch on a screen just as one of the Phene troopers calmly lifts their gun, aims at the camera as if at me, and shoots. The screen pops to obliterating black.

"Go!" snaps Alika. "And answer your damn pings, like Percy would have."

There's Only One Body Outside

Sun balanced in one of the Wolverines, gripping a rail as Isis drove the vehicle at a bone-jarring pace through the forest. No speed could be fast enough to suit her, so she was grateful the coniferous forest was light on ground cover, mostly snake grass and ferns. Other vehicles hurtled along to either side, spread out through the trees in a flexible, open formation. The engines were built to run as quietly as possible. Even so, the speed of their approach made a fair bit of noise.

The academy network had long since dropped out when Alika pinged her.

THE HOSTILES ARE ON THE GROUND. He attached a clip of two Phene troopers shooting out surveillance cameras, with a pin marking their position on a map.

GUNSHIPS? She pinged James. His blip moved parallel to her a half klick south of her unit, exactly where she expected him to be.

CONTACT. He pinged back a live image. One of his wasps had found a ship landed atilt in a clearing half a klick from the eastern edge of the industrial park, less than a klick from where she was now. Figures were shepherding human-sized cylindrical lifepods down a damaged ramp. Smoke eked from the fuselage. This must be the ship hit by the second alert fighter.

Without warning the view disintegrated. Wasp down.

"I want that ship," she said.

Isis did not take her eyes off the ground ahead. "They'll blow it up before they abandon it. You have a brigade of untested cadets. How many lives is it worth to you?"

"Right now it's the only Phene ship we have."

A shattering roar boomed across the heavens. Dust, debris, and smoke churned above the canopy. The sky-tower had fallen.

Sun shouted, "Direct the vehicles in the center to go in unmanned! Use screening agents for concealment!" She fixed the telemetry helmet's air filter over her nose and mouth, then pinged Alika.

"Whales moving," he replied, all business, no show. "The park network is dead. I can't get an overhead view to see if other ships have set down."

"James, get more wasps out."

"On it."

Visuals flashed past in Sun's ring network. Wing was being buffeted by grit from the collapsed tower, view veering crazily. A wasp sighted down a long straight avenue where janitors trundled as in parade, cadets advancing in their wake wearing telemetry helmets and body armor. Their formation was tight and steady. It looked good. It looked courageous and bold. A surge of certainty flooded through her. Lee House wasn't the only one who had access to Channel Idol. They didn't get to control the narrative. She clipped out a tight signal to her Companions: ALIKA. JAMES. HETTY. VISUALS OF EVERYTHING. WE MAKE OUR OWN STORY.

She said to Isis, "I'm going in."

"I can't recommend you place yourself in such danger, Your Highness."

"The Phene have lorded their superiority over us for generations. Now they're trampling on our soil and mocking our inability to stop them. I will stop them."

Isis didn't bother to argue. She dropped off the back. As cadets abandoned the vehicles at the front of the line, the ones designated to go forward under remote control, she rounded them up into squadrons.

Thumps marked the release of smoke bombs and swirling light shimmers. Shielded by these screens the leading unmanned vehicle raced into the clearing and was immediately punched to a halt by rail gun fire. Its big wheels deflated, and it tipped sideways.

A two-wheeled Fox raced past and, knocked off course by heavy gunfire, collided with a landing strut.

The forward wave of the debris cloud from the sky-tower's collapse boiled out of the trees from the other side of the clearing to obscure the ship. Sun steered the Wolverine into a dense streamer of smoke and blasted into the clearing. She released a wide pulse from her stinger. Its parabola dulled the stinger's impact, but she only needed to stagger and stun.

"Move! Move!" shouted Isis from the trees. "The princess is in there alone."

A stuttering round of shot from the Phene defenders hammered into the base of the Wolverine, pitching Sun sideways. As she hit the ground the shock of impact throbbed through her shoulder, but she rolled into it as Octavian had taught her and came to rest on her knees amid ferns. The Wolverine turned incandescent beneath the full fury of a hailstorm broadside. She scrambled up and ran for cover behind the nearest tree. The trunk crackled as a pulse of heat seared across its bark. Needles burst into flame and fiery branches rained down around her. But she wasn't dead or mortally wounded, so the burning sting didn't matter.

Two unmanned Wolverines barreled out of a hedge of smoke. After them ran a squad of cadets on foot, bent over as they popped off bursts of fire. One dropped, hit in the torso, but the rest kept running. Sun fell in alongside to race through the noxious debris cloud. A landing strut loomed up through the billows like the leg of a monstrous beast. Isis already had a squadron crouched under the struts. Of course.

As Sun slid in, Isis gave her a tip of her chin in acknowledgment.

"Give me covering fire," said Sun. "I'm boarding the ship."

"Let me. You need to find the lab."

Annoyance flickered in Sun's heart at the thought of shrinking from any challenge, but Isis was right. "I'll keep moving."

Isis said, "You five, with me up the ramp. You five, lay down covering fire and create a perimeter. Everyone else with Sun."

Sun and the cadets assigned to her raced for the far tree line.

Isis went up the ramp amid a racket of fire. Sun glanced back. The last cadet on the ramp toppled sideways, back carved out by a shot from out of the trees. Her people. Her command. Response must be immediate. Sun sighted back down the trajectory and slammed out bursts until she caught a target. A figure flailed in the haze and vanished.

She sprinted to where she'd seen the movement. Under a spruce rested two dead Phene. One was tangled in webbing with blood spattered over body armor. The other was an older woman with age lines easily visible on her pallid skin and a starburst scar on her chin. Her clear helmet was high-end military gear, meaning she was an officer, although the Phene wore fewer markers of rank than Chaonians or Yele. She lay as still as the other corpse but with eyes closed peaceably, no mark on her. A cadet stepped carefully over the sprawl of extra arms to check for signs of life.

"Make sure they're dead. Especially that second one."

"No pulse," said the cadet.

Sun pinged Isis: STATUS.

No reply. Before Sun could turn back to the ship, a big Bear rumbled out of the smoke from the left flank, packed with cadets. James jumped down. He'd taped his flatcap onto his telemetry helmet.

"I've got a second gunship. It landed." He blinked coordinates and an image from a wasp. A ship had set down next to an unexceptional factory block on a plaza one klick due west from the eastern edge of the park. Not far from her current position. "If that's where the lab is, the Phene must have been tipped off."

"It's likely, yes. The other gunships?"

"The second wave of gulls is keeping a third ship busy aloft. No sign of the fourth."

"A group of Phene and lifepods came off the damaged ship behind us." She considered Isis's situation, but the second gunship took priority. "Send wasps to look for them and leave sentries. You and Alika get control of the roofs and approaches around the plaza."

She did a scan of her ring network. James beside her. Alika at the depot. Isis inside the ship, dead or alive. Hetty safe at CeDCA with Tiana. Candace a swift-moving blip in the air headed for the park. Zizou far away in the forest. She pinged Persephone, a blip near the depot, but got no response.

"Either she hasn't figured out how to use the ring or she's the Phene collaborator," said James with no mockery or anger, just focus. He tapped two fingers on Sun's arm in a gesture of intimacy she only allowed her Companions. "Do you think the Phene came here for Prince João?"

The thought of her father in danger made her resolve grow as sharp as the razor edge of a scylla's teeth. "Maybe. But I think they're here for Zizou."

"*Zizou?* He's cute but not *that* cute."

No time for his cheap joke. "Why else raid deep into our territory? They're desperate. They've done something weird and complicated to Zizou and maybe to other banner soldiers. Things they don't want us ever to find out about. Go."

She waved her unit forward. James took the vehicles under his command in a swing south, so they could flank the Phene position while Alika swung west.

Sun and her people emerged from the forest into the dying storm of the sky-tower. Ash and dust swirled into their faces, clogging filters and smearing grit over eye masks. Beneath the roar of the storm pulsed the muted hooting of an All Alert system someone had finally gotten going. A racket of shooting added to the din. They drove their two Bears, three Wolverines, and four Foxes to the terminus of the nearest avenue and lined them up just out of sight around the corner of a factory block. Her imbed did a cadet count: fifty-one. Because their faces were masked against ash and smoke, all she saw were eyes fixed on her, waiting for orders.

James linked her into the feed of a wasp flying over the park. The second gunship had landed in a plaza one klick due west down this very avenue. The Phene had extended deployable shields around its position, giving them commanding lines of sight. Six visible snipers had set up on the roofs around the plaza. A straight assault would be a bloodbath. But only a straight assault would be fast enough to stop the Phene before they grabbed and got out.

She pinged Alika. WHERE ARE MY WHALES?

ALMOST THERE.

Just as the ping faded five Whales appeared north of her position on the outer road, rolling toward her. She found Persephone's blip. The mechs and janitors were still working as a moderately effective screen for the unit that was pushing down a north-south avenue under withering fire toward the landed gunship. Good tactics.

On the plaza, Phene troopers were off-loading lifepods and guiding them in through the block's access gate, sited at the northwest corner facing onto the plaza. One of the roof snipers shifted, gun barrel swinging up with a flash as they took a shot at the wasp. The panoramic image snapped out.

Sun pinged. "Isis?"

No reply. Her gut twisted with anger; never with fear, never that. Keep the target in mind. They had to keep moving. Two more Whales rumbled into view, coming up the outer road from the south.

Isis's ping lit her network like a stab of relief.

SHIP SECURED. IT IS A PHENE IN-SYSTEM GUNSHIP WITH EXTERIOR DISGUISE AND FITTED WITH A BEACON DRIVE. I'VE NEVER SEEN ANYTHING LIKE IT. SHOULDN'T BE DOABLE. CASUALTIES TO COME.

A beacon drive! Gunships were in-system vessels powered by torch drives, not interstellar travelers. A hundred possibilities raced through Sun's mind, each rapidly discarded. She replied:

SEND COURIER INTO COMMS RANGE OF CEDCA. GUARD GUN-SHIP UNTIL SECURED IN MILITARY CUSTODY. IS THAT 2 MORE PHENE IN ADDITION TO THE 2 PHENE KIA OUTSIDE?

YES BUT THERE'S ONLY ONE BODY OUTSIDE.

Isis transmitted an image from Wing's cam, showing a Phene corpse on the ground where Sun had left them.
Sun pinged, THERE WERE 2.

ON IT.

Sun pinged James. LIFEPODS?

NOTHING BUT TREES AND SMOKE. I HAVE 3 WASPS LEFT.

DIVERT 2 TO MAIN BATTLE. Finally she pinged Hetty. STATUS.

THREATCON DELTA. NO FURTHER SIGN OF ENEMY. GROUND-BASED FIGHTERS & QRF ON WAY ETA 29 AND 47 MINUTES. ANALYSIS OF ENGINE NOISE CONFIRMS HOSTILES ARE PHENE GUNSHIPS.

AFFIRMATIVE.

"Your Highness!" a cadet shouted. "Incoming!"
All eyes looked up. High above, an enemy gunship hurtled out of the sky. The cadets dropped to the ground, using the vehicles for cover, but Sun remained standing because it wasn't headed toward their position. It strafed along the edge of the eastern forest about a half klick south, shredding branches, splintering trunks. Right around where James was moving into the built zone for his flanking attack.
She pinged Candace and got an immediate voice reply.
"We're coming in now." Candace's voice was squeezed and tinny-sounding.
The enemy ship changed course as the six remaining gulls came streaking in, headed directly for it with a bravado that made her smile.
"Fourth ship?" Sun asked just as the gunship fired.

"Unknown. Jade Kim has a plan—"

Candace's voice cut off. The sound of an impact smacked through the air. The leading gull jerked sideways and spun toward the trees as the pilot fought to pull up on a damaged wing.

As the gunship overshot the remaining gulls, still in their V, the trailing gull broke off from the formation. It pitched into a steep dive aimed for the plaza with the landed gunship.

"Son of a bitch," said the cadet who'd spoken before.

The gull's ejection seat popped, and a parachute bloomed. Sun stepped out around the corner to look down the avenue. Drifts of smoke made it hard to see clearly, so she tugged a filter across the goggles of her telemetry mask to adapt for the haze. Strikes from a rail gun and searing blasts from a heat seeker in the rear of the gunship raked up the body of the diving gull, but it was too late. Phene troops scattered, diving for cover.

With a shattering boom the gull drove into the grounded ship. The walls of the buildings on all sides of the plaza cracked. Pieces of ship tore off. Windows crumbled as the shock wave boomed outward.

"Down!" Sun ducked back around the corner. Everyone crouched along the wall as the blast wave boomed past, its roar melding with the rumble of five Whale barges as they lumbered up at last.

At three meters wide and ten long, each carrying a three-meter-tall hopper or container on its cargo platform, the barges made formidable obstacles. She waved the first driver forward. With a grinding of gears the leading barge lurched around the corner. As soon as the cadet had locked the barge's steering to a course straight for the wreckage, she jumped out and dodged back. A sniper shot took her in the back, sending her sprawling.

Sun leaped out, grabbed the cadet's ankles, and dragged her back around the corner as rail gun bursts peppered the wall above her head. A second Whale swung around behind the first, then the third, then the fourth.

"Move!"

Her squad packed in at the rear of the fourth barge, with the

Bears and Wolverines and the rest of the unit falling in behind and the last Whale bringing up the tail.

Even damaged as they'd been, the Phene soldiers hadn't lost their skill. They pounded the forward Whale until it smoked from heat, but the other barges shoved it forward relentlessly. Pulverized wheels scraped the pavement with a painfully endless screech.

James pinged in, hooking her to a wasp buzzing over the objective. A crater took up much of the plaza, debris everywhere. Bodies lay amid settling dust. The main gate into the factory block—right at the northwest corner—was crumpled and twisted, gapping open. A group of Phene survivors had set up behind an intact gunship strut to block the entrance while also firing down the four avenues of approach. It was a solid defensive position.

The wasp's view rose to hover over the factory block's roof, a flat expanse where tables and chairs were arranged haphazardly for meal breaks. Several squads of cadets were moving in over the nearby rooftops. Past the boiling smoke of the fallen sky-tower could be seen three intact smokestacks: the view Zizou would have seen when he'd been taken out via aircar by Lee House.

Was Persephone complicit?

James linked her to a second wasp. It had followed the Phene inside the targeted factory block into a big processing plant. A catwalk spanned an assembly line floor. At one end of the cavernous space, doors opened onto an emergency stairwell beside a pair of freight elevators. Phene soldiers were shooting down into the stairwell, flashes of light answering from defenders below. One trooper turned and took a shot at the wasp. The image vanished.

The driver of the second Whale rammed the crippled first barge against a factory wall, then bailed out as the second barge accelerated forward into a fresh barrage of Phene fire. They were over halfway there.

A time came when you had to make the decision and charge in. She opened a voice line on the ring.

"Persephone Lee. Reply with the green tab."

"What? *Sun?* This tab? Fuck."

It was jarring to hear Persephone's curt reply instead of Perseus's laughing insouciance.

"I need cover so I can take the northwest gate to the factory block. Lab inside."

No reply.

"Do you copy?"

"Uh. Yeah. Over."

"Out."

By now the engine of the second Whale had turned to slag from the heat of Phene fire, and the pressure of the third barge pushing it forward had caused it to slew sideways to block half the wide avenue. Sun waved forward the fourth barge to help push, thinking together they could shove the second barge all the way to the plaza like a moving shield. But the Phene had finally gotten some kind of big armor-disintegrating weapon set up. With an ear-popping thump, almost like an implosion, the second Whale juddered and collapsed sideways as its leading edge disintegrated into shards. The third Whale crunched over the debris. One hundred meters of open ground littered with smoking wreckage to go.

Sun waved the trailing barge forward and sent all of the Bears and Wolverines unmanned on either side, hugging the walls, crackling over glass from shattered windows. She led her squadron at a run, using the vehicles as cover, as the Phene at the factory gate hammered the incoming Bears and Wolverines with a hailstorm. Axles broke, wheels shattered, and vehicles reeled off to slam into walls. A cadet went down hard and bloody over to the right.

"Keep moving!" Sun shouted without slowing as she started to get out ahead of the squad.

A wheel spun backward, knocking another cadet sideways. Sun broke back to grab the girl and drag her behind a crippled Wolverine as rail gun fire peppered the roadway, chipping up asphalt. A second hollow thump sent a wave of pressure through the air. The third barge slumped to a stop, the big hopper on its back cracking from a direct hit. Raw ore poured out in a cascade. More obstacles, and the Phene knew it. They were just buying time for their operation. She needed a brilliant idea to break the attention of the Phene rearguard position even for ten seconds, long enough to bridge the gap and drive them back into the factory interior. Alika and James were moving in effectively, but they could not attack the gate on the plaza.

A soft whump caught at the edge of her hearing. A moment later a big white sack came hurtling over the plaza from the north-south avenue that ran perpendicular to the one she was on. The sack seemed directed at the factory gate's makeshift blockade.

Fire from the Phene split it open. White particles rained in a brief shower.

"What was that?" said one of the cadets. Seven cadets had crowded in to crouch beside her and their fallen comrade in the shadow of the Wolverine.

Two more sacks came flying from the other avenue. One fell short of the Phene position. The second flew past it and was torn open by a blast of fire. A cloud of pale green particles whooshed on the breeze.

"That's fennel," said Sun. "Oh. I see. They're using the spices from the train."

"They're launching spices at the Phene?" One of the cadets laughed, halfway to hysteria.

But Sun grasped the wild unpredictability of the plan in an instant. "Finding their range."

Two more sacks came flying. The first smacked down short of the Phene, but the second was arcing toward the strut when a set of shots punched through the sack and it dissolved into a red-brown mist of powder that swirled down into the wreckage like a work of art being prepped for Channel Idol.

To the cadets she said, "Use a full seal on your masks."

"That's only five minutes of oxygen."

"That's all we need. They've got their range. On my signal we advance."

She held up a hand and braced, ready to leap. Waited. Waited.
Two more sacks, each shot down, were followed immediately
by a barrage of sacks marked with the characters for black and
red pepper.

GO

She leaped over debris scatter and charged across lumps of ore
as sacks of pepper burst above the enemy defensive line. A gust of
heat sizzled past from a Phene shot gone wide. It was followed by
a series of loud sneezes.

In Which the Wily Persephone Reflects That No One Who Grew up in Chaonia Could Fail to Recognize Him

"I can't believe that worked," I say to Solomon where he crouches beside me behind a barrier made by the last six remaining janitors. With their unit cohesion disrupted by the pepper attack, the Phene have retreated inside, while Sun's sunburst has reached the gate. In a weird way it's just like old times, me and Solomon cooperating for field exercises, only people are actually dying and he's still a backstabber.

"There's something off about this, something we're not reading right," says the backstabber. "Even if the Phene are playing for time, where do they go now? Nothing in the playbook suggests Phene do suicide runs."

"That's what they have the Gatoi for," I say bitterly, thinking of Zizou. Wondering where Zizou is now, wandering alone out in the forest with only Sun's mysteriously powerful ring network to track him . . . "Wait. You're onto something. Why would a top-secret lab have a single entrance inside a heavily trafficked industrial zone? Dammit. How stupid could I be?"

I flash on that moment when the Handsome Alika sneered at me. Stupider than I care to admit, but that doesn't mean I don't learn fast. I use the green tab to ping Sun.

WE SHOULD BE LOOKING FOR A SECOND ENTRANCE.

There's a pause like a glitch in the system. Somehow I can feel Sun turning my remark over and over in her head. The ring lights up as she replies.

I'M TAKING MY COHORT AND RETURNING TO THE CAP-
TURED GUNSHIP. THEY LANDED THERE BECAUSE THEY
KNOW WHERE ANOTHER ENTRANCE IS, NOT BECAUSE THEY
CRASHED. ALIKA, WITH ME. JAMES AND PERSE, BLOCKADE
THE FACTORY BUILDING.

"The Phene hit both entrances while we got suckered into following them here," I say to Solomon as I scroll back through a
record of the pings I missed.

"Auwe!" He jumps up as he signals the squad forward. I think
we're going to create a standard siege pattern, but James pings me
within seconds.

I'M INSIDE. FACTORY FLOOR IS EMPTY. HEAD FOR THE STAIRS.

"I had no idea the Honorable James was so reckless," I remark
to Solomon. "His older brother is a notorious hard-ass about
proper procedure. Or so Resh always told me."

He gives me a look I can't interpret.

"I'm still mad at you," I say quickly. "This is just lighthearted
battlefield chatter, not forgiveness."

"It's not like you to bring up your illustrious connections so casually. I guess you're back in the circles where you really belong."

Abashed and annoyed, I snap, "Move it."

After directing most of our people to set a blockade, Solomon
and I follow James's squad inside across an eerily silent manufacturing floor. Line mechanicals have frozen in odd positions. A
piece of cloth flutters, caught in a breeze. Solomon jolts sideways
and clips it with a burst. It ignites and spins down all in fire.

The big metal stairwell descends into darkness. The clank of
running footsteps echoes up. I lean out to get a look down the well
before Solomon hauls me back.

"Good way to get yourself shot in the head."

He starts down at point, me at his back with my decidedly not-
junk stinger on narrow focus. Ay has joined up with us by now.
I send her with the rest of the squad up to the roof. I should stay

behind to take charge of guarding this zone, but I can't stop thinking about how the woman who took Zizou out of the lab was almost certainly my aunt Moira. If anyone can find evidence of Lee House perfidy I can, and I will.

The base of the stairwell opens into a rectangular room that includes the two freight elevators. Opposite them, big insulated doors stand open, breathing cold from refrigerated storerooms. A third door hangs ajar, scorched and off its hinges. It looks into a control room with a bank of screens that would be relaying images and metadata from the factory floor if they weren't melted and hissing. The only sign of life is an overturned cup with tea sprayed outward in a wet splatter whose shape oddly reminds me of Chaonia's second-largest continent.

Ikenna is trying to coax a signal out of the least damaged screen.

"How'd you get here?" I exclaim.

He offers a cocky grin and talks at his usual racing speed. "After my brief but exciting sojourn with the Handsome Alika, star of Idol Faire, I got rolled over into the squad of the Honorable James Samtarras. You know who the hells he is, right? Highest of high grade, son of Crane Marshal Zàofù of Samtarras House and brother of that perfect specimen of fancy officer the Honorable Captain Anas Samtarras—"

Solomon makes a mocking raspberry in my direction.

"Hey!" I snap.

He winks at me and moves back into the foyer.

I say to Ikenna, "Is this area clear?"

Ikenna gives me his famous side-eye like I'd just suggested he date a girl. "Of course it's clear. Would I be talking to you otherwise? Why does the Honorable James wear that stupid cap?"

"Honorables are a mystery to us all."

"I guess you would know," he says, with a little too much bite for my liking.

A *pop-pop-pop* signals fighting in a distance muffled by passages, walls, and doors.

From the foyer Solomon calls back, "The elevators stop here. There's no level beneath this one."

Ikenna grunts, turning back to the fried console. "So the controls claim. I'm checking it out to make sure there are no floors hidden beneath, because there's an echo. I think there might be concealed chambers below this level."

A flash of image tweaks the ghostly gray of the screen Ikenna is fiddling with: figures moving down a stairwell.

"Ay's up on the roof with a squad," I say to Ikenna and leave him to it as I cautiously follow Solomon through the fourth door. It opens into a break room with couches and a galley. Four tables have been flipped sideways to form a barrier in front of a metal door marked with an emergency exit sign. The keypad lock has been blown out and a fifth table shoved into the gap to hold the sliding door open. A bloody handprint smears the tabletop. A tech in a lab coat sprawls there, a bloody eruption of fluids around their left eye where they were shot with deadly accuracy. Just a drill. Just a drill. This isn't real. We can't really die.

"Cover me," says Solomon.

Ahead lies a featureless corridor. My imbed informs me that it runs twenty-three meters to a change room suitable for sterile labs. Both seals are jammed open with more overturned tables. I cover Solomon as he runs forward to crouch behind the first set of tables. When he's in position I race up to join him. A cadet from a different barracks, whose name I don't know, is braced in a corner of the change room and waves us forward. We ease past quarantine suits and emergency probes, and into a decon airlock.

A second sentry places two fingers to her lips, then makes the hand signal for *hostiles ahead*.

The door opens into a warehouse-sized space crowded with observation chambers, transparent cages, extensive lab benches, and ancillary furniture, including heavy-duty work tops fitted with restraints. Several big nets drape from a ceiling catwalk like so much fanciful artwork. Most of the cages are blasted open. Several wall banks have been cut away to liberate consoles too big to carry, unless you have a lifepod to stow them in.

We hear a hollow *pop*. As one, Solomon and I drop to the floor, rolling to get behind quarantine suits. A firefight breaks out, light flashing from stingers dialed to kill and a hail of old-fashioned bullets hitting bulkheads and smashing glass. The ring network is flatlined, blocked by powerful shielding within the lab.

After a final burst all the noise stops. A second echoing *pop* shifts the air pressure. We brace, but nothing happens. Silence settles. I peek around the door and into the chamber.

A lab bench is tipped over, tools and vials scattered over the floor. A pair of cadets lie behind it. One is twisted onto her side with the ragged fragment of metal sticking out of her neck. The blood has just begun trickling like a crack in a dam that's about to start gushing. My mind goes blank, and my skin goes cold.

"Cover me," says Solomon.

His voice cuts through my daze. As he darts forward I sweep the chamber with bursts from my stinger. There's no answering fire. He flattens down beside the two cadets. The other cadet, also wounded, has opened an emergency hemostatic seal. Together they and Solomon pull out the fragment and pack in the agent. The injured cadet spasms, then relaxes—dead, or unconscious.

My gaze catches on a flatcap lying on the floor beside a big console workbench placed ten point three meters farther into the chamber. In the thirty-eight-centimeter gap between console base and floor I sense the shifting of movement.

I ping. JAMES? ARE YOU UNDER THE TABLE?

The ring network is still blocked.

Solomon signals me to advance to the console while he covers.

I sprint forward, doubled over, and race past his position to throw myself down alongside the console. An overturned metal chair gives me a scrap of cover.

"James?" I whisper.

A faint scrape answers me. James is slid under the console trying to work a small rectangle free from underneath. Like a tumor, it has tendrils.

He whispers in a remarkably calm voice, "Breaking a bomb lock."

The sour taste of bile surges up my throat. I want to bolt away, but I force myself to stay still. "Phene?"

"A crude slap-on. They'll trigger it remotely. Most of the raiding party were clearing out as we came in. An unknown number of hostiles got trapped in one of the side rooms—"

A spear of heat hisses above my head. Return fire yammers from Solomon, followed by a thud. I peer between slats in the chair. A Phene soldier has collapsed in a doorway 23.4 meters farther down. My vision automatically telescopes in for detail. As I wince away from the splatter I see where the Phene soldier was headed: trying to cut across the big room to a lone passageway on the far wall. Fitted with a decon airlock, it must be the exit corridor leading to the second entrance. We have to close it.

To our right, a cadet jumps up from behind a bullet-pocked console and races toward the airlock controls as Solomon bursts covering fire toward the door where the dead Phene lies. The nose of a weapon slides into view around the door. With a single shot an unseen trooper pegs the cadet in the back of the head.

I look away. But Solomon thrusts up from his position and runs flat out toward another workbench. In the side door, the weapon shifts position, targeting him. Desperate, I fire frantic bursts with my stinger to keep the enemy's head down.

Solomon throws himself into a slide just in time as shots pass through where he was just running. He uses the momentum of the slide to roll up, and slaps the airlock controls to close the exit, then dives sideways as fire hammers the bulkhead.

We are sealed in with the remaining hostiles.

Solomon finds cover behind a workbench with a better angle on the side door. He catches my eye from all the way down the space and signals me to advance. A spiky voice worms into my head: What if he's still working for my family? What if they've told him to kill me by any means necessary? What if he means to lure me out so the Phene can shoot me?

Can I trust him? It's time to choose.

I dodge from the workbench to an overturned chair. Both Solomon and the injured cadet throw up covering fire that allows me to reach a workbench where I have a clear view at the Phene trooper. I pop off a shot, but it goes high. The trooper pulls back into the unseen room. Solomon scrambles forward, signaling me to join him beside the door. When I reach him, he crouches while I stand. Frigid air billows out from the chamber.

We both swing our sights around. I get a swift impression of a storeroom fitted with empty mesh cages. One cage gaps open with a green-lit lifepod beside it. Two Phene troopers are using the cage and lifepod as cover. I've stuck my head out too far. A weapon winks into view as a trooper aims, but instead of dropping or shooting, I freeze. All I can see is that cadet getting shot in the back of the head.

Solomon pops off a series of bursts that drives the troopers down. His shots slam into the lifepod's ceramic casing. Light coruscates from the impacts out across its surface like a splintering web.

I'm still standing there, mind blank, limbs numb, an easy target.

Behind the two Phene, a nozzle in the wall peels soundlessly away to reveal an eyelid opening. A man wearing a flashy tunic steps neatly out of a shaft with a ladder leading to a hidden level beneath, just as Ikenna had suggested. A shadow like a monstrous snake made of inky smoke swells forward from the newcomer to engulf the Phene troopers.

There's a sound of crackling paper, then a rattle like beads shaken in a gourd. When the smoke dissipates, the two Phene lie unmoving. The man who came out of the wall peers at the lifepod controls, then presses its touch pad. The lifepod exhales as its shield cracks open.

Solomon grabs hold of my arm and leads me into the storeroom. "Perse?"

My legs give out. He lowers me against a bulkhead.

"It's all right," I mumble. "I'm fine now."

"Fine now is dead one minute ago." He shakes his damn head.

In so many noble stories of young soldiers getting their first taste of war, people vomit after their first taste of death. Then I remember Octavian and Navah. This isn't my first taste; it's the second course. Why am I even thinking this? What's wrong with me? My mind is a riot of thoughts wrestling across the floor in a death battle whose outcome I can't predict. My hands convulse, and my right hand closes on a small bundle discarded on the deck: a pair of socks knitted in rainbow stripes. The soft fabric feels so humbly soothing that I can finally catch my breath and, after a moment, stand.

"Lab is cleared of explosive devices," James says from the doorway, tugging on his cap as he scans the chamber. Seeing the man in the flashy tunic, his eyes widen, and the cap comes off again. "Your Highness! So you did survive!"

No one who grew up in Chaonia could fail to recognize Sun's father, Prince João, a man known as the great indiscretion of Queen-Marshal Eirene. His exceptional looks and the Gatoi neural patterns pulsing beneath his skin mark him together with the way he stands like a mass of coiled energy barely held in check. All manner of decorative chains hang from his well-tailored coat in a pattern that ought to look chaotic but instead attracts the eye.

To James he says, "Is my daughter here?"

"Yes, Your Highness. She went to find the second entrance."

"It took long enough for someone to respond. Did Eirene not realize my messages had stopped arriving? That a rival clan attacked the lab and trapped me?"

"I don't know, Your Highness."

João addresses Solomon. "Cadet, Colonel Evans needs attention."

Solomon hurries forward to the lifepod. Seeing the person inside, he flinches, but then obediently helps a Gatoi soldier out of the lifepod's cradle. Besides the usual neural patterns, she has a gleaming artificial jaw, rank markings glowing down her right arm, and a ceramic medical vest encasing her torso.

She looks ashen and anemic as she assays a trembling salute, hand to heart. "Your Highness."

"You did well, Colonel Evans." The prince's gaze falls upon me.

I take a step away from the fierceness of that stare, deciding I don't need to be in this room any longer.

"Lee House betrayed us," he says, and he shoots me.

What Is Done Cannot Be Undone

However furious Sun was at herself for not taking into account the likelihood of a second entrance, that water had been spilled. So as she and her group raced on Foxes toward the captured ship, it was no surprise to see the fourth gunship finally appear, skimming impossibly low above the treetops. A rumble of thrusters shook through the ground as the ship set down nearby, out of sight

She pinged Isis. STATUS

FOUND IT. HOSTILES SET UP A PERIMETER AROUND A CONCEALED ELEVATOR SHAFT. WE'RE TAKING HEAVY FIRE. WE'VE GOT NO WEAPONS ABLE TO PENETRATE ITS HULL.

Sun replied,

HOLD YOUR GROUND. DON'T TARGET THE LIFEPODS.

?

MY FATHER MIGHT BE IN ONE.

Her squad sped past a unit of the perimeter guard Isis had set up. Its Wolverine had been torn apart by concentrated fire. Three wounded cadets huddled behind the wreckage amid fallen branches. Two corpses stared open-eyed at the shattered canopy.

She took in the sight and set it aside for later, racing on.

Isis had created a command post by concealing a pair of Foxes in the spread of a large flowering bush. She had inserted a tube through the leaves to get a view of the clearing, which she'd triangulated with images from Wing, perched in a tree overlooking the elevator opening. The elevator was a square shaft so overgrown with vines that only its door was visible. The door was open, revealing a metal freight elevator.

The gunship had set down vertically. Its hatch was already popped to create a ramp. The Phene ground team was scrambling to guide lifepods on board, covered by absolute withering fire from the gunship's emplacements. A Phene soldier stood at the top of the ramp as the last lifepod was wheeled up. She was an older woman with age lines easily visible on her pallid skin and a starburst scar on her chin. A clear, hard helmet covered her ears and neck.

"She was the other KIA," said Sun, noting the harpoon gun the woman carried using her two lower arms. "She had no pulse, so the medic said."

"Anyone can be mistaken. Cadets more so."

As the last four Phene soldiers backed up the ramp, the older woman surveyed the clearing and trees. She lifted a hand in the time-honored gesture known throughout beacon-linked space: *Fuck you.*

As the ramp began to close she turned her back to the meadow. Within the frame of the helmet, open to both front and back, another face came into view on what should have been the back of her hairless head. This face was distinct in its differing features: wider-set eyes, a flattened nose, a thinner mouth, as if the features hadn't quite filled out into a full human face. Intelligence dwelled there, piercing in its intensity and yet remote. Unreachable by ordinary people. Unfathomable in its capacity.

"*Rider.*" Isis spoke the word, then hissed softly.

The Rider studied the clearing, the scorched snake grass, the dense leaves of the bush behind which Isis and her forward group crouched. She raised a pistol with an upper hand and, using an arm backward, shot Wing.

"Fucker!" whispered Isis.

Sun slapped a hand onto Isis's shoulder to keep her from leaping up as Wing's body crashed through the branches and hit the ground.

The Rider did not smile. Riders felt no joy, no pain, no anger, no fear, no love, so the sages said. Emotions belonged to their host, while they were merely a malign intelligence hopping a ride.

But Sun wondered as the ramp clanged shut. As thrusters boosted the gunship up. As snake grass curled into ashy heaps beneath the heat and pressure of its lift. The Phene were also the children of the Celestial Empire. All populations had come in the Argosy fleets powered by knnu drive across the great ocean to a new home. That their descendants didn't all look exactly the same didn't mean they were different at root.

The third gunship raced past overhead, now ignoring its trailing flock of gulls. It had succeeded at its task: keeping the gulls distracted from the fourth ship.

Isis said, "I left a cohort of cadets on guard at the downed ship but pulled them out of the ship and back to a safe perimeter because in my experience—"

A series of shocks shivered through air and ground alike, coming from the direction of the downed ship.

"For that reason," said Isis as the noise of the blasts faded, "the Phene destroy equipment rather than leave it behind. But I couldn't identify where they'd placed the explosives."

"Dammit. They'll have rigged the lab to blow too, won't they?"

"Almost certainly, to erase all trace of the raid and any research they weren't able to grab."

Sun flipped the autopilot controls on the Foxes and sent them ripping through the shrubbery and into the meadow. The vehicles tracked back and forth across the ground between the elevator shaft and the flattened ground left by the gunship. She had to make sure the Phene hadn't dropped deadly puffer fish antipersonnel charges on the ground, but it seemed they'd been moving too fast to make the effort.

A flutter disturbed the ground at the edge of the meadow. A flash of a small animal moving. Wing was still alive.

Isis looked at Sun for permission.

"Go."

Overhead the gulls dropped away as the other surviving gunship pitched steeply heavenward in the wake of the ship carrying the Rider and the lifepods.

Engines roared, approaching their position. Alika pinged HERE just as the bulky shapes of Wolverines and a Bear loomed up within the shadow of the trees.

He hopped down from the lead vehicle and ran over to her.

"Have that Bear do one more crossing through the clearing to make sure they didn't drop any mines," Sun said.

He waved the Bear forward. Everyone backed a safe distance away.

"I don't get it." Alika studied the silvery shapes receding into the hard blue sky. "Gunships are too small to house the energy load for a beacon drive. So how are they intending to get out of the system?"

"They have a beacon drive on board."

"That's impossible."

"Not impossible if they've done it. Good tactics too. I'd guess they disguised themselves as in-system merchant freighters so they could attach to a Remora transit barge. Then when the Remora cleared the Chaonia beacon, traffic control wouldn't have thought anything of them detaching alongside other small freighters. We can figure out where they came from by tracking which beacon they used to enter Chaonia System. James? *James?*"

James didn't answer on her ring network, nor did his location show. Persephone had dropped off too. But Zizou was exactly where she hoped he would be.

"Hetty?" she said.

HERE

"Get the academy shuttle running. We're chasing the Phene."

ROGER. QUICK REACTION FORCE INCOMING.

It was odd Hetty wasn't talking to her by comm when it was unlikely she was in a situation where she couldn't speak out loud, but Sun kept her focus on what lay directly ahead of her.

Isis trotted back over. Wing was cradled in her arm, blood spattered along its right side but demonstrably alive and making clicks of distress. "That hells-cursed Rider only clipped her wing. Damned if I don't wonder if she left her alive on purpose."

"Like a taunt?" Alika asked.

Isis said, "More like a warning. She could have killed it."

"Or she missed," said Sun.

"Riders don't miss, Your Highness."

Alika whistled with a jolt of surprise. "There was a Rider here? Why would they risk a Rider on an operation like this?"

The shaft doors slid closed.

Sun whistled everyone to alert. "All weapons trained on the elevator. Use the trees for cover. Shoot at my command."

A clunk sounded from the shaft. The doors opened onto a freight space that Sun's network measured as five by five meters. Every weapon focused on the interior where, under the glare of an overhead, a short person stood blindfolded and with her hands tied behind her back. Persephone's pomegranate icon popped back into view.

"What in the hells are you doing in there?" Sun called.

"Your royal father doesn't trust me, Princess." Persephone's voice was rough, like she'd been coughing. "Sent me up first as a fail-safe. He said to tell you Lady Chaos will not be calmed by false words."

It took Sun a few more breaths for her racing heart to settle so she could reply. "All right. What's the routine? There's always a routine with him."

"What the fuck did he shoot me with? I'm going to be sick." Persephone Lee stumbled out of the elevator, veered to one side, dropped to her knees, and vomited.

With a prim grimace of disgust, Alika covered his nose, but Sun strode across the crushed snake grass.

Persephone flinched when Sun set a hand on her shoulder. "Fuck. Don't come up on me like that."

"Thoughtful of you to vomit off the main path so we don't have to step in it." Sun undid the blindfold. "What are the instructions?"

Persephone staggered to her feet. "He said you'd know what to say. There's a comms unit that bypasses the lab's shielding."

Sun scanned the interior for signs of a heat trap or puffer fish mine, but there was nothing. The comms unit had a keypad and a simple on/off voice switch. Flipping it on, she said, "Lady Chaos gave her child the Tablet of Destinies and fastened it to their breast."

A voice replied. "Sun?"

She swallowed several unseemly remarks and a sob of relief, and managed a calm tone. "Yes, it's me, Father."

"We're coming up."

She scrambled out. The doors shut, forcing her to wait as she impatiently tapped her foot.

"Your Highness, you should move back in case it's an ambush," called Isis. "You can't trust Lee House."

Sun glanced at vomit-stained Persephone. The Lee girl had braced herself against the side of the shaft, breathing raggedly. "It's not an ambush, Isis. I stake my life on it."

"It's still awfully convenient Perseus's twin came into your orbit right after his death." Isis stroked Wing's head as she gave Persephone an up-and-down measure finished off with a shake of the head.

"After his murder? Do you think Lee House killed their own son? I'm not so sure."

"Lee House had access to this lab. The banner soldier's appearance at the wedding banquet is evidence of that. Prudence dictates a more cautious stance in regard to this elevator and the testimony of Persephone Lee."

Sun gave her a look. "Maybe prudence does dictate that, but I'm not prudence."

The elevator clicked into place. Sun tidied her rumpled clothing as best she could, squared her shoulders, lifted her chin.

The doors opened. James emerged, holding his cap in front of him. The fabric was weighted with two small devices.

"The Phene left these to blow up the lab. They didn't expect our group to come in so fast. Points to us." He grinned.

A haggard-looking Colonel Evans herded out a squad of cadets, four being carried on improvised stretchers. The cadets seemed to trust the colonel even though she was Gatoi.

Last of all the prince appeared, flamboyant in his usual dress, decisive as he strode out into the sunlight, smothering in the way he studied her to make sure she was unharmed.

"Sun, why is this Lee girl among your Companions? Moira Lee sent in her thugs to take over the lab. They disrupted our work and murdered six of my soldiers. That Lee bitch would have killed me if she'd been able to find the entrance to the under-level."

"Ikenna was right about there being an under-level," muttered Persephone, earning herself a scorching glance from Prince João. She winced and glanced toward his left hand, but he'd holstered his weapon.

"Hand the Lee girl over to me, Sun. You can't keep her beside you."

"Persephone is mine now. It's for me to judge her fitness to be one of my Companions. With all respect."

"Lee House betrayed the lab to the Phene," he said furiously.

"If Lee House was working with the Phene there'd have been no need for a raid that would throw the entire republic into alert. They'd just have smuggled them out."

"Then what was the point of Moira Lee taking over the lab in secret?"

"To discredit you by suggesting you're a traitor trying to train banner soldiers to take over Chaonia. That would discredit me, and it would leave the path open for Manea's child to become queen-marshal after Eirene."

"Ah, I see what you're saying. A simple power play." He often annoyed her, and when he grasped hold of a grudge he never wanted to let it go. But he understood the deadly currents of court intrigue better than anyone. "Hmm. Well, then, we'll revisit the issue of Lee House later. Getting back the lifepods and the consoles must be our primary goal."

As always, the fraught reunion with her father had left her with a sense that she hadn't managed to greet him with the correct etiquette, as if etiquette mattered in the middle of a hells-cursed battle with the hostiles getting away. But it would, to him. He wanted her obedience, and he was right about the lifepods and the consoles, but it would be disrespectful to tell him his concerns had all occurred to her already.

Fortunately, a ping from Hetty popped up in her network just as the *chutter* of a Hummingbird caught at the edge of her hearing.

INCOMING. THEY WANT A FLARE AT YOUR LOCATION.

Sun strode over to one of the stretchers and set a hand on the brow of a cadet with staring, empty eyes. "Alika, record this."

As the focus of all their gazes she seemed to grow in stature, to fill more space, to shine with a greater light.

"I am Sun, daughter of Eirene, the queen-marshal of the republic, as you are sworn to serve. We have just witnessed a craven attack by Phene raiders on a peaceful town. Who among us would stand aside and allow the Phene invaders to shoot down our brave pilots and trample our buildings and lands? Not the cadets of CeDCA. The cadets did not hide in the shelters. They took the attack to the Phene and pursued the raiders, even at the cost of their lives."

She stepped to one side to give Alika a better angle on the dead youth's slack face and the academy badge prominently displayed on the bloody uniform. Alika scanned the other wounded cadets and the ranks of the ragged squadrons who had gathered in the clearing now that the fighting was over.

"Two Phene ships these brave recruits took down. Two remain at large. The Phene have stolen what belongs to us: territory, people, knowledge. We won't let them brag of how they slapped us in the face and escaped unharmed. We won't rest until we get back what is rightfully ours. Because we honor Chaonia and our ancestors. I make an oath on the sacrifice made by these noble cadets that their deaths will be avenged. Who is with me? *Who is with me?*"

With a shout, the cadets called out her name, eager now that they had survived the shocking assault. Determined to get pay-back and to prove themselves.

She nodded at Alika, and Alika nodded back at her.

As the sound of the incoming Hummingbird grew louder it be-came clear there were at least three vessels about to arrive, filled with senior officers who would do nothing but get in Sun's way.

"Isis, assign someone to track down Candace. She's out there dead or wounded. And immediately retrieve the pilot who para-chuted out, the one whose gull hit the Phene ship in the plaza. Perse, were the sacks of pepper your idea?"

"No, it was Solomon's idea."

"Bring him." She tapped through her ring. "Hetty, get every gull pilot who survived onto the shuttle."

She beckoned to a squad of cadets. "Send up a location flare. Lead the QRF to the other entrance. Father, it's best if they don't find you here. Come with me."

She clambered up on one of the Wolverines and took control of the steering stick. Prince João leaped up beside her, holding on to the railing as the Wolverines rumbled into gear and headed into the forest.

"Where are we going?" he demanded, voice pitched to carry above the engine's grind.

"You'll run interference with the queen-marshal while I and my Companions take the academy's shuttle into orbit and com-mandeer the *Boukephalas*."

He was watching her with that irritating look that mixed pride and admonishment. "Sun, the enemy certainly has a plan to shield themselves from pursuit. And they have a head start. How do you intend to follow them?"

"I'm way out ahead of the race. I baited a hook. I'm already tracking them."

31

Everything Gets Torn Away

To Zizou, the sky is disorienting. Its blue color seems painted on even though he knows blue waves of visual light are shorter and thus get scattered more. Everything seems to scatter planet-side: wind, moisture, light, sound.

But he likes the trees because their trunks are stationary. Like bulkheads, they provide a measure of order and dimension. Branches and leaves cut the sun's glare from reaching the ground in full force, leaving dappling and streaks of light.

He runs through the forest for exactly ten minutes and stops, stock-still, beneath the branches of a tree his network takes three minutes to identify as a deodar cedar. Its rich scent reminds him of the wood used in the temple of Lady Chaos.

The spin of an engine catches his ear, building in volume. One of the invading ships appears over the treetops, skimming so low it clips off the top of a tree. He's shocked when the ship halts overhead, hovering above the trees. A hatch opens. A small chariot, an oblong base with railings for sides, lowers out on its hover base. It drops straight down, snapping branches with abandon as it descends. He jumps back to avoid getting hit by debris.

The chariot spins a half circle, and its driver maneuvers dexterously through the trees right to him. Every banner soldier hired to the Phene is chipped in the hope that at the very least something of them can be returned to their home wheelship if they die. Only now does it occur to him how much the chip benefits the Phene officers. No banner soldier would run from a fight; that would be dishonorable. But if one did, the Phene could track that person down and collect them. As they have just done to him.

He closes his right hand over his left, hiding the ring the Royal gave him. He can't hide from the Phene. Princess Sun must have known. Yet she left the ring with him.

A Phene officer stands braced on the chariot, flanked by two soldiers sweeping for enemy combatants. The only things moving in the forest are the wind in the trees and a wasp that's been shadowing him since he left the others. It's buzzing down by his ankle, half-concealed by his leg.

The chariot halts a body's length from him. The officer holds a wand, a sigil of rank. The pulse of light within the wand's length echoes in the neural threads woven into Zizou's body.

"Soldier, state your rank, your banner, and your purpose here."

"Recruit. Wrathful Snakes Banner. I was captured by Chaonians and brought to a laboratory where they are carrying out experiments."

"What happened to your uniform?"

"They took our uniforms." That's true enough.

"How did you get out here if you were captured?"

He considers his options, measures the words he's said and what would be unexceptional for him to know. "I escaped when there was a power drain. I ran."

He's wagering they've not seen any footage from the wedding banquet. Princess Sun and Persephone Lee said it was being censored.

The officer frowns.

"Long way to run that fast that far, if the power drain came at the initial attack," remarks one of the soldiers.

"Not for the likes of his kind," says the other soldier. "They're beasts. You know what they say about them. Heh."

"None of that," says the officer sharply to the soldier before turning to face Zizou. She holsters the wand at her belt. "We're going to put you in restraints, just as a precaution. You understand."

"Yes, ma'am." He closes his hands to fists and sticks them behind his back obediently. The gesture also conceals the ring. Obedience is duty. Duty is obedience. Like the Ouroboros-class ship he grew up on, the wheel is simple and infinite.

One of the soldiers—not the one who called him a beast—hops down from the chariot to fix a restraint around his wrists. He wonders: Should he thank the officer for rescuing him? Should he banter with the soldiers as he did with Colonel Evans and as he would with his own arrow? But at the training camp for Gatoi recruits, the Phene officers acted as distant, elevated figures. He can't afford to make a mistake so he says nothing except to carefully crush the wasp under a heel so it won't follow and be discovered.

They hoist him onto the chariot. It rises with majestic ease. Once he's above the canopy he gets a clear view. Smoke gusts from the ground habitat three klicks away where wrecked buildings burn. Then he loses sight of smoke and sky as they get sucked in through the hatch into an airlock, which they pass through into a cargo hold. The smell of cedar and pine is overtaken by the cold metal taste of a space-worthy ship. The chariot settles into a cradle. They gesture him off, letting him walk by himself, a courtesy he appreciates.

Inside it is immediately apparent this is not a freighter and never was one. Six chariots sit in cradles, powered up and ready to go. A bank of empty wire cages spans one wall, enough to safely cushion and "coffin"—as the Phene say—an arrow of banner soldiers during a beacon drop. He's been in a ship like this before, when his squad was transported to their patrol zone. It's a specialized gunship made for in-system strikes: small, cramped, and loaded with weaponry.

"Strip him, rinse him down, and give him fatigues," orders the officer, then signals to the soldier who'd said "beasts." "Not you. I personally have a one-strike policy. No rubbish sex talk like that in my unit."

"Prig," the soldier mutters in an undertone that Zizou hears because of his enhanced aural capacities. Maybe the officer hears it too, but Zizou is already being led through a hatch into a passageway. He relaxes a little, comfortable within walls.

Two soldiers take him to a bank of showers, where they free his wrists and give him 120 seconds of water, more than he's used to from home. All this is accomplished while the ship is moving. He and the two soldiers steady themselves on the array of handhold bars, necessary for zero-g, that are standard in every gunship's compartments and passages. Because nothing among the Phene is boringly utilitarian, even these humble bars are decorated, in this case embossed with symbols representing the elements. The chariots are painted with scenes from the long-lost Celestial Empire: serious ministers walking through gardens beneath parasols; laughing hunters riding velociraptors as they chase down a wounded griffin.

A blast of air dries off his bare skin.

The fatigues they give him are sized for a short Phene. The too-long torso bags over his hips until they hand him a belt. The sleeves reach his fingertips, and the two extra sleeves flap at his sides.

A bell rings four times. The hull shivers like a vast creature caught in a blast of cold air.

His minders hustle him back to the equipment hold and stow him in one of the wire cages, which is barely wider than his shoulders across and another head taller. He hasn't even strapped himself in when the bell rings again and the ship upends. Were he not in the cage he'd fall; the Phene grab hold-bars with their four hands and kick out to anchor their feet on rungs as the ship lands.

He gets an elevated view down the main floor of the equipment hold. A big hatch opens to create a ramp. A rush of air washes in, swirling with pine needles and chaff. The air stings with weapon fire. Leaves are burning and hot ash blown by the wind burns on his upper lip. Soldiers pile in with well-drilled discipline, securing lifepods in racks and getting out of the way. A last group scrambles in. As the ramp closes an officer wearing the clear helmet of highest rank walks in. She's easily distinguishable because of a starburst scar on her chin. The bell rings, and she catches a hold-bar and pulls a mesh cushion around herself as the ship thrusts upward.

After some time the acceleration eases and the ship pitches forward until the floor is almost horizontal again. Crew members worm out of mesh cushions and hustle about their tasks.

The newcomer's gaze snaps over to his cage. He's not afraid of anything, not even death. Every child of Lady Chaos falls into the Gap in the end. But there's something about her fixed look that disturbs him.

She peels away the mesh cushion and heads straight for him. The way she walks has a slight hitch, as if there's a transitory lag between thought and movement.

As she approaches his cage he presses against the back as if to strain himself through the wire mesh and through the molecules of the bulkhead into the safety of an adjoining compartment. But of course he can't do that—no human can—so there is no escape.

The officer halts a handsbreadth from the cage. Her breath stirs the air. Her gaze traces the neural patterns on his face.

"What have we here?" she asks.

"Recruit. Wrathful Snakes Banner." His voice remains steady.

From behind the officer, a whispery voice speaks words he can't catch. There's no one else near them, no one else it could be.

Not until the officer turns.

She wears a different face on the back of her head, framed by the transparent helmet. It is a distinct face and yet eerily unformed, as if it wasn't left for quite long enough in the oven of creation. All four arms, uppers and lowers in unison, reach out. In unison all four hands grip the mesh.

"Come closer," the Rider says in its whispery voice, gaze on his face.

He hesitates. She clenches the wire mesh just out of reach, but even to consider leaning forward sends tiny charges of stimulation through his skin preparatory to a fight-or-flight response.

"Let me touch you." It is a command, not a request.

He stiffens, but he obeys. His nose brushes the wire mesh. The fingers of her upper right hand probe his cheekbones, the corner of his eye, the bridge of his nose, the center of his forehead. Her skin against his feels dry, ordinary, and yet it takes every clenched fragment of his self-control to reveal by no flicker of movement the terror that hits like a blast storm.

He chips off a sliver of a calming agent deep in his neural network so he won't light up, a sure tell. In his head he prays with all the sincerity of his youngest days, when every trip to the temple of Lady Chaos was a walk into the maelstrom.

For my transgressions, Lady, please forgive me. Be gracious. Shelter your child under your wings of peace.

The Rider withdraws her hand, licks the fingers she touched him with, but does not otherwise move. Her gaze scans him like an imaging machine, top to bottom, side to side, in long sweeps first and then in shorter ones. When she finishes she takes a single step back, although her uncanny gaze never leaves him.

There is a long pause. In the background, voices murmur, tools clink and clunk, interior hatches whir open and thunk closed. He doesn't dare look away, so he stares at the curve of her head below the eyes. This face doesn't really have a jaw or chin. It definitely has no starburst scar.

"Look at me."

He tenses, then looks up. The eyes of her riding face have the depthless inexorability of a void. They see him, and that is the most terrifying part of all.

If one Rider sees you, then all Riders can.

She blinks three times, like a coded message.

He knows Riders can't read the minds of other people, and not even the minds of the people whose bodies and brains they ride. But he's sure every thought he's thinking, and the secret of his association with Princess Sun, must be as clear to the Rider as if the words are hanging like fire on the air.

"Processing," says the Rider. "Identify subject."

He takes in a breath, releases it slowly, emptying his lungs.

The ship lurches left, then right, then pitches steeply. The Rider grabs hold of the mesh to steady herself. Everyone is slammed with g-force. The acceleration presses him back into the wire mesh. His lungs feel weighted with sand. Each breath is like raking through sludge. The Rider's face goes as blank as if it's been emptied.

An impact hits the ship. An alarm blares.

An intercom pings, and a voice says, "We are all destined for death. Let us honor our comrades who have given their lives for the mission."

They are still accelerating.

He's lost count of time, but as he opens his clock a glitch scrapes through his imbed system as its visual twists into an unreadable helix. The ship's gravity drops out.

Stunned, he realizes what's about to happen. It's impossible, of course. A gunship doesn't have the size or energy capacity to accommodate the huge energy load of a beacon drive. But he sees what he overlooked amid the confusion: ligaments woven into the walls of the ship, in patterns and composition not unlike the neural system woven through the bodies of his people.

This ship has been outfitted with a beacon drive.

The Phene are the cleverest of people, and they are wealthy beyond compare, so if anyone could pay that energy cost, they could figure out how to do it.

His thoughts fly back to Sun and the way she trusted him. To Tiana, who treated him kindly. To Hestia, who fed him. To Persephone Lee, who confuses him with her sharp words and the other story, the potent and beguiling story her body speaks when she's close to him. He'd like to talk to her some more, but she's been torn away, just like his squad, whom he had barely gotten to know.

Torn away.

Everything gets torn away.

The universe goes black.

They've dropped into the beacon.

He can feel his body but not see any part of himself or the ship. He might as well be suspended in a formless, timeless abyss. Maybe he is. Maybe they all are.

Wisps of light curl past. Shapes whisper out of the dark and get absorbed back into the living womb of Lady Chaos from which all life arises and dissipates. A voice is speaking, but he can't hear the words and anyway they are a language long lost to human knowledge, or maybe they are just gibberish.

The universe rings like a bell whose vibrations mark the ending and beginning of this cycle of time.

Then he's back on the ship, lights on, air still tinged with chaff and ash from the planet drifting as motes in zero-g.

The intercom says: *All hands. All hands. Battle stations.*

The Phene officer who captured him in the forest pulls herself over to where the Rider is hanging from a hold-bar. "There's a battle in progress."

"Yes," says the Rider in the clipped tone of a person who already knows and can't figure out why you're bothering to tell them. "Our raid was timed to coincide with the attack on Molossia so we would have a clear getaway. Your report?"

"We retrieved twelve Gatoi prisoners, five researchers, and four consoles. All seventeen humans are alive and stable within the lifepods for now. But we have to get out of the battle zone before we can examine the subjects to see if we retrieved the specific individual you are looking for."

The Rider's flat gaze shifts to fix on Zizou. "I have just now had it confirmed through the council. We have him . . . right here."

32

All the Wily Persephone Lacks Is a Club in Her Hands

We race away before the Hummingbirds of the quick reaction force land in the clearing. I'm still woozy from whatever Sun's father shot me with. My mouth tastes sour, and my throat burns, although that might also be because of the debris cloud we've been breathing. Solomon sits crammed in beside me at the back of one of the Wolverines. It's being driven by Ikenna, who has all the reckless panache I lack. We zig and zag through the forest, the wheels spitting up coniferous needles in our wake. Sun is driving the other Wolverine. When I look over toward where she's speeding through the trees I get nauseated, so I close my eyes and hunker down.

"Perse, you need to work on your reaction times," says Solomon.

"Fuck off," I say, but the battle, the aftereffects of the jolt that felled me, and the memory of dead cadets whom I sat beside in class and ran beside in PT have scoured the heat right off my tone. To my ears, I just sound tired.

"No, I mean it, Perse."

I almost tell him to fuck off again, a little more enthusiastically this time, but that thing in my mind that loves linking up transportation systems fires off, giving me pause. This is a puzzle that needs to be solved. "You were talking to a man. The same man every time?"

"It was a male-coded voice, but it could have been disguised. I guarantee it wasn't any of my uncles. You just thought it was. I never corrected you."

"Did they identify themselves as Lee House?"

"Why would they identify themselves? They made the threat—"

"What was the threat?"

"That they had information on my family's extralegal dealings and would turn them in to the gendarmes."

"Their silence being bought by reports about me. Anything else?"

His turned-down mouth and haunted expression make him look as guilty as fuck. "Nothing else. I make an oath on it."

"Like that reassures me."

He tries a grin to soften me, not that it's working. "Yeah, I get it. What's weird is it was the most mundane stuff. The only normal thing they asked for was wanting to know if you ever contacted anyone outside the academy, like family, friends, moneylenders. But how was I to know that? And anyway, you never did. Did you?"

"Like I'm going to tell you."

The Wolverine lurches hard to one side. Ay, who is clinging to the forward rail beside Ikenna, shrieks and cusses him out, but they're both laughing hysterically. Maybe laughter is their outlet to burn off this shattering adrenaline rush. The vehicle bursts out from under the trees and into a view of the academy hazed by dust. For years I oriented my life by the sky-tower and the twin pagodas. The sight of the wreckage unmoors me.

The Phene will pay for this.

And their secret ally will pay too. Someone told them about the lab. Someone who doesn't love Chaonia.

Solomon's last words finally penetrate the sludge of my mind. "Wait. The blackmailer wanted to know if I'd contacted my family?"

"Yeah."

"But if it were someone from my family who put you onto me, then they'd already know I hadn't contacted them."

"Yeah, that's right. Huh."

We speed along a cargo lane toward the still-smoking depot. The six surviving gulls, battered but not broken, have been parked off to one side. The academy shuttle is out on the tarmac, powered up, air shimmering around its sleek lines.

Captain Vata is standing on the portable stairs face-to-face with someone inside the shuttle's number 1 airlock. A security detail flanks him, people retired from the military in favor of a low-intensity job patrolling a peaceful settlement in the middle of a lightly inhabited continent.

Sun's Wolverine roars up to the shuttle. She jumps off and charges through the hapless security detail. Captain Vata holds his ground. I can't hear what's being said as Ikenna pulls a swerving stop that makes a painful squeal and almost throws me sideways onto the tarmac. But by the time Solomon, Ikenna, Ay, and I clamber down and run over, the captain has given way and Sun's group is already up the ramp and onto the shuttle. The red airlock light is blinking as we dash in. It seals behind us.

"Buckle in," Sun orders, like we don't already know what to do.

The shuttle has a utilitarian cargo hold with banks of acceleration couches, padded cradles, and equipment lockers. Isis is tenderly settling Wing in a cradle. Is that blood on the pteranodon's little body? It's clicking in distress. In the last hour I've crawled and run past injured and dead cadets and kept going with grim resolve, but the sight of the wounded animal floods me with tears.

My rack-mates have already strapped in beside Alika. Five shock-faced cadets in facing seats must be the surviving pilots. James is building an information tower by pulling brightly colored code out of his open palm.

I ping Minh on the academy network but get nothing back. I hope it's just that she's still out of range.

I look around for the princess. Hetty stands in the open hatch that leads into the forward compartment and the cockpit. She has an arm out, braced across the door, blocking Sun, who is clearly trying to get to the cockpit.

As I move toward them down the cargo hold I hear Hetty's angry whisper, meant only for Sun. "Never disrespect me so again. You think to keep me safe, but all you do in sparing me the battle is to show all others that you think I am not fit."

"That's not true!" Sun's words are soft, but her body is tensed.

I can't tell if she's upset, or mad, or just trying to get to the cockpit and annoyed that Hetty hasn't given way and let her through.

I don't care about their argument, so I push between them.

"And what about Naomi?" I ask Hetty, ignoring Sun.

Sun takes in a sharp breath, like I'd meant her to, because it diverts her annoyance from Hetty to me. I don't wait for her answer because the fate of Aunt Naomi is out of my hands. Instead I give Hetty a nod, meant to be sympathetic, and move through the forward compartment with its tactical tables and from there to the cockpit. I am absolutely stunned to find Tiana leaning on the navigator's chair wearing a charming smile for the pilot.

Jade fucking Kim.

"What a hero you are," Ti says with her most glittering smile. "You crashed your gull into one of the Phene ships. How did you manage to get out unharmed?"

Jade slants a glance back, noticing me, then targets Ti with the lazy smile that roped me in the first time. "I'm just that good. What did you say your name was?"

"I didn't say." Ti hooks me by the elbow and tugs me back as Sun strides in, followed by the ominous Prince João.

Sun addresses Jade Kim. "I requested you specifically, Cadet Kim. That was a brilliant and perilous attack."

For the first time ever in my acquaintance Jade Kim shifts uncomfortably, hands twitching on the console like an ordinary person would do if they were nervous. "Thank you, Your Highness. I figured it was the only way a gull could disable a Phene gunship."

"How'd you guess they were gunships?"

Jade loses any trace of shyness when the subject turns to qualifications. "I took double honors in Pilot and Intelligence rating. I know my guns. Those were Phene guns. Disguising the exteriors as freighters had to be easy enough even if it hurts their aerodynamics. It's also the only way they could sneak in-system for a raid. Pretty smart, if you ask me. And just like the Phene to change the exterior look, isn't it? But they couldn't disguise their guns."

"My thinking exactly," says Sun with an approving nod. To my disgust she slips off the ring once worn by dead Navah and offers it to Jade Kim. "I'm assigning you to me for the duration."

Jade can't resist a quicksilver smirk in my direction, knowing I've witnessed this triumph. I offer a two-finger gesture in rude reply. Ti taps my arm scoldingly like she's the boss of my etiquette.

If Sun notices the exchange she ignores it. "We're going after the gunship."

Jade Kim slips on the ring and cocks a perfect eyebrow in my direction before smoothly addressing the princess. "Your Highness, with respect, this shuttle can't catch a Phene gunship, as I am sure Your Highness must already know, so forgive me for mentioning it."

"We're headed to a Tulpar-class cruiser."

A bell rings with an incoming priority signal. Jade glances at the console, eyes widening. "The queen-marshal is on approach. This shuttle is ordered to stand down and wait until the royal air-car has landed."

Sun's frown lowers like a wall of rain sweeping down on the wings of a storm.

Prince João taps his left cheek with his left forefinger. "Ah, so this is why you brought me. So I can handle Eirene."

"Yes. In fact, I want you to take Persephone Lee with you."

"*What?*" I take a belligerent step toward her, but she gives me a don't-bother-me-with-this glance. She's not one bit threatened by me physically. "But you said—"

"I did say, and I meant it. You are one of my Companions now. I won't let your family take you. But you have access to Lee House. I need you to figure out if Lee House was involved in calling the Phene to the lab. If not, who is the traitor? Who is in league with the Phene?"

I'm honestly bludgeoned by surprise. Words slip soundlessly off my tongue, and when I finally speak, what I say isn't what I intended. "How do you know you can trust me?"

"That's right," agrees Prince João. "How do you dare trust her?"

"Because I do dare," says Sun without an iota of humor. Her gaze isn't what the poets would call bright; it's severe, even harsh.

She waits as my heart takes its measure. From this moment on, I will either dive into her gravity well or my family's grip will tighten on me forever more.

I nod. "I'm in."

"Get it done, Perse." She indicates the door.

Tiana leaves the cockpit with me. Jade Kim doesn't even notice Ti going, being so dazzled by the presence of Sun. As I cross through the forward compartment Hetty catches my eye.

In her low, melodious voice, she asks, "Who is that bold cadet and why are they so sure they'll be the cynosure of eyes?"

"The asshole Jade Kim, you mean?"

Hetty hides a smile behind a hand as she taps my arm lightly with her knuckles. I've won a point.

Made reckless by this flash of sympathy, I forge on. "Top double honors, number one in the graduating class. All earned, I'm sorry to say. Relentlessly hardworking. Backstabber extraordinaire. Beware."

She nods in acknowledgment of my vast wisdom. I nod back, then hurry on with Tiana into the cargo hold, following Prince João. Seeing my rack-mates, I hesitate.

"What hey?" says Ikenna, he and Ay looking first at Ti, of course, and then at me with wide questioning eyes as the airlock cycles open.

"You're with me," I say, because I am a Companion and I can have my own damn retinue. My mouth can't quite bring itself to ask Solomon, so I give a quick jerk of my chin to the jerk. He sucks in a breath, unstraps, and leaps up to follow.

Chest tight, I ping Minh on the academy network to make sure she's alive. She pings back immediately: On hospital duty. Got a gull pilot here, name of Candace, one of Princess Sun's people. What hey there?

I got the rest of the rack with me. More later when I know more.

We hasten onto the tarmac behind Prince João and stand back as the shuttle taxis away. It lifts wheels up just as a military aircar painted with the sixteen-pointed sunburst of the queenship sets wheels down. For an instant, I think the royal aircar is going to chase the shuttle, but instead it roars to a halt.

Prince João smiles. "Now the day gets interesting."

The ramp of the queenship drops. Eirene appears like lightning out of a thunderhead. She stamps down the ramp and bulls right up to him. He's disheveled and flanked by the worse-for-the-wear Colonel Evans, not much of an honor guard to signal his glamorous importance. Yet somehow, as he presses a hand to heart as in greeting, she is the one whose cheeks color with emotion. Her artificial eye has gone full obsidian, charged with light deep within, but he calmly meets and holds the gaze of her organic eye, which is a limpid brown.

"Eirene," he says, her name almost a purr from his lips, although the words that follow are spiked with the tang of a sweet poison. "I thought after what passed between us in private after our public parting in the command node that I'd never see you again."

She slaps him, a solid smack.

Her anger makes him smile more broadly, which makes her cheeks flush even more. Her gaze fixes on us four cadets and Tiana, where we are standing a few steps back trying to be unobtrusive. We say nothing because there's nothing to say.

Her attention snaps back to him. "Sun behaved with reckless disrespect and insulted our guests and hosts at a public banquet. Is that how you raised her?"

"Did you really not defend her from Moira Lee's provoking insults? Did you really try to kill her in a drunken rage? Our daughter, Eirene? That capable young woman, on whom the future of Chaonia rests? You know she is your right and proper heir, even if she infuriates you at times. But you've been swayed by this unseemly obsession for Manea Lee, a girl half your age. What lies has Lee House been pouring into your ear, stoked by the passion that drives you, always drives you, so you just can't ever quite keep it under rein?"

"Enough, João." Even so, there's a taste of arousal in the snap of her tongue. "You're jealous."

"Why would I not be jealous, knowing what you and I shared when first we met in the Temple of Furious Heaven?"

She laughs with a harshness that reminds me of Sun. "Fine. I'll not argue that. So where in the hells is Sun going? I ordered her to stand down."

"To track the Phene who raided the lab. This is serious business."

"Of course it is serious! Why do you think I came myself?"

"Leaving the marriage bed? Indeed, a crisis."

She gives him a look that makes me wonder if she is about to trigger the weapon in her artificial eye and obliterate him with a burst of contempt, but instead she shifts the uncomfortable glare of her attention to me.

"So. You are Persephone Lee. I haven't seen you at court with your brother. I am sorry for your loss."

"Your Highness," I say with a bow, for although the queen-marshal is first among equals in the Core Houses and treated thus by her Companions and citizens, who have the right to speak freely in her presence, she is also mother of the republic and thus must be treated with the respect due to an elder.

Her gaze settles for just a little too long and lingeringly on Tiana before she returns to the prince. "João, I need you to shut down the lab. All news reports of its existence will be binned."

"Censored by Lee House, I imagine. Lee House, who are directly responsible for the deaths of four of my banner soldiers and two Chaonian marines. What answer have you for that, Eirene? Will there be consequences? I presume it was nothing more than an ugly, petty power play to discredit me and Sun—"

"Sun spoke with great rudeness and a complete lack of restraint."

"You think it was not a petty power play? Do you believe Lee House is in league with the Phene?"

She stares at him as if he has begun speaking the arcane and barbarous language of the Skuda, who live at the farthest boundaries of beacon space. "Of course Lee House isn't in league with the Phene."

"Moira Lee's act has strengthened the hand of the Phene."

"What's done is done, João. Now we contain the damage. This conflict must not be allowed to interfere with or slow down our preparations for the Karnos offensive. You will erase all trace of the lab and stay out of sight until I contact you. In return I will not have Sun arrested for insubordination. She's flouted my authority in public and pretended to set a killer on my bride. You try my patience too far with your defense of her. In the days of my great-grandparents, such a troublesome heir would have been dropped into a terminus prison and left to rot—"

"Like your nephew?"

"He's not in prison. He lives in a perfectly comfortable villa on Pelasgia Terce for his own safety, as you know perfectly well. I was urged to execute him outright because of the treachery of his Hesjan mother. But enough! I don't have time for your meddling. This is a pointless distraction from serious matters—"

She breaks off and holds up a hand, listening to something on her net. Her expression creases with a look of perplexity that shades rapidly to alarm. We all stiffen. I glance around, expecting a fresh attack to drop out of the clear blue sky.

She blinks back to us. "João, go now. We've a new emergency. Do as I say."

"Sun left this Lee girl behind so you can restore her to her family."

"Sun needs a Companion from Lee House."

"Not this one," he says so smoothly I'm not sure if he is baldly and effortlessly lying or if he has decided to undercut Sun's decision.

The queen-marshal shrugs, uninterested in debating such a trivial issue, and gestures for me to embark onto the royal ship. I walk thirty-two paces before halting to address my rack-mates out of earshot of the queen-marshal.

"I don't know what's going to happen next. You three are probably better off staying here and taking your original postings."

Ay gives me her hard-ass stare. "We might never get another

chance like this. Princess Sun said we cadets will get special honors, and that's nice and everything, but it's that asshole Jade Kim who's up swanning around with the heir. Sticking with you would be a leg up for us."

"I know, and I will be back for you. If I survive what's coming next."

"The drama queen speaks," says Ikenna. "Holy hells, Perse, I can't believe you didn't trust us and kept all this . . . fucking Lee House . . . a secret from us. Don't try to push us back now."

"We don't even know if Princess Sun is going to survive the week," I say. "Keep your heads down and get hold of Minh. Your actions won't be forgotten. I promise."

Solomon still hasn't spoken. In fact he's not even looking at us. He's staring at something behind me, and to judge by his expression it must be a threat more horrifying than the Phene. I turn to see the half-ruined depot. A tall figure is striding across the tarmac toward us: Aunt Naomi. All she lacks is a club in her hands.

"Let me go with you, Perse," he says in a breathless tone. "You need a bodyguard."

"I'm her cee-cee," says Ti with unexpected force.

Solomon counters, "If someone in Lee House is the one who hired me, then me showing up with you may shake loose their guilty ass. You know I'm right, Perse."

"Shit," I say, because Eirene is headed for the ramp. I'm headed into a skirmish without a club, too, and people might show me more respect with Solomon at my back. "All right."

Ay and Ikenna offer ironic salutes. Solomon, Ti, and I jog for the royal ship, which we reach before the queen-marshal only to be halted by two soldiers standing at the base of the ramp. They wear the round silver shields of the queen-marshal's elite ground forces.

"Let them on." Eirene walks past us.

We hustle up in her wake. An adjutant waves us to acceleration couches to get us out of the way. The main cabin of the royal aircar isn't nearly as fancy as Lee House's personal aircars. It's a soldier's utilitarian tool kit, a mobile marshal's platform stripped down to essentials and utterly without decoration.

Eirene settles into a chair fitted with a console and various en-hanced projectors. The door into the cockpit remains open, but the queen-marshal doesn't pilot; she conducts. The power flows through her, and she directs it to its destination.

"Take us back to Argos. Condition 1."

She turns to address the three Companions who are traveling with her. "A courier just arrived in-system. It came from Aspera, via Troia and Molossia. The Phene have launched an overwhelm-ing attack against our positions at Aspera Drift. By the time the courier dropped into the beacon, 20 percent of our forward fleet was already crippled."

The others murmur in shock.

"I must take charge of the response. However, we can't just let the Phene get away with an attack on Chaonian soil, so I've as-signed my heir to track down and destroy the raiders. We'll know her worth by the measure of her success. But even so, the raid is at best a coincidence and at worst a diversionary tactic meant to dis-tract us from the real conflict. If the Phene want to accelerate this into immediate war, if they think to surprise us before we launch our own offensive, then they will find out Chaonia is more than ready."

33

We Are But Insignificant Objects Surrounded by the Vastness of Space, All Except One

The shuttle docked in the bay of the *Boukephalas*. Sun left the cadets behind in the cruiser's stateroom suite to sort out quarters under the command of Isis. She headed directly for the command center. Jade Kim blithely maneuvered ahead of the Companions in order to walk alongside her.

Cadet Kim had a smooth voice and a smooth presence and a smooth look, almost too smooth. "I thought the *Boukephalas* was doing its trials in Molossia System, Your Highness. I got my posting to this very ship."

"Right out of CeDCA? That's unusual, isn't it?"

"I work hard for my family. All their hopes are pinned on me." The statement managed an impressive blend of braggadocio made palatable by humble filial duty.

Sun glanced back. James had caught Alika's gaze and mimed sticking a pin repeatedly into his own eye with a grimace. Hetty elbowed him, although not hard, and her normally complaisant mouth had developed a surly curl. Was she jealous of the undeniably attractive Jade Kim? Would Hetty, James, and Alika gang up on any new Companions if Sun brought a full complement of seven into her household as her parents wanted and custom allowed? Those three and Percy had been together a long time. They'd gotten comfortable, even complacent. Complacency stuck you where you were. The advent of Persephone Lee and the ripples her presence caused within the household made Sun think it was time to shake things up.

Crew members stood aside to let their little procession pass, giving their blood- and dirt-stained garments the once-over.

"Were you the ones who drove off the Phene down-planet?" an eager ensign asked, so dazzled by Jade Kim that he didn't notice the quiet princess. Cadet Kim was smart enough not to speak for Sun.

James, however, gave a tug on his cap and his quirky grin as answer. A scattering of applause rushed like wind through boughs, punctuated by a single whooping cheer. Then everyone rushed onward to their duty stations.

The command center was a high, open, circular compartment with a strategos dais in the middle where the captain kept an eye on space and ship. Eight consoles were set in curves around the raised dais like petals around a pistil. The compartment's bulkheads projected a static virtual sphere so the crew could orient themselves within the complex realities of four-dimensional battlefields.

"Captain Tan, I'm commandeering this vessel again," said Sun as she strode in. Every head turned to watch her approach the dais.

To earn the captaincy of a coveted Tulpar-class cruiser, any officer had certainly spent years commanding lesser ships and won renown in Eirene's campaigns. The queen-marshal did not suffer fools and incompetents. Yet in the presence of the heir a captain must step aside. Senior Captain Tan, a quietly competent man who spoke only when needful, gave way without a word. The princess ascended two steps onto the strategos dais as he vacated it.

Alika said, "Hetty, take a step to the left. That gives me a better composition with Sun just a little off-center."

"Tulpar-class battle cruisers are classified," objected Hetty, ever the rules quoter. "You can't film much less broadcast from here."

"I'm not broadcasting." His *yet* remained unspoken.

James found a backup console and plugged himself in.

For all Jade Kim's cocky self-importance, the cadet had halted upon entering the command center with the look of a glassy-eyed innocent overwhelmed by the magnitude of the situation. Sun watched Hetty's lips pinch with a glint of gratification as she noted how awkwardly the otherwise suave cadet was gawking.

Feeling Sun's gaze, Hetty glanced at the princess, who gave her a nod of command. Hetty sighed infinitesimally, but she would never allow Sun to look bad for having one of her entourage in the way because they didn't know where to go. So she directed Jade Kim over to an acceleration couch, then hesitated.

Sun could trace the course of Hetty's thoughts in the slight upward roll of her eyes and the way she puffed out a breath through her lips. Imagine the manifold dangers of leaving inexperienced social climbers unsupervised on the deck of a Tulpar! After a moment's consideration, and another sigh, Hetty strapped herself in beside Cadet Kim. Perfect.

Sun turned her attention back to the strategos platform. She settled the network's webbing over her head. The mechanism allowed her to insert herself into a grid of sensors and satellites that spread across the system from the farthest tracking sensors at the heliopause to the big comm satellites that orbited the major planets and moons. But she didn't need a system-wide view right now. She needed a tight focus on the receding planet of Chaonia Prime and its spiral beacon, military and civilian orbital stations, civilian ship lanes, and military patrols as they responded to the emergency.

"Get me a track on the two gunships." She pushed a visual toward a Lieutenant Ruiz at track control. She'd flagged the gunships' initial trajectory as the enemy speeded away.

"That can't be right." Lieutenant Ruiz beckoned the captain over to her console. "The two gunships are headed for the beacon. The *Catubodua* is moving to engage them."

"Lock down any Remora barges making ready to go through the beacon," ordered Senior Captain Tan.

Lieutenant Ruiz shook her head. "The last Remora caravan went through on schedule hours ago. There are no barges in the queue."

"It's got a beacon drive," said Sun.

"With respect, Your Highness, that's not possible," said the captain. "Gunships can't carry the energy load of a beacon drive. Helm. Accelerate. I want to cut in front."

"Captain!" the comms officer broke in. "The Phene just blew up one of their own ships right in the path of the *Catubodua*."

Lieutenant Ruiz's voice tightened with the rush that accompanied action. "The explosion has forced the *Catubodua* to alter vector. They have some systems failures. We've got incoming debris."

The captain said, "Helm, steady as she goes. Shields front."

A chief wearing a CeDCA alumnus badge below his stripes flagged the captain. "Unscheduled beacon flash."

"Who is it?" said comms.

The chief said in a shocked tone, "The gunship dropped into the Molossia beacon."

"Follow it through," said Sun.

Questions and data careened through her head that she battled to weave into a meaningful shape. Why fly a small, vulnerable gunship into a massively militarized solar system?

But even that wasn't the crucial question. For two hundred years the Phene Empire had controlled multiple sectors of beacon space, the common name for all the regions linked together by the Apsaras-built beacon network. The Phene had wealth to spare, resources abounding, and a population genengineered to fit various environments. But their rarest and most precious resource was the one thing no other confederacy or population possessed: instant communications between Riders.

So why risk the Rider who was aboard that gunship?

The captain scratched his head. "I don't see how a single gunship thinks they can get through our sector reserve fleet, much less the Eighth Fleet."

She said, "Because we are headed straight into major action in Molossia System."

"But we just came from Molossia, with you, Your Highness," said the captain. "Everything was on standard alert, no hostiles, all quiet."

"That was two days ago. A raid on Chaonia Prime is audacious but not beyond the capacity of Phene special forces. But the only reason—*the only reason*—you put a Rider on a vulnerable raid like this one is so you can coordinate multiple actions across the vastest of distances. The rest of us are limited to intersystem communication by courier ships via beacons. But Riders aren't. I will bet my right lung the gunship expects to meet a Phene fleet in Molossia System."

The captain considered her words for five seconds. Then he signaled the boatswain's mate of the watch. The klaxon began blaring.

Comms crackled on. "General quarters. General quarters. All hands, man your battle stations. Set Condition 1."

The battle cruiser accelerated. Sun glanced over in time to see Hetty tightening her fingers over the straps with her usual pre-drop nerves.

Jade Kim had recovered a cocky equilibrium because the cadet said something to Hetty accompanied by a condescending smile. Sun could use the ring network to eavesdrop, although she rarely did. She dropped into the ring she'd given to Jade Kim in time to hear that glib voice offer a reassuring lecture to the Honorable Hestia Hope.

"You never dropped through a beacon before? It's fine. Nothing to worry about. It just all goes black, and before you know it you've fallen into a new system."

Hetty did not consider herself a violent person, but by the way she gripped the straps even more tightly Sun expected she was about to slug the cadet's handsome face for the obnoxious display of condescension.

Hetty needed a job to do. Sun pinged her.

GET ME AN UP-TO-DATE LIST OF ALL UNITS PRESENT IN MO-LOSSIA SYSTEM

The officer of the deck said, "Set beacon stations. Transition in ten minutes."

Sun stayed on the strategos dais, fastening the webbing that anchored her legs to the platform.

"Five minutes."

Hetty began to route an organized list into Sun's ring, neatly boxed off so it wouldn't interfere with the other visuals and information the princess was processing.

"Take all weigh off the ship."

People hooked their feet under stability rails. The gravity cut.

The comms officer said, "A courier ship just came through from Molossia."

The transition bell rang. The ship rolled once, and everything went black.

No sight. No sound. No breath of circulated air on her face.

Only a void empty of sense and existence. Like a life without glory or success.

The instant they dropped out of the beacon Sun oriented herself, an insignificant object no larger than one of the passive sensors, surrounded by the shockingly vast distances of Molossia's solar system:

A G-type sun, a yellow dwarf. Six planets, five of which anchored a beacon.

Molossia System had superseded Chaonia and Thesprotis as the center of the navy some fifty years ago. The main naval command orbital station orbited Pánlóngchéng, the fifth and only beaconless planet, with its metal-rich resources, while an auxiliary NCOS had been constructed in orbit around Yǎnshī by Great-Grandmother Metis to help retain control of Troia System.

Èrlǐtóu and Èrlǐgǎng, the first and third planets, anchored beacons whose destinations had been lost in the beacon collapse eight hundred years ago. For this reason Èrlǐgǎng, with its deadly atmosphere and scattered domed outposts, had been given the munitions depot and orbital shipyards.

The beacon to Thesprotis System was anchored to the sixth planet, a bit out of the way.

The Chaonia beacon, the one they'd just come through, was anchored to the fourth planet, called Xièchí by the locals but officially designated Molossia Prime.

The new Tulpar-class technology had a clarity the previous strategos grid had lacked. Even so, at such scale her eye was not fine-grained enough to pick up detail. She compressed the solar system around her, able to move fluidly wherever she wished, taking in telemetry at real time even as new telemetry was processed and slotted into the grid with the usual distance delays so information coming from the farthest edge of the system had happened hours before the movements of ships closer at hand. She searched for the gunship amid a jumble of shifting points. Her ring network was the most powerful tracker she knew, limited only by distance delays. Zizou's blip blazed clear although the gunship was light-minutes ahead.

She flagged the target for the captain.

He said, in real time and close at hand, "Look at its acceleration. The thrust is undermining the hull's integrity. It must have taken damage in Chaonia System."

Her gaze tracked back along the wake of the Phene gunship. Pieces of its outer hull were breaking loose only to puddle in the acceleration wave of the wake.

The *Boukephalas*'s comm cut in.

"Incoming debris. All hands brace for shock."

A shudder jolted through the ship as it took an impact from a fragment of hull. The shields threw off the debris. Sun tracked back to the gunship. The sections coming off were revealing the real ship beneath with its distinctive double-helix torch drive and the flash of a beacon cone winking at the bow.

How had the Phene solved the energy problem?

No time for such questions now.

"Captain, a Phene light cruiser is approaching the gunship," Lieutenant Ruiz said. "She's braking hard."

"A preplanned rendezvous, just as you'd guessed," Senior Captain Tan said to Sun before turning back to his crew. "Give me max thrust. We'll run down the light cruiser first and then reverse thrust to catch the gunship. Charge forward cannon batteries. Arm javelins."

Sun zoomed in and highlighted the contact. "I need the gunship's cargo and personnel intact. Burn a hole through their propulsion system, match velocity, and send in a boarding crew. Can you manage that, Captain?"

"My turret crews are the best in the republic, Your Highness," the captain replied primly. Then he added, to his crew, "Have the aft starboard gun start working a fire-control solution for the gunship."

Sun left the captain and crew behind, expanding her field of vision back into the entire solar system. Sensor feeds poured into the strategos grid as the program identified and flagged all military targets. The first comm traffic hit, a bounce back from the signal node of the beacon they'd just passed through. A hundred signals voiced at once, smashing into each other. It took her a moment to filter out Channel Idol.

Royal wedding updates! Color schemes for your block party!
We're getting hit by debris.
Mayday. Mayday. We have incoming bogies and have lost contact with—
Bake these Double Happiness cakes!
No answer from the bogey. Can you secure a visual?
Seeing anomaly in sector 3.05, *Lanippe,* can you confirm? *Lanippe,* do you read me?

Every beacon had a control node attached to its outer coil. The node's crew hailed the *Boukephalas,* cutting through the frantic background chatter.

"*Boukephalas,* you are secure past the beacon aura. Are you the reinforcements? Where are the reinforcements?"

"This is Captain Tan of the *Boukephalas.* What reinforcements?"

"A Phene fleet has attacked Molossia System."

"Where did they come from?" the captain asked.

Sun cut in. "Have you tracked back on the route of the Phene light cruiser? Its arrival had to be timed to rendezvous with the gunship."

The *Boukephalas* had dropped into the system via the beacon anchored to Molossia Prime. Sun spun out a tendril of attention toward the Troia beacon, anchored on the second planet, Yǎnshī. Measured on the plane of the ecliptic, Yǎnshī was currently at a ninety-degree angle from Molossia Prime, and nearly on the opposite side of the sun from the third planet, Èrlĭgǎng, with the munitions depot.

There was no unexpected activity to be seen in the vicinity of Yǎnshī, although of course she was seeing it as it would have looked an hour or more earlier. That meant the Phene hadn't entered Molossia's space through the Troia beacon. But that scenario was unlikely anyway, since the palace on Chaonia Prime would already have heard via fast courier if a Phene fleet had hit Troia before dropping into Molossia.

There was something else going on. Something entirely unexpected.

She tracked back the comms traffic to the mention of *Lanippe*, and flung the name at Hetty, who replied immediately with a visual of a fast frigate called *Lanippe*, seconded to the Molossia reserve fleet.

Sun ran the telemetry backward to find the point of generation: Where had that piece of chatter come from? How long ago?

And there it was, utterly shocking and remarkably brilliant.

A Phene fleet had entered Molossia System from beyond the heliopause, into sector 3.05 near the fifth planet and its naval command orbital station. Now the rest of the incoming information began to make sense.

"Captain Tan! Let the gunship go for now. We can catch it later. We have bigger problems."

"Your Highness?"

"A Phene fleet entered Molossia System in sector 3.05 and has attacked the NCOSP. Get hold of Crane Marshal Bahram, or any ship captain—"

James said, "My brother Anas is with the Eighth Fleet, getting ready to ship out to Troia. He's in command of the *Melandria*. He should be at the munitions depot."

"Captain! Hail the *Melandria*. Get me Raven Marshal Radomir at Èrlĭgǎng Depot."

"Sun," Alika interrupted, "how can a Phene fleet have entered the system undetected?"

"Because they didn't come through a beacon. They're using knnu drives."

"That would take months of travel from their nearest port of call."

"That's right. Months of travel, out of sensor range, unseen, unexpected. All of it coordinated by Riders. That's why there's a Rider on that gunship. I don't know how long ago the Phene learned about the lab's existence. But I guarantee the raid on the lab was coordinated to rendezvous with an attack the Rider Council and the Phene military already knew was coming, because it had to have been launched months ago. That's why they think they can get away with it."

She flung visuals toward the captain's console, showing how a line of attack would allow a fleet to strike the fifth, third, and second planets efficiently and with relative quickness given the current orbital positions of the planets. Data piled up as readouts from hours ago piled into their system: a sudden call to alert, a scramble of call signs as ships tried to launch to meet the threat, frantic maydays, calls of distress cut off suddenly, ships and habitats silenced.

The comms officer tried to patch a call through to Crane Marshal Bahram's high-priority line at NCOSP, but no ping returned. In her heart Sun heard the roar of obliterating flames even though she knew the moment the atmosphere systems were breached all fire would have been sucked to nothing.

"Your Highness, I have contact with a Commander Baber of the assault frigate *Hábrók*, stationed at NCOSP."

Breaking protocol, she grabbed the comms herself. "*Hábrók*, this is Princess Sun on the *Boukephalas*. Report in." She went back to the strategos grid and sent out additional messages, seeking other survivors. Replies popped in according to distance delays.

A steady comms voice said, "This is *Hábrók*. Roger. Wait. Out," and a moment later a new voice came in. "This is *Hábrók* actual. Are you the reinforcements?" Commander Baber sounded out of breath. A klaxon sounded in counterpoint. "Secure that alarm, Ensign!"

"Report in. How many Phene ships?"

Again she waited. Every exchange became intertwined with other exchanges, a complex web more like leaving paper notes and picking up replies later.

"Hundreds. They hit NCOSP with salvos of missiles and kinetics. There were over one hundred Chaonian naval ships moored there and at nearby orbital dry docks. All of us hammered."

"Are you still docked?"

"No, but we were docked when it happened. The Phene hit with multiple strikes and accelerated on. Smash and run. Pure accident this ship survived."

Finally Sun got a fix on NCOSP with enough resolution to see how the situation had looked tens of hours ago—the wrecked orbital was venting atmosphere and slowly spinning in the wrong direction, soon to start a death spiral toward the planet. Ships drifted, powerless. Debris began inexorably turning into the gravity well.

Ships were moving away from the wreckage, forming up into squadrons and tracking down lifeboats.

"Commander, all ships able to fight immediately join up with the *Boukephalas*. We'll send you our bearing."

"The hells!" exclaimed Senior Captain Tan as a new wave of information rolled in. "We found the Phene fleet. They've hit the munitions depot at Èrlĭgăng. There have to be at least five hundred enemy ships."

James dragged his cap off his head and slapped it against his thigh. "Anas and his task force were taking on munitions at the depot."

"James, see if you can patch through a private comm to your brother. Captain Tan, try to get any comm open to the munitions depot or to any command ship . . ." She trailed off as a new telemetry shifted through the grid, giving her a telltale path.

"The Phene fleet is slingshotting around Èrlĭgăng to get extra speed toward Yănshī. Which means they intend to exit the system via the Troia beacon. And that means . . . that means . . ." Her mind sped through the ramifications, shuffling in and discarding information until the patterns started to make sense. "Why would they bottleneck themselves through Troia when they would know Troia will have warning by now? Unless . . . they've hit Troia already from either Kanesh or Aspera."

Hetty said, "We passed a courier ship on our way out."

"That's right. It dropped into Chaonia just as we went out to Molossia. I want to see the message that was on that courier."

Seconds ticked past like hours before the classified message flashed up as a visual:

FLASH FLASH FLASH ASPERA SYSTEM UNDER ASSAULT BY MAJOR PHENE FLEET. MARSHAL SARNAI IN RETREAT. SEND REINFORCEMENTS.

The crew had taken the shocking circumstances in stride so far but broke out now into a hum of murmured exclamations and speculation. Sun was beyond being surprised. It all fell so neatly into place.

"We must get to the Troia beacon before the Phene fleet here in Molossia reaches it. We will cut them off." She assessed shifting ship movements on the grid, but there was too much to absorb with one pair of eyes. "Lieutenant Ruiz, get me an analysis of Phene fleet movements."

"The Phene fleet has taken damage at Èrlĭgǎng. It looks like they're blowing up their damaged ships. Some of their light cruisers are falling behind to scoop up lifeboats from the abandoned ships. There's a group of about eighty Chaonian ships ahead of them, running a fighting retreat from Èrlĭgǎng, headed toward Yǎnshī."

"James? Any response from your brother?"

"Waiting." He'd crumpled up his cap into his right hand, working his fingers against the fabric like it could squeeze out a faster reply, although there was no guarantee Anas had survived the initial attack.

"Comms, hail anyone in the group retreating toward Yǎnshī, all channels."

A ping landed, routed by James onto Sun's ring network.

"Captain the Honorable Anas Samtarras of the *Melandria*. James, are you on the *Boukephalas*? Is Chaonia on alert? We need reinforcements."

"Anas, this is Sun on the *Boukephalas*." She continued to track the unfolding battle as they waited for his reply.

"*Sun?*" The Honorable Anas's tone had something of the flavor of a person discovering the promised feast is really a broom given to them so they can sweep up after others. James winced. "Captain Tan of the *Boukephalas*, are you there?"

Tan looked toward Sun, said nothing.

Sun smiled, reverting to formal procedure because she knew it would annoy Anas. "*Melandria*, this is *Boukephalas*. What is your situation, and how many ships do you have?"

As they waited she checked on the status of Commander Baber. The ships he'd gathered were beginning to move away from the shattered NCOSP and toward them.

The pause stretched for longer than needed to accommodate distance delay.

"*Melandria?*" Sun repeated. "Time is of the essence. What is your situation?"

Something clunked in the audio background.

"He's thrown something, like he does when he gets pissy," remarked James.

When Anas Samtarras replied, his voice had a thorny prickle to it. "The munitions depot and a number of neighboring shipyards have been hit by a Phene attack of at least 438 ships. Raven Marshal Radomir is confirmed KIA together with the on-duty command staff. The Phene admiral detached about 100 ships to strike targets of opportunity among the shipyards. The rest of the fleet has slingshotted around Èrlǐgǎng and are headed on a trajectory that suggests they are aiming to strike COSY. Senior Captain Black of the *Rakhsh* is gathering up survivors at the depot and the shipyards. By most recent comm she has 109 viable ships. I have command of 137 ships. We are engaged in a fighting retreat trying to lay down an obstacle between the Phene and Yǎnshī. They have no heavy frigates, no heavily armored ships except ten dreadnoughts, so they're having trouble breaking through my formation."

"Very good. In the absence of Bahram and Radomir, I'm in command. When I give the order, I want you and your ships to break formation and retreat in disorder toward Yǎnshī and the Troia beacon."

"We're perfectly capable of holding our ground."

"Of course you are. A feigned retreat. You know what purpose it serves. I'll signal you when I want you to break the feint. Do you understand?"

A hefty sigh burred into static. "I execute a feigned disorderly retreat toward Yǎnshī. When you give the order, I reverse and attack."

"Very good, Captain. Await my order."

Hetty pinged her a hailing frequency to Angharad Black, having anticipated her needs the instant Senior Captain Black's name was flagged.

"Angharad, what a day to meet! This is Sun. What's your situation?"

While waiting for the reply she surveyed the grid for other surviving Chaonian ships. "Captain Tan, what happened to the Phene light cruiser that was trying to take on the gunship?"

"Confirmed hits by our javelins. We've stripped their shields. It's returning fire. We have counter shields up. We'll cripple them with a volley from the forward batteries."

"Keep tracking the gunship."

"Yes, Your Highness."

An ensign brought her something to eat. She watched the captain finish the engagement with the light cruiser, a smaller and lighter ship outmatched by the *Boukephalas*.

"Hail from the *Rakhsh*," said the comms officer.

A brassy voice boomed through the comm. "Fuck this shit, Sun. Those fucking Phene came in like fucking locusts and just bombed the fuck out of us."

"Fewer fucks, more info." But Sun's lips quirked up. A swearing Angharad was an Angharad who still had her wits about her, the best tactician and toughest fighter Sun knew besides her mother. "The Phene just conducted a small-scale raid on Chaonia with four gunships outfitted with beacon drives and carrying a Rider. The surviving gunship from that raid is in Molossia System now—"

"Engines of the light cruiser now disabled," said the captain to his bridge crew. "Hit their weapons systems, and leave it behind."

Sun nodded to acknowledge the action and went back to Angharad. "We must stop the hostiles from dropping through the Troia beacon. Anas is using a feigned retreat to draw the Phene after him. I'm pulling in as many ships as can fight to form up with me. We will harass the rear of the Phene fleet with hit-and-fade attacks. They're a raiding fleet, mostly lightly armored ships. So I need you to make directly for Yǎnshī on a trajectory that avoids the Phene but which will get you there before they do. Burn as hot as you can."

While waiting for Angharad's answer Sun tracked the trajectory of the battle.

The NCOS in orbit around Pánlóngchéng had vented fully, the first victim of the bold assault. Commander Baber's ships collected from that region headed for the meet point she'd indicated.

Repair and rescue boats were lifting from the surface of Èrlǐgǎng en route to the orbital shipyards. Wreckage from the munitions depot drifted past mute sensors untouched by the attack. A breached lifeboat winked red as it began to fall into the planet's gravity.

Angharad's ragtag fleet accelerated at hard burn for Yǎnshī, while the ships under the command of Anas Samtarras had broken into a disorderly retreat in front of the advancing Phene fleet.

Closer at hand, the light cruiser drifted, its engines drafted. It fired one last volley in a final act of defiance, which the *Boukephalas*'s active defense systems easily swatted out of the heavens. Then it fell behind them, its heat fading as internal systems failed and shut down.

The Phene gunship was still closing with the light cruiser, but the gunship would soon realize it was stranded and outmaneuvered. Its commander would have to make a decision about which way to run. Their options were limited.

At some point a medical officer cycled back through, handing out more stimulants as the hours flashed past and the minutes dragged on.

Hetty updated the list of available ships and weaponry as stragglers sent in hopeful messages, waiting for orders in the increasingly chaotic situation. Senior Captain Tan capably fielded all the queries Sun didn't need to hear.

The Chaonia beacon, now far behind them, flashed. One by one a quick reaction force of seven fast frigates, two courier ships, and a single heavy cruiser slid in-system from Chaonia. Comms lit up as the beacon's control node sent out its distress call to the new arrivals. One of the fast courier ships pitched on its axis after it took on the most current information and made ready to drop back to Chaonia to deliver the news to the queen-marshal and her military.

"This will not go unanswered," said Sun, looking at Alika.

He was recording everything, creating a narrative, making sure she got the credit she deserved for being the first to understand the scope of the enemy's audacious offensive. Together they'd make sure no one in the republic would ever listen to Moira Lee's slurs about her and her father's ancestry ever again.

If they survived this battle.

34

The Wily Persephone's Face Is Going to Burn Off— In Fact, It Would Be Better If It Did

"No," says Tiana. "You absolutely will not return to Lee House wearing blood- and smoke-stained clothing that makes you look like you just came off shift from a black market slaughterhouse in Camp Nine on Tjeker."

We're on the royal aircar, hiding in a lavatory with our duffels. How Tiana has managed to keep the duffels with her this entire time I don't know, but it's an impressive display of efficiency under fire.

"I want them to see what the cadets at CeDCA sacrificed." I keep flashing on the train cars ripped off the tracks, the smoking wing, the shattered gull. It's somebody's fault, and I want them to pay.

"Solomon can represent the heroism of the citizen cadets in his blood- and dirt-stained uniform." She touches her elbow to my arm like a nudge of conscience. "He's a better representative of CeDCA anyway, don't you think, Your Honorableness?"

"Ouch. That stung."

"I'm not lying."

Clothing appropriate to a scion of Lee House sits neatly folded on top of my duffel, a skin I have to put on. "I liked being Persephone Lǐ."

"But you never really were her, were you?"

I glance around the lavatory with its tunable wall, a cushioned bench, side-by-side sinks, a shower stall, and a partitioned-off toilet. The tiny chamber isn't visually fancy or loaded with extravagant extras, but no one would mistake it for anything but what it is. It's astounding to think we are flying on the royal aircar with the queen-marshal herself. Or it would be, if I had actually started life as a dirt-poor orphan in possession of nothing but her bundle of grit.

"Anyway," Ti goes on, "if you show up looking like that, Vogue Academy will strip me of my license."

She tunes the wall to mirror mode. Even in the workaday clothing we borrowed from Solomon's family she stands tall and elegant, having given the bland khaki trousers and loose work tunic a stylish look with a midnight-blue silk scarf wrapped as a cummerbund around her waist, and a second scarf, in a contrasting lighter shade of heaven blue, tied as a tignon over her hair. Practical and yet striking. Beside her, I look short, rumpled, and dull.

She shakes out the military trousers and long jacket and runs a de-wrinkler over them as I strip and shower. It takes her far more time to get me dressed properly and my hair into a topknot than it does for her to change into a simple floor-length tunic, slit up each side and worn over silk trousers, and touch up her makeup.

I stare at my face. It's a good face, with a good bone structure. I wonder if I like it because it reminds me so much of my dead sister.

"Do you think I'm a clone?" I ask in a low voice.

"A clone?" She pauses, hands in her hair where she's fastening three silk flowers in a curved vertical line placed to emphasize the pleasing shape of her face. "Oh, that's right. Princess Sun said so, didn't she? She didn't like you at first. She has the personality to say such a thing just to get you riled."

"She didn't know me, and didn't expect me to be assigned to her like that, much less when she is still mourning Percy. But why *that* accusation? It's so random. She meant it, Ti. I have to wonder, how much did my family keep from me when I was growing up?"

"You do look a lot like the eight-times-worthy Ereshkigal Lee. Maybe like the Honorable Manea too, though she's taller and heavier, so it's harder to tell since the only images released of her have been in full wedding garb with her face painted with bridal flowers. What if you are a clone?"

"Clones are illegal in the Republic of Chaonia. That would make me illegal."

"Then your cousin Manea would be illegal too. That being the case, Sun's accusation isn't going to fly with the queen-marshal. It would look as if Sun is doing to Manea what Lee House did to her: challenging her legitimacy."

"The clone issue is yet another question that needs an answer. And I have a lot of questions. Who suborned Solomon to spy on me, and why did they bother? Was Perseus's death an accident, or was it murder? If murder, who did it and why, and were Percy and Duke the targets?"

"Perse, slow down. Take a deep breath."

I go on breathlessly, too well launched to stop now. Because as urgent as these questions are, I keep looping back to Zizou, programmed to attack me even though he doesn't want to. "Where was Prince João getting those Gatoi prisoners from? Everyone knows banner soldiers would rather die than be taken prisoner. Whether it's compulsion or honor it still means they die. So who was supplying him with experimental subjects? And how did Lee House find out about the lab? And why take it over like that? No, wait, that one's easy. Factional infighting to discredit Prince João so Manea's child can get the fast track to the heirship."

She rests a hand on my forearm. Her fingers are warm. "I call that pretty ruthless factional infighting. People were killed. That's even before the Phene raided."

"Of course it's ruthless. Didn't you study Chaonia's history? Or do they censor that part in citizen schools in favor of our glorious heritage? But even so, *even so*, that still leaves the biggest question of all."

The hum of the engine changes key as we begin our descent. I nervously reach back to tug on the complicated topknot, but she slaps my hand away before I can do any lasting damage. She gives herself a last once-over in the mirror before she tunes it back to its opaque setting.

Then she turns to face me. "What's the biggest question?"

"Who betrayed the lab's existence to the Phene? And why?"

"Hey." Solomon raps on the closed door. "We're about to land."

I rest a hand on her forearm. She meets my gaze with a calm assurance I envy.

"Whatever is going on, there's a good chance I'll end up in combat again," I say to her. "You can terminate your contract, no hard feelings."

"I get combat pay, remember?"

"You don't get combat pay when you're dead."

"My family gets my combat pay and a death bonus if I die."

"Are things that desperate for your family?" I realize I don't really know her and can't fathom what drives her.

She examines her left hand, as if expecting to see an answer there, then says pensively, "Yes, things are. I'll tell you sometime. Are we going?"

When I unseal the door Solomon gives me a startled look that shifts to a gape-mouthed stare of utter bedazzlement as he takes in Tiana.

She offers him a heavenly smile. "Might I ask you to be so kind as to carry the two duffels?"

"Uh. Sure."

"Shut your trap or catch wasps, squarehead," I say.

He closes his mouth.

Every head turns as we reenter the main cabin. I pretend not to notice as I seat myself and strap in. They're not looking at me, of course. I'm just a disobedient child being dragged home in disgrace. Their distraction gives me a chance to study Eirene's Companions and their cee-cees and her staff without their noticing. Three of her Companions are seated in the main cabin to guard her physical person and because she likes their company. People want things from the ruler, and her Companions have always had the most precious commodity: access. That's why she trusts them more than anyone else, more even than any of her four consorts.

Sun has offered me that trust.

Sun, who raced away in pursuit of the Phene raiders. Who might be anywhere by now, dead or alive, broken or triumphant. Yet I cannot imagine her broken. My mind can't shape that image or that outcome.

The Companion nearest me is a familiar face, the Honorable Marduk Lee, a cousin down a branch line of Lee House. He leans toward me and murmurs, "Where did you find *her*?"

"Vogue Academy." I fix him with my steeliest glare, which makes a man of his age and experience raise his eyebrows with amusement. "Isn't your cee-cee a graduate of Vogue Academy, Elder Brother?"

"My cee-cee is a military asset," he says congenially, indicating a person about his age who is dozing, mouth slightly open. They're both wearing flight suits without any badge. Companions don't need badges, though I can't help but notice that none of them wear the rings Sun gives to her own people.

His gaze slides back to Tiana. She has folded her hands in her lap and is gazing into the middle distance with the serenity of an awakened one whose presence lights the path for the stumbling masses.

Then he adds, "So you're Moira's other child?"

The question startles me since, as far as I was ever told, my aunt Moira has only the one daughter, Manea. "I'm Perseus's twin."

He pats my forearm without really getting into my personal space. "Ah. Of course you are. That's right. It happened too suddenly."

I realize I haven't thought about Perseus since first getting hit with the news. My brother's passing slotted him into the fog of old memories, when we were children hanging over the railing of a moon bridge to watch the bright koi swim past below. Out of sight into the water of eternity.

The old knot of shame tightens. Did I do enough to protect him, as Resh told me I must before she shipped out to the fleet? Mother always went on and on about how Percy was the weak one. Now I wonder if that's why he was sent to Sun, because it was Mother's way of discarding something unwanted while intending it as an insult to the heir she disliked. Sun cultivated his good qualities and helped him thrive. She did better than I did. She took care of her own.

With a burst of thrust the aircar pulls up and we land. The ramp peels down. Everyone gets up to disembark with the haste of people who have tasks to accomplish in short order. I gesture at Ti and Solomon to stay seated, thinking we'll be conveyed separately to Lee House.

Marduk pauses at the ramp and beckons. "We're all getting off here."

He doesn't wait for my response. The queen-marshal's Companions have better things to do than to usher around hapless honorables who have set foot in the royal palace only twice in their very short lives. Once when Perseus and I turned eleven and he was presented to the heir to become her Companion, and a second time when the entire population of Lee House stood in our white mourning ranks as Channel Idol broadcast the state funeral for Resh.

The palace's architecture is a mystery to me so I hustle after the queen-marshal's entourage. We cross through a garden lush with manicured beds of black peonies, scarlet poppies, and gold chrysanthemums. The entrance into the queen-marshal's inner courtyard is a gate made of two facing tulpars whose wings curve over their heads to form an arch.

It's dusk by now. An inner courtyard with alcoves and paths has been lit in the archaic style, flames burning from wicks set into bowls of oil. The waft of heat and smell of burning hits me with a vivid image of the collapsing sky-tower. My step stutters.

Ti cups a hand under my elbow.

Solomon says, "Perse? You all right?"

People have gathered in the inner courtyard. The air buzzes with chatter about the raid and, spreading like fire, the news of the attacks on Molossia and Aspera. I keep my eyes on the queen-marshal. She pauses to nod at this official and that official and to brush a greeting kiss to the cheek of a Companion before heading into one of the intimate dining rooms. No one stops me as I step over the threshold into a chamber adorned with golden light and a gentle river's flow of music being played by a musician on a sixteen-string zither.

What a lovely tableau greets my eyes! The queen-marshal bends down beside seated Manea and lifts her new consort's hand to her lips for a delicate public kiss. Eirene is a hard woman, a tough soldier, and a ruthless diplomat. But given the way her eyes soften as she smiles down at her bride, I have to grudgingly admit she seems to genuinely care for Manea. That doesn't mean my family didn't encourage the match. That doesn't mean they don't intend to cut out Sun as soon as they can, given rumors of Manea's pregnancy. That doesn't mean they didn't try to goad the queen-marshal to imprison or even kill Sun at the wedding banquet. After all, Lee House runs the Ministry of Security, Punishment, and Corrections. They possess all the tools to make it happen.

It does seem a bit like overreach that they would clumsily attempt to murder Sun with an embargoed weapon that killed Octavian instead. Aunt Moira has always been a cautious manager. She likes to keep her dirty work out of the public eye. Yet at the same time, it's true one of Lee House's responsibilities in the republic is extrajudicial murder, while the queen-marshal looks the other way and pretends she knows nothing about it.

Yet Eirene's drunken rage struck me as unrehearsed and impulsive. It's Lee House I don't trust. Sun showed her military promise at Na Iri. If Lee House waits too long, if she distinguishes herself in a way that can't be ignored, then they'll never be able to discredit her in favor of an infant who will need years to grow up.

Chaonians love a winner. It's what Channel Idol is all about.

A dozen people are seated around a table laden with platters of food. The aroma makes my stomach growl. Aunt Moira registers my presence with such a lack of surprise that clearly someone already informed her I was coming.

Aisa Lee—my mother—looks up and sees me.

"Persephone!" She presses the back of a hand to her forehead, sways alarmingly, and almost tips over her chair, which is caught by an attendant. Then she slumps, closing her eyes as if she has fainted. I know her tricks. She's waiting for me to run over to her to make sure she's all right.

I snag an empty chair beside Aunt Moira and sit down.

Eirene glances at my mother, then at Moira, who gives the queen-marshal a shake of a head. The queen-marshal turns back to Manea, who to her credit hasn't twitched at Mother's embarrassing display.

"Must you go so soon?" Manea asks Eirene in a slightly breathless voice that is one of the most effective forms of flattery I know, and which I never use because I detest it.

"I must. I want you to return to Lee House until I get back. You'll be well guarded there." The queen-marshal is no fool. That's how she survived her rocky ascent to power.

As they murmur a few more inaudible endearments to each other, I load up my plate with 'ulu curry, sesame peanut noodles, and fried squash. I hand that plate back to Tiana for her and Solomon to share and prepare a second for myself, adding green beans sautéed in oil and garlic. While doing so I watch my aunt look over Tiana and Solomon, but there's nothing suspicious in the way she marks and dismisses them as hired hands. If I had to guess, I'd say she's never seen Solomon before and has no idea who he is or that he's anyone at all.

"What are you doing here, Persephone?" Moira asks. "You're supposed to be with Princess Sun."

"She got rid of me. Why did you blackmail someone to spy on me at the academy?"

"Why would we need to spy on you when we knew where you were?"

"You didn't know where I was!" My voice squeaks horribly, cracked by indignation.

"Don't be naïve, Persephone. It doesn't suit a child of Lee House."

I planned so carefully! Covered my tracks!

She leans a little away from me, as if I have begun to exude an unpleasant odor. "Oh dear. You didn't really think you'd concealed yourself at CeDCA, did you? My goodness, Persephone. I thought you the cleverest of the children, and now I fear you are just the most egotistical."

Mother's eyes crack open to check why no one has come to her rescue. She tries a new gambit. "My precious Persephone! Come give your old mother a kiss. Or are you ashamed of me? Is that why you ran away?"

"Where is Father?" I break in, because I *am* ashamed of her. It's even worse with Ti and Solomon here to witness.

Mother begins sobbing, covering her face with her hands to disguise the crocodile tears meant purely to manipulate us.

"Manea, could you be a darling and take your aunt home?" says Moira in the steadiest of voices. "You know how her nerves are. Then you can get everything settled as you wish."

To my surprise Manea rises, makes a composed farewell to the queen-marshal, and, with an unexpected display of soothing patience, guides my weeping mother out of the room. She is followed by the other household guests and all but three of the attendants: one gray-haired man remains behind with Ti and Solomon. Even the musician hastens out, leaving her zither behind on its stand.

"Perseus's death hit your mother hard," says Moira to me.

"Oh, please, don't pretend she didn't despise Percy. I'm sure she's just upset because she can no longer leverage social invitations on the strength of him being one of the heir's Companions."

"You have a heart like your father's," remarks Moira as she sips from a cup of tea.

Anger goads me on. "My father? Is he—"

I break off, remembering I am on assignment for Sun. It takes me a moment to compose myself by imagining I am back at the academy preparing for inspection: rack tidy, uniform neat and clean, standing at attention with arms at my side.

"Is he . . . ?" Moira prompts. The corner of her mouth twitches. She's enjoying my discomfort and anger.

In a cool tone I say, "I thought he would be here too, given the honor shown to Lee House by Manea's marriage."

"He had work to complete and means to join us later. We'll

have to see him at Lee House." She rises. "Eirene, is there anything else I can do for you or the fleet?"

Eirene breaks off from a communication she's been receiving while she picks through the squash, beans, and 'ulu left behind on Manea's plate. "Zàofù will have the list. Can you find Aloysius for me?"

It takes me a moment to recall that Aloysius is Baron Voy.

"I lost track of him at the wedding banquet, and he hasn't been back to his suite in the palace," Eirene goes on. "I know he was intending to move full-time to his compound at Sublime Point. Perhaps he's in transit, although it's odd he's not answering my ping."

"Why is he needed now?" Moira asks with the prim disapproval that seems to be her preferred expression.

"I need him to convey to the Yele League my extreme displeasure at the news that Admiral Manu has defected to the Phene."

"I thought the defection was just a rumor."

"There was a confirmed sighting on Hellion Terminus seven months ago. It's taken this long to reach us by back channels. Although I find it strange it would be confirmed exactly when the Phene make a major surprise attack."

The queen-marshal for the first time looks directly at me. I can't say I like being the focus of her interest, the way her organic eye examines me in the flesh while her obsidian eye measures me by some metric I can't see.

"So you hid this one for five years at CeDCA. That's very good optics. A real citizen soldier, with street credibility. Well executed, Moira."

"It would have played out better had Perseus not died," says Moira.

"Is there any more news on the investigation?" the queen-marshal asks.

"Father told me his death was an accident," I break in.

Both women stare at me, surprised I am discourteous enough to interrupt, then exchange a glance with each other. Even though Moira was required to give up her position as Eirene's Companion, it's clear the two still trust each other. I've forgotten how deeply these connections run, because I stepped away for so long. Because I worked so hard to pretend I wasn't part of them.

But Ti is right. I was never Persephone Lī. I just played her as would an actor on Channel Idol, and I probably got all the details wrong.

"You and I will discuss that issue later," says Moira to me.

She and Eirene give each other a kiss on the cheek, the kiss of trust and reciprocal loyalty. Moira Lee may have tried to shame and insult Sun to ensure her unborn grandchild's future standing at court, but I would swear on my eight-times-worthy sister's honor that my aunt is a loyal Chaonian and not a traitor serving the Phene.

The queen-marshal leaves.

Moira snaps her fingers. "Come, Persephone."

The inner courtyard has cleared of people. Everyone has a job to do now that the queen-marshal is riding to war. The five of us make our way at a brisk walk toward a secondary landing field. Moira and I walk three paces ahead.

"I know you took over the lab to discredit Princess Sun and her father," I say. "But who betrayed the lab to the Phene? That's treason."

"So it is. It's possible Prince João betrayed us when he realized he'd been found out. We never discovered where he was hiding, although he emerged as soon as he had Eirene in his sights. She's always had a weakness for his . . . personality."

"Why would he betray his own research to the Phene? Him being complicit doesn't make sense. I reject it as an explanation. You know what I want to know?"

"I don't, but I sense you are about to tell me."

Rack tidy; uniform neat and clean. "How did *you* find out about the lab?"

"Manea has a gift for pillow talk."

I laugh. I've underestimated my cousin, a girl I neither liked nor disliked growing up. She was so different from me I never knew what to say to her, and so we weren't close even though we grew up in the same compound.

"Why is that funny?" Moira demands, bristling.

I glance back. Ti winks at me with a smile surely powerful enough to drag secrets out of the most laconic mouth.

"I thought the answer would have more to do with skullduggery and surveillance and less with sex," I answer.

Moira's not a smiler, and she doesn't smile now, but her eyes wrinkle up. "You of all people should know better. How many lovers did you have at the academy? That one, I must say . . . Jade Kim, is that the name? Incredibly gorgeous."

My face is going to burn off. In fact, it would be better if it did.

Solomon chokes down a laugh. I flash him a glare deadlier than serpents' venom, but it has absolutely no effect on his smug amusement. Tiana wears the blandest mask imaginable, while Moira's gray-haired attendant looks bored.

"I never told anybody anything secret!" I protest, losing hold of my composure.

"No, it seems you didn't, because no rumor of your presence there ever kissed the lips of Channel Idol. I kept expecting the gossip to hit, but it never did. Impressive self-control, in that department at least."

She's needling me, and as much as I want to like her for it, I don't hear any affection in her voice. Resh offered me warmth and security, which is the reason I grew up knowing what love feels like.

We reach the landing field. A Swallow awaits us. Is it the same one that was sent for me? Its factory-issue voice has a fresh sheen of eagerness.

"Peace be upon you, welcome, and please be seated. Welcome, Moira Lee. Welcome, Persephone Lee. Welcome, Putra Sì Almari. Welcome, Tiana Yáo Alaksu." The voice ceases in a whir of distress as the ship tries to identify Solomon in reference to its current registry.

"His name is squarehead," I say, because I'm still furious at him.

But if it wasn't my parents and Moira who used him to spy on me, then who was it? And why? Why would anyone care about the disobedient daughter who thought she'd run away but really hadn't run away at all?

Ti takes the duffels from Solomon and stows them into the lockers, then takes a seat beside Solomon, who is staring around trying not to look out of his league. Putra Sì Almari takes the pilot controls, while my aunt sits in the copilot's seat. I wedge into the navigator's chair. The hatch seals. As we wait for our turn in the queue, aircars lift off around us as officials and officers head for new assignments, rearguard security posts, and the front.

Where is Sun now?

"Is there any news from Molossia?" I ask, then remember that James broke the lock on my net access. I do a quick trawl, but I don't have high-end military clearance, and news of the crisis is being censored.

In fact, Channel Idol has started its Idol Faire coverage as if no crisis is going on at all. The first round's entries are flooding in: Ji-Na the smiling ribbon dancer, odds-on favorite to win this year's event; a family of cousins doing acrobatics in the ancient theatrical tradition of the One Hundred Skills; an extremr attempting a sixteen-second exposure to vacuum; an all-terrain race between teams of raptor riders across the badlands of Thesprotis Terce. Seeing the cheery ads and hearing the *chirp, chirp* commentary of the announcers hits me like whiplash. In my mind, an image of the dead cadet in the lab darkens my vision: the way the blood pooled in viscous crimson around his elbow; a lock of his long black hair come loose from the regulation bun to stick to his bare neck.

The Swallow takes flight, the pressure jolting me out of the memory. I must focus. We stay low for the flight across the bay. It's a windless day, and the water gleams, a window into another world. The shadowy bulk of a charybdis swims deep beneath the surface like the family secrets that have been hidden from me.

"Aunt Moira, I'm a legal adult now. I have the right to the highest security access of Lee House."

"I'll grant you access to the basic security grid once we reach Lee House."

In my lifetime Moira has always run Lee House although she is the youngest of the three sisters. It was always understood my mother isn't fit for the duty. I've never sat alone with my aunt in all my life—as alone as this is, with three people attending us—and in the world of the Core Houses it's almost the same thing. After five years I'm finally ready to ask the question I only whispered to Resh, who told me we must not question the burden we'd been given.

"Why is my mother the way she is?"

Moira gives me a candid look. "I don't know. The behavior started when she was a girl. She can only see other people in reference to how they make her feel. It's a narcissism we could never eradicate. When she brought back your father after a trip to Yele we thought he might stabilize her. In his own way he does, mostly by overseeing the supervisory post we've given her. He keeps her division running smoothly. That keeps her occupied so I can oversee the ministry without her interference."

"She brought him back from Yele? It wasn't a match arranged by the family?"

"With the seers of Iros, that dubious sect? Hardly. We vetted him before we allowed the legal binding. Well, to be accurate, Nona vetted him, and Nona allowed it."

My aunt Nona, murdered by terrorists according to what I was taught. A war criminal responsible for the slaughter of unarmed refugees as well as being my progenitor, according to Sun.

"I was against allowing Kiran into Lee House, even with the obvious benefit to us in having a seer of Iros to conduct interrogations. Your father is not a nice man, Persephone. He's Yele through and through. Arrogant, contemptuous, and aloof."

"At least he's always been honest with me."

"If that's meant to be a dart to prick me, know I have very thick Chaonian skin. As do you, Persephone, and never forget it. We do no favors to our republic by bringing in these foreigners to dilute our strength."

But her comments run right off me as my thoughts keep circling back to what Sun said. Am I a clone of Aunt Nona? Is Manea? Was Resh? This is not the right time to ask Aunt Moira such an explosive question. Anyway, we have bigger problems.

"Where is my father? Why wasn't he at the royal palace?" I ping him.

"He should be answering," says Moira. "He's at Lee House."

Neither of us receive an answer.

35

In Which the Wily Persephone Is Ready to Move Fast If Need Be

We put down outside the family hangar. Kadmos is waiting. When he sees Tiana and the duffels the two exchange a complicit smile as at a job well done. When he sees Solomon his eyes narrow. He shakes off whatever he's thinking and turns to address me.

"The Honored Consort Manea let me know you have returned to us, Honored Persephone."

"She did? I'm surprised she would have bothered."

In the low voice he uses when he means to admonish without scolding, Kadmos says, "The Honored Manea has the gift of thoughtfulness."

"There's a trait," mutters Solomon.

I flash a rude gesture at him, and his answering grin is all taunt and teeth. At that instant I forgive him. Holding on to my grudge isn't worth it. In this world we can't afford to lose the companions who have our backs. Everyone makes mistakes; everyone succumbs to pressures, many of which are out of their control. What matters is whether he would stab me in the back. I believe him when he says he never told more than the most mundane details. The question then becomes: Why did his blackmailer only want mundane details about my life?

"Persephone?" Aunt Moira has already walked on. She pauses at a round gate. "You'll come with me. Kadmos can see your people are taken to the proper venue."

I ping Kadmos on the school net with my  only to have the message bounce back. I've been kicked off the school net at some point in the last seventy-two hours. Sun's ring vibrates gently against my skin. A ping from Tiana drops in.

LET ME KNOW HOW TO PROCEED.

I ping back: HOLD FOR NOW. BE READY TO MOVE FAST.
I do a quick broadcast ping to the entire ring. ANYONE THERE?
In any other network I'd get back an off-line signal for people who had dropped through a beacon, which naturally cuts them off from any intrasystem net given the vast interstellar distances leaped by the beacons.

The ring says: WAITING FOR CONTACT.
Years or decades from now, if we're still alive, will the ping have worked its slow route across space to reach them?

In silence my aunt and I walk through the family garden and past the dining gazebo and two beautifully decorated salons where friends may gather for an evening of music and poetry contests. A ping on the ring network startles me, because I was sure Sun took everyone else with her.

CANDACE REPORTING. IS THIS PERSEPHONE LEE?

HOW ARE YOU???

BROKEN LEG, A BRUISED SPLEEN, AND HEMATOMAS. I'LL
HEAL. MEANWHILE ALIKA HAS DROPPED A BIG ASSIGNMENT
INTO MY IMMOBILE LAP. BY THE BY MINH SAYS WHAT HEY.
SHE SAYS TO TELL YOU SHE TOLD ME YOU'RE FUN WHEN YOU
WANT TO BE & ONLY OCCASIONALLY A SACK OF DICKS.

LATER, I ping back, feeling unexpectedly warm and supported.
BE READY TO MOVE. YOU CAN TRUST MINH, AY, AND IKENNA.
"What are you smiling about?" Moira asks.
"Just happy to be home."
"I don't need to be a seer of Iros to know that's a lie."
She leads me upstairs to the inner compound's barrier wall.

We stand at a railing looking over the interior lagoon. Fish flash around bright coral. The sunlight soothes my face, and a lazy breeze cools me with its salty kiss. The fine white sand of what we all call the baby beach beckons with its shallow swimming area netted off from the main lagoon.

Moira says, "You never liked it here. I could never understand why. I thought you had what it took to be named as next governor of Lee House, to take my place in time."

"You had Resh for that. She was the obedient daughter."

"How poorly you understood her. She was the worst rebel of all. Her recklessness contaminated you and even Manea, I'm sorry to say."

"Reckless? Resh was the least reckless person I know."

"*Pff.* You were too young to see her for what she was. Ereshkigal's act of heroism was an act of suicide that shouldn't have worked."

"That's not true!" My hands clench. I want to punch her, but I breathe myself down.

"Let's not debate her death now. It served Lee House well enough at the time."

"Her death served you well? Is that how you think of it?"

"You took it too hard, Persephone. You went to CeDCA because you thought such a journey took you closer to her, but she has waited here for you all along."

She's chosen this balcony because of its proximity to our household altar. We descend a spiral staircase to the room where we keep images and remembrances of Lee House ancestors alongside bronze spirit tablets. Since Perseus's tablet will go to the palace, that means Resh's is the most recent. I wonder if anyone has figured out that the one here is a forgery, because I took the real one when I left five years ago.

Moira dutifully lights a stick of incense and steps aside so I can light one as well. The scent tickles my nostrils, a reminder of the respect we owe to our ancestors and the virtues we should cultivate in ourselves.

As for Moira, she wants something from me. It's why she brought me here.

"You said you would give me access to the security grid," I say.

"Yes. This way."

We descend past the family quarters into an underground level, past two security gates, and to a chamber where lesser scions of Lee House work at consoles and monitor surveillance screens. These people belong to branch lineages, and I realize that Moira might be desperate. The gamble with Manea marrying Eirene means I am the last child of the three sisters' direct line who can take over the governorship. If I don't, my refusal will trigger a war among the secondary branches. The winner will be elevated to the place Moira now holds. It happens in every Core House at intervals. If I recall my gossip correctly, it's how Alika's branch of Vata House got exiled to a grim posting on a terminus system two generations ago: they lost a takeover bid.

Moira leads me into an even more private room. A security officer stands as we enter and, at a nod from her, leaves us alone. The door seals behind him.

"Sit. Put both hands on the surface. Look directly into the aperture. I know you bought a retinal adaptor and got a palm print seal to alter your signature, so the old one we have on file for you isn't sufficient."

I do as she says and let the console imprint me. When it finishes it blinks green.

I say, to test it: "Locate Kiran Seth de Lee."

A message flashes into my net: Kiran Seth de Lee is resting in his private chamber under privacy filter.

According to its timeline he has been there for eleven hours.

"That's not right," says my aunt with a frown. "I spoke to him eight hours ago. He was going to finish the interrogation of the company representative from the firm on Molossia who did maintenance on the tender."

"The tender?"

"The tender . . . the little boat attached to the yacht. Perseus and his cee-cee died when its engine exploded."

"Then why did my father say it was an accident?"

"That's the official line and will remain so until we have proof it was rigged to malfunction."

She blithely overrides the privacy filter to my father's personal rooms. Cameras sweep through the suite, investigating every nook and cranny of its three sparsely decorated rooms.

He's not there.

Her eyelids flicker. Her lips press together, and she makes a noise in her throat like a growl of annoyance. The image shifts to my mother's suite. Its gaudy décor assaults the senses: too much gold, too many sparkles, too many drapes. Mother is reclined on a couch, arms limp at her side, head tilted back. Manea sits beside her patiently dabbing her forehead with a damp cloth and murmuring platitudes as Mother sucks in tremulous breaths and lets them out in shaky wails. The sound is unbelievably grating. I wish I could find something to like in her, but I can't, although I'm impressed by Manea's fortitude.

There's no sign of my father in her rooms.

Aunt Moira is looking quite disgruntled.

"Where else could he be?" I ask. But I'm already formulating a theory. Transportation systems link up in logical ways if they're well built. The links between this series of events and their lacunae is starting to make an ugly kind of sense to me.

"Come with me." It's a command, not a request.

We leave the office and descend through two sealed doors and down a long flight of stairs to the deepest security level, where Moira uses a retinal scan to unlock a final door. As I cross the threshold, Sun's ring network cuts out.

A surveillance walkway overlooks twelve cells that are sheersided pits. Seven are lit red, unoccupied, while five are green. It's here the family meant to confine Sun. Three of the prisoners are sleeping. A fourth crouches by a waste bucket, licking feces off his left hand.

I recoil. "What did you do to him?"

She doesn't answer, doesn't even pause, but at the adjacent cell she halts to look down.

"That asshole," she murmurs.

The asshole in question is reclined comfortably on a cot, engrossed in reading a paper book and looking entirely too relaxed. I have no idea what the prisoner is confined here for—they might be an innocent political prisoner or a vile mass-murdering traitor for all I know—but I admire their insouciance.

At the end of the walkway there's a thirteenth chamber, larger than the others, with a baffle of mirrors to bring sunlight into its pit. The walls currently display a landscape of towering horsetail trees swaying in the wind. There's a shelf with a rolled-up futon, a sling-back chair, and a fold-down table laden with a tray on which sit a bowl, cup, and spoon. Metal glints in the shadows: a mechanical has been dismembered and spread out, gears and pistons arranged in a spray like a fractal, oddly unnerving.

A person whose age I can't determine is seated in the pool of light rolling a toy van back and forth, in and out of shadow, gauging the line between light and dark. The prisoner is humming, but I don't know the tune.

"Kiran isn't here either," says Moira. "He spends more time with her than anyone else does."

"He spends time? Like hanging-out time? Interacting time?" He rarely spent time with me!

Moira is too distracted to register my peevish tone or the gist of my words. "He can often coax fragments of sense from her."

"Who is she?"

Her frown darkens as she studies the woman's round, pallid face and its odd lack of expression. "Your cousin. My firstborn."

"Your *firstborn*?"

"Born three years before Ereshkigal."

"I . . . I didn't even know . . . I thought Manea was your only child." I lean against the wall to steady myself. "Why in the Eighteen Hells do you hide her down here? That's grotesque!"

"It's for her safety." She speaks flatly, but her eyes are haunted.

"What does that even mean? You don't lock people up to keep them safe."

"She has a rare illness brought on by the beacons. Your Aunt Nona's only child had it too. That child died before its first birthday."

All my life the household altar has included the spirit tablet for my eldest cousin, born years before Resh, a ghost at the table. I'm reeling from the revelation that there's a cousin I've never known existed. How do people keep secrets like that?

Moira goes on. "Your mother had several miscarriages before Ereshkigal. So did I. So did Nona. Any weakness in a ruling line will be attacked by rivals from within and without. We raised you children to do your duty, did we not?"

I cannot close my mouth, which is popped open in utter shock. "I . . . I . . ."

"Always 'I' with you, isn't it, Persephone? Let's go. Your father's not here."

My father. The hells! Time is ticking, and I have a job to do. One thing at a time. This locked family closet I must deal with later. "Take me to a console that allows me to access visual records."

"We'll go back to my office."

I race up the stairs, a mere 178 steps, and then have to wait at the sealed door because Moira gets winded before she reaches the top.

"You're fit," she says grudgingly as she pants up beside me.

"You could give me the codes."

"It's early days for that, don't you think?"

When we reach the office I triangulate a search of the external walls of the Lee House compound on the day of the wedding banquet. It looks pretty damning, what with lines of armed guards taking potshots at the boats we are fleeing in. When I find the segment I'm looking for it's obvious Navah is signaling with her bracelets to someone on the wall.

"Where did Hestia Hope's cee-cee come from? Her name was Navah."

"Was?"

"She's dead. Where did she come from?"

Moira sniffs. "She came from Yele with the Honorable Hestia

Hope. Hestia is half Yele, you know. Her Yele father is an obscure scholar of linguistics. So Yele of him. Studying meaningless minutiae as if such things matter just because they belong to the forgotten languages of the Celestial Empire. But those Yele always walk around like we lesser beings ought to be grateful they bother to speak to us, much less share their exalted philosophy and scholarship with us impoverished ignorant souls."

"She was a spy."

"Hestia? I would be delighted to get proof of that, if you have it!"

"No, not Hetty! If you think that, then you're . . ." Bigoted, but this isn't the time to launch that argument with my aunt. "You'd be a fool to think Hestia is anything except Sun's most loyal Companion. I meant Navah. The cee-cee."

"Princess Sun favors Hestia Hope too much. There are rumors the two are lovers. Companions are never meant to be lovers. Sex does nothing but complicate the pure and trustworthy bonds of friendship."

There's such a sour edge to her tone that I look at her in surprise, wondering what I'm missing. She shoots me a dagger's glance.

"Was Navah spying for you?" I say with a smirk, pleased to have gotten under her skin even if I don't know quite what set her off.

"For Lee House? Of course not. We don't hire or allow foreigners to work here."

"The queen-marshal lost her temper *at* the banquet. But lost tempers cool. Did you try to kill Sun after we left the banquet?"

"Kill her? As tempting as that might be, such a drastic action would backfire on us. Sun was well on her way to undermining her own position with her reckless temper. Our plan was to imprison her and let Channel Idol spill gossip to poison her reputation."

"How nice. Well, as it happens, someone tried to kill her as we were fleeing Lee House."

In a defensive tone Moira says, "The guards were only using stun guns and beanbag projectiles."

"Uh-huh," I say. "Except for the late bloomer."

Her chin comes up sharply. "What are you talking about?"

"Someone shot her bodyguard, Octavian, using a late bloomer. I believe they were aiming for Sun."

She touches the wall to steady herself, then sits, gaze flat. "A late bloomer," she mutters. "Persephone, how could you possibly think we would use such technology?"

"Oh come on, Aunt Moira. You're concealing your own child as a prisoner in your deepest dungeon. Don't pretend you're not capable of it. Manea is pregnant. You want her child to be heir instead of Sun."

"And why wouldn't I? A true Chaonian—"

"A clone's progeny!"

Moira slaps me. "Who said that?"

My cheek smarts, but my heart is clean and strong. "Zizou is the proof."

"Who is Zizou?"

This is too much, too soon. I need ammunition in reserve. So I change tactics. "Never mind. I didn't mean anything by it, just getting a rise out of you."

"How like your mother," Moira says, trying to get a rise out of me, but I'm too busy clicking layers of facial recognition over the security people who were running along the walls and shooting at us. It doesn't surprise me when I get a match.

My father was supposedly secluded in mourning with my mother. Instead, he stands on the wall-walk imperfectly disguised in a spruce-green Lee House gendarme uniform with a hood pulled tight around his face. He sights a weapon on the boat I am steering.

The surge of pure visceral loathing is almost like triumph. Her, who bullied Percy mercilessly until he was saved by being sent to court. Him, for letting her do it because he cared more about his agenda than his children. One pulls the trigger while the other covers it up.

In my calmest tone I say, "Who else knew about the lab's existence?"

"Why are you still on about the lab? Manea told me, of course, and . . ." She breaks off, seeing Kiran's face on the screen.

"Aunt Moira, who did you tell?"

"I told Aisa," she mutters in a harsh voice.

"She would have told my father. Did it ever occur to any of you that my father might be an anti-Chaonian Yele agent who'd found the perfect way to worm himself into Chaonia's secretest ministry—as a marriage partner? Was my aunt Nona that stupid? Just because my mother is out of control and you thought it made your lives easier to have someone else around to manage her?"

"You have no idea how much worse Aisa was before Kiran." Moira's already starting to tap on the console's input pad, calling up information I can't see. Her lips are pressed as tight as if she's choking down a gush of catastrophes. "The seers of Iros belong to a religious order. They are apolitical."

"Sure."

Her expression closes into taut concentration as she hammers through the information pouring into her feed. "Aloysius Voy has always counseled accommodation."

I'm feeling pretty damn vindicated. "Sure, there's a whole contingent of Yele politicals and philosophers who counsel alliance with us. But there's always been that other contingent who hate us, hate the queen-marshal, and hate everything we are. Don't you see the connections? Two botched murder attempts on Sun. The Phene raid on the lab. A surprise attack on our forward positions in Aspera System. And who knows what else is coming down the pike?"

I jump forward to today's visuals. First I search the boat hangar—all boats accounted for, and according to records nothing has been taken out in the last day, not even by maintenance. I drop in an algorithm to scan through the visual feed to make sure there's no footage missing, but I'm betting against the boat. My father has never liked the sea.

Moira says, "He didn't take an aircar. All are here."

"Did you check for a glitch in the time stamps?"

"Goodness, Persephone, that would surely never have occurred to me after all my years of experience."

Her sarcasm rolls right off me as I find what I'm looking for. A cargo train left seven and a half hours ago. I don't bother to check our end. He'll have managed a simple workaround to get on without being seen. The line ends at our dedicated transit warehouse just outside the military spaceport that keeps the queen-marshal and her high officials able to head into action at speed.

Scanning the operator logs I count twelve stevedores and twenty mechanicals who unload, service, and load the train. At the end of the one-hour turnaround, thirteen stevedores depart the train. One splits off from the break room to go to a lavatory, then departs the warehouse to the street. Facial recognition isn't giving me a match, but he'll have ways around that.

At first I think the wandering stevedore is going to transfer through the security gate to the military side where a Lee House shuttle sits in a hangar. Instead, wearing workaday clothing and with a hoodie pulled up over his head, the figure walks briskly out of the warehouse compound. I lose sight of him. When he doesn't appear at the nearest station I panic, then trawl the next three adjacent stations and finally find him because I recognize his posture and stride. After that it's easy to follow him through the train lines, even when he reverses direction and changes clothing. I know this system like I know my own heart. Although maybe that isn't the best metaphor.

When I realize where he's headed I sink back with a kick of triumph. "Five Prosperities Station."

Five Prosperities Station connects to the single civilian spaceport on the outskirts of Argos, which is tasked for high-value deliveries and time-dependent foreign or business delegations that aren't being escorted in via military courier. Everything else goes up and down by space elevator.

Moira exhales sharply as she reads her virtual screen. "The commercial vessel *Weak Execution* captained by a Toby Cheek departed Reliable Winds Spaceport fifteen minutes after what appears to be Kiran's arrival there. It latched onto a Remora freighter, which made a routine scheduled transit drop through the Molossia beacon less than an hour before the Phene raid on the industrial park."

"Baron Voy seems to have gone missing too. Do you think he's on that courier?"

"Never trust a Yele bearing gifts." She stares at the console for fifteen seconds, although it seems an eternity. "Persephone, I have to lock down Lee House. We've been compromised. Only I as the governor have the authority to do a complete reboot. You go at once to Eirene with this information. Tell her in person. Preface your briefing with the phrase 'frost on the ground' so she'll know it comes from me."

"Sun guessed," I say.

My aunt isn't listening as she loads her report onto a hornet drive, the kind that will sting any unauthorized user, and hands it to me.

"Eirene's shuttle leaves in fifteen minutes. Chaonia's security is in your hands."

36

A DISPATCH FROM THE ENEMY

Dear Mom,

I don't want to die, and you don't want me dead, I know that. But please promise me that if I do die you will release your repro-lock and have the second child you always wanted. Find a nice person, like the mechanic at Tranquility Harbor, because he totally has a thing for you even if you pretend not to notice. I bet he'd be an involved parent. His sisters always made me welcome at their table. I guess if I'm being honest I'd have to admit how much I always wanted a sibling. I'm so grateful for my rackmates here, Cricket, Deadstick, and Splash (I can't tell you their real names). They have become friends, and they have my back.

Don't forget to lay an offering for me at the altar of Saint Arthas the Cursebearer. I hope I have lived up to your dedication of me to the Path of Arthas, but if I'm being honest I'm not dying for the homeland. The thing is, I will never let the other lancers down. Please stay safe, and don't mourn me too much.

Suited, sealed in, and tubed up, Apama sat in her lancer as the *Strong Bull* jolted from an unknown hit. The silence drew taut as they waited. Sometimes pilots died when they were crushed, suffocated, or burned alive in the launch tube. Before her thoughts could fall into that horrorscape, the private internal comm crackled.

Delfina cleared her throat. "You don't have to answer, but *do* you have some weird secret in your past? I didn't ask before because I didn't want to seem rude, but we could be dead in five seconds and I'm really curious."

Apama was grateful for a distraction. "You mean, why did I get this assignment right out of flight school with no combat experience, unlike every other lancer pilot on this ship? Why did the fleet wait three days for me before launching?"

"You have to admit it is odd, even with your great scores."

"I honestly don't know. Like I told you, my mom's people were grunt shipyard workers. When she was sixteen that big accident happened at Tranquility Harbor. All her family was killed, so she had to strike out on her own—"

The ship jolted again, throwing Apama so hard sideways her shoulder smacked the side of the cockpit.

Voice tight, Delfina said, "You think we're ever going to be launched?"

Under stress Apama's mind became suffused with an icy clarity. "I hope so. I'd rather die fighting."

The command comm crackled in tandem with a triple burst of bell tones, the alert for launch. Tower chimed in, "Heads up, Maces. We've got a debris field right as you launch. But don't worry, it's all former bad guys."

"Dyusme," breathed Delfina. The readout for her pulse quickened as her adrenaline surged.

Apama's whole body tensed, so she took in a five-count inhalation through her nose, held it for a five count, exhaled on a five count through barely parted lips, and held her lungs empty for another five before starting again. She'd practiced this calming exercise so many times. *So. Many. Times.*

Mom had worked hard to pay for her schooling, to give her this chance.

I will not let you down.

"Mace Sixteen, you are fourth in line to launch."

Telemetry bloomed within the membrane that sealed her into the lancer, giving her an operational sphere of view onto surrounding space. The Phene assault fleet had swung around the third planet and was now racing toward the second planet and the beacon through which they'd exit into Troia System. Jewel colors represented the escort groups that accompanied the high admiral's flagship, a behemoth named *Choki's Beauty*. The fleet moved in a disciplined formation like a school of armored and armed fish in a dark ocean. Two scattered groups of Chaonian ships seethed at the edges of the Phene fleet, one retreating in disorder and the other an undisciplined pack nipping at the fleet's wake.

A garnet gleam marked the *Strong Bull*, which with her escort of light cruisers was holding a rearguard position together with her twin dreadnought, the *Steadfast Lion*. The Chaonian ships in pursuit were mostly frigates and corvettes, but they were persistent enough that the *Bull*'s captain had sent out the lancers to slow down the harrying. The reds, blues, greens, and yellows designating each individual lancer in the *Bull*'s flights had scattered like chaff on a solar wind. It sure didn't look to Apama as if there were sixty dots remaining. They'd been told the engagement in Molossia System was meant to be the easy part of the double-pronged attack, for the lancers, at least.

Had the high admiral miscalculated the speed and ferocity of the Chaonian response? Yet as the ancient sages said, no plan survives contact with the enemy.

The tube clunked, rolling them halfway over.

"Mace Sixteen, you are go."

They were kicked free and released into space agleam with ships on the move.

They slid straight into debris.

"Evade!" Delfina's voice blasted in tandem with the bleat of the collision alarm.

"None of this can puncture us. Let's use the cover to get a look round." Apama manually switched off the collision alarm to blessed silence.

They reported in to Mace leader. The debris had separated them from the rest of their flight.

"Do you see the ship this debris came from?" Apama asked.

"Saints protect us, that's one of our own." Delfina's whisper was so faint Apama barely heard it above her own ragged breathing.

A suited lancer pilot, torn membrane melted half away, tumbled past like an acrobat in a low-g spectacle.

"We are all destined for death," Apama murmured. Her throat felt choked, but she swallowed and shook it off.

A bulkhead heaved into view from the direction Apama had labeled zenith. As the damaged hulk of one of their own light cruisers passed, a few red lights blinked deep within jagged gouges where life-control systems were struggling to survive.

"Looks like it took two direct hits to the drive compartments," said Apama.

The light cruiser's debris cloud enveloped them, objects thunking into their shield as the lancer shuddered and shook. They spun and wove an evasive trail out to the string of lit beads the dying ship had expelled: lifeboats and lifepods set adrift like glittering tears spilled into space. The silence always seemed eerie to her, who had grown up on a planet made bright and lively with sound. She scanned the telemetry. The *Strong Bull*'s reassuring bulk blocked her view of the stars in one octant, its escorts flashing fire in a curved net around it.

"Do you see any cutters coming to pick up the lifepods?" she asked.

"Pakshet! Chaonian assault frigates incoming!" Delfina flagged the movement on the telemetry sphere. "Seven hostiles."

A hail of javelins streaked past their lancer, headed for the *Strong Bull*, followed by bursts of cannon fire that couldn't do much damage to the much more massive heavy cruiser.

Apama spun the lancer as the lead hostile came into range. The lancer's close-range weapons wouldn't do more than tickle a fleet ship, but they had four powerful missiles.

"I can't get a better shot than this."

Delfina grunted assent.

Apama released missile one, then tumbled the lancer into the shield of the dying light cruiser. The lancer's ovoid shape and four-jointed propulsion system made the maneuver fluid, and its heat baffles and modest dimensions made it hard to spot in the chaos.

The lead frigate seared out return fire, clipping their missile. Abruptly, all the enemy frigates started braking and laboriously cut hard flip turns. That would shake up their crews! Her lancer's wobbling missile missed the lead frigate by about a thousand meters and detonated at the edge of the warhead's kill radius. The blast shook the frigate, debris and melted chunks of metal sloughing off the ship's hull as it accelerated away.

The frigates retreated toward a mob of indistinct flares that Apama at first mistook for more debris. Only then did she realize there were more Chaonian ships chasing them than the telemetry was showing, as if new ships were arriving faster than the telemetry's lag time. The enemy were mostly frigates, darting in and out in predatory packs like the group that had just fired at the *Strong Bull*.

The bold tactic was working. Two enemy javelins hit *Strong Bull*. The shields on the big ship held the initial impact, but explosions blossomed on the hull, impact from the cannon rounds timed to hit after the javelins had compromised the shields. The dreadnought slowed momentarily but reaccelerated to match the rest of the fleet by diverting power to the engines.

"Mace, form up around me." Gale Force's order came in calm and clear. "The hostiles are punching in and fading back. Harass the incoming ships to keep them busy while our big girls hammer them."

Their flight spun off in pursuit of a fresh group of frigates that had darted in from a different part of the octant, but the enemy pulled back before they could initiate contact, and Mace leader did not want them to venture too far from home base.

Tower from *Strong Bull* piped in, "Hostile incoming. Bearing two four six zero mark one one eight three."

A big Chaonian battle cruiser loomed out of the ship scatter in the fleet's wake and swept in at high acceleration. It was one of the new Tulpar class, almost as large and fast and powerful as Phene dreadnoughts. It easily outpaced its cloud of frigate escorts. When it reached the invisible line where the other enemy ships had flipped and retreated, it kept coming, accelerating past the *Strong Bull* and actually inside the fleet's formation.

What was its captain thinking? Such an audacious charge left it an easy target, easy to smash, easy to kill.

Lancers scattered to get out of the way as the huge ship cut a brutal brake and spin that allowed it to launch its rear payload across the path of the *Steadfast Lion,* which was now behind it. As the lancers tried to splash as many of its missiles as possible, the big Chaonian ship retreated, thrusting at a punishing burn ahead of return fire. The lancers couldn't catch everything it had launched and could do nothing against the cannon rounds. The enemy's payload slammed, slammed, slammed into the *Lion.* The impacts hit with such a hail of force that Apama could see the *Lion* slowed by each strike. The *Lion* fell back, falling out of formation, dropping behind.

"Mace flight, incoming hostile headed for home base. Retreat and protect."

"They will not let up," said Delfina, spinning the lancer onto a new trajectory.

They raced in a tight path back toward the *Strong Bull,* using the long lag to suck down energy gel, run a systems diagnostic, and bite down on a stim pack. Ahead, a flurry of lancers released all their missiles at an incoming group of enemy ships, frigates and a Chaonian light cruiser. By the time they got into weapons range one enemy frigate was venting from multiple holes, and several frigates were damaged. But the enemy light cruiser had broken through the gnat-like defense of the lancers with a devastating turret fire. It began to exchange fire at close range with the *Strong Bull.* A full payload of missiles from the light cruiser hit all along the *Bull*'s starboard flank, followed up by volleys from the accompanying frigates. The dreadnought juddered from multiple shocks even as its return fire chewed through the light cruiser, whose engines cut suddenly as it began to drift, hulked.

But the damage had been done. Cracks radiated out from an impact site on the *Strong Bull.* Atmosphere vented from a breached compartment. Apama's sphere lit up with internal hails from all over the *Bull.* In her head Apama heard the scream of klaxons, but inside the lancer she heard only the rapid breathing of Delfina.

The *Strong Bull*'s beacon cone ruptured. Fluid erupted, boiling, then turned to a shower of ice crystals glittering where their surfaces caught light from the Molossian sun.

"Fuck that," said Delfina. "Let's take these fuckers down."

They spun back into formation with the remnants of their unit: Cricket and Deadstick, Gale Force and Spot, Skinny and Croak. But just as they split into a four-pointed star, the better to target the enemy from four directions, the surviving frigates cut hard around and, at high burn, retreated toward the pursing line of Chaonian ships and safety. No lancer could keep up.

Their sphere lit up with an incoming message from home base. "All lancers, RTB."

"Ours not to reason why," muttered Delfina, but her imprecations, elaborate curses, and logorrheic swearing accompanied them as they followed their pod back to the flight deck of the crippled dreadnought.

They made their slot, sliding in, jerked to a halt. The seal hissed open, and the membrane constricted to pop them out like seeds expelled from a pod. Deck crew grabbed Apama as she went tumbling feet over head. Gravity was gone.

"Clear!" shouted one of the deck crew.

The lancer got shunted onward into a holding slot, clearing space for another lancer to come in. But none did.

How many lancers had survived the onslaught?

"What happened to gravity?" she asked, and realized she was shouting to be heard above the klaxon. At least there was still atmosphere.

"Lieutenant Apama At Sabao!" The captain appeared, tethered to an anchor line. The actual ship's captain. How did he know her name? Why did he know her name?

His face held a grim determination. His dark hair was coming undone from its regulation braids, strands stuck to his cheeks. "Back in your lancer, Lieutenant. Ba Hill, out. At Sabao, you're taking a passenger to *Choki's Beauty*. Evade all challengers. Your only job is to get to the flagship."

"Yes, ma'am."

Delfina was gripping a rail a few meters away. Meeting her rack-mate's gaze, she shrugged.

Bewildered, Apama pushed off in the direction of the launch tube. Gears churned busily as her lancer was pushed back into position. Just as she got there the passenger appeared, wearing a Yele-grade flight suit with a full vacuum membrane. He had only two arms, which always looked strange to her eyes. The flight suit's faceplate mirrored her own features back at her: the oval face and strong chin and perfectly contoured eyebrows all came from her mother, together with the black hair she had buzz-cut the day she'd gotten her acceptance letter to lancer training.

"Don't see eyes like yours much out here, fancy that," said the passenger. He spoke with a distinctive Yele lilt, and his voice was warm and jovial, as if this was the greatest entertainment he'd had in years.

The cruiser shook, rolling a quarter turn sideways.

Comms sang out, "All hands prepare for knnu drive activation in three minutes."

The captain was already gone, vanished to deal with every other emergency. What could be so important that he had come here in person to give her the order and see off the passenger?

"Hammer One has launched. Mace Sixteen, you are next in line."

Hammer One was the colonel's lancer.

The passenger had already sealed into Delfina's seat. Apama looked around. Seeing Delfina and Renay and Ana, she raised a hand in farewell, wondering if she would survive the transit to the flagship, wondering if the *Strong Bull* and her rack-mates would survive the transition to knnu drive now that their beacon drive was destroyed. Wondering why in the Cursebearer's name she had been plucked for this duty.

But it *was* her duty.

She slid down into a seat still warm from her body heat. The deck crew sealed her in. The lancer clunked hard, rolled halfway over, and kicked. Her passenger laughed as the dreadnought jettisoned the vessel.

She identified Hammer One with a visual and settled into its draft. The wake jostled her lancer constantly like flying in turbulence. The thought made her recall a famous piece of music about the turbulent winds of a lonely terminus planet that had become popular across the empire last year even though the musician was Chaonian.

"What's your name, sweetheart? Apama? Is that it?" He pronounced the initial *A* too flat, and the syllabic emphasis was off, and he didn't even wait for her reply. "I have a daughter about your age. Flies a Spitfire in the Yele air guard. You'd like her."

"It's Lieutenant At Sabao." She snapped out the words, all her focus on keeping close to Hammer One, keeping her transponder dark so it wouldn't trigger Chaonian search sweeps even though obviously her engine would be flaring with the brightness every torch drive had. Anyway, what did he know about who she would like?

He chuckled as she slammed the lancer side to side and jolted it up and down to weave through a debris whirl piling up amid the Phene fleet. The pursuing Chaonian ships were taking heavy damage, yet they still kept coming, darting in and fading away. Meanwhile, the *Strong Bull* fell back and began to reorient in the direction of the heliopause. Smaller ships of the line formed up alongside it, most spilling icy clouds from shattered beacon cones, a few intact.

"Can you get my half of the sphere working for me?" he asked with irritating persistence, still in that big charm tone. "I don't have four hands. I need to see the big picture. I don't know who in the Eighteen Hells is in charge of the action that's pounding us with the strike-and-fade tactics, but it's cursedly effective. Have you noticed how they're deliberately going after the beacon drives? Smart move."

To shut him up so she could concentrate, she projected a copy of her sphere into his half, easy enough to do although there would be a tiny lag. He expanded the scope of the display to encompass the entire solar system, far more than a lancer needed. She gave up on trying to figure out what he was doing and concentrated on flying. They pulled away from the debris whirl and finally out of range of the hit-and-fade pursuers.

"Your ships are in such a rush to reach the beacon they're falling out of formation." The man was evidently a person who could not endure long intervals without hearing the sound of his own voice. She'd heard a lot of the Yele were like that: in love with their own brilliance and locution.

But he was correct; gaps had opened in the Phene fleet. Smaller task groups held together in groups of eight and twelve clustered around the dreadnoughts while the vanguard began to string out in its race toward the Troia beacon. Sunlight reflecting off the second planet was slowly revealing the curve of Yǎnshī. The distant blips of Chaonian ships could be observed running hundreds of klicks ahead of the forward group of the Phene fleet, exactly the way an overwhelmed force would collapse during a rapid retreat.

"The Chaonian ships that are ahead of us are panicking and running," she explained as Hammer One picked up speed. They had a clear path to the flagship. "We're too much firepower for them."

"That's not what's going on at all. They are executing a classic Eirene move."

"What's that?"

"Don't they teach you kids history? You were alive for this." He sighed expansively. "They're collapsing on purpose to lure us into losing cohesion. The hit and fade at our rear is part of the plan. So I have to wonder where else there might be surviving Chaonian ships and what they are doing right now. I'm seeing a lot of coordinated movement . . . Does this thing go backward down the time stream, so I can catch the telemetry all the way back to our initial entry in-system?"

"Not now." She rolled hard enough to choke the breath out of him.

The flagship loomed at zenith, Hammer One winking out its landing code. As a Behemoth-class dreadnought *Choki's Beauty* didn't have launch slots but rather an actual landing deck. She chased Hammer One in and hit her brake thrusters harder than was strictly necessary, just to keep her passenger's mouth shut. But she did have her pride, so she set down like a feather beside Hammer One.

Flight crew came running. Her passenger squeezed out a laugh meant to be hearty but sounding more like the wheeze of a man trying to sprint when he's never even jogged.

"Clever trick with that roll, Lieutenant. Sabao is an unusual name. I haven't run into it before."

"No, ma'am, it's unlikely you have."

"Ma'am? I'm a sir."

"*Ma'am* is fleet standard for all ranking officers, ma'am."

He laughed again. Could an individual get *more* annoying? "You lot have some peculiar customs, that's for sure. So why is it unlikely I might have run into your name before?"

Fortunately the deck crew arrived to unseal the lancer and help them out. The hangar of the dreadnought had the dizzying grandeur of one of the basilicas dedicated to the saints. Without anyone to report to, she found herself corralled by her passenger as he shed his membrane and removed his helmet.

"Nice flying, Lieutenant At Sabao." His grin was a klick wide and almost too genuine to be comfortable. His teeth gleamed whitely against skin darker even than her own, and his eyes were darker than wine; she wondered if they were artificial. Rumor had it the Yele replaced parts in bodies with the same ease that techs switched out failing gears and cogs in mechanicals. He raised an eyebrow inquiringly, and she realized she was staring at him.

"My apologies, ma'am," she said. "I don't know your name."

"Ah."

"Admiral Manu!" An adjutant wearing flagship colors hurried up. "This way."

"Come along, Lieutenant," her passenger added as if concerned she might try to escape him.

As they crossed the hangar, people paused in their work to stare. And why not? Admiral Manu was the most celebrated tactician of modern Yele and indeed considered the best military man the Yele League had produced in a hundred years. Some said he was

nothing more than a mercenary who would hire out to the highest bidder. Others said he was a true Yele patriot who hated the
Chaonian yoke so much he had reached across the Gap to make
common cause with the Phene even though the Yele League and
the Phene Empire had themselves been at odds on and off for two
hundred years.

Colonel Ir Charpentier hadn't even gotten out of her lancer
as flight crew swarmed around the vessel, checking for damage,
sealing a leak, and packing in a new missile by hand, a perilous
undertaking in the best of times.

Seeing Apama and Manu, the colonel nodded. Apama headed
for the ladder, expecting she would be assigned as the colonel's
double to return to the *Strong Bull*. If they left right away they'd still
be able to return to the *Bull* before the knnu acceleration kicked
in. But just as she reached the lancer, a pilot she didn't recognize
pushed past her to get in.

"Lieutenant At Sabao, you're staying here," the colonel said.

Apama opened her mouth to protest.

"Orders from on high," added the colonel, who knew her pilots
well enough to read Apama's expression of frustration and distress. "See you on the other side."

Why did this keep happening to her? A terrible worm of suspicion ate into her heart. What if even her acceptance into lancer
training was part of this same unwanted string of interference?

"Lieutenant?" An adjutant wearing a lieutenant colonel's stripes
beckoned to Apama. "This way."

They stepped through a hatch and went up a ramp to an observation room that looked over the hangar and its bustle of activity.
Admiral Manu gave her a smile so cheery she had an unexpectedly
raw desire to punch him. Then she saw the people who were waiting for him, and her throat froze up. One was High Admiral Choki
Ne Styraconyx, the rich syndicate boss and influential politician
who had concocted the audacious plan to strike the Chaonians
where it would hurt them most.

The other was a Rider.

The high admiral glanced at her. She stiffened to the posture of full submission, both pairs of arms clasped behind her back to leave the belly, heart, and throat vulnerable.

"Who is this?" the high admiral asked with a harsh frown.

The Rider spoke in a thin, whispery voice that chased like a nightmare deep into Apama's brain. It felt like someone were tapping on a closed door in her head, one she was determined never to open. "This individual is no concern of yours, Choki. She has been evacuated on the order of the Rider Council."

On the order of the Rider Council? Blessed Arthas, what could that even mean?

She dropped her gaze to examine the floor with its pale bronze sheen lightly etched with a floral pattern of fantastical flowering trees and vines so it was like walking across the faded memory of a garden. Riders couldn't read minds, everyone said so, but you never, ever wanted to have a Rider notice you. That's what everyone said, what everyone knew.

But the Rider turned away, shutting his riding eyes as if he were listening to a voice very, very far away.

"Enough pleasantries," Admiral Manu went on, because he did always go on. "High Admiral, your ships are getting strung out between a pursuing force—the one behind us—and the force ahead that lies between us and the Troia beacon."

"Yes, I am aware. There is also a third group of enemy ships approaching from our flank. Is there something you wanted to add?" Choki Ne Styraconyx had all the age and burnished privilege anyone could expect from a person born directly below the line of He. His rise in the administration of the empire had resulted in him being granted permission by the council to raise a syndicate fleet under his own flagship.

"Eirene has won two victories using feigned retreats," said Manu.

"One against a Yele fleet you were commanding, Admiral."

"Indeed, which is why I recall it so well. That I hate the harness by which Eirene has yoked my beloved Yele doesn't mean I hold her capabilities in contempt. Quite the contrary." Manu did not fix his arms behind his back, not that the Yele in general were likely to submit to anyone given that they considered themselves the light and pillar of beacon space, the most advanced and cultivated of confederacies. He also did not mince words. "The Chaonians are doing real damage to this fleet. Your lack of heavily armored ships is costing you your advantage."

"Are you somehow of the opinion I haven't noticed? It's true the Chaonian fleet hasn't been as disordered by the speed of our attack as we hoped. That part of our plan has failed. But I have still inflicted an impressive amount of damage on their readiness and industrial capabilities."

"You've lost numerous ships, more than the plan called for."

"We've taken hard losses. Seventy-three ships reported dead in space and abandoned. Twenty-nine ships have lost their beacon drives, so I have ordered them to engage their knnu drives and retreat under the command of *Strong Bull* back across the Gap to Hellion Terminus. But I am still on track to get at least three-fifths of the fleet through the Troia beacon to support the companion attack in Troia System."

"But Eirene—"

"Eirene isn't in command. It's no coincidence our attack was timed to coincide with her wedding. She won't have had time to reach the battle yet. Her weakness is that her marshals are good but they're not bold, not as she is. They will hesitate to directly attack my behemoth. That's why my escort group is dropping back to protect our rear while the rest of the fleet pushes faster toward the beacon. That's what you are misinterpreting as loss of cohesion."

"I meant to say, Eirene has apparently put her daughter, Sun, in command."

"Princess Sun? She's scarcely out of childhood, inexperienced and callow. No match for us."

"If you pull your dreadnoughts to the rear, as you're doing, you're not going to have enough firepower to break through the heavy armor of their assault frigates in time to get through the beacon. I'd like to request command of a squadron of assault cruisers. We must take the battle to that third force, the one slingshotting in.

It'll be close, but if I can slow them long enough before they can combine with the other two groups then you should be able to get half your ships through."

"Admiral Manu, you were allowed on this mission as an observer, not as a commander. I'll use my dreadnoughts to block any attack from the third Chaonian group while the bulk of our fleet pushes past the resistance and drops through the beacon. Once the fleet is clear, I'll follow. Chaonia's forward fleet in Troia will be crushed in the two-pronged attack, caught between me and the Tanarctus Fleet. It'll be a victory as resounding as our predecessors' acclaimed victory six generations ago at Demon Walls over the Karnos command fleet."

Under his breath Admiral Manu said, "And thirty years after that my illustrious forebears beat the socks off your magnificent fleet, sending you home like whipped curs."

Then he sent Apama a swift grin, like they were secret allies.

Styraconyx was still waxing eloquent, oblivious to Manu's remark. "For the first time in over one hundred Anchor years, we will take control of Troia System once again."

To Apama's amazement, Admiral Manu had nothing else to say.

The high admiral gestured toward the command table. "Coffee is about to be served. Please join me. I know you in particular will enjoy watching these upstart Chaonians go down in ignominious defeat."

37

Hard Left Rudder

Sun read the telemetry with the lightning blend of instinct, impulse, and Octavian's regimen that served her well. Damage and casualty reports were streaming in, capably handled by the *Boukephalas*'s experienced crew. Hetty and James were scanning the reports and flagging details of particular interest. Alika filmed and edited a record of the action, for later. Every nerve and every cell of her body, every breath brought in and released, felt seized and carried up to a great height from which she could survey all, comprehend all, be all.

She keyed an open channel to Senior Captain Black, Captain Samtarras, and the captains of the ships that, with her, had been running in pursuit of the Phene fleet.

"Anas, let their vanguard escape through Troia beacon, then reverse course and cut through their line so the rest are stalled. Angharad, bring your ships in to make a gauntlet of fire that any ships that want to get through the beacon will have to run. My unit, bring up all fast frigates and light cruisers to attend the *Boukephalas*. We must push past the Phene rear guard and close the gauntlet from behind to envelop them. It will take a hard burn. Captain Tan, the *Boukephalas* will engage the flagship personally. A battle cruiser is the only ship with the firepower to hurt it. They're counting on that behemoth to hold us back. It won't."

The captain said, "Your Highness, we've done more damage than anyone could have expected. Now might be the time to collect our scattered forces and follow the Phene into Troia in a more orderly formation."

"I will not disgrace my great-grandmother's achievement in holding on to Troia System against all odds by allowing the Phene to wrest control of Troia from our fleet for even one hour. Anyway, if we slacken our attack and let all of them through, they will fire on us as we follow them through the beacon. We hit them now while we have this window of opportunity. Make sure you cripple the flagship's drive compartments. *Execute.*"

Everyone was already at battle stations, strapped in, padded for acceleration, stimmed up. A visual of the battle-space lit the central display along the ceiling of the command center. So many lights moving, blinking, winking out. Distress signals thumped in at steady intervals.

"All ahead. Lock fire-control solutions on the flagship."

Sun's body was pressed into the strategos webbing as the *Boukephalas* drove forward. A shower of javelins and a smoke screen of exploding flail mines gave them cover. Confused scraps of comms traffic bit at her ears, but she focused her attention on the behemoth as they approached, on its stark lines and impressive mass. The *Boukephalas* shook, absorbing a fresh set of shocks, but did not lose its forward momentum. The 1MC crackled, "Investigators out from repair lockers two, nine, fourteen, twelve," as damage reports from across the cruiser blew in like storm swell.

Sun scanned the telemetry, enduring the lag, waiting to see the other two Chaonian forces make their move; a move they were making even now even if she couldn't see it yet. Time ticked past, caught in a weightless space that elongated interminably, and then suddenly they were close enough to make a hard left rudder as they readied a broadside.

Another series of shudders jolted through the ship. With a groan of metal under strain and a disorienting head-over-heels turn the *Boukephalas* flipped direction, preparing to retreat as it lashed out with its defensive batteries. Phene missiles flashed on-screen as they were destroyed, but the enemy was ready with a second volley, this time rail gun rounds targeting the emplacements that had just defended the *Boukephalas*.

A massive impact bounced Sun in the webbing. Smoke flooded

the command center. A containment breach alarm shrilled. A powerful wind tugged at any loose item: a stylus missed Sun's nose by a hair; a tablet whirled past; James's cap slapped the ceiling. Sparks stung her cheek as she shut her eyes and shielded them with a hand. A voice screamed, the sound cut off by an unpleasant thud. A crackling noise like fireworks drowned every other sound for approximately fifteen seconds, and when it fell silent, the wind ceased. Suppressant spray hissed over the command center's bulkheads. Smoke pooled in pockets. A valve clunked down onto the floor from inside a broken locker.

She looked first toward the crash bench where Hetty had been seated. Hetty was still there, still alive, gesturing at the empty air as she scrolled through her augmented-reality screen for information Sun could not see. Blood welled on her forehead from a scrape. Otherwise she looked unharmed. Unperturbed by the chaos, Alika was catching it all on visuals. Where was James? Ah. There, scrambling to grab his cap off the floor.

Others of the bridge crew were not so lucky.

No time to dwell on casualties. Her eyes streamed from the smoke as she manipulated the circle to give her a 360 of their dire situation.

In a calm voice, Senior Captain Tan delivered orders to his crew. On her display Sun watched as the *Boukephalas*'s few remaining defensive emplacements opened fire yet again.

The captain turned to Sun. "Your Highness, the enemy flagship is hit but has released a new barrage of missiles at our position. We are too close to evade . . . we are preparing to launch the last of our ordnance."

"Very well."

So be it. The fight wasn't over yet.

More shudders rocked the ship. The air became thick with particulate matter and the stench of fire suppressant. In her peripheral vision Sun noticed damage control and medical personnel entering the command center, but she was too busy clawing through the strategos grid. Its scope had somehow gotten expanded to the entire solar system, but she needed a tactical view.

Everything reduced to her against the Phene flagship and its high admiral.

She pulled the view down. Tight. The fast frigates that had escorted her in drifted, dead in space, their vented hulks further testament to the accuracy of Phene gunnery. Streaks of light raced toward the limping *Boukephalas*: the incoming missiles. Death swinging for her.

"All shields to the rear," said Senior Captain Tan, still in that calm voice.

Voice shaking, an operator called out, "All hands brace."

Another Tulpar heaved into view, accelerating at the limit of human tolerance. Sun's comms snapped open with a hail on her personal frequency. Captain Angharad Black's booming voice stabbed into her ear like a peal of thunder.

"Sun, what the fuck are you doing? Even you can't take down a behemoth."

"What are you doing over here when your flank is meant to be enveloping their line?" Sun demanded.

"Saving your precious ass," said Angharad with a laugh.

The *Rakhsh* cut between the *Boukephalas* and the dreadnought, firing as it passed the enemy. What missiles it did not shoot down it absorbed on its shields and hull. A large explosion flared at the front of the enemy flagship..

Sun said, "Captain, was that their beacon cone? Is it down?"

"It's gone, Your Highness."

The *Rakhsh* came back around for a second pass. Both Tulpars were badly wounded but still alive and breathing.

"Captain, have we launched the last of our ordnance yet?"

"Not yet, Your Highness."

"Then launch it now. The Phene will learn better than to ever invade Chaonia's territory again."

38

A BRIEF DISPATCH FROM THE BELEAGUERED ENEMY

Dear Mom,

All lights went out in the high admiral's chamber and in the hangar beyond. The hiss of vents ceased. Apama sucked in a shocked breath as her suddenly nerveless fingers lost hold of her tablet. It floated. She began rising, unmoored, and grabbed for her chair's arms. A bubble of warm liquid popped against her chin, and a second bubble with stronger surface tension rolled across her lips like the promise of a kiss.

An ominous rumble ground through the deck and bulkheads like the growl of a wounded beast. Comms crackled, and died. As power cycled through emergency reroutes the gravity came back in. Her tablet hit the deck with a smack. She tasted coffee as the bubble smeared against her partly open mouth. Her arms tensed reflexively so she could guide her rear end back into the chair. A personal light popped on, illuminating Admiral Manu's face creased with a stern expression. He swung the beam around the oval table at which the command staff was seated. High Admiral Ne Styraconyx sat frozen, black coffee splashed over the front of his splendid gold-and-white uniform. As if galvanized by the light, the high admiral slapped the tabletop with an angry oath.

The lights came back on. A telemetry sphere coalesced over the table. Apama's personal system was suddenly integrated into the flagship's reroute and her voice comm overwhelmed by a riot of voices calling out for damage reports and fire control.

In the telemetry sphere a strange and silent ballet unfolded. A battle cruiser, maybe the same one that had damaged the *Strong Bull,* had just hammered the flagship with a crippling broadside. It was now shifting vector to turn and run back the way it had come, to the safety of its comrades, but such a maneuver couldn't be done quickly with a vessel of that size.

A voice spat as if out of thin air, from the distant bridge. "High Admiral, we've taken several serious hits. Damage report incoming—"

"Destroy that ship, Captain."

"Targeting." That was weapons.

Apama leaned down, picked up the tablet, and slipped it into her sleeve pocket. Everyone in the chamber seemed to begin talking at once, except her, of course. She stared at the shifting lights within the sphere, ships outlined in ghostly shimmers and painted with colors appropriate to their hostile versus friendly status and any information known about their damage and readiness condition. Now that she knew to look for a third flank attack, its angle of entry seemed inevitable. The three Chaonian formations created a funnel around the entire Phene fleet. The forward Chaonian group— the retreaters—had reversed course and now attacked the forward ships of the Phene fleet with a cross fire. The pursuing hit-and-fade group now pressed relentlessly forward to push the trailing Phene ships up into the cross fire created by the other two groups. The third group had just made contact, sealing them in. As Admiral Manu had warned, the Phene fleet had lost cohesion and gotten enveloped. Its vulnerability became obvious as weapons fire poured in from every octant.

"Salvo released."

The high admiral smiled. "We've got that Tulpar dead. It's the *Boukephalas.* The princess's ship."

A second Tulpar spun furiously into range, burning incredibly hot. This ship raced into the gap between the flagship and the first Tulpar to literally interpose itself between the missiles and the *Boukephalas.* At the same time it launched a barrage of its own into the heart of *Choki's Beauty.*

A massive hit jarred the behemoth. Apama was flung sideways

against the transparent wall that overlooked the hangar. Sprawled out, she stared down onto the flight deck. Hammer One had long since departed, leaving Mace Sixteen behind. Her lancer was lashed down, readied for beacon transit. Apama couldn't help but bitterly compare herself stuck here with the high command instead of among her comrades where she belonged.

The lights snapped out again, and again the ventilation failed, to be succeeded by the dull red glow and wheezing bellows of emergency power. Three different alarm systems—bells, bugles, and the emergency klaxon—shrilled together in a cacophony so loud it hurt her ears.

A hand settled on her shoulder. "Lieutenant? Are you hurt?"

Of course Admiral Manu hadn't been taken by surprise. He helped her up.

High Admiral Ne Styraconyx had fallen back into a chair as if he had himself been mortally wounded. As it was his ship, and his fleet, maybe in every important way he had.

"Both our beacon and knnu drives are crippled," he said in an oddly calm voice. "Put out the call to abandon ship. All personnel to deploy to other vessels on emergency standing. I need three volunteers to remain behind with me."

"The Tanarctus Fleet is already fighting in Troia System," said the Rider, who had remained silent until now. "What should I tell my colleagues? How many of your ships will make it through to Troia?"

A pallor of death recognized and accepted had settled in the high admiral's face. "Take my courier. It's fast enough to outrun anything the Chaonians can throw at you. I will do my best to get as many of my ships through. We are all destined for death."

The Rider said, "Admiral Manu, come with me. Bring the girl."

Apama would have followed regardless; she was too stunned to do anything else. But Manu kept a hand on her forearm like a guiding light, or a shackle, as they made their way out of the chamber and down the ramp's spiral into the hangar.

"What is your interest in this young woman?" Manu asked as

they hustled into the hangar, where people were abandoning their stations and headed for auxiliary vessels and lifeboats.

The Rider turned his riding face away from them. Apama looked into the bright eyes and sardonic smile of an ordinary, normal face, the man whose body and brain this was, who had been born an infant with a half-formed face on the back of his skull. Somewhere in the Phene Empire his shocked family had dutifully registered the child with the authorities, and the Rider Council had sent a team to take the baby and compensate the family for their loss.

This man's gaze rested briefly on Apama. The curve of his strong jaw and the slightly hooked shape of his nose had a vague familiarity, but he looked away with disinterest, finding her no more worthy of notice than the bulkheads. It was the Rider who found her interesting, and she didn't know why. In fact, she really did not want to know why, not now and not ever.

The courier was cramped with ten passengers strapped into acceleration cushions crammed any which way amid the huge energy generators that gave couriers their speed despite their tiny size. Couriers were the fastest way to get information from one system to another via the beacons, except of course for the Riders. And Riders were only born within the imperial Phene population.

The courier launched within the cover of escaping lifeboats and jettisoned debris. The two big battle cruisers were circling like sharks, continuing to fire into the dying behemoth, while the bulk of the pursing Chaonian fleet had pushed past the flagship's death throes to keep pressing the rest of the fleet.

Apama hated being a passenger, passively observing while dependent on the actions of others. Watching was almost worse than not knowing, but she had nothing to do except watch. She'd been given a stray single seat laced in between bare-bones pipes and tubes. The others were talking among themselves, Manu quizzing the pilots like the only thing that would shut him up would be a javelin through the mouth. She was alone with only a fuzzy, low-resolution sphere to keep her company.

Acceleration pushed her into the cushion. The pilot was excellent, weaving in and around debris. More ships than she'd realized had been damaged; the Chaonians were aiming for drives, determined to stop as many as possible from reaching Troia. Any ship with an intact knnu drive was powering it up, meaning to flee the debacle that way. They would take months to get home, but they might survive.

After a thrust that weighted Apama's lungs, the courier dropped g alongside eleven fleeing Phene light cruisers. The last thing she saw before the emptiness of beacon transit was the flagship going dark section by section as life support and power cut off. An abrupt series of internal explosions lit the ship, a sign of deliberate core overload. It bloomed into an incandescently brief lantern, a short-lived star, as Admiral Ne Styraconyx used its death throes to cover the retreat of his remaining ships.

39

What the Wily Persephone Experiences Deep in the Heart of a Black Nothingness That Is Transition

The transfer from the Lee House Swallow to the royal shuttle at the military base moves smoothly. My cousin the Honorable Marduk Lee gives Tiana a dazzling smile before remembering to greet me. I give the hornet drive to the queen-marshal, who takes it without a word and ignores us. We're shown to a cramped bank of acceleration couches in the back. There we sit amid adjutants busy organizing a streaming river of intelligence to which we're not privy.

I'm suddenly exhausted. As the worst pressure eases when we cross the mesosphere I doze in bursts, dropping in and out of sleep like falling through passageways too heavy to navigate while awake.

Bells wake me as we land inside the flagship, the Tulpar-class battle cruiser *Shadowfax*. Flight crew and deck crew go about their work with efficiency and seriousness. Every surface is clean. An ensign is delegated as our escort, a fresh-faced graduate of the royal military academy, the institute I should have attended. We follow at the rear of the queen-marshal's retinue.

The ensign shades several glances at me, then says, "My pardon, but you look a lot like the eight-times-worthy hero."

"May I live up to her stellar example," I reply with creditable calm.

It's funny because as a CeDCA cadet I'm outranked by the ensign, but my status as Companion to the heir means every officer in the royal flagship has to step carefully around me. That's not even considering my aunt's brief discussion of making me heir to the governorship of Lee House, a prospect that congeals in my gut like a venomous stone.

We're allowed to follow the queen-marshal to the command center. No one questions Tiana's presence as my cee-cee, and Solomon in his battle-stained cadet's uniform gets a pass.

There's an observation bank of couches for dignitaries, diplomats, and transferring officers, as a courtesy, set out of the way. I've never been on a Tulpar-class ship. To work on its beacon drive would be an honor, not that I'm qualified for such a level of responsibility. Not yet.

I take in every piece of the gleaming command center: its hexagonal arrangement of consoles surrounding a top-of-the-line strategos dais; flat screens and projection spheres; the hum of activity among well-trained and disciplined people who are ready to fight and know they are the best.

Compared to the superior and advanced Yele League and the wealthy and powerful Phene Empire, the Republic of Chaonia is a junkyard hatchling trying to make good on a playing field we should never have had the temerity to enter. But we did, and under Queen-Marshal Eirene we have proven ourselves time and again. I may hate the part my family plays and the methods they use, but I can't deny I'm proud of my sister's sacrifice, that I'm proud of Chaonia. That's why I went to CeDCA.

Now the Yele League resents our success, and the Phene finally understand we are the first serious threat to their hegemony in two hundred years.

That's what this is all about: the spying, the raid, the surprise counterattack on Aspera System. The Phene and their allies are desperate to disrupt Eirene's decisive and effective leadership.

"Incoming courier from Molossia," says the officer of the watch.

There's a moment of silence as Eirene, her Companions, and all top-clearance officers receive whatever message the courier brings.

From somewhere in the command center a shocked voice says, "Holy shit."

The captain of the *Shadowfax* says, "Your Highness, should we abort the transit? We could be blown open the moment we drop through."

"The task force under my command proceeds," says Eirene. "Make ready to fight."

Tiana grasps my hand.

On my other side Solomon swears under his breath, then whispers, "I hate this. Give me a gun and a battlesuit any day over being stuck here strapped into a seat."

I pass him my tonfa. "This converts to a stinger. You're better under fire than I am, so you take it. In case we're boarded."

"Take all weigh off the ship," commands the captain.

The helm cuts acceleration, brakes just the right amount. My body unmoors as gravity loosens its grip.

Everything goes black. I can't see myself or anything around me. All I can feel are Ti's fingers curled against mine.

No one knows how the Apsaras Convergence built the beacons or how the beacons work. Probably no one will ever know, because the secret died when the convergence collapsed, taking whole sections of the network with it.

But I fell in love with the beacon network the first time I went through a beacon transition, many years ago. Not everyone sees it, because I've asked.

But I see it.

I see the ghost of the network deep in the heart of a black nothingness that is transition. Faint traceries like infinitesimal gleaming arteries shimmer in a void. Ships like droplets of water slide along whatever passages beacons create between each other. The seers of Iros like my father say we fall through the beacons no matter which direction we enter; there is no up and down, no forward, no return. But I'm not so sure. Direction and volition always matter. If I could get closer maybe I could see the lost networks that link together the forgotten beacons in the regions now known as the Gap. Maybe I could find the lost, or fabled, homeworld, She Who Bore Them All, where the Apsaras hid their secrets. Maybe I could fix the network and restore its glory and reach.

But there are dangers in getting too close to the Gap. It's rumored but never been confirmed that other presences live inside the network, minds that either aren't human at all or that once were human and were fractured when the inner system collapsed and they had nothing to cling to except the insubstantial web that weaves in and out of the physical universe. This branching network has become their skeleton, their scaffolding.

A cold exhalation touches me, the mouth of the Gap pressed like ice on my lips. It's trying to breathe into my mind.

Let me in.

The universe reappears as we drop into Molossia System. My heartbeat thunders, and I break out into a sweat. Screens leap to life, too dizzying for me to comprehend. An alarm cuts through my confusion.

"Incoming debris. All hands brace. All hands brace."

Tiana stiffens. Solomon swears under his breath.

The ship jolts as it takes an impact.

Without a clearance for the queen-marshal's network all I see are images on a set of screens. Space is a big place, and ships are minuscule. There are so many points of light it's impossible for me to make sense of them. The command center crew works in a silence as intense as pressure on my skin. Tiana licks her lips nervously.

Eirene stands on the strategos dais, gesturing in the air as she moves her field of vision to take in the entire solar system. We can't see what she sees, but a slower visual field feeds across the screens.

A Phene light cruiser floats dead in space. The vessel is surrounded by a debris field.

"Absolute devastation of the NCOSP and the munitions depot," says Marduk Lee, who is seated at a console. Companions are officers of a kind; they are trained to fight as is every Chaonian. "I have reports collating. At least five hundred Phene ships, ten dreadnoughts accompanied by cruisers and fast escorts, transitioned out of the heliosphere running on knnu drives. Have to give them credit for audacity, and the patience to make such a long journey. They took our stations by surprise."

"Make for the Troia beacon," the queen-marshal says in a tone of admirable calm. "We cannot and will not let the Phene invaders drop through into Troia System. I see it: a plan to cripple our shipyards and command centers and then follow it up with a pincer attack via two beacons against our fleets massing in Troia."

"General quarters. General quarters. All hands to battle stations," the 1MC blares.

The call galvanizes me; my pulse races, and my cheeks flush. Solomon nudges me, his expression caught between a grin and a grimace. We've only heard this announcement in simulations. If it weren't for the bruises and scrapes I sustained in our assault on the lab, I'd almost believe we were in a simulation now. It seems so unreal.

"I hate sitting here," he mutters again, shifting restlessly.

I show him how to unscrew and rescrew the tonfa to become a stinger. Then I lean toward Tiana. "You okay?"

Her eyes have gone glassy, and her complexion a little ashy, but she nods.

"Phene don't generally kill civilians," I whisper. "Rumor has it civilian prisoners are often resettled on isolated planetary systems where they need more population—"

"Perse, we're on the queen-marshal's ship. Isn't it more likely they'll blow us up?"

"It's more common to disable and refit hulls given the high allotment of resources and labor to build from . . . oh."

"Do you overexplain everything?"

"Yes," says Solomon just as I say, "No, I only explain necessary information such as—"

A chief shoots a look in our direction that shuts me up. There is nothing to do but wait as the *Shadowfax* thrusts. No ship in the fleet can match her speed. Doing a few calculations of my own I find that the second planet, Yǎnshī, where we're headed, is currently orbitally close to the fourth planet, Xièchí, better known as Molossia Prime, where we dropped into the system.

I doze, then wake when a new flood of information bursts onto the screens. We are approaching a running battle. The Phene fleet is racing toward the Troia beacon while a ragged group of

Chaonian cruisers and frigates pulls back in an apparently undisciplined retreat in front of it. Meanwhile a persistent Chaonian pursuit made up of frigates and gunships under command of a battle cruiser targets the enemy ships at the periphery of their ellipsoid formation.

"Eirene, that's the *Boukephalas*," says Marduk.

The queen-marshal grunts. "Of course it is," she says with an irony that might signify anger or resignation. She doesn't seem pleased.

Newer information feeds in; lifeboats are getting picked up, some by the enemy and some by us. Damaged Phene ships peel off in small groups, engaging their knnu drives to leave the system by this slow but sure path rather than be picked apart by the deadly skirmishers. They've taken a lot of damage. But I guess they can afford to. The empire is so wealthy and populous that they never seem to run out of ships or crew.

The silence in the command center shatters as officers and crew exclaim in excitement and surprise. The *Boukephalas* has rushed forward ahead of the line and like an overeager raptor stabs at the Phene behemoth that is clearly the flagship.

The queen-marshal stiffens, looking a few minutes into a future the rest of us can't yet see. Her obsidian eye gleams, tracking information no one else can perceive. She says, clearly and yet speaking to herself, "Reckless, unrestrained, disobedient . . ."

Then she laughs, and a proud smile creases her usually grim expression.

"Bring us in, Captain," she says to the *Shadowfax*'s commanding officer.

The visual feed blurs before popping back into focus with updated information. The battle resolves into new lines. Whatever numerical superiority the Phene fleet may have had at the beginning has dissolved into a mad race for the Troia beacon. Meanwhile they are being hammered from multiple sectors. A few Phene ships are managing to slip through the Troia beacon while others transition to knnu drives.

"What are your orders, Your Highness?" the captain asks.

"We're too late to make a decisive difference in this battle. Open a channel to the *Boukephalas*."

The Phene flagship shudders. Couriers and lifeboats spray from it. Soon after, the huge ship disintegrates into a rapidly expanding and colossal debris field right in the path of the pursuing Chaonians. A patch is scrolling up along the side of the viewing sphere listing estimated ship, habitat, and personnel casualties in constant updates. Chaonia has taken heavy losses. Yet in the death of the behemoth and the desperate retreat of so many of the enemy fleet I smell a Chaonian victory.

"This is Captain Tan of the *Boukephalas*. Grey, you missed the fun."

"Don't get cocky," says the queen-marshal before the *Shadowfax*'s captain can respond. "Is Princess Sun on board?"

"Your Highness!" says the startled Senior Captain Tan.

A fresh silence, leavened by a background noise of fire-control alarms and the wheezing of emergency respirators, lasts just a touch longer than it needs to.

"Put Sun on visual," Eirene adds in a voice no one would dare disobey.

After the distance delay, a hologram shimmers into view. Sun stands at attention, hands at her side. A virtual representation can clean off all blemishes and stains, but Sun eschews such flourishes. Her left shoulder is bandaged, and a smear of blood leaks from a gash on her chin. The alarm heard in the background cuts out, but a wheezy emergency respirator keeps up its frantic *whoosh, whoosh*. Images of the *Boukephalas*'s command center ghost in and out of view. Several bodies are lying on the floor where a medic kneels. Consoles are spewing flame retardant; James is waving his cap to clear the air in front of his face where he's patched into a battered console. Alika is playing a rhythmic accompaniment on his ukulele like this is some kind of Channel Idol op, and maybe it is. Because it's a dramatic setting.

Sun says, "Your Highness. We have driven off the Phene and prevented the bulk of their fleet from dropping into Troia System."

"Very good," says Eirene in a tone that could mean she is

pleased or enraged; studying her expression from across the room I can't tell. She has her battle face on. If Sun is the arrow in flight, all motion and will, then Eirene is the bow, strung and weighted, because however sharp the arrow is, it needs a bow to loose it.

"What is the status of the *Boukephalas*?"

"Temporarily disabled."

"Very well. I am taking the fight to Troia. Your Companion will be sent over to you in a shuttle. Return to Chaonia."

Eirene gestures to her nearest adjutant. The ensign who was assigned to us hurries over to collect us. As we leave the command center I hear the queen-marshal broadcasting on a wide net calling to all operable Chaonian ships to form up on the *Shadowfax*.

We board a personnel shuttle, a twenty-seater meant for cross-fleet hops and quick jaunts between orbital habitats. It doesn't have wings for atmosphere, but its windows offer an incredible view as we approach the *Boukephalas* and the *Rakhsh*. The two battle cruisers are drifting side by side. The *Boukephalas* has taken damage. Impact scars and a breach in the hull being patched over by mechanicals extruding sealant mar the predatory lines of its exterior. In constrast, the *Rakhsh* is a hulking brute of a ship pitted with impact scores from its many battles. According to fleet scuttlebutt, it's a point of pride for the *Rakhsh*'s crew that any damage that doesn't compromise the integrity of the hull has been let be, like a veteran choosing not to have battle scars removed. One of her drive compartments is absolutely gutted with a venting wound. The *Rakhsh* won't be going anywhere except to a repair yard.

To my surprise Sun is at the hangar. Then I realize she's not here to greet me. She's saying goodbye to a large, imposing, and very loud captain who I instantly recognize as the famous Angharad Black.

"That's one kick on the head that won't knock any sense in you," Angharad Black is saying to Sun as she slaps her heartily on the shoulder.

Sun laughs. It's odd to see Sun grin in such a carefree, light-hearted manner, unintimidated by a person a full head taller and many kilos heavier. "It worked, didn't it? But you saved my life and that of the ship. I won't forget it."

"I'd better get the fuck out of here since Eirene is calling." Angharad Black catches sight of me and does a double take. "Holy fuck, you are the spitting image of Ereshkigal Lee. You must be her sister."

"Persephone Lee," I say politely, taken aback.

"My newest Companion." Sun tilts her head to the left to give me a considering once-over. Then, with a purse of her lips I can't possibly interpret, she draws the big captain aside for a few words and afterward waits respectfully until the woman embarks on her shuttle. Only then does she turn to me.

"Walk with me."

She's limping, although the hitch in her stride doesn't slow her down as we head toward the command center. Ti and Solomon follow in our wake with the duffels.

"You really got hit," I say.

She shrugs. "That's not important."

"Wait until you hear what I learned!"

"Not in the passageway."

She guides us to a suite of rooms whose entry doors are marked with cranes, which means these staterooms are meant for flagship command and staff if the *Boukephalas* is ever deployed as flagship in a fleet. Crew are working so furiously in the galley that I wonder how long it's been since anyone on board has had a regular meal. Sun collects a tray from Isis, who is evidently as at home in the galley as on the battlefield. She leaves Ti and Solomon in the wardroom with full plates and leads me into an adjoining cabin. The spacious compartment is split into two spaces, a small bedroom with a perfectly made bed and an untouched desk and a messy lounge with sofas placed for conversation beside a strategos tabletop with eight chairs. She clips a privacy seal into place, sets down the tray, and pours for us both.

I sniff suspiciously at the brown liquid. "Is this . . . coffee? It smells of aniseed. Is that normal?"

"It's a variety called *barako*. It seems to be popular among Phene officers. I got a taste for it during the Na Iri campaign and brought some back from supplies confiscated on captured ships."

I sip. Sun chuckles when I wince. "They got tea in that galley?" I ask.

"You need to buckle up and take what life throws at you, Perse. Here's fresh paciencia. That should help." She slides over a platter of pale drop cookies. "Now. What did you learn at Lee House?"

I dip a cookie and pop it in my mouth to help me think about how I want to say what I need to say. The meringue both crunches and melts, and it cuts the bitterness of the coffee.

"My father has gone missing in a suspicious way. I think the anti-Chaonian faction of the Yele League wants to disrupt Chaonia."

"Anyone could tell me that."

"What I mean is, this anti-Chaonian Yele faction decided killing you would be a means of disruption, while sowing distrust between you and the queen-marshal would be another option."

Her eyes flare. "Are you saying Lee House is in league with Yele?"

"No, just my mother and father."

"Hmm." She drinks thoughtfully, savoring the strong taste. "Aisa has reason to be angry at the throne because it refused to affirm her appointment as governor of Lee House after Nona Lee."

"The throne refused? I thought it was the Lee House council."

"After Lee House refused to consider her for the position, Aisa appealed to the throne, and was rejected. I'd guess Moira and Eirene were working in concert."

"That's the kind of thing my mother would never forget or forgive."

"It could be. But are you certain your father is involved? From what I've heard, and what James can dig up, everyone thought it was a prudent match. The seers of Iros are meant to be apolitical."

"Sure, that's what the seers say. Maybe most are mediators, or head-in-the-clouds scholars like the Honorable Hestia's father.

By the way, I will give an oath on my eight-times-worthy sister's memory that Aunt Moira knew nothing about this particular plot. Although Moira certainly would be happy to see you discredited in favor of Manea's child. Did you know she has another child, older than Resh, who is being held in secrecy in the underwater confinement wing in Lee House? Because she has an incapacitating disorder?"

Sun stares at me for an uncomfortably long stretch, then blinks several times not as if she's checking something in her imbed but as if she's flummoxed. Never in our brief acquaintance have I imagined I could take her off guard.

She leans toward me. Her gaze heats up in intensity until I think I'm going to get burned. "Moira said it was her own child?"

"She did."

"Did she say who the other parent was?"

"She did not." I tilt a fraction toward her. "What does it matter to you? I guarantee the individual is not a clone, in case that's what you're thinking."

She sits back, takes a sip of coffee, and sets down the cup. "I'm not thinking that at all. I'm thinking the person is my cousin, an unacknowledged, unclaimed, and unidentified child of Queen-Marshal Nézhā."

"But that would mean . . ." I set down my cup.

"You didn't know?" She whistles softly. "No wonder you don't trust your family. They never tell you anything. Yes, my uncle Nézhā and Moira Lee had a thing when they were young."

I slap a hand to my head. "Oh my hells. No wonder Moira was required to resign her Companion status. Sexual relations between rulers and Companions are illegal."

"There's no law that makes them illegal," Sun says in a sharp tone. Her gaze flicks toward the sofas. Blankets have been left in an untidy heap where, no doubt, her Companions have been sleeping when they've had a chance to rest. "Such intimacy is deeply frowned on because it could create favoritism, which can be damaging, but it isn't illegal. It makes much more sense if Moira was required to resign not because of the sex but because she got pregnant by Nézhā. Such a pregnancy would have angered and even threatened his legal consort."

"But Nézhā already had a child by the consort."

"Yes, my cousin Jiàn. The consort might have feared her boy would be endangered by the existence of a fully Chaonian child, even an illegitimate one. So *she* might have been the one who demanded Moira be stripped of her Companion status."

"And it was afterward that she betrayed Nézhā and got him killed in battle."

"Maybe it was her revenge. I don't know. Jiàn was barely five when his father died, so obviously he couldn't become queen-marshal."

"The topic seems volatile. Your father mentioned it to her, on the CeDCA airstrip, but she shut him down."

Sun shakes her head. "My mother genuinely loved her brothers. She didn't see her nephew as a threat."

"So she exiled him to grow up on an isolated outpost on a terminus system, maybe sweetened with a friendly collection of guards loyal to her?"

"He's alive," said Sun. "Anyway, I had no idea about this other child. None. I wonder if Moira kept it a secret even from my mother."

"Wow. *Wow.*" I clutch both hands to my head. "I can't get over how wild this is. A doomed, twisted, clandestine Lee House romance at its best."

"What kind of disorder?"

"Beacon sickness," I say, lowering my hands.

"I thought beacon sickness was a myth."

I'm so delighted to discover a fact I know that she doesn't that I take a big swallow of coffee and don't gag this time. "I'd call it a myth in public if I didn't want people to be afraid of beacon travel. It's rare, but even so, it's pretty horrifying, isn't it?"

Yet the image that flashes to my mind isn't of my toy-pushing cousin but of the prisoner who was eating his own feces. What forms of brutalization has a mind endured to drive it to such an extreme?

Sun dips a paciencia but doesn't bite. Instead she contemplates the cookie as if wondering if it's tainted with poison. "That adds a wrinkle to the tally of claimants, does it not? A half Hesjan traitor's son who lives in internal exile. My half-Argosy brother who no one expects to see ever again since his mother took him away when she left Chaonia. And now this mysterious extralegal cousin."

"Until Manea gives birth," I point out.

Sun's eyes flicker. "Moira Lee is sure intent on grabbing for a royal blessing, one way or another. But let's get back to this plot to kill me. Why do you think your mother is involved together with your father in the anti-Chaonia Yele business? Aisa's not gone missing. Isn't she more likely to be an innocent dupe cleverly manipulated to be used as cover?"

I hesitate. In stories, angry princes kill messengers who bring bad news.

She gives me a sharp look and sets down the disintegrating cookie. "Say it."

Now or never. "He fired the late bloomer that killed Octavian."

A tremor passes through Sun's frame like a spasm of fury.

I say nothing, just wait it out.

She clenches a fist, exhales, and opens the hand. "That's a serious charge."

"I know."

"And it doesn't necessarily make her complicit."

"She gave him the alibi that allowed him to do it without anyone suspecting. And now he is missing, along with Baron Voy."

"Aloysius has gone missing?" The information startles her.

"A ship with a Yele merchant registry departed Chaonia through the Molossia beacon before the battle would have started. I'm sure my father is on it. As for Baron Voy, he never checked in with the queen-marshal. This is what I can't figure out, though."

"What's that?" Her gaze doesn't leave my face. She's a missile, tuned to strike.

"I understand how and why Prince João could have convinced Queen-Marshal Eirene to give him the security and the resources for the lab. He's no ally of the Phene, and he wants to liberate his people from Phene control. Very noble."

"Go on."

"So sure, the queen-marshal trusts your father enough to give him the means to disrupt Phene control of Gatoi mercenaries and maybe enlist them to her own cause. But the Gatoi are almost impossible to capture. Where and how were these soldiers captured? Did Prince João have a procurement arrangement with some mysterious supplier? Chaonian agents under cover? A Hesjan cartel that doesn't scruple to trade in bodies?"

She frowns as she considers. "My mother said she had an unexpected source but not what it is. At least not within my hearing."

"And your father didn't bother to tell you? I didn't think he kept anything from you," I remark gracelessly.

Sun sets a hand on my shoulder, the pressure firm and insistent. "Say nothing of any of this to anyone, not your cee-cee, not your friend. No one. Until I say otherwise, everything we've discussed here is between you and me alone."

I imagine myself locked in a steel-walled pit beneath the Lee House atoll, water above me and rock below, never again breathing fresh air or seeing the sun except through baffles that mirror it down from a surface I can never again touch. If I'm lucky I might get a toy van to play with.

"All right," I reply, "but what about Zizou?"

"Zizou? What's your interest in Zizou?"

My cheeks heat.

She tilts her head to the left in that questioning way she has. She's not going to let up until she gets an answer.

"He's one of us," I say, feeling the burn as she shoots a glance heavenward as if asking herself why I'm not being honest.

"I thought you hated the Gatoi, Perse."

"He's not what I expected." I can still feel the flush in my cheeks.

"A lesson for us all," she says, so deadpan I can't tell if she's amused or bored by my transparency. "Don't worry. The Phene picked up Zizou, just as I knew they would. I have a powerful tracker on Zizou." She taps her ring.

I glance at the ring I wear. "Where does this ring network come from, anyway?"

"It's a gift from my father. Banner technology."

She stands. Our cozy chat is over. I slug down the rest of the coffee. The flavor is starting to grow on me. Sun leaves the tray for someone else to clean up. We collect Ti and Solomon on our way out. Isis sticks her head out of the galley to give a hand sign to Sun that I don't recognize.

It's a short walk from the suite to the command center hatch. As Sun walks up, the hatch cycles open. A caustic swirl of chemical-tinged air stings at my eyes as we enter. The first thing my gaze catches on is Jade Kim actually seated in the tertiary pilot's seat like an authenticated crew member. As luck would have it Jade glances around just as we enter. A smile is as good as an air-kiss of scorn, sent to me across the crowded, noisy space. I gesture a quick *asshole* sign. The charming smile widens. I hate the way that smile still has the power to stir me. Fortunately Jade then raises a hand to make sure I see the ring they are wearing, an exact match to my own as if CeDCA graduate Jade Kim now has the same status as the Honorable Persephone Lee does. We'll see about that.

Then the reality of the scene crashes in on me. I'm ashamed by my petty thoughts. The bodies I saw in the virtual feed are gone, but dried blood still stains the deck because no one has time to clean in a battle. Crew are bent over working consoles while mechanicals and maintenance chiefs cluster around damaged equipment. James is half inside the guts of one of the consoles, his cap hanging on a cable. Alika has put away his ukulele and taken Sun's place on the strategos dais. Hetty is standing by Senior Captain Tan, holding a clipboard manifest on which she's collating information.

"Captain!" Sun calls as she strides in. "What's our ETD?"

"We'll be beacon-worthy in nine minutes, Your Highness."

"Beacon-worthy?" I examine the shambles that is now the command center. "Shouldn't this ship be headed to a shipyard for repairs?"

"The shipyards are in worse shape than we are. Anyway, I'm not done yet."

"The queen-marshal ordered you to return to Chaonia."

"Set a course for Troia beacon, Captain," says Sun, ignoring me. "The Phene gunship is seven hours ahead of us. I will recover the lab consoles, researchers, and captured banner soldiers. The Rider who led the raid hasn't beaten me yet."

Hard Landing

Zizou grips the mesh as the gunship rolls in multiple tumbles. Despite his strength he is slammed repeatedly into the padded bulkhead, head whiplashed back. His system pumps adrenaline and blockers until he can't feel pain. A ghastly shudder shakes the entire ship. A metallic clank rings out as an object strikes the hull. An auxiliary power cube set in the middle of the hold spits a spray of sparks, hisses smoke, and goes dark.

Silence.

Is the ship about to break apart?

Like all recruits chosen by the fleet council for the honor of earning a battle name, he learned how to speak Imperial Phene as well as Common Yele as part of his training. So even locked in the cage, helpless and battered, he can understand the shouted commands and stray chatter over the comms as the pilots get the stabilizers back on track and put on a burst of acceleration. The intercom blares, "The enemy is breaking off; they're turning back."

The crew springs into action to make repairs. Zizou watches intently as techs examine the big cube, which routes power from the auxiliary engines into the beacon drive. But he doesn't know enough to follow what they're doing.

The Rider fetches up by the consoles stolen from the lab. These blocky storage units have weathered the attack fairly well, lashed with protective webbing against the opposite bulkhead. The Rider straps herself into a safety harness with her riding face toward the consoles and her ordinary face looking into the hold.

After months of intense training spent building the psychological shields that allow him and his brethren banner soldiers to leave behind the only home they've ever known, Zizou thinks he can sustain anything. But it's creepy to see the ordinary face settle into patient repose as it gives up control of its body, to see the arms reach behind the back to manipulate the console's lock pad with perfect ease.

It's peculiarly disturbing since he now knows his own corpus has an override built into it that set him multiple times to attack Persephone Lee. Like every recruit, he underwent a neurosystem alignment after being sent into Phene service. He was told it was a routine procedure that would accelerate agility, enhance strength, and make banner soldiers more able to withstand the rigors of battle. It's what the Phene are famous for: engineering human beings to fit an environment with alterations like four arms or exoskeletons. For recruits like him, the environment is battle.

But slivers of time and action have gone missing from that period of his training. He could have done things he doesn't recall, things he didn't want to do, things wiped from his memory by Phene engineering.

The Rider's ordinary face glances his way, marks him with mild but brief interest, and looks toward the far end of the cargo hold. Phene technicians are huddled with the ship's commander around the power cube. An eerie quiver passes through the Rider's body. Abruptly the shoulders come forward and the arms shift trajectory so they're moving in tandem with the front-facing face again.

But that doesn't mean the Rider isn't still awake and in charge. Because the Rider walks across the hold to the wire cage and turns so its riding face studies Zizou. The gaze of that unfinished face has an odd liquid feel to it, like it leads through gaps and baffles and reflections to a listening post much farther away.

"Recruit, where were you captured? Who captured you?"

He swallows. His orders are clear. "I'm not allowed to give out that information."

"Answer me."

"According to banner law I answer directly to my commanding officer."

UNCONQUERABLE SUN · 419

"I speak for the Rider Council. We govern the Phene Empire. You work for the Phene Empire. Answer me."

He keeps his right hand in a fist, thumb tucked beneath the curled fingers to hide the ring. Sun will come for him, and for the lifepods and the consoles. It's his duty to keep the Rider ignorant of these plans for as long as possible.

"Recruit. Wrathful Snakes Banner. My battle name is Zizou." He pauses, but the Rider doesn't know the language of the banners or the proper response, not as Sun does. "I am sworn to the service of Lady Chaos."

The Rider's eyes flicker, like lights toggling on and off. Then she says in her whispery voice, "You creatures are more trouble than you're worth. But I do my duty, just as you do yours."

She looks toward the commander, who is consulting with the techs by the power cube. "Commander! Make for the Troia beacon."

The commander pats the side of the cube. "She doesn't have enough power for a second transit. Surely the fleet can detach another vessel to pick us up."

"The battle isn't going as planned. We are small enough to sneak through the Troia beacon while attention is elsewhere. We mustn't be captured."

"We will almost certainly blow our remaining engines with the overload."

"Find a way we can get through intact. We don't need to make a third drop, just get us into Troia System." The Rider pauses, attention shifting inward, then snaps back to the officer. "Arrangements are being made for us to be picked up by allies on the moon of Tjeker."

Only physical objects can carry messages across the vast distances between solar systems, and only ships piloted by humans can pass through beacons. But there's a saying whispered in the barracks by the recruits: what one Rider knows, all Riders know, so never let a Rider know.

The commander gives the appropriate orders, then goes back to the techs at the power cube while the Rider returns to poke at the consoles.

Relaxing, Zizou allows himself to doze.

A klaxon's blare interrupts his rest.

The commander walks up the deck to him, slogging against an accelerating thrust. She snakes a pliable mask through the mesh. "Fix that over your nose and mouth. It's primitive, but it'll keep you breathing."

He takes the mask.

Satisfied, the officer calls to the Rider. "Close up your helmet, Your Eminence. We may lose oxygen in the transit. I'd be happier with you in a crash couch up front."

The Rider considers, then moves to the forward hatch.

"You'll lose your face if you lose that one," says the Rider as she and the commander wait for the hatch to cycle open.

"I won't lose him or the rest of the cargo. I get why we needed to take down the lab on Chaonia Prime. But what's so valuable about this particular one?"

"We're using him, and ones programmed like him, to track down an enemy asset we need to eliminate."

An enemy asset? What does that mean?

The hatch closes behind them, leaving him in the hold with the lifepods and the consoles and this new question. The techs are still working on the cube. They've wrapped strapping around their bodies so any impact will bounce them away from hard surfaces. Busy with the repair, they're not looking at him.

With the precision that won him his battle name, he flares his neuro-threads with a blast of strength. By wedging a shoulder into a forward corner of the cage and his feet into the diagonal backward wall, he shoves with a strength no unthreaded human could ever have. Bolts shift. Metal groans under pressure. The stiff steel mesh starts giving way.

The techs pause at their work, but he's already released and pressed back against the padding. He pretends to look around the hold for the source of the sound.

"What was that?" asks the stockier tech, scratching at an ear with a lower left arm. Both glance nervously toward Zizou.

He keeps his eyes half-closed, running a diagnostic through his body. A bruise is starting to throb on his shoulder. He chases a dose of anti-inflammatory to the site. The techs walk a circuit of the cargo hold, shining a tool-light into every corner and behind insulated pipes. They edge close enough to take hold of one of the cage's bars to verify that it is solid; of course they can't budge it at all. He gives them a friendly smile that makes them skitter away like children frightened by their attempt at entry into the salt maze in the temple of Lady Chaos. The Phene may be the imperial masters of much of beacon space, but that doesn't mean individuals don't fear him for what he is.

Finally they go back to work, chatting.

"I swear an oath on Saint Cid that if this farting tub doesn't break apart when we drop, and if we survive this saints-cursed mission, I will study properly for my quals and get out of the service and go back to uni like my family wanted me to. No regrets!"

"Our sector isn't releasing anyone from the service right now, not with the Chaonians scrambling to loot and pillage like the jumped-up roaches they are."

"Ei, hand me that wrench."

They work at the innards of the cube. He doesn't have the technical knowledge to understand what they're doing, but it's interesting to watch how well coordinated their hands are, the interplay of arms. Their "this wire, that bolt" conversation veers twice into asides about an officer they both dislike. Their casual chatter reminds him how much he misses his people, the easy way he was brought up among folk who knew each other's business. He even misses his squad and their crass joking.

A bell rings to signal a beacon approach.

"Let's hope that holds for the length of the transit. Alea iacta est." The techs pack up their tools and they, too, exit the hatch, leaving him the only conscious entity in the hold.

The ship loses g. His head softly bumps the top of the cage.

The universe goes black.

Wisps of particulate matter curl out of the void and whisper into his neural pathways like echoes coming home to roost. A honey warmth settles deep into his bones.

The universe rings like a bell.

Then they're out, alarms blaring so loud it hurts. The hull shudders. He's flung back against the padded bulkhead then forward face-first into the mesh, smashing his nose. Blood trickles into his mouth.

Gravity fails.

The intercom crackles. "All life-support systems fail. All life-support systems fail. Engine breach. We are adrift. Emergency measures."

He can't catch his breath. Coughing turns to wheezing before his right elbow snags the tube of the clear mask. Oxygen. His hands fumble at the mask, but for all his usual dexterity he can't get a grip on it. He tongues a burst of adrenaline through his system, enough to give him a spot of clearheaded focus. As he tugs on the mask he inhales. His breathing steadies. The lifepods' power lights gleam green, their inhabitants untouched by the oxygen drain. There's a leak in the hold, a whine of escaping gas that, horribly, fades as all the air leaves. The cold of space seeps in. Drops of blood from his nose boil away into crystals that float past his eyes. His neurosystem starts pumping heat, sucking energy out of his cells; the skin starts sealing, trying to protect him against the creep of vacuum.

His pulse pounds in his ears, sluggish, sludge.

A tremor shudders through the bulkhead; the wheel of the hatch has started to turn. The hatch opens with a whoosh of warm, rich atmosphere. Three individuals wearing full-body membranes pull themselves in and dog the hatch behind them. They spray a glittering liquid that is immediately sucked in three directions, toward unseen breaches. A strangely noxious odor stings in his nostrils and lances right up behind his eyes. Before he can kick in a counter-valence, he passes out.

He comes to when the gunship hits atmosphere with a turbulence that shakes him into consciousness. Straps pin him to the bulkhead's cushioning, which is a mercy, because they are pitching and yawing and rolling so wildly he expects to crash at any moment. Someone has fastened a full-body membrane around him.

The gunship lurches. The webbing that grips one of the consoles tears at a corner, and the console rips free and comes banging across the hold to slam into the wire cage just to his right. An impact alarm blares over and over. The comm whispers, but he can't hear words.

They hit the ground and bounce once, twice, three times, and finally belly through with a screech of abused metal. The loose console smashes to the new center of gravity. With a final lurch, the gunship comes to a halt. It has survived the descent, but it's badly damaged.

The big cargo hold door cracks, then groans as its hydraulics give way. The ramp peels down and thuds to the dirt. They're already aswirl in a cloud of dust from the crash. Its grit racks him with coughs. The rank smell of an organic atmosphere filters through the membrane. He checks for composition; it's a marginally breathable atmosphere, survivable with no filter, but the mix of contaminants and dust will pit the lungs after prolonged exposure. Beyond the ramp spreads a rocky plain littered with random piles of debris. Something's moving out there, and he cycles his vision in until he gets a view of an old scavenger mech making a slow circuit.

He spies a distant habitat, low-slung khaki-colored barracks tents squatting beside a city of glossy domes and shining towers. The buildings and tents drift in and out of view through blowing dust. The ship has come down on a slope somewhat higher in elevation than the city. He's not sure of the dimensions of the domes and towers, but he guesses the city is about ten klicks away. An easy walk, even as bruised as he is. He tests the cage door with a knee; it's ready to pop. The way is clear. He can break the straps and vanish into the haze.

But he doesn't. He has a job to do, even if he isn't quite sure what it is.

The hatch clears and the crew emerges into the hold, wearing membranes and filters. One group of techs pulls out the coils of the beacon drive, the most difficult-to-replace part of the gunship, and bundles them into oversized lift-crates. Others remove the lifepods and load the consoles onto hover-lifts. Another crew member sets charges in the hold. They're abandoning ship.

"We'll be captured in two heartbeats," says the commander to the Rider.

"You assured me you released enough debris to mask our descent."

"For now, and only because there's fighting in-system. It'll be some while before they winnow all the chaff and find us. But they will eventually find us. How long do we have to stay hidden?"

The Rider's attention shifts inward, then snaps back to the officer. "Longer than I'd like. The Molossia gambit turned into a rout of our forces."

"A rout? How is that possible? High Admiral Choki Ne Styraconyx was in charge . . . I have kinfolk pledged to his syndicate . . ." The officer catches herself on a bulkhead, takes several calming breaths, and straightens back up. "We are all destined for death. Now what?"

"As I said, Commander, the Rider Council always has a backup plan. I want this gunship decontaminated and demolished so it can't be traced to the raid on the lab."

"Already in progress," says the commander.

"Any sign of pursuit?"

"None showing up yet. It's likely to take them days to track us, given everything else going on." The officer looks Zizou's way. "What about that one? He's a wild card."

"He'll obey. That's why we purchase them from their home fleets, so we can leash them via their neural systems as needed to fit our purposes."

Purchase? Banner soldiers are chosen through a strict regimen of training and testing. It's a momentous and consequential honor to leave home to protect those left behind. When recruits leave their homes they know they likely will never return, that their duty lies in service far from their kin. But for the first time he wonders how the Phene see soldiers like him: As people with lives as valuable as their own? As valued allies? Or as expendable *purchased* tools that can be replaced with each new set of recruits? He'd never thought to question these verities until now.

The Rider produces a wand and flicks it on. A hum vibrates in his bones. His nerves tickle as if they've been charged with electricity, and the sensation disgorges half-forgotten memories of training when he was run through mazes with his limbs not under his own control. Nausea swells in his gut, not bile but revulsion. He breaks out in a sweat.

"He'll be passive now," says the Rider. "I've leashed him."

He tries to move an arm, but it doesn't move. He tries to move a leg, but it doesn't move. The Rider watches him strain, then nods at the soldiers.

"Bring him. But keep him restrained as a fail-safe."

Two soldiers undo the cage's door. They have to wrench it open, and the torqued hinges grate. As if he's a slab of meat they transfer him to a hover-stretcher, strap him in, and push him outside with the lifepods. Again he tries to twitch his feet and wiggle his fingers, but nothing happens.

The wind picks up, dust stinging his face when he cannot even turn his head to shield himself from the worst of it. Lights flash at the tops of the distant towers.

The Phene crew efficiently unloads the gunship, cleansing it of telltale organic markers. Charges burn through welded seams, leaving it vulnerable to scavenger mechs who will pull it apart to recycle its valuable metals and ceramics.

The Rider walks through the ranks of lifepods, pauses to study him, tunes the wand a bit higher. His tongue stings.

"Blink," she says.

He blinks.

"Again."

Again he blinks. The dishonor rankles. His mouth still works, raspy and slow. "I am not a puppet. I am an honorable banner soldier."

"You are a weapon we have bought, nothing more."

The words explode like fléchettes into his head. "No!"

"Your fleet councils sell you to us. You're the excess, the surfeit they have no resources for but which we can use until we've used you up. But they don't tell you that, do they? They stuff you full of honor and duty until you're gorged on it. I almost pity you."

She walks away.

He isn't a puppet. He's an honorable man.

Sun sees him for who he is, not just what he is. He won't let her down.

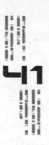

41

In Which the Wily Persephone Unwittingly Races up the Charts

The only person in the Republic of Chaonia who can gainsay the heir is the queen-marshal, and she's not here. So after the *Boukephalas* has dropped out of Molossia System into Troia System but before Senior Captain Tan reports in to Crane Marshal Qìngzhī Bō, the cruiser jettisons a shuttle. Sun is on that shuttle, having shed everyone except her Companions. Hetty is piloting, with asshole Jade Kim in the copilot's seat wearing a ring just like the others and me.

Now that we're in Troia System, the beacon we've come through is called the Molossia beacon; they're always called by where they drop you. This particular beacon is anchored to a gas giant. The planet's swirling orange expanse fills our screens as we race away. The *Boukephalas* vanishes from visual range.

"The main action here in Troia has moved to the vicinity of the second planet and the Aspera beacon, on the opposite side of the sun from us," says James. He's seated in a crash couch next to Sun, throwing lines of data back and forth with her like a fiery badminton match.

"Good," she replies without looking away from the data. "That means no one will be hunting for us."

"You seem awfully chill," I remark, "what with a major battle taking place elsewhere in this system."

She shrugs. "My mother is in command of a strong and disciplined military, which she built. And she's pissed. And although we sustained heavy losses in Molossia, we put a spoke in the wheels

428 · KATE ELLIOTT

of their Troia gambit. My guess is the Phene will cut their losses and retreat to Aspera. Let's keep the focus on our mission."

She unfolds a grid so we can follow Zizou's ring.

"I've got it." James tugs his cap to his favored jauntily triumphant angle. "The signal is showing up on one of the moons orbiting the gas giant. They're grounded. Just as you'd hoped."

"Just as I'd planned," corrects Sun.

James notices me watching and winks at me, like we're friends sharing a sliver of delight over the predictable way Sun corrected him. The way he includes me worms a cautious sense of belonging into my stony, untrusting heart.

"There are six inhabited moons," he says to the shuttle at large. "I can never tell them apart."

Tiana lifts her chin. "There are seven inhabited moons, named after seven auxiliary ships attached to one of the old Argosy fleets, the Mopsos Argosy. The moons are Ekwesh, Peleset, Shardana, Shekelesh, Teresh, Tjeker, and Weshesh. May I see the grid you have there, Honored James?"

"Please, just call me James," he says with a flourish immediately spoiled by a blush. His shyness makes me like him. He's kind of a jerk, but he's our jerk. And he's really good at what he does. He expands the grid to show the gas giant Colophon and its thirteen moons.

"The signal's on Tjeker." Ti glances at me, where I am seated beside her with nothing to do except snark. "That's where I grew up."

"How well do you know the moon?" Sun asks.

"There's one major city. It grew up around an old Phene military compound that's now a Chaonian staging point, training ground, and industrial park. There's a huge refugee camp there. It's the only place Phene can go more or less unnoticed."

"How's that?"

"There are always Phene refugees sheltering in or near the hostel administered by the saints basilica in Repose District."

"Useful for Phene fugitives and spies," says Sun. "Hetty, take us in."

We descend into a swirl of clouds that look like vomit ice-dried to grit and being run through a planet-sized fan. Being buffeted by winds makes me think of Alika's song "Turbulence." The handsome and talented winner of last year's Idol Faire is seated in a crash couch, plugged into the comms console. Ignoring me, thank goodness.

Waves of comms traffic cascade out of the battle in progress by Aspera beacon, spilling over each other like too many notes roaring past. He flicks his fingers through invisible threads, untangling the massive river to find what's useful for Sun. It's weird to know there's a battle going on at the other side of the system, while here it might be any ordinary day.

Hetty pilots the shuttle with the same skill she showed with the boat when we escaped Lee House. Her calm expression never wavers as winds buffet us, pitching us up and then sideways. She's got game.

As always, Jade Kim can't keep from commenting on the performance of others, which is never up to toppest of top cadet standards. "Have you considered—"

"I know what I'm doing." Hetty's shoulders tense as she keeps her attention on her task. Notably she doesn't seek backup from Princess Sun, who is in the third row, tapped into the intelligence feed.

"Fuck off, Jade," I say softly.

Jade offers a quick two-finger gesture in my direction that might be insult or invitation. Hetty casts me a grateful look. Sun glances up, gaze touching on each of us in turn, but says nothing as she goes back to her feed.

Troia System has no habitable planets; two are gas giants, one is a toxic hells-scape, and the other two are burned-out shells lacking atmosphere. Colophon's habitable moons became famous for all sorts of black market activity here where, for generations, the systems that make up the Hatti and Karnos regions bordered the territories under the rule of the Republic of Chaonia and within the zone of influence of the Yele League.

Two hundred years ago the Phene absorbed Troia into their empire. They used the system as a staging point for their invasion of the Yele League, a war they were winning for decades before they shockingly lost the battle of Eel Gulf. After the defeat instigated a rumored bloodbath within the Rider Council, the empire had to retreat. Of course even after they lost to the Yele they still controlled Chaonia for quite a long time. Naturally the Yele didn't lift a finger or risk a single ship to liberate the Republic of Chaonia from Phene overlordship. We had to do that ourselves.

On archaic beacon maps the Troia system is listed as *Ilion*, but after the Phene took over it began to appear on maps as *Troia*. A *troia* is an entertainer, a person who offers their services in a wide variety of capacities. Once the Phene installed military bases there were a lot of personnel temporarily barracked on one or the other of the moons. Since temporarily barracked personnel use a lot of services, the name *Troia* stuck. Maps changed. Refugees whose lives in orbital habitats or planetary domes were disrupted by war began migrating to the moons. In the last twenty years the bulk of the refugees have been required to settle on Tjeker, because it has a gamma-class breathable atmosphere, which means it kills you slowly and thus gives the government plausible deniability with respect to cause of death.

We get clearance to land at the Tjeker military base.

The clouds part as we come in, offering a view of a semiarid plain sprinkled with rows of windbreak trees and carpets of tough plants being seeded into the dusty soil. I'm too nervous to remember the names of the flora even though I aced the semester course on terraforming strategies. The round ponds of a waste treatment plant dot the northern flanks of the conurbation. We fly over the central city with its sealed domes and gleaming cylindrical towers. The military base is huge, with ten landing strips and a small city's worth of sealed buildings and connecting roadways.

So as we make a wide turn to come around to our designated runway, the sight of the hectares upon hectares of tent city shock me. We didn't learn about these in class. The uncovered paths and roads look disturbingly naked. People are out and about in unfiltered air. Instead of solid, seamless floors, walls, and roofs made of ceramic, the refugees live in big rectangular fabric tents. The tents line up in row upon row upon row upon row. Intersections become ganglions of market and admin and medical tents, swollen up as if they're infections. Open ground is scarce inside the barrier fence. Outside spreads a debris field that extends to distant hills.

Then we bank around, losing the view. A wind hits us crosswise. Wings rocking, the shuttle lands with a few staccato bumps. That roll of the eyes is classic Jade Kim, but fortunately no words leave those perfect lips. Hetty's cutting side-eye toward her copilot confirms I have a new ally in Jade-hating.

Isis has been in the back with Solomon, prepping a set of mini stingers suitable for concealing about the body. As we unstrap she nods at him. "You know your weapons, Cadet."

"My thanks." He holsters a pair of stingers and slings two small rail guns over his back.

We all unstrap.

Sun says, "Jade, you stay with the shuttle."

"But—"

"I want her ready to go at a moment's notice."

I catch Jade's eye and waggle my eyebrows mockingly. It's petty but satisfying.

In a stiff tone, Jade says, "Yes, Your Highness."

A royal attaché and a puzzled Guard captain await us as we disembark. They're both wearing filter masks while we cough into the rough air. My lungs feel hollowed out after only fifty steps. A merciful door offers entry to a long, low admin building where we're shown into a chamber furnished with a strategos table and chairs.

"How may I help you, Your Highness? I got no word you were coming."

"I'm on a classified mission. If you'll guard the door, Captain."

He takes the hint and goes out, taking the attaché with him.

James sits at the strategos table. Its glossy black surface measures five by five meters. After he taps a keypad and the surface lights up, he builds a topographic model of the conurbation, a remarkable simulacrum of the view we saw from the shuttle. Sun swoops the view down and down, zeroing in on an unblinking blue light that marks Zizou's position. It shines in an area that seems to bridge the gap between the refugee camp and the main city.

Sun studies the map. "This is a low-regulation market area. It should be easy to get in and out without being noticed."

"If I may, Your Conclusiveness."

Sun's eyes crinkle up and her lips quirk. She's about to smile, but she doesn't. Instead she nods to indicate Tiana has permission to approach.

Ti slides in beside the princess. She finds a pointer stylus hanging from the table, unhooks it, and uses it to delineate an area. "This is the low-reg market, yes. But that's not where the ring is. This area here isn't part of the market. That's Repose District."

"Give me more information on Repose District."

"Can you make the map bigger, James?" Ti irradiates him with a brilliant smile.

He blinks as if he's been blinded. "Of course."

She uses the stylus to guide us on a circuit around the rectangular plaza and side streets of Repose District. One narrow end of the plaza is entirely taken up with an ancestors' hall and, behind it, the Temple of Celestial Peace. Facing it, at the far end of the plaza, lies a spacious repose garden whose green foliage and bright flowers stand in stark contrast to the barren ground outside the domes. As for the rest, the builders of the district have made sure there is a respectful sacred place for almost everyone. There's a lion of Al-lat, a colonnaded Bel temple, a house of healing marked with twinned holy snakes, and a saints basilica with the proper sixteen alcoves. Shining golden walls painted with a border of bright flowers marks a theatron dedicated to the Great Mother Queen of Mishirru, she whose names cannot be numbered; the entrance is flanked by images of her sister gods Fire and Splendor. A complex henge in the Hesjan style rises in stately majesty, paved in mown grass and split into three sections by the two main entry paths that fork like a snake's speaking tongue. There's even a shifting maze, wreathed in a glaze of shadows, in which the brave and reckless can walk perchance to dream or if they are unlucky even to meet Lady Chaos.

Ti speaks. "The air on Tjeker is breathable, but it will scour your lungs if you breathe it for long periods unfiltered. It's a slow and grueling death. The tents that house the refugees are sealable, as long as they're in repair. If you can afford it you can get better air pumped into your personal tent. If you can afford it. Usually several families share an air line, either because they share a tent or because they share the air between several different tents. There are also filtering masks you can wear for outside work, or even inside if you can't pay for an air line. Refugees can't go into the domes, which of course have the best air. Breathable air is a perk for citizens."

"The domes don't use refugee labor?" Sun asks.

"Dome and tower jobs are set aside for citizens. As you know, all citizens receive a basic allowance of air, water, medical, and shelter. Refugees have no such rights, so they pay for every metered delivery and every service."

James looks shocked. "They make people pay for medical care?"

Sun waves him to silence and turns back to Ti. "What does Repose District have to do with this?"

"The Phene established Repose District when they ruled here. In fairness to them, the empire observes a strict policy of religious tolerance. But I'd guess they like shoving the temples cheek by jowl into a single district so their administrators can keep an eye on the temple establishments. The thing about Repose District here on Tjeker is many of the temples offer free services to the refugees. Different ones specialize in different offerings."

Sun nods. At the heart of the Republic of Chaonia's social compact with its citizens is that our love and respect for our ancestors must translate to care for the living, so the living can properly honor the dead who are still with us.

"For example, Repose District has good air, and it's free to enter," Ti says.

"So refugees without access to good air can become very devout, is that what you're saying?" Sun asks.

"That's right. They can get free clean air for an hour a day."

"That's where Zizou is? Why that frown?"

"You have to pass full-body security scans to get in. The thing is, however long the lines are, the air is good even when you're standing in line. So no one minds long lines because they can breathe. But if Zizou is still with the Phene—"

"I think he is."

"—then the Phene will have agents watching the entry."

"I'll get military access."

She laughs. "No offense, Your Certainty, but the temples have real power here. There is no military access to Repose District. It's part of the deal on the moons. The cooperation of the religious leaders keeps the gears greased and running smoothly. If you don't believe me, look here."

She gestures to James, and he zooms in the view. It's a real-time view of the temple district. Translucent figures like ghosts move along the streets and alleys, fading in and out, hard to get a grasp on.

"Interesting," says James. "Someone is running a scrambler through the visual. Compare the real-time images from the camp, which are precise and being routed through military channels."

Ti nods. "Like I said, the temples have power. Enough power to limit surveillance by the military."

Sun raises a hand. "That's all very well, but there's no way a gunship load of Phene special forces in company with lifepods, consoles, and a captive banner soldier stood in line for full-body scans."

Ti smiles. "The temples have individual private keyed entrances for spiritual personnel. So who among the temples is likely to have Phene agents or sympathizers?"

"The basilica."

"Too obvious. And as you can see, that's not where the ring is." Ti indicates a modest hermitage with actual stone walls that lies opposite a lane crowded with souvenir stalls. "He's here, in a community of the seers of Iros, where people can get mediation for disputes."

"The seers of Iros." Sun glances at me, then at Hetty.

"The enemy of my enemy is my friend." I tip my chin toward

the map. "Did you not believe me when I said my father fled town just like he was painted in guilt?"

Abruptly Hetty speaks. "My father is not here. He has retired to quiet reflection in the fatherhouse that stands on Yele Prime. He is not here."

"I never thought he was here." Sun touches Hetty, two fingers brushing her forearm like a promise. The delicacy of the gesture makes my face heat, as if I've seen an interaction that ought to have been private. Sun breaks the moment by turning to me. "So your father really is a traitor?"

"He'd say, not to the Yele. But I think this is bigger than my father."

"You still think Baron Voy is involved?"

"I guess we're about to find out. Ti, I'm wagering you have a suggestion for how we can get in."

She arches a playful eyebrow at me. "Why yes, I have access to a back way in. There's a Campaspe Guild annexed to the House of Healing Waters. I worked there for a few years."

"You worked as a campaspe?" I can't decide if I'm surprised Ti got her start as a sex worker. James blushes, looking away. Hetty crosses her arms, looking a bit prim and prudish, but maybe that's her Yele upbringing. Of course Alika's not paying attention to the rest of us lesser creatures; he's deep in the comms doing I don't know what except he's whistling softly under his breath, working out a melody I've never heard before. Isis isn't interested in anything except our weapons. Solomon gives Ti a brief nod, as in solidarity, making me wonder what kind of off-license work he did for his family's illegal enterprise when he was younger.

Ti gives me a look, disappointed in my response, and I'm immediately ashamed of myself. "It was the best work a girl in my circumstances could get when I was fifteen, and we were really desperate for money. It worked out well for me. The guild sponsored me into Vogue Academy, so I'm grateful to them."

"It's honest work and nothing to shame someone for, as you all ought to know," says Sun with a wave meant to scold us. "Ti, what does this mean for our mission?"

"It means I still have my access key to get into the guild annex through its private entry. Which gets us into Repose District without going through the security line."

"Ah! That's what I want to hear."

"But you all will still stand out, dressed as you are."

"That's your other job as Perse's cee-cee. Get us outfitted so we blend in."

"As much as you'll ever blend in, Your Distinctiveness."

Hetty gives her a sharp look. Ti's teasing smile widens, and she holds the Honorable Hestia Hope's gaze until Hetty relaxes and chuckles.

"You have a style that lesser lights might envy," says Hetty.

"Then not you, Honored Hestia," says Ti so graciously that I swear a faint blush of sweetest rose brushes Hetty's pale cheeks.

"Enough talk," says Sun, jumping to her feet. "Let's go."

"There's one hitch. I don't have the key on me. I left it behind when I went to Vogue Academy. It's at my family's tent."

"You really grew up in the tent city?" James drags his cap off his head and presses it against his chest.

"I really did. I can go alone."

"I'll go with you," I say.

Sun says, "We'll all go. James, you'll stay here to monitor the environs in case there are any unusual movements we need to know about."

Ti glances toward Isis. "The camp is a no-weapons zone."

"I can get clearance for that," says Sun. "You get us into Repose District."

So it is that an hour later we're walking the dusty streets of the tent city like a heist crew in a Channel Idol crime serial. We're all carrying laden tote bags to suggest we've been shopping. Filter masks conceal our faces, which is fortunate because at every ganglion intersection between a confused gaggle of enclosed food stalls, permit kiosks, and dry goods stores we pass screens projecting the latest results from Idol Faire. I didn't even realize the contest started thirty-six hours ago.

What's even more shocking is that while ribbon-wielding

fresh-faced returnee Ji-na is in number-one place, the number-eight contestant is "Princess Sun and her Companions." We're racing up the charts with what is evidently our first entry, a montage sequence of the battle at the industrial park that finishes off with Sun's stirring speech to the cadets underlaid by music that enhances her phrasing. Candace must have uploaded it from her hospital bed.

There's even a spinning image of the ten of us posed like any other idol group. It's an animated rendering with Sun positioned in the center, bold and bright, the Handsome Alika at her right hand, and the rest—James, Hetty, Isis, Ti, Candace, Solomon, and a stern Octavian at the very back—arrayed around them in various dramatic positions. The person that's me is crouched with chin resting on a gloved fist. I have never owned a pair of glittery gloves in my life, although I have to say they look pretty great and, even better, are the color of pomegranates. There's a fade-out behind me that winks in and out with a ghost outline of Perseus and Duke.

What a kick in the gut. I can't believe he's dead. The concept of death doesn't compute. It's more like I haven't seen him for years, which was how we lived anyway. Has Sun commissioned a spirit tablet for him yet? Where will she place it?

Did my parents ever love him, even a little bit? Did they miss him after they sent him away? I doubt it.

Did they miss me?

"Hey, Perse." Solomon snags my elbow. "Don't fall behind."

A thrill of panic rushes through me as I realize the others have vanished. But Alika has brought his ukulele in its hard-shell case and slung it over his back, so we follow its curve bobbing through the press of the crowd. Sun's in the lead with Ti guiding her. Isis strides right behind her, followed by Alika and Hetty, who walk with heads together, conferring. Solomon's been given the privilege of rear guard. All our weapons are concealed in bags or tucked into deep pockets of the long canvas coats Ti found for us in one of the military storerooms. I've strapped my tonfa on my forearms, hidden under the sleeves of the duster I'm wearing.

"Isis must trust you," I say to Solomon as we hasten to catch up.

"She trusts I can defend the princess. Nothing else matters to her. She's all business. I checked her military record. It's pretty intimidating."

"Really?"

"Really. Did you know Colonel Isis is House Samtarras too? Like the Honorable James? Except she's from a minor branch, the kind that's one ladder rung up from having to sign off as an ordinary citizen. Like what happened to Asshole Kim's family line. That's why she's a cee-cee and not a Companion, I guess."

"Right."

It's midday, windy with a constant pall of dust, but the streets are as busy as if a work shift just changed. About half the people out and about are wearing filter masks, most of them grimy, pitted, and worn with age and rust. Those without masks look haggard, ashen circles dark under their eyes and sweat beading on their brows even though it's not hot. Fever stalks those without clean air.

The deeper we walk into the camp, the more people are out without masks. The scrubbed-clean tents near the main gate give way to older tents repaired with glossy sealant. Farther on, fraying tents are patched with squares of repurposed fabric sewn or taped to walls and roofs.

The food stalls lose their sealed enclosures; sellers who can't afford masks wrap cloth over their noses and mouths. The stores become awnings draped with clear plastic walls with reverse fans sucking out the worst of the grit. The locals glance at us but, with our faces behind the masks and our unremarkable gear, no one pays us much mind. A janitor mech grinds past, sounding on its last gears as it nuzzles along the ground for litter and waste to toss into its rubbish bin.

Ti whistles. The mech halts, reverses, and trundles over to her. She rests a hand on its forward picker.

"This is one of my dad's," she says proudly. "He repairs mechs that've been discarded as too old or broken down to bother with."

"How can you tell it's one of his?" I ask.

She traces a doubled chevron burned into the metal. "This is his mark.. It brings the bin back to him and we sort and sell anything of value."

Sun examines the street with its patched tents lining the packed-dirt street. Her head tilts as it does when she's thinking hard, running whatever calculations go on in that formidable mind. There's nothing here except people subsisting day to day, waiting for something to change in their lives. Even the poorest neighborhood in Argos must seem paved with glory compared to this. No wonder the people stuck here are desperate enough to endure the fenced-in barracks at the industrial park. No wonder Ti talks the way she does about the money she gets paid, even in death.

Two tents down a boy stands behind the clear plastic window of a tent's entry porch, a kind of airlock between the street and the air-sealed interior of the living quarters. He's staring down the other direction of the street with a wistful expression, watching a pack of children about his age kicking a ball up and down the street. Ti glances in that direction and sees him.

I've seen her polished smile, her friendly grin, and her serious profile. What crosses her face is new to me: a flash of alarm in the flare of her eyes that she immediately shutters away, succeeded by tenderness as her lips press together in a pained, compassionate, loving smile.

42

The Heat of the Wily Persephone's Lust

Ti releases the mech and hurries toward the tent. The boy notices the movement, then her. A grin breaks wide on his face. He starts bouncing up and down but stays behind the seal as Ti lets a lock-strip read her retina. When the strip blinks green she peels it open and steps inside. He flings himself into her embrace with an open, tactile enthusiasm that isn't Chaonian at all. It reminds me of people in Phene dramas, always hugging and back-slapping and spilling their emotions all over everything and everyone like so much sticky syrup that will have to be laboriously peeled off the skin when it dries.

"What are you doing out here?" she asks him in a low voice. "You shouldn't be out here."

"Ma said it was okay if I just look with my eyes."

She turns him to face us as we politely file onto the porch. Plastic mats cover the dirt, and there's a rack to put shoes on before you step up onto a raised floor where another sealed entry, this one opaque, leads into the interior.

"Princess Sun, this is my brother, Kaspar. Kas, this is Princess Sun and her Companions."

"You're on Channel Idol," he says, taking us in.

Sun considers the child gravely. "In eighth place, for now. But we're going to win."

"How do you know?"

"Because I win."

"Oh. Okay." He's a stocky boy, thick through the middle, wearing an oversized tunic meant for an adult that's been hemmed up so it hangs to his knees. A striped knit cap covers his head. "Did you really fight that battle at the broken sky-tower, or was it just a made-up story?"

"We really fought. People who think it's all right to build a reputation, or an idol campaign, on fake battles aren't to be respected."

He shifts, like a ripple in his torso, then scratches his chin as Ti watches him anxiously. "Do you want to see my drawings? I can't go out, so I draw."

"Of course I want to see them," says Sun, "but we don't have much time."

He looks at me, studying me closely. He's not as dark as Tiana, and he doesn't resemble her, his features being lean and long and with a cute beaky nose he'll have to grow into. His eyes are hazel instead of brown, and his hair is entirely concealed beneath the knit cap, which is pulled down over his ears all the way to his neck.

"You are the Honorable Persephone. Ti works for you, doesn't she?"

"That's right, little brother," I say, deciding to treat him with respectful informality. "How about I go with you to get the drawings while your big sister takes the princess to get the thing she needs."

"What do you need?" Kas asks.

Ti tweaks his nose affectionately. "Classified. Where's Ma?"

"Inside."

"Are we going in?" Sun gestures toward the sealed entry flap that hides the interior.

Ti bites her lower lip. Alika is scanning the porch, the view of the street as seen through the plastic, and the fresh-faced boy.

She takes in a deep breath. "Princess Sun, please let there be no images of this street, this tent, or anyone in my family."

Sun says, "Are you ashamed of your living conditions?"

Ti lifts her chin. "I'm not ashamed."

"Yes, I didn't get that impression before. If anything, you've been quite insistent on describing the plight of the refugees and the conditions they labor under. Giving Alika full access can help educate people, don't you think?"

"Educate them in service of your Idol Faire ratings, do you mean?"

The boy's mouth drops open at this plain speaking.

Sun's steady regard does not waver. Maybe Ti's words have angered her, or maybe she's intrigued. I don't yet know the princess well enough to tell. "How can citizens learn about what needs to be changed if they're never allowed to see it? I would suggest you have a responsibility to educate people."

Ti's in full statuesque mode, posture proud and stately, face a study in composure. It's hard not to admire her and the cool, clear way she answers.

"You say that, Your Gloriousness, because you don't comprehend how dangerous it is for people like us to come to the attention of the authorities."

Sun raises both eyebrows, then lowers them. "Alika, erase whatever you've recorded here. Very well. Let's get what we came for so we can finish this mission."

"Tiana? Is that your voice I am hearing? What brings you home?" The interior flap is pulled aside. A woman appears in the opening. She looks so much like the boy, with that same lean, long face and long torso, that it's evident to everyone who she must be. Her shock on seeing us clamps off whatever she meant to say next.

Smoothly, Ti says, "Princess Sun, may I present to you my mother, Nanea kin Kavan."

It's a Karnoite name style, identifying themselves by their clan rather than a surname and place name. Nanea is tall like Tiana, but her extreme slenderness and long torso gives her height a more ethereal sense, unlike the weight and impact of Ti's presence.

Leaving Solomon on guard duty on the porch, seated on a cheap reconstituted bench, the rest of us take off the grubby shoes we're wearing. Ti wouldn't let us keep on our military boots; she said footwear is a dead giveaway in a place like this.

Inside, the tent measures eight meters by fifteen meters. I'd expected it to be crowded with several families, but instead it feels spacious because it is sparsely furnished. There are a pair of double racks for sleeping and a curtained-off double bed. A long shelf is neatly lined with clear boxes. The only other furniture is a black table for eating and viewing. Braided throw rugs cover the plastic flooring, giving the room a bit of warmth and texture. Most surprising is a remarkably elaborate kitchen that takes up the rear third of the space, with four ovens, eight burners, a double sink, lots of stainless steel counter space, and a large refrigeration unit. Loaves of bread are cooling on a sideboard beside a tray of crescent-shaped pastries. The smell makes my mouth water.

"Ma has a baking sideline," says Ti, sounding nervous for only the second time since she and I have met.

"Please, Your Highness, have a pastry," says her mother, who is watching our group as if we all have stingers hidden about our persons and are bringing her a wealth of trouble. "I've got a barley-and-squash stew ready to heat, if you'd honor us by staying for a meal."

Sun hesitates. To turn down an offer of hospitality is the height of rudeness.

"Ma, there isn't time. We can come around later, but right now we're in a hurry."

"My apologies," says Sun. "Your offer is generous. Only the urgency of our situation prevents me from accepting."

"What have you been getting yourself in with, Ti?" Her mother grasps Ti's elbow with a loving concern that makes me envious. My mother never cared about me except insofar as my activities or performance reflected on her.

"I need my guild key."

"Your father decided to store it in the lockbox in his shop. But let me go first, and warn him. He'll be . . ." She breaks off. There's a vent at the back of the kitchen that I assumed led to a toilet, laundry, and shower area, but it rips aside now and a big man pushes through, saying, "What's going on in here? Did I hear Ti's voice?"

He stops short, comically stunned. He has to be Ti's father with such a similar complexion and build. She got her beautifully long-lashed eyes from him. Past the open vent I can see into a second tent, exactly as big as this one. Two big worktables, a wall of mech arms, and shelves stacked with random parts and baskets of bits and bobs fill the back half of the tent. Farther forward, an opaque front wall is rolled up so passersby can see in. Several people are in the tent, one bent over a worktable and another at the front talking to a pair of customers. The person at the worktable looks up toward us; he looks enough like Ti's mother that he could easily be her brother. Ti's father shuts the vent to block the view.

"Your Highness!" He taps his right arm to his chest in salute. The hand and arm below the shoulder are a crude mechanical, stark metal, not even a basic cosmetic replacement. "Corporal Vontae Yáo Alaksu. Third Battalion, Scorpion Company, Republican Guard."

Sun nods regally. "Where did you lose the arm, Corporal?"

"Lukka Prime, second day of the attack on the Esplanade in the Fourth Kanesh campaign."

"Surely as a citizen who served honorably and was disabled in the line of duty you are due something better than that basic attachment."

He glances toward Nanea. "Life's a complicated set of choices, Your Highness. How may we help you?"

"I need my guild key, Dad," says Ti.

He blows out air through pinched lips, looks at Ti, looks at Sun, then steps back. "I'll get it."

Sun walks after him. "We'll come with you and your daughter."

A small hand grasps my wrist. Staring hopefully up at me, Kaspar says, "I thought you were going to look at my drawings?"

I catch Sun's eye and gesture toward the boy. "I'll stay here with Kas and his esteemed mother."

He tugs me to the long shelf with its boxes. His mother hurries to an oven to get out a batch of cupcakes, the smell so appetizing that I lick my lips involuntarily. She brings a cooled pastry over on a tin plate, and I can't refuse it and don't want to anyway. It's flaky, moist, and delicious with an almond-and-sesame-seed paste.

"Mmmm. This is so good."

She smiles. Her accent is a curious one; she's not Chaonian, that's for sure. "I was able to invest in this new kitchen with Tiana's employment bonus. But I beg your pardon, Honored. I have a batch of batter needing to go in."

"Please, go on with your work. It would be a shame to waste such mouthwatering food."

Surreptitiously I examine the woman as she works. She wears a faded blue dress that falls to her ankles, cut close to her long body and narrow hips. She's got a dead-on eye for pouring out batter into small molds without spilling a drop.

Kas sets a box on the table and opens it. I wasn't sure what to expect, but it isn't this: actual physical pictures, on real paper, using physical pencils and brushes. All the images are landscapes and cityscapes, rendered in exceptional detail with a few tiny human figures here and there as if for scale.

"Wow. How old are you?"

"Thirteen."

"These are really good."

"Do you think so?"

"I do. You must spend a lot of time on art. I guess you really love it."

He shrugs. "It gives me something to do. I don't go to school." He flashes a look toward his mother, as if hoping she will hear and be sorry for denying him this chance.

"Why not?" I ask.

His mother interrupts from the kitchen. "Kaspar has the asthma. Also he is displaying four of the precursor symptoms to developing pit lung. It is not safe for him to go outside."

"Not even with a mask?" I ask, thinking of how awful it must be to stay cooped up in a tent all day every day, and even worse for a curious, restless kid.

Her look of alarm shames me. It's not my business. I don't live here, struggling to make ends meet, much less breathe, and to keep my child from developing a degenerative and fatal disease of the lungs that I can't afford proper treatment for. So I turn my attention back to the art.

The landscapes look strangely familiar, but I can't pin a memory on where I've seen them: a monumental promenade lined with stone beasts sculpted in imitation of the mythical animals of the Celestial Empire; a white tower crowned with horns; a flat salt plain at twilight with three moons rising; a forest of fiercely green bamboo pierced by a walkway that branches into three paths, each mysterious and tempting; a gleaming three-cornered plaza elevated high above the ground on a cushion of air and illuminated by hovering lanterns in the shape of koi.

The interior of a vast basilica with sixteen floridly decorated alcoves dedicated to the holy saints of the Celestial Empire, looking down the nave toward the main entry doors.

"They're not right yet." The boy leans on the table, examining the paintings with an artist's skeptical eye. He points to the bamboo forest. "Like here. I'll never be good at leaves until I see a real one. Wouldn't it be nice to go there for real?"

"Is that a real place?"

"Yes."

"What's it called?"

"I don't know."

"Do you copy these from things you've seen on the net?"

"We don't have the net," he whispers. "It's too expensive."

His mother breaks in. "The net is not allowed except through a censored shunt. This shunt the authorities are always monitoring. And it *is* very high in cost, too much cost for what you are receiving."

In Chaonia basic net access is provided to all citizens. People could no more function without it than they could function without medical care, food, and shelter. I scan the shelves and spot actual physical books, rarely seen outside of archives and museums. But when I walk over to study the titles, none are travel books with pictures for a homebound child to copy. Seven are classical fashion books with antiquated titles like *Dictionary of Design Innovation* and *Traditional Style in the History of the Celestial Empire*. Two are old-fashioned reading primers, one for children and the other for Karnoite language users learning Common Yele, the language of scholars and traders and anyone with pretensions of being sophisticated and civilized. One is encased in a clear sleeve, its spine labeled in a script I don't recognize and which the net can't identify. I'm oddly reluctant to ask, although my fingers itch to slip the book off the shelf and page through it as through a mystery.

"That's my favorite," says Kas, who has followed on my heels like I'm the most fascinating thing that's ever happened to him, which possibly I am. "But I'm not allowed to touch it. Do you want to see?"

Before I can answer he pulls the slender volume off the shelf and carries it back to the table. There he opens it with the tender care one gives to very old people. From the book's inside pocket he unfolds a diagram.

My heart stops, or it would, if desire twinned with shock could stall the atria. It's a beacon map so old that discoloration has warped patterns into the print.

"Where did you get this?" I ask hoarsely.

The mother straightens up by the oven, where she just slid in a tray of unbaked cupcakes. Her voice sharpens. "Kaspar, what do you have there?"

"Just showing the Honorable my drawings," he lies.

I can't bear to betray him, and anyway I want to touch it, but I'm afraid that if I do the heat of my lust will scorch it to ash. I am staring at an artifact from a lost archive.

For two thousand years after landfall, humans expanded out of the queendom of Mishirru into a rich, worlds-heavy region. Local systems were able to retain autonomy because although the vast distances of space were bridgeable by the knnu drive, the passage between systems took months or years. That all changed when the Apsaras Convergence invented, or discovered, the beacons.

I like to think of the beacons as interstellar stations on an invisible rail system we no longer fully comprehend. Conceptually it works on the same basic principles. Stations link together to form lines that follow set routes to specific places. A beacon has to be gravitationally anchored to another object in a solar system, like a planet. And of course they are anchored within systems in sets of prime numbers, or one.

Any line ends ultimately in a terminus, a single-beacon system; a ship can come in from and go back to the same place, but it can't go farther, not by beacon drive.

Janus systems have two beacons. They're the backbones of the system, like local stations on the Chaonian rail lines. A long single-stage route of janus beacons runs like a river through ancient Mishirru from its glorious capital all the way to the isolated terminus system of Landfall where the Argosies that fled the Celestial Empire found a first planetary haven, long before the beacons were built.

A cerberus system has three beacons, as Troia System does, for example. Now the route possibilities begin to branch out by creating complicated intersections, since a beacon might link you not to a nearby system but to one much farther away.

Chaonia, Molossia, and Thesprotis are all scylla systems, each with five beacons. The Republic of Chaonia parlayed its liminal space between frontiers and its Tinker-Evers-Chance convergence into political and military might.

Karnos System is a hydra, with seven beacons whose tendrils reach out into the resource-rich Hatti region and back into the heart of the Phene Empire. That's why it's so valuable.

The Phene and Yele, who each control an eleven-beacon system, can send out multiple tendrils of influence that have allowed them to become the most powerful of confederations.

Every main hub and branch line of the current beacon system is burned into my mind. I know the map by heart. What makes this map amazing is that it shows the beacon network before the collapse.

The collapse came suddenly. Whole route sections vanished into what we now call the Gap. Of course Argosy fleets powered by knnu drive still ply their slow roads through what is not really a gap but just normal space, guided by the ancient art of celestial navigation, a skill the Argosy guilds guard jealously and never teach to outsiders. When Solomon's family lost their little fleet, they lost their sails.

But even more incredibly, this map must date from the point of collapse because on this map the Apsaras home world, She Who

Bore Them All, is marked with thirteen beacons. It was originally built with eleven. Many have speculated that the construction of twelfth and thirteenth beacons in a single system is what overloaded and crashed the network.

Scholars have reconstructed most of the lost routes. Even though no one can use them, it's the kind of thing people want to know. And here are the old beacon lines as they were at the peak of the Convergence, overlaid on a faded star chart that marks the main routes taken by Argosy trading fleets in their glory days, when their ships were the lifeline that linked worlds. A person who possesses this chart might be able to use it to find She Who Bore Them All.

"Where did you get this?" I ask again.

The vent into the repair shop rips open. Sun charges through in the lead with Isis and Hetty and Alika behind her. Kas snatches the map out of my hand, slides it back into the book, and shoves the book onto the shelf.

"Can't I even take an image?" I whisper, angry that I didn't think to record it.

He shakes his head. I'm about to try to wheedle him when Sun strides up to us.

"Time to go," she says, and then her gaze jolts to a halt as she takes in the paintings. "Who did these?" she demands.

Kas manages a nervous smile. His lips don't move, but I'm sure I hear a strange whisper of sound. His mother drops a pan, a clatter that whips Isis around.

Sun splays both hands on the table and studies the illustrations. "These are all views of famous landmarks in the Phene Empire. That's the processional way on Anchor Prime. That's the famous horned lighthouse on Sogdia Limit. That's the plain of triple-headed Cyclops, in Auger System. And that is the floating concourse on Axiom Prime. It's off-limits to anyone except high-ranking Phene military and administrative officers and members of the Rider Council."

"How do you know what it looks like?" I ask. "You're none of those things."

"That's right, you didn't grow up at court. For three years a high-ranking Phene official took refuge at court with their son, Bartholomew. Bar and I became friends."

"What happened?"

"The official got tired of me asking questions about the empire. And they really weren't pleased when they found out Bar was showing me interdicted images of places no outsider is meant to see. So they separated us. Not long after they got recalled when the political enemy who'd had them exiled died abruptly. You know how that goes."

"I don't, really. I was at CeDCA for five years, remember? So I wouldn't have to know how it goes."

"Don't kid yourself, Perse," says Sun with the measuring tilt of her head. Am I being found wanting? "We of the Core Houses don't just walk out of that life and those connections. They make us what we are."

"Yeah, yeah, I already had this lecture from Tiana. I don't want it from you."

We both glance toward the back of the tent.

Ti stands at the open vent, embracing first her mother and then her father. Kas slouches over to them, looking as sullen as only a thirteen-year-old can. Sun examines his gait and chubby torso through narrowed eyes, then shakes herself and steps away from the table. She slips a court token out of her sleeve and sets it on the gleaming kitchen counter.

"If you need anything, this token will get you access to me personally."

I look longingly at the shelf and the slender book, but there is no possible way to get an image now. I don't want to get Kaspar into trouble. The poor, isolated boy couldn't resist showing off. But now I know it exists and where it is, and because Ti is my cee-cee I'll have an excuse to come back here.

Tiana leads us out of the camp by a different route. She's silent, brooding, as we reach a large nerve center filled with market stalls, enclosed shops, wash facilities for those who can afford the exorbitant water cost for clean clothes and clean bodies, and endless lines leading into various administrative centers where refugees can purchase temporary ration cards, travel and work permits, and urgent medical care.

There's a line to get into the line for the security gate to Repose District.

Ti leads us past hundreds of resigned, exhausted people whose faces are wrapped in gauze or wheezing filter masks running down their last charge. She heads for an establishment advertising itself with an elaborate neon lotus flower whose petals open and close. There's a main door carved with various symbols: an ichthus, a butterfly unfolding out of a cocoon, womb boats and phallic towers, a caduceus with intertwined snakes, and a pair of hands. But Ti leads us around a corner and down a shadowed alley. She uses her key to unlock a nondescript door.

We enter a service hallway. Voices speak in the distance: laughter, sobbing, whispered intimacies, cheerful chatter clattering from a kitchen. I'm hungry, and I can't stop thinking about the pastry. Twice people approach us down the long corridor. Ti gestures with a sign, and they sign back and ignore us.

The corridor ends in a square, featureless room with an airlock and a lock pad. Ti unlocks the entry and we cycle through, emerging into a room so exactly like the one we just left that for an instant I think we have simply walked a full 360 through the gate and come out where we started.

Sun pauses, checking in with James, then turns to the rest of us.

"Hetty, you go with Alika . . ." She trails off as Hetty gives her a look that would singe a lesser luminary. "Isis, Solomon, Hetty, with me. We only get one shot at this."

"We're taking out the Rider and the remaining Phene special forces, Your Highness?" Isis asks. "The four of us?"

"Zizou is our secret weapon."

"You're sure he'll obey you, and not the Phene? He works for them, after all."

"Among the banners, an oath to a Royal overrides all other orders. The Phene haven't figured that out yet. If the banners have anything to say about it, they never will. Perse, you go with Alika."

"What are Alika and I doing?" I ask, trying to sound perky instead of dismayed.

"You two are the flanking maneuver."

Alika looks at me, gives a skeptical sigh, and says, "You need to work on your visual presence, but for now set your stinger on stun and act like my backup."

"My favorite assignment," I say in my most sardonic drawl.

He adds, "If you can't smile then that sullen look will work almost as well for the wasps."

Ouch.

I'd exchange a meaningful eye roll with Ti, but she and the others are already out the door. We follow into a dim corridor. I pull my filter mask up off my face and suck in deep breaths of air so rich it makes me a bit heady. The corridor ends in two doors, side by side. One opens into an alley and the other into a tiny campaspe shrine. The Campaspe Guild is a labor union, not a religion, but some people bring offerings and so a clamshell grotto sits in Repose District for those who may find it needful. Sun and the others hustle away down the alley, but Alika leads me into the back of the grotto. Tucked into the hinge of the grotto's clamshell architecture rests a couch heaped with pillows embroidered with images of acrobatic sexual postures, many of which I've tried and an intriguing few that are new to me. Beside the couch stands an altar table made of rose quartz and laden with flowers, bites of food, and drams of arrack, soju, and golden rum. Alika pauses to examine the space.

I say, "You're not thinking of recording yourself singing here, are you? Doesn't that seem a little . . ."

"It's a fantastic venue, intimate and suggestive."

"Disrespectful?" I don't like being on the receiving end of the Handsome Alika's scowl. It makes me want to touch my face to make sure there's no unsightly snot or drool to disgust the world.

"You seem to be under a misapprehension, Persephone Lee. We're at war with the Phene. Don't be precious."

"Your call, since you're in charge of this flanking maneuver." I slip out my tonfa and twist them together into stinger configuration. "I just take orders."

"On second thought, we can't get enough disruption in here. The space is too small. We'll go out to the fountain plaza."

We pass through light showers of water interspersed with gauzy curtains rippling in a wind generated by a mechanism at the back of the grotto. The curved rim of the giant shell segues into steps that lead down onto a vast plaza. An eight-tiered fountain in a pagoda style stands at the center of the plaza. Its tip touches the high clear dome that seals in the air of Repose District. Bits of torn sky serenade us from beyond the dome's curve, but mostly the light is yellowish and dim, occluded by gusts of dirt and sand that scrape across the outer surface of the dome. It's quite tranquil here beneath the shelter of the dome. I think of Ti growing up out there, and me growing up always in here, or places like here.

Alika heads across the plaza for the fountain. People stare at him because he's still wearing his filter mask, here where no one needs that protection. There are so many people loitering on the plaza it's impossible to tell who is here for an hour of free air and who is here to worship, make an offering, or seek the revelation of serenity.

"Oi. Persephone. Pay attention!" We've reached the steps of the fountain. "I need you to do the recording. Focused on me, of course, but it's crucial to get the background and the audience. You know how to record, right?"

"Sure," I lie, and immediately ping Ti.

My ping gets shot back at once with a BUSY. CAN'T.

Alika climbs up onto the rim of the fountain and strums the opening chords of a song he made famous last year. People standing nearby turn in eager surprise. When he pulls off his filter mask, it leaves a smear of grit around his perfect features, but the grime only enhances his presence because he's got that kind of flair. People turn to gape as he launches into his interpretation of an ancient poem, his voice and the ukulele amplified by a means I don't understand.

"Wherever you stand, be the soul of that place."

Grown folks cry silent tears at the sight of Idol Faire's most beloved performer standing among them, who are the least and the forgotten. Raggedly dressed children, faces ashine with innocent wonder, are lifted up onto adult shoulders so they can see. More people hurry into the plaza.

I need to start recording. I launch into the net to open Channel Idol's streaming Idol Faire coverage. A spike of commentary has already started building and soon will become towers of squee scratched down at intervals by the usual ranks of ironic too-cool-for-you critics. "Princess Sun and her Companions" has climbed to number six in the ranking on the strength of public feeds, and Alika has only just completed the first verse.

I clumsily toggle through recording options as I scan the plaza with its many different architectural styles all crammed cheek by jowl, just as Ti said. For example, the campaspe shrine is built below the towering wall of a saints basilica identifiable by its flying buttresses and guardian gargoyles.

That's when I realize I *have* seen images of the basilica Kas painted. It's the original basilica built on Anchor Prime by the first Phene rulers almost a thousand years ago, rebuilt and expanded several times over the centuries. We saw images of it in class, in third year, when we studied the history and culture of the empire, the better to know your enemy. What's weird, though, is that every image I've ever seen of a basilica's interior has sighted down the nave from the entry doors toward the apse. No one but Riders can enter the apse, so it's unexpected that Kas has painted a basilica from a point within the apse looking back toward the entry doors.

At that very moment I unexpectedly glimpse my father.

He's deftly maneuvering through the edge of the crowd. A scan of the menu reveals that the Iros hermitage lies off a nearby side street festooned with flags, but he walks past the side street and climbs the stairs to the portico of the saints basilica.

I abandon the singing Alika, shove through the adoring crowd, and run toward the basilica on the trail of my father.

43

A Brief Handoff from One Body to Her Other Half

Sun followed Tiana as the cee-cee led her, Hestia, Isis, and Solomon down a lane lined with souvenir shops displaying prayer flags and beads, silk-flower necklaces, and miniature henge pillars carved with inspirational sayings like "Go with all your heart" and "A tree starts with a seed." They paused outside a shop displaying every size and shape of bell.

Sun exchanged tote bags with Hetty.

Hetty hefted Sun's bag, testing its weight. She hadn't been certain Sun would assign her to this part of the operation, given its small numbers and big risk. That she'd never wielded a weapon except in training gave her pause, but Octavian's tutelage of the young people in his charge had been thorough and exacting.

Isis pinged through to James. CAN YOU GET US A MAP OF THE BUILDING?

"There is no map, they keep the layout hidden," said Hetty in a low voice before James could reply. "Since every seer is blind to visual light, so every hermitage must be laid out on the same plan with all the same proportions. I know the plan."

"How can you know, if it's secret, Honored Hestia?" Tiana examined her with the skepticism of a person who may feel uneasy about trusting her life to hearsay. It was difficult not to feel intimidated by Tiana's disciplined beauty and precisely measured elegance, and yet Hetty admired it as well.

"My father was a seer. He is a seer. He fell in love and left the hermitage. He married. They had me. And all was well. Until my other father—"

"Alika's started to play," Sun interrupted. "No time for talk."

Lambent notes rose alongside his distinctive voice. Around them, guests and visitors and loiterers browsing the stalls stopped what they were doing. People's heads came up, their postures straightened with astonished excitement, and an aura of energy sparked in the air. A trio of wizened old folks sporting grimy filter masks pulled down to their chests whispered excitedly among themselves, then turned as one body and hastened toward the plaza. A customer set down a statue of thousand-armed Mercy as the shop's merchant apologetically began rolling down his awning and security screen.

"Idol Faire here, on our very own plaza! This might never happen again in my lifetime."

A ping dropped in from James: a map marked with the rectangular exterior outline of the hermitage's footprint. The interior remained opaque except for a pinprick of light marking where Zizou's ring was located.

Tiana said, "The green door eleven stalls down, on the right, accesses a delivery entrance into the hermitage."

"How do you know that?" Isis murmured with a warning glance at Sun.

Tiana shrugged. "Even seers of Iros on occasion request the private services of a campaspe. There's an entry vestibule and two small receiving rooms. Beyond that I don't know."

"There is no vault or cellar, just one floor." Hetty sketched a rough drawing of an architectural plan into their shared ring network. She left two-thirds of the rectangle blank and concentrated on the layout of the back third of the compound which had branching corridors splitting around rooms of different sizes. "This portion is reserved for daily life. These cells for sleeping. Toilets. Laundry. Baths. The kitchen's here, and a refectory. Here's Zizou's signal, in the infirmary hall. See here? It sits beside the medicinal garden."

"Are there any secret escape routes?"

"If there is one my father never told me."

Sun studied the pattern of corridors and rooms. From the delivery entrance there was, curiously, no direct route to the kitchen or infirmary. "We'll split up and take two approaches. Isis, with Hetty. Solomon, with me. Tiana, once we've entered you go back to the street. James?"

HERE.

"Are the marines in place?"

AFFIRMATIVE. SEALING OFF THE SIDE STREETS AND ENTRY GATES AS WE SPEAK.

"Await my signal."

The crowd roared from the plaza as Alika flourished through the end of his initial offering and segued into a new song: "'I went down to Saint James Infirmary, and saw my baby there. Stretched out on a long white table. So cold, so sweet, so fair.'"

Sun pushed on down the souvenir lane against the tide of people flooding out toward the plaza. Hetty kept pace, determined to keep up, but while Sun had the presence of a missile loosed upon the field, Hetty had to work hard to tamp down her anxiety. She didn't underplay the skills she had, but battle wasn't her forte. She just didn't want to mess things up when she was the one who had demanded not to be left behind.

Sun glanced at her but said nothing: no encouragement, no warning. With Sun you were either there, or you weren't there. You succeeded or you failed. Action and outcome ruled. Everything else was pointless chatter.

For a thinker like Hetty, who lived so much in her mind, Sun's focus was a heady brew. She could drink it down like sunlight and never be filled up.

They reached the hermitage's delivery door set into a windowless exterior wall. Its security had a retinal scanner and a comms lock to force visitors and supplicants to enter by the main vestibule at the hermitage's public front entrance. Tiana's Campaspe Guild key unlocked the comms unit as the others stood outside of visual scan. When the comms light blinked green the cee-cee spoke.

"I'm so sorry I'm late," she said in a throaty voice, all raw promise. "There's a disturbance in the plaza, and I got caught in the crowd. I'll make up the lost time."

The comms clicked over twice. Then a youthful voice said, unsteadily, "Who are you here for?"

"Didn't he leave my calling card? I was told . . ."

Tiana heaved a sigh, like an actress in a serial, only it was different watching it in the flesh as she brushed a hand over the top of one breast. More visceral. More inviting and arousing, stirring heat in Hetty's chest. But the doorkeeper had to be a seer, even if a novice, which meant he was blind to the visual spectrum. Either Tiana was using her voice to full effect or somehow manipulating her own body heat.

She went on so breathily that Hetty had to stifle the impulse to laugh. "I need this job. The prime's approval is so important."

"Prime Deo?"

"Is there another prime in residence?"

"N . . . No."

"It will garnish my campaspe rating. I could throw a quick something in for you, as thanks, or send another guild member around later if I'm not to your taste. I know novices can't afford us otherwise. That seems so unfair. We all deserve pleasure."

Sun touched a finger to her brow, shaking her head as if to say that such a blatant ploy could not possibly work. But the doorkeeper's voice suggested youth and inexperience. The seal popped. Attached on hinges, the door swung open just enough to offer space for a body to squeeze through.

Tiana signaled for the others to be ready, then slipped inside and out of sight into darkness. "My thanks. Do you mind if I touch your shoulder so I don't trip? I can't see anything in here."

An indistinct reply was followed by an audibly excited inhalation.

Solomon grabbed the door before it could close. Isis took out the doorkeeper with a single blow and moved on. Sun and Solomon stepped over his body, but Hetty paused. He was young, with a beardless face and hair cut short in the style of novices. Trusting and naïve—that's how her Yele father had described himself to her once, remembering his youth in the order.

Tiana said, "I'll drag him into a receiving room so he doesn't get hurt, poor kid."

"That's good, but then you must get back outside," Hetty said. "We can't chance that you might be taken hostage."

"Got it." Tiana's expression was serious, even grim.

Sun and Solomon vanished into the dark interior down the only available corridor. Hetty tugged on a stealth mask concealed in the tote bag and toggled her view to infrared. The shift in view was immediate and surprising. The lightless passage sprang to life with strips along the floorboards, energy bands visible with enhanced sight and thus making it easy to negotiate the windowless hermitage if you were a seer.

Isis tapped her on the shoulder. They padded past symbols painted on closed doors, turned left, turned right. A long passage ended in a three-way junction. Sun and Solomon headed left. They would go through the kitchen, which had a door into the infirmary hall.

Isis and Hetty turned right. There was a left-turning corner eight meters ahead. Isis crept toward the corner as if weightless and frictionless while Hetty felt each of her own footfalls as a thunder. A murmur of voices, speaking Phenish, drifted to them from around the corner. The people were arguing, if tone was anything to go by, and speaking too quickly and with too much choppiness for her translator to register more than individual words tossed up onto her net like verbal flotsam. Her palms felt greasy with sweat as she clutched her stinger.

A final sharp command—"Guard this entrance" in Phenish— was followed by the sigh and snick of a door opening and closing.

Isis pinged into her net rather than speaking. ON MY MARK.

A foot scuffed ahead, someone approaching just out of sight around the corner.

Isis hissed as softly as air escaping through a slit in an airlock's skin. Hetty's shoulder bumped into a wall. She felt Isis's heat beside her; then the soldier catapulted away from her. A muted grunt of surprise was followed by a limp body being slung onto the floor.

"Fff." That was Isis making a noise between teeth and lip as a signal.

Hetty found her calm place and slotted into it as if fixing gears gone out of true. Too late to turn back now. You were either there, or you weren't there.

She dropped flat and pushed around the corner to slide in beside Isis, who was using the prone body as cover. The individual had two arms.

Twenty meters down a straight passage, a heat source stood by a closed door into the medicinal garden, the door they needed to get through. Isis rolled a small heat-seeker ball down the passage to distract the sentry. Hetty shot four times, missing three, hitting once. The figure slumped, then recovered, straightening to put their weapon into play. A hissing whine marked the enemy's shot at the heat seeker. The glowing ball sparked and sputtered in a swift display of fireworks as it was taken out, but the distraction worked. Isis took down the sentry with a single shot.

They ran forward. This individual also had two arms, so they hadn't encountered any Phene yet. What if Sun's theory was wrong and there were no Phene here? And yet why were the philosophically pacifist seers acting like soldiers?

Isis eased open the door; all the doors in a hermitage had hinges. A line of sunlight from outdoors hit like an impact. Bent over, half-blinded as her eyes fought to adjust, Hetty slipped out the door and dodged behind the screen of a manicured hedgerow always grown in this location in hermitage medicinal gardens. Isis let the door close, staying inside while leaving Hetty on guard outside.

HOLD YOUR POSITION. YOU'VE GOT THIS. I'M GOING TO THE KITCHEN TO JOIN SUN. GET A BEAD ON THE INFIRMARY DOOR. LET NO ONE OUT. MARINES INCOMING ON SUN'S ORDER.

You've got this. Hetty took a few calming breaths as she scanned her surroundings. The garden was a glasshouse, sealed off from the outside world like the rest of the hermitage. Beyond its roof of ribbed glass she could see the high curve of the dome that sealed Repose District against the slow-killing atmosphere of Tjeker.

Movement flashed to her left. One side of a double door at the far end of the hedgerow lane—the other door into the infirmary hall—cracked open. The barrel of a rail gun poked out, two arms holding the weapon, a third bracing the door open, the fourth resting on a holster: a Phene soldier making a quick sweep. She flattened herself below the prickly leaves. Her hesitation could have killed her, but the soldier was already turning back, answering a voice from inside the hall. The door closed.

The Phene were truly here. Hetty was genuinely shocked at the idea that the seers of Iros were complicit with the Phene. Did her father know? Surely not. He was the most apolitical of scholars, gentle and kind and vulnerable, so she ruthlessly spiked the thought.

Hetty shifted position back to give herself an unobstructed shot down the narrow lane to the infirmary door. The door she'd entered through was a meter ahead of her, to her left, framed between a pair of dwarf cypress. Now she had to wait as Sun, Solomon, and Isis moved to the kitchen along the inner passageways. One minute, two, three ticked past.

The passageway door clicked and eased open a finger's breadth. Hetty held her position, and her breath. A man in seer's robes leaned out. She shot him in the torso with a silent, nonlethal blast. He slumped sideways, caught by cypress branches, the door held ajar by his trailing legs.

The door shifted. A figure half-seen against the darkness of the passage addressed her hesitatingly, speaking Imperial Phene with a slow clarity her imbed easily translated. "Pray, friend, do not shoot. We agreed between us—"

Hetty released a pulse just as a second seer leaned into view. He toppled forward. To her horror he was an elderly man wearing the prime's collar. The head of the hermitage was involved in the plot! His wispy hair, lined face, and air of fragility rattled her. She sucked in several tight breaths. Stay present. Don't drift. Be in the moment.

As if in answer, Sun pinged a command into the local military channel:

GO

Go meant Sun would be charging into the kitchen and from there into the infirmary hall. From inside the hall, right on schedule, shouts of surprise transformed into the noisy clamor of a vicious fight. The clatter of hailstorm guns. Cracking and splintering as objects got broken. A scream of pain. Hetty wanted to run to the infirmary door and charge in like a rescuing angel, but she held her position, following the plan.

A flash popped overhead. The glass roof shattered. Soldiers outfitted in the sleek camo-armor of Chaonian ground troops smashed through, deploying short-range boot thrusters as they dropped to the ground amid shards of falling glass.

Its Oleaginous Contents

Sun kicked open the door into the kitchen and charged in. James had full visuals through her helmet with its diadem of cameras giving a full surround view.

SEVENTY-FIVE. TWO. He whispered in coordinates.

A sweep from her stinger took down two Phene soldiers standing sentry by the far door into the infirmary, at a seventy-five-degree angle to her entry point. Solomon sprinted past her as she took down three seers to her left who were apparently cooking for the visitors. As he fell, one of the seers caught at the edge of a big kettle. His weight dragged it off the stove. With a crash, the kettle hit the floor and its slippery contents gushed out like a flood tide over the floor, cubed vegetables racing to catch her on a wave of creamy green-tinged liquid.

Solomon had already crashed through a door set into the opposite wall and into the infirmary. By the time she reached its threshold he had kicked over two metal examination tables polished to a sheen. He crouched behind one. The other, lying crosswise to the first, reflected a blurry view of the infirmary hall.

Surprise gave the attacker a brief advantage. Solomon got off a jackhammer of shots while the Phene dove for cover behind tables, cabinets, and the very lifepods and consoles Sun was determined to recover. A startled seer got hit in the first burst of return fire, falling with a scream as a Phene hailstorm tore through him. His body absorbed most of the chaff. The rest of the enemy burst peppered the two tables with a shattering sound that almost covered a splintering noise from outside.

OUR MARINES INCOMING, James pinged.

Isis pinged: I'M COMING THROUGH THE KITCHEN.

Sun brushed away a flicker of annoyance that Isis had left Hetty alone to watch the other door. The battle was now. Zizou's ring was straight ahead.

Solomon laid down a stream of covering fire as she dashed forward to duck behind the nearest console. Isis came through the door shooting, pulling attention off Sun. The princess risked a glance toward the far end of the room, where stood two huge apothecary cabinets up against a wall. Poised between the cabinets, Zizou was holding a heavy wooden chair as a barrier in front of the Rider, who was crouched behind him against the wall.

Zizou saw Sun.

The secret of the banners was their Royals, whom all banner soldiers must obey according to the covenant. The Phene wouldn't know what hit them.

"Zizou!" she commanded. "Capture the Rider."

"Kill her," said the Rider. A wand flashed in her hand. Zizou spasmed awkwardly, fighting whatever the Rider was pouring into his body. He lost the battle and leaped toward the console behind which Sun was crouched.

He shouted, "Royal, I'm leashed by the Phene——"

Isis hit him with a stinger blast that tumbled him sideways, not enough to keep him down for long but enough for Sun to dive to the shelter of a neighboring lifepod as the Phene soldiers opened fire. A flash of heat seared across Sun's thigh, the worst of its burn siphoned off by the knit armor leggings she was wearing under the loose working-folk trousers Ti had disguised them in. She landed atop an unconscious Phene soldier in ship's uniform who was bleeding from the neck. A hailstorm slammed into the lifepod with such a concussion of hits that the whole thing shuddered. Its power light winked from green to red, and its seal popped with an ugly gasp of defeat.

A four-armed figure loomed up behind her. She spun and shot straight up into an enemy face, then kept turning as James fed her positions, kept shooting. Where was the Rider? Live capture was the goal, but dead was acceptable. No Chaonian had ever captured a Rider, alive or dead.

The double doors to the medicinal garden blew open.

"Don't shoot the Gatoi!" Sun shouted as Chaonian marines flooded in.

The surviving Phene used their own bodies and whatever furniture they could move to create a ring of protection around their precious Rider. Rolling smoothly up to his feet Zizou cast a helpless, angry glance at Sun. He knew her but he was under the Rider's control, puppet to programming that overrode *even a Royal's command.*

A small painted door in one of the apothecary cabinets popped open to reveal the shockingly familiar face of Kiran Seth de Lee.

Effulgent Heaven. Persephone had been right.

In a cool, collected voice, as if they were entering a teahouse, Aisa Lee's spouse said to the Rider, "This way, Your Eminence. They tracked you here, so one of your people must have a tracker on them."

He retreated back into the darkness.

The Rider dropped to her knees by the cabinet door, making ready to crawl in. The unsettling glimpse of her riding face with its strange, half-formed features cast a pall over the infirmary as if, like a late-stage medusa, she could freeze people in their tracks. Every figure seemed to hesitate, wondering who to shoot first and who not to shoot.

"The tracker must be on the Gatoi," said the last remaining Phene officer, who crouched next to the cabinet with a weapon braced on a lower arm. "The ring."

The Rider tapped her wand against the cabinet and spoke in the soughing voice of her riding face. "Take off the ring."

Zizou doubled over as if he'd been slugged in the stomach. He stripped off the ring and let it fall, a soft clink onto the tile floor.

"Follow me. The rest of you, destroy the evidence. We are all destined for death."

Because Sun had told the marines not to shoot him, Zizou was himself the shield the Rider and the officer used to escape into the cabinet, after which the young banner soldier followed them inside.

The remaining Phene turned their weapons on the consoles and lifepods. In a rage at losing Zizou, losing her chance to rescue her father's work, losing face to the perfidious Lee clan, Sun unleashed the full fury of her people on them. It took thirty seconds to kill them all, far too long.

In the grim aftermath, smoke hissed from scorched lifepods and slagged consoles. Power monitors blinked warning orange or glowed red. Only three lifepods were still green. The kicker was the failure slamming her in the face. The fourteen lifepods and four consoles had been neatly stacked along one wall, awaiting pickup in an orderly fashion. It was her arrival that had skewed the plan and resulted in the deaths of her father's researchers and subjects.

"We need medics and engineers," she barked at the nearest marine.

The two apothecary cabinets were riddled with holes and striped with scorch marks. Fragments of leaves, roots, and powder lay scattered on the tile floor like an Idol Faire art project. Blood seeped from sprawled bodies to mingle with shredded brown leaves from a drawer labeled *Tobacco*.

She picked up Zizou's ring and slipped it on her left thumb before ducking down, meaning to crawl through the cabinet's still-open door to wherever it led. She would catch up to the Rider and capture her if it was the last thing she did.

Isis grabbed her arm and yanked her back.

"Princess! Let me run a scan first. They'll have triggered traps in their wake."

Sun was shaking, adrenaline coursing alongside wrath in her body, but she waited in a tense crouch as Isis rolled a heat seeker into the darkness. After three seconds it thudded into something, followed by a clunk, a leaden thump, and a hot puff of rancid air that blew back in their faces.

"That could have been your head," remarked Isis congenially.

What if it had been Octavian beside her? He'd have said, "Breathe, Princess. Don't let your temper control you."

She sat back on her heels. "We need a disposal technician."

"Sun! I captured the prime." Hetty appeared from the garden, dragging behind her a stumbling, elderly man who did, indeed, wear the prime's collar. He had a bruised forehead and a bloody nose.

As soon as she saw the slagged lifepods Hetty stopped short, expression caught in a grimace. She grabbed the prime's robe and shoved him around to face the red lights. "What monstrousness to kill that which is helpless."

The prime wouldn't even look at the slagged lifepods and their dead. Instead he scanned the broken drawers and their scattered contents as if detritus mattered more to him than human lives. Sun considered the ring on her left thumb. The Phene leash, the effects of the wand she'd just seen used on Zizou, was surely part of the answer to the mystery of mounting Gatoi "savagery" over the last thirty years. No wonder her father wanted to neutralize the neural control the Phene held over their Gatoi auxiliaries—so that they couldn't be mere detritus left behind in the wreckage of battle.

"Hetty, take charge of the lifepods and consoles. They must not be handed over to anyone except my father. The Phene fear what we will learn. As for what comes next, they'll do what they must to save the Rider."

The dead Phene soldiers were testament to that. Their deaths gave her no gratification. She respected their loyalty.

The prime was a different matter entirely. Hetty released him into Isis's custody and rushed over to examine the lifepods as a pair of medics joined her.

Sun gestured to Isis. "Bring him here."

Isis frog-marched him over.

Even furious as she was, Sun addressed him with the deference due to elders. "Your Wisdom, why are you harboring Phene hostiles in your hermitage?"

His look of alarm did not seem feigned, but how was she to know? "They came upon us suddenly."

"Yet here I find kidnapped people and stolen information neatly stacked, which means there was time to bring them inside in an orderly fashion. This room is prepared for illegal and criminal smuggling. You have a secret tunnel in your apothecary cabinet!"

"I had nothing to do with it," he said, breathing raggedly, sweating with fear. "The orders came in unexpectedly. I could not refuse them."

"From whom did the orders come?"

"On an encrypted channel. I don't know the source."

"You'll show me the message."

"It was a code with a four-minute grace period before dissolving. There is no physical remainder."

"How convenient for you."

The wrath surged back. Criminals and spies deserved no consideration. She raised her stinger as if it were a club. He shrank back, falling to his knees like a coward who didn't have enough honor to admit to deeds he'd knowingly chosen to commit.

"Where does the passage lead? You have one answer. It had best be the truth."

He scooped up a vial from amid the blood-soaked tobacco. Before Sun could take a startled breath, just as Isis grabbed a broken drawer off the floor labeled with the ideograms for *late bloomer,* he broke its oleaginous contents into his mouth.

45

In Which the Wily Persephone Has to Make a Decision in Forty-Two Seconds

It's hard to get up the basilica steps because of the push of excited, chattering people flooding out, lured by the promise of seeing the Handsome Alika. I flatten myself against a pillar and wait impatiently, unable to make headway against such a determined tide. As it slackens I start up the steps, fretting. I've lost my father. Not that I ever had him in a meaningful way. Even the brief interaction I witnessed between Ti and her father carried with it a thousand times more heartfelt connection and emotion than all the years built up between me and the man who, in his cold, detached way, parented me.

What business does a seer of Iros have in a saints basilica? Why would Zizou's ring show up in the Iros hermitage? I'm obviously right about Kiran Seth de Lee having been an agent of the Yele all this time.

Just as I reach the portico a second wave surges out, somber and silent and with a significant percentage of disgruntled-looking people. I allow the movement to carry me sideways until I'm pressed against one of the open doors. The basilica is emptying out even though temples never close but are always open for worshippers. The concept of sanctuary is one of the eight venerable traditions brought from the Celestial Empire.

I work my way inside and slip into the first alcove to stay out of sight while I get my bearings. I've never physically been in a basilica before. It's not part of the tradition I was raised in. While there are basilicas on Chaonia they are found in provisional districts, foreign population centers, and orbital habitats where trade and merchants cycle through. Of course at the academy our instructors discussed the history of beacon space, and of pre-beacon space whose histories are more fractured, and even earlier than these the oldest layer of archives, the broken memories of the Celestial Empire, these fragments that shore our ruins. The legacy of basilicas grew up in Phene territory. Scientists and laborers pieced together out of shattered archives their best scholarly recreation of old beliefs and powerful saints from the Celestial Empire, the home territory out of which humanity fled millennia ago to escape the plague of corrupted blood that had overtaken the lands where humanity was born.

This particular basilica was built by the Phene when they controlled Troia System. Its architecture is magnificat, the same as every basilica anywhere. There's a long, lofty nave with a vaulted ceiling supported by towering pillars with an aisle on either side. Sixteen alcoves, eight per side, are set into the aisles. Each alcove is devoted to one of the sixteen saints to whom people dedicate themselves. They hope the saint's specific qualities will aid them or burnish them or give them what they need in material or spiritual ways. The massive pillars glow with a soft golden light. Shining spheres float like peaceful bubbles above the entrance to each alcove. I'm suspended in a momentary sense of awe, of being transported into a plane higher and deeper than my meager self.

One hundred and thirty meters away, at the far end of the nave, the basilica ends in a space called the apse. As I recall from lessons, the apse remains empty because it represents the official Phene policy that no god or whatever is described by the word *god*, no supernatural being of omnipotent and omnipresent existence and power, exists in the universe except insofar as human belief brings it into being. The saints are well enough; they are humble, they live close to the people; they serve a purpose.

I don't agree. No Chaonian would, since the ancestors who brought us forth still live in us and around us, insinuated into our lives and made present through our actions. But we are who we are, and they are who they are.

Because the apse is a place of absence, no one may enter it. In fact, no one *can* enter it because it is separated from the rest of the basilica's interior by a shimmering curtain of lethal energy, impossible to cross.

As I peek out from where I'm hiding in the first alcove, I see four people standing just outside the shimmering curtain of lethal energy.

One is Zizou. I have been acquainted with him for only a few days but would recognize him anywhere by the way he stands as if he might leap in the blink of an eye with spring-loaded steps.

Two are Phene, both wearing the clear helmets that mark high-ranking Phene.

The fourth is my father.

I ping Sun: BASILICA NOW. ZIZOU HERE.

Behind me, as by magic but more likely by a simple electronic mechanism, the entry doors close with a resounding thunk. My ears pop as if a seal has engaged. We are locked in.

A stripe of white light snaps on in the apse and travels down the nave as an imaging resonance. When the stripe reaches me where I stand in the shadow of the altar dedicated to Saint Cygna, a sphere hanging over the alcove's entrance flashes yellow.

I don't move. It's better to see what they will do. As far as I can tell the basilica is empty except for them. And of course me.

Sun pings back. ON OUR WAY. BEWARE. ZIZOU IS LEASHED BY PHENE TECH THAT OVERRIDES MY COMMAND.

My father holds a wrist to his ear, then speaks to the others. He starts walking down the nave toward me. I'll have to make a decision in forty-two seconds. Shooting him with my stinger won't solve the problem, and I'm doubtful I can bring myself to shoot him anyway. He *is* my father.

But my attention is wrenched away from his approach when the shorter of the two Phene steps sideways into the shimmering energy field. I brace myself, expecting the Phene to spasm and collapse from a fatal jolt. But they don't.

This Phene is a Rider. With a face looking in each direction, its gaze can be read by the energy field simultaneously on both sides. It's a locking circuit.

An unseen mechanism clicks. The shimmering curtain vanishes. The floor shifts, taking on a muted glow. A gleaming eight-sided cylinder rises out of the floor. When it reaches seven feet it halts. A section splits open like an orange segment to reveal a cavity within, containing what looks like two stasis couches of the kind used in lifepods. Injured soldiers get placed in stasis until they can be taken to a proper medical facility. Spacers whose ships have undergone catastrophic failure and who need to survive a long stint in space with minimal life support use stasis.

I understand the rationale in an instant. Riders are the empire's most precious resource because they are so rare, because the empire is built on their ability to communicate instantaneously across the vastest measures of space. Stuck on a hostile planet, any Rider must salvage the most important part of their mission, which is saving themselves. Basilicas are safety hatches, a last-ditch hiding hole, a place to survive for days, weeks, months, and perhaps even years.

This Rider means to conceal herself right beneath our noses, in stasis, until she can be rescued.

I ping Zizou on the ring network, but he doesn't look around or even tense. When I check his status, the blue circle that identifies him in Sun's ring network isn't here in the basilica. It's on the move, leaving the hermitage. Sun has his ring, and she's headed our way, but she won't get here in time.

The Rider raises a wand. Zizou takes a rigid step forward toward the apse, then a second. He moves like an automaton whose joints are freezing up. He moves like a man being forced to walk against his will. She's controlling him. He's leashed.

No wonder the Gatoi fight to the death. Their Phene masters don't allow them to stop.

Sun has lost him, and the Phene clearly want him alive.

My father is two-thirds of the way down the nave as Zizou takes a third stiff, struggling step into the apse. In three more paces he'll enter the opened cylinder, lie down in a stasis couch, and be sealed in. If I don't do something now, I'll lose him.

I step out from the alcove into the nave. My father halts, scanning to make sure there is only one intruder. Because he is blind to visual light and I haven't spoken and I'm not wearing anything that marks me to his vision as being part of Lee House, all he can see is the heat signature of an individual. I might be anyone. I might be Octavian instead of Sun. He raises a stinger, tuned red.

I start walking toward him, speaking in a loud but calm tone. "Father, don't shoot. It's me, Persephone. You were right all along. I'm sorry I didn't understand it before. Let me join you. I'll come home. I'll do whatever you ask of me."

Father hesitates. I'm surprised and honestly relieved that he seems to have a smidgeon of paternal feeling.

Hearing my voice, the startled Phene glance my way. Whatever rats they expected to find slinking out from the dark aisles of the basilica, I wasn't one.

The Phene officer unholsters a small hailstorm gun, although why any Phene would spray off a round in this holy basilica I could not tell you.

I keep walking, picking up my pace, needing to get closer. I will not let them take him. He doesn't belong to them, or to Sun, or to me. He belongs to himself.

"Zizou! It's me."

Zizou looks over his shoulder.

He sees me.

He sees my face.

46

You Might Hear the Whispers of All That Had Been Lost

The basilica doors were shut. Arriving on the exterior portico, Sun spared a glance for the plaza and the crowd that, packed together like so many vibrating molecules on the verge of exploding into gas, had gathered to watch Alika's concert. He'd segued into an extended tale-telling song that demanded audience call-and-response, a good way to keep their attention on him and not on Sun stymied at the closed doors of a religious edifice meant to be always open for worship.

"Is there a side way in?" Isis asked.

Solomon said, "I'll run a circuit of the exterior."

"Don't bother." Sun grabbed Isis's restricted-grade weapon out of the cee-cee's hands and blasted a red-hot hole through a beatific image painted on the door depicting Saint Cygna the Lifebringer and her loom of creation. She shoved the gun back to Isis and charged through the ragged gap, unholstering her favorite stinger.

The gulf of the nave's staggering height swam in half-light as her eyes took in the vault. She dropped and rolled just out of habit, rising to one knee in time to see Zizou slam headlong into Persephone Lee. His hands wrapped around the Lee girl's throat.

At the far end of the edifice, 130 meters away, the Rider stood *inside* the boundaries of the apse. But that was impossible.

Then Sun realized the Rider was standing beside a blocky, cylindrical object risen out of the center of the apse where normally was only a floor mosaic. The cylinder was a large lifepod, set vertically into the floor and equipped with two stasis couches.

Ah.

A trick of acoustics threw words the length of the nave. The Rider said to the Phene officer, "Shoot the girl he's attacking. When we get him back under control, he can take out the others."

Before the officer could raise her gun Sun shot her. The impact sent her stumbling, but her body armor splintered the pulse into shock waves. Isis and Solomon scrambled up behind Sun. A squad of marines swarmed into the basilica in their wake, sprinting for cover in the alcoves. The Phene officer ducked behind a pillar.

Sun released a nonlethal pulse at the Rider. Staggered, the Rider dropped the wand she held, slumped backward, hit the edge of the lifepod, and collapsed backward onto a couch. With a pneumatic hiss, the couch sealed over her.

The lifepod gave a loud click and shut. The cylinder sank into the floor. The curtain of lethal energy that enclosed the apse shimmered back to life.

Sun's glare had no effect on the process, could not stop it. The Rider's presence had clearly triggered both the opening and the closure. Given Phene technology it would probably take a major bomb to jar it loose, one that would flatten all of Repose District.

"Surrender," Sun called to the officer, still out of sight behind a pillar. "Hand over your weapons. You will be treated humanely in detention and your wounds cared for until such time as hostilities cease or a treaty for exchange is sealed. Your Rider has abandoned you."

A silence followed this declaration, succeeded by scraping sounds, a pop, and a gasp.

Sun shook her head. What a waste of a good soldier. She waved the marines forward to complete a sweep of the space.

"Did we know about hidden lifepods in the apses of basilicas?" she asked Isis.

"I never heard of such a thing."

While Sun's attention had been on the Rider, Isis had thrown an altar cloth filched from the nearest alcove over Zizou's face. He lay unconscious on the ground, face concealed by an image of Saint Chell surmounted by a banner on which the words FACTA,

NON VERBA were written in the blocky alphabet used colloquially in the Phene empire.

Persephone Lee was lying on her back on the floor, breathing raggedly. She tried to speak, coughed, groaned, and winced.

"Let me help you up." Sun grabbed her left wrist and dragged her into a sitting position. "That was smart and foolish at the same time. Which seems true to you, now that I'm finally getting to know you."

"Gah," said Persephone, tentatively probing her neck. Her voice was hoarse and brutal. "My father . . ."

"Your father?"

"Yeah." Persephone's voice grated. "I positioned myself behind my father so Zizou would hit him on his way to me. Isn't he here?"

"Solomon, find him."

Solomon called over a squad of marines and started searching.

"The Phene definitely have a leash on the Gatoi," said Persephone.

"I know. Call them banner soldiers from now on," said Sun.

"Oh fuck. I guess if he'd crushed my windpipe I wouldn't be able to breathe."

"Wait beside him until he comes to."

"Me?"

"He'll listen to you. Just make sure he stays blindfolded."

"Whoa, thanks, Princess. I might have forgotten if you hadn't reminded me."

Sun flashed Persephone an appreciative smile, then signaled Isis to walk with her down the length of the nave. The marines were searching all sixteen alcoves for the missing seer and apparently not finding him.

"Look for a secret tunnel," she called to Solomon, who was scratching his head and looking frustrated. "There should be a disposal tech at the hermitage by now. Once they clear the entrance of traps from that end we can trace his escape route. Once you've cleared the interior, do a perimeter sweep outside. Check for a concealed under-level."

She spared a moment to watch the cadet as he rounded up the marines and set them on their way. He had good skills.

When she reached the far end of the nave, the energy curtain prevented her from entering the apse. The wand had rolled beyond the curtain, out of reach. It gleamed, still powered up. The floor had been restored to a pleasingly symmetrical floral pattern of tiles with no hint of a secret chamber hidden beneath.

What had such hiding places been called in the Celestial Empire?

"Priest holes," she said aloud. "Safe rooms."

Isis paced the length of the curtain and back. "Seamless. Every basilica I've ever been in has this same energy curtain. The apse is meant to be empty as a symbol of the invisible reach of Phene power, or their belief in a godless universe, or just because they like it as a visual aesthetic. I had no idea it is really a fail-safe hiding place for Riders. Which do you think came first—the worship of the saints, or the Riders deciding to construct fallbacks that no one would guess were safeholds?"

Sun turned to look down the length of the nave. The piers holding up the roof reminded her of the ribs of the Titan-class ships that had brought humanity away from the suffering of the fallen Celestial Empire to seek a new home, a safe haven. She felt at ease in the basilica, as if this edifice were a crack in the wall between the opaque world of the living and the secrets of the dead.

"It's safest never to insult gods and spiritual forces, however they manifest," she said to skeptical Isis. "The ancestors speak to us through worship and ritual even if we often can't understand what they are saying. The saints once lived in the Celestial Empire . . ."

She trailed off as the angle of the view struck her.

"Your Highness?"

She signed for silence. Took a step back.

"Careful!" Isis looked alarmed at how close Sun's back was to the curtain.

Sun stared down the length of the nave to the entry doors. "Does this angle look familiar to you?"

"What angle, Your Highness?"

"The view from here."

Isis shrugged. "Every basilica is arranged the same way, the alcoves in the same order, Saint Hrothgar the Near Dweller and Saint Cygna by the entry doors, Saint Arthas and the twins here by the apse, and the other twelve between always in the same order. The general architecture of entry, nave, aisles, and apse is the same. Sometimes there's a transept, sometimes there isn't. Just like the Honored Hestia said about the hermitages having the same layout. I guess it makes it easy for worshippers to know where to go."

Sun looked at her feet. The paving was stone, like the rest of the nave, expensive but durable, and laid out in a pattern of squares: regular and dull. Only in the apse did the pattern of the paving change to the elaborate circular mosaic that disguised the slot for the hidden cylindrical lifepod.

"What are you seeing, Your Highness?"

Sun dropped her voice to a whisper. "Bring Tiana here at once."

Isis gave her a surprised look but left.

Sun pinged Hetty. FIND TIANA. YOU AND ISIS ESCORT HER TO ME.

Then she pinged James by voice. "Has my father landed yet?"

"Are you expecting him to land?"

"Really, James?"

"Oh. Of course he's coming." His silence ticked over like gears running an engine. "You sound out of sorts. Do you need medical assistance? Metrics say you're wounded."

"Don't be an ass," she snapped. She glanced at her left thigh. The field bandage Solomon had slapped over it was containing the blood and the pain.

"I'm not being an ass. You're being an ass."

Her temper trembled on the edge of explosion, and then she laughed. "Never change, James. Has my father landed, as I already asked you once?"

"Not yet. Orders?"

"We remain on lockdown until this is resolved. No one can

know what's going on in here, not even the local military command. Make whatever excuse you need."

Last of all she pinged Alika. KEEP THEM FOCUSED ON YOU.

LOCALLY WE ARE MOVING UP FAST. THAT WILL HELP OUR NUMBERS WHEN THE COURIERS TAKE THIS REPUBLIC WIDE. A FEW PROTESTS ARE BEING FLAGGED THROUGH OFFICIAL LAYERS, SAYING THE "SUN AND HER COMPANIONS" GROUPING DIDN'T REGISTER AS AN OFFICIAL IDOL FAIRE COMPETITOR BEFORE THE DEADLINE.

She filed away the information for later and, feeling a twinge of pain in her leg, looked for a place to sit. An unpadded bench in the alcove of the twin saints gave her respite to mentally walk back through the attack. Was there any point she might have acted more decisively and thus not lost any of the lifepods? If only Octavian were here to question her down to the tiniest detail.

Grief is a beast, and she would not feed it. She would honor him as he would have wished to be honored: by using the training he'd instilled in her.

The sound of footsteps brought her head up.

Hetty.

Lit as by the vault of heaven, with the loft of the nave as her glimmering backdrop. Her dark hair in its braid: disheveled. Her chin smeared with a line of dirt and a stippling of dried blood. Her gaze lambent. Her mouth—that secret pleasure—was already moving with her usual pragmatic tug back to earth.

"There are you, and here we are. Alone." Hetty had a hand tucked into Tiana's elbow in a gesture that might look sociable to the casual eye but which gave her leverage with which to steer the cee-cee.

Being no fool, Tiana understood she was in informal custody. For once her sheen of perfection and poise had cracks. Her skittish gaze flashed all around the basilica as if she expected clowns to leap out and murder them. Sun did not rise nor did she invite Tiana to sit.

"Attend me, Tiana," she said.

Hetty's mouth made a little *o* of surprise. She released Tiana's arm and took a step back, positioning herself so if the cee-cee broke and tried to run she could body block her. Sun examined Tiana, who looked first at her and then, nervously, at the lovingly painted life-sized statues of the twins, to whom the benighted might pray for relief from Anguish and Pain. In the opposite alcove, beneath an imposing status of Saint Arthas the Cursebearer, the marines who hadn't gone with Solomon sealed a security webbing over the dead Phene officer. How fitting that the officer had died under Arthas's gaze, for her homeland.

Sun remained silent until the marines carried away the dead soldier. She wanted no witness for this.

"Tiana Yáo Alaksu. What is your womb parent's name and story?"

Tiana flinched, not so much at the question Sun had asked but at the question not asked. "My womb parent was named Rose Tarawele Alaksu. She was a combat veteran who took her own life two months after I was born. I have made my peace with her memory because my father loved her. He says she must have been in a great deal of pain that she'd concealed from everyone around her. However, her family called her act shameful and wanted nothing to do with me. My father's parents raised me in my early years on the kalo farm while he continued to fight with the Chaonian military. He lost an arm in the service of the republic, as you saw. The republic having no more use for a one-armed soldier, and him not having the money to replace the arm with a proper prosthetic, he was discarded."

"He could have gone home, but he chose to remain in Troia System. I know what you are hiding."

A tear slipped from the cee-cee's left eye, but with impressive discipline she did not raise a hand to wipe it away nor by any other expression or gesture or movement further reveal her fear.

"You have something to do with the Phene, do you not?" said Sun.

Hetty slipped a hand up her sleeve where she kept a stinger

strapped to her forearm. "Is she involved with this conspiracy, Sun?"

"I've nothing to do with this!" cried Tiana in a burst of emotion, voice catching in the echoes of the nave.

Down by the doors Persephone Lee sat cradling the unconscious Zizou's head in her lap like a madonna in a maudlin teledrama. Hearing Tiana's exclamation she looked up, stiffening.

Sun pinged, STAND DOWN. SHE'S IN NO DANGER. DID SHE TELL YOU NOTHING OF HER SITUATION? WHY SHE NEEDS THE MONEY? TOOK SUCH A DANGEROUS JOB?

YOU SAW THE REFUGEE CAMP.

In other words, Persephone had no idea.

The princess turned her attention back to Tiana. "You will be escorted to your home and bring your brother here immediately."

The cee-cee hid her face behind her hands and sobbed in a burst of sheer terror. Hetty gave Sun a critical look. Sun shook her head, and Hetty responded with a puzzled shrug, to show she was willing to wait it out even though she, too, had no idea what was going on.

Tiana lowered her hands. People like her were still beautiful when they cried, and Sun didn't think it was artifice, just chance.

"Don't do this, I beg you, Your Highness. They'll come for him."

Sun rose. She wasn't as tall as Tiana, but her presence always filled whatever shape she willed it into.

"They will have to get through me. He's too valuable for me to lose now that I know what he is. Do you understand me?"

"Is that a threat, or a promise?" Tiana asked hoarsely, but with pride. "Just so I know where I stand."

"That depends on how you and your people decide to come to me."

Tiana touched a hand to her eyes, released a slow breath, and lowered the hand to reveal a cool, bland expression. She had recovered her composure out of the depths of her rigorous training at Vogue Academy.

"How did you guess, Your Highness? We've been so careful."

"His paintings. The one of the basilica could only have been painted from a point of view at the back of the apse. I have discovered that Riders can enter the apse. What one Rider sees, all see. How is it possible you've kept him secret all this time?"

"He wears the knit cap. If he must take it off we make sure there is no visual marker to give away his position, no background noise that would allow the Rider Council to trace us. Poor Kas. He never leaves the tent. It's a terrible life for him. It's why she ran. She didn't want to give him up."

"Is Nanea kin Kavan truly Phene? She only has two arms."

"She's a stunt. That's what the Phene call people born with just two arms. But babies born with two faces can come from anywhere within the population of the descendants of the original founders of the triple alliance of Anchor, Auger, and Axiom. What they call the imperial Phene."

HIS NIBS INCOMING IN A FRESH OUTFIT, pinged James, flashing the tiara made of entangled gold snakes he used to represent Sun's father.

"Hetty, take Tiana with Isis. Only those two. Collect the family and return here. They may bring only what they can carry. They won't be going back."

When she used that tone no one gainsaid her. Even Tiana gave her a hopeless, hopeful look before Hetty led her away.

Sun wanted to sit—her leg pained her—but she remained standing as the minutes ticked past as she considered the basilica empty except for Persephone Lee, Zizou, and the Rider sealed in the hidden lifepod. Empty except for the intangible affirmations offered by the saints to those who begged them for strength and intercession. Dreams had power to breach great distances. How else could humanity have escaped the plague of corrupted blood that threatened to extinguish it? If a person listened hard enough, they might hear the whispers of all that had been lost across the millennia-long passage. So much of the road had been covered as with blown sand, obscuring the route and the landmarks. Just as entire sections of the beacon routes had been lost in the collapse of the Apsaras Convergence, so fragments were all that remained in human memory of the Celestial Empire. Some said it had never existed at all, that it was just a story. But plants grow from seeds, and humanity too had grown from roots germinated out of ancient kernels.

Enough. Time for contemplation later.

She piggybacked on the ring network to look through Alika's eyes. He was halfway through a tour de force rendition of a dramatic narrative song describing the last voyage of a courier ship caught in the great beacon collapse of eight hundred years ago, how the ship had tried to outrace the failing beacons as they shut down one by one like lights switching off, and how in the end it had become caught in the Gap, never to be seen again.

The epic would keep the crowd busy for long enough.

She limped down the length of the nave to Persephone and Zizou. The altar cloth had been tossed aside in favor of a leather blindfold binding his eyes. Zizou was lying facedown on the floor. Persephone knelt beside him, stroking his short black hair as if unaware she was doing so.

"He's awake," said Sun, reading the twitch of his feet and the hitch in his breathing.

Persephone pulled her hand away but let it settle on her knee, near his head.

"I'm sorry about the ring, Your Highness," said Zizou. "The Rider took it from me. Is it true what she said?"

"What did the Rider say?"

"That the Phene buy soldiers from the banner fleets. That we're nothing more than tools to be bought and sold. That we're the excess baggage the wheelships don't have resources to support. That's why none of us return. Not because we die with honor but because we're made to fight until we die whether we chose that path or not."

"You aren't any of those things," said Persephone. Her fingers brushed his mouth as if to peel away words she wished he hadn't felt he had to say.

"Where did you find that handy blindfold for his eyes?" Sun asked.

Persephone gave a one-shoulder shrug, as if to brush off the comment. More to the point, she blushed, which was interesting since Sun had not taken her for the blushing kind, although she definitely struck Sun as the kind who would become dramatically infatuated with a handsome enemy who'd tried to kill her.

Voices sounded from the portico. James ducked in through the hole in the door.

He swept his cap off his head as a form of respect as he looked around the nave with a spritely gaze. "I miss all the fun!"

"There's more fun to be had. You're on Alika duty until I say otherwise."

"*Sun!*"

"Do it."

He twisted his cap askew to make sure she fully grasped the intensity of his distaste for the assignment, and slouched out. After he left her father ducked in and, taking a noble stance, surveyed the situation with his usual critical eye.

"How many survived?" he asked without greeting or preamble.

"Two of the consoles—"

"What do I care for the consoles? Lives cannot be replaced."

"Three of fourteen were green when I left. Hetty stayed back with two medics. It happened so fast so I don't know the extent of the damage, but she might have been able to revive some of the others."

"Well, I'll soon know the full toll." He looked at Persephone, frowned, then indicated the banner soldier on the floor. "Is this Zizou? It's an honorable name among the people. Elegance with precision. Why was he not confined in a lifepod?"

"He's the anomaly," said Sun. "There's a whole other layer of engineering on him. I'm turning him over to you with the surviving subjects to continue your study."

"If Zizou agrees," said Persephone sharply. Definitely infatuated.

"He'll agree, because I'm a Royal telling him to agree," said Sun in her best attempt at a patient voice. "Prince João will find a securer venue in which to do research, will you not, Father? A venue that even Queen-Marshal Eirene doesn't know about and thus can't betray through careless pillow talk."

Her father said, "Eirene has to know. I need funding, and I need her to owe me. You need her to owe me too, a reminder of how valuable we are to her."

"We," murmured Sun.

"You can be supplanted by another heir, Sun. Or have you forgotten your tantrum at the wedding banquet?"

"How do you know about that?"

"How do you think I know about it? I know how to survive. I wonder about you when you give way to your anger in such an undisciplined manner."

"You're the one who taught me we can't just let them insult us and do nothing. Honor and respect is stripped from the one who makes no protest."

"Mmm. Well. You're wounded and clearly running on fumes. I insist you sit down and have the injury looked at. If you don't take care of yourself you'll collapse one day and have only yourself to blame for it. Where is Hestia Hope?"

"On a mission, fetching the other part of your new research mission, the one you absolutely must keep secret from my mother."

"That's simple enough if she has the banner soldier project taking up the front of the stage, the one that will clearly benefit her war effort. What is this other project?"

"Easier to see than to explain." She pressed the ring into Zizou's hand. "Zizou, I'm giving this back to you."

"If—" interposed Persephone in her annoying way.

"If you want it," said Sun.

But she knew what Zizou would do. Obedient to tradition, to his banner, and to his upbringing, he slipped on the ring.

"Zizou, you'll be leaving with my father as soon as the others return. Stay here to guard the door. Allow only my Companions and those they escort inside. Father, accompany me, if you will."

He walked beside her down the nave toward the apse. Her leg was really starting to hurt. They both glanced back as Persephone rose and, quite unnecessarily, took hold of Zizou's hand to help him to his feet. Their faces were so close, almost touching, rapt and anticipatory, as if proximity had come to them as a fresh language never known to any other individuals in the long history of humankind. It made her remember the first time she had kissed Hetty.

Turning away, Sun said, "Give them some privacy. Did you see our Idol Faire rating?"

"Why aren't you in first place?"

"We will be." She pinged James. His feed gave her a view of the plaza, the crowd singing along with the proper responses, his cap being waved.

THIS IS FUN FUN FUN, he pinged. I HOPE YOU HAVE MORE FUN IN STORE FOR ME.

"Just you wait," she answered, and her father said, "What?"

"James being James."

"Don't trust his brother Anas. He's too ambitious. In fact, don't trust Zàofù or any of that grasping Samtarras family. Did I mention Zàofù is almost certainly the one behind the plot to throw Eirene and Manea together? He probably put Moira Lee up to it, not that Moira can't be ambitious on her own count, given her history—"

"Could we just sit, Father?"

His glance was narrow-eyed, chiding, but he sat on a bench beneath the eyes of the twins, and she sat next to him. For a mercy, he did not give his usual lecture about what she could have should have would have done, the endless litany she couldn't imagine growing up without: her father's scolding and pushing and her mother's testing and competing. Yet his presence brought comfort, for she never doubted even in her darkest moment that he had her back.

At last the others returned. Sun felt Hetty's arrival in the lightening of her heart, in the smile that lifted her mouth unbidden.

Prince João watched the group approach down the length of the nave. In a low voice he remarked, "Hestia Hope always manages to accomplish exactly what you ask of her with no fuss, no bother, and with a full comprehension of your aims. I had reservations when Hope House insisted she return as your Companion after her father died, but I am satisfied with the situation now."

Sun glanced sharply at him, waiting for the other shoe to drop.

"But remember, part of a queen-marshal's duty is marriage, which brings useful alliances and resources to the republic. You can't marry one of your own Companions, much less one who is half Yele and from a minor branch of the House."

"Father—!"

"Not now." To show he expected no reply and no argument, he crossed his legs and clasped his hands in his lap.

In an odd way, the comment eased her. He'd guessed, or seen, and he was just warning her about what she already knew. Anyway, there was nothing she could do about it now. There were more urgent matters to deal with, specifically the family clustered around Tiana that had come to a halt before her and her father.

The boy, Kaspar, was nervous because his parents were terrified, but he was also beside himself with exhilaration and curiosity to see a world so long denied. He kept staring around, fidgeting and twisting as he tried to take in every painted statue and handmade flower wreath laid as an offering. The parents stood stoic and frowning.

Sun rose.

"Corporal Vontae Yáo Alaksu, you are under my command now. You'll be promoted to captain. You and your family will join my household and receive the benefits thereof. I know you'll serve me well. Do you understand?"

Tiana's father understood, although his partner, Nanea kin Kavan, struggled to hold back tears.

Sun addressed her separately. "You have done well to rescue

the child from the fate that awaits him in the Phene Empire. It's in my interest to protect him and keep him alive."

"Yes, Your Highness. But this task you are wanting him to complete . . . this curtain . . . it will reveal his existence to them. We have managed for so long, since his very birth, to conceal him."

"In choosing to hide him for all these years you have already made him a hostage to fortune. Better you come under my protection because I will allow you to stay together. Prince João will escort you to a place of safety. The Phene can't manage another raid into Chaonian territory anytime soon, not with their forces in such disarray."

The parents wanted to protest, and Sun respected them for that, but they looked to Tiana. She made a sign Sun could not read but that was known to them, and so they kept silent. Of course they did. The matter had been settled the moment Sun realized what the boy was. She escorted him to the shimmering curtain that shielded the apse. He pulled off the knit cap, which had a silk lining sewn inside.

He had tufts of hair atop his head like a crest, but the back of the skull was as bare as his own face. The eyes of his riding face were closed, the lips sleepy, the expression lax, the whole face shriveled and sunken like an atrophied muscle.

"Both sets of eyes must be open," said Sun. "Is it always in this stupor?"

"I hope so," said Vontae sharply. "It's an evil thing that the boy never deserved."

"Riders aren't evil," said Sun. "They are what they are. Kaspar, do you ever speak to it?"

He shook his head, looking frightened now that he was exposed, that so many people were staring not at him but at the part of him his parents had caused him to hide for all these years, the shameful, dangerous part. "Sometimes it whispers, trying to get my attention," he said softly. He grasped his mother's hand. "But I never say anything back, and it can't get into my mind. If it could, it would have found me."

"But you see what it sees, what the other Riders see, don't you? That's where your paintings come from. From their eyes."

Tiana kneels before her brother, grasping his other hand. "Do it, Kas. You have to, and it will be better later. The princess will take care of you and Ma and Dad. It will be better, I promise you." As she finished she shot Sun a glare whose bitterness would wither the strength of any soul but Sun's.

"Wake it up and step into the curtain." Sun clapped her hands, the resonant sound startling everyone.

The sleepy eyes opened with a look of confusion.

Kas grimaced as if in struggle. A tear slipped from one eye. With a forceful exhalation he released his mother's hand and, still as if fighting for control of his own limbs, sidestepped into the shimmering curtain. The shimmer did not part so much as absorb his presence. The riding face seemed to gain form and sharpen as its gaze flicked from side to side, trying to absorb where and what it was. Who it was. Trying to fully wake up.

"No," said Kas, to himself. Beneath his loose, heavy tunic, his stout torso shifted, angling to either side like elbows sticking out. Of course his parents would conceal his second pair of arms by binding them against his torso.

The shimmering curtain vanished as his paired faces unlocked the circuit.

The floor clicked, and the cylindrical lifepod rose.

Sun held out the knit cap. The boy snatched it. A struggle ensued, his hands jerking back and forth as he tried to raise the cap to his head while being stymied in a way that reminded her of Zizou struggling against the leash. Then he hissed with a spark of rage and snatched the cap down over his head, covering the riding face.

At once he fell forward to hands and knees, weeping. His mother gathered him against her. The lifepod clunked into place and opened, revealing the stasis couch in which lay the wounded and unconscious Rider. Isis and Hetty moved at once to unmoor the lifepod. With the help of Tiana and her father, they carried it out of the apse. Prince João grabbed the wand just before the energy curtain re-formed.

Victory.

"Father, James has arranged transport for you. Wait until we've drawn off the crowd."

She pinged James and Alika. COMING NOW. I WANT EVERY PERSON AND WASP ON THE PLAZA AND EVERY EYE ON CHANNEL IDOL TO LOOK MY WAY WHEN I WALK OUT OF THE BASILICA WITH A CAPTURED RIDER IN MY CUSTODY. GIVE IT FLAIR.

47

The Space They Stand in Is So Vast

Persephone Lee had offered a hand to help Zizou up, although he doesn't need any aid even with a blindfold on. Once standing he cannot quite bring himself to release her hand. He isn't sure why he leans toward her, not boldly but with a sigh of relief. It is all the invitation she needs. She puts her arms around him, and they stand like that, mostly alone except for a murmur of voices from the far end of the basilica. The scent of flowers and incense drifts on the air, reminding him of home.

Was his grandmother proud of him when she signed off on his departure, when she declaimed the traditional poems in his honor at the leave-taking promenade? "Let those we leave behind remember us in the days to come."

Or was she just glad to get rid of him so she would have enough food to eat and air to breathe? Did she choose him specifically from among her grandchildren to trade away? Had she ever truly loved him? What does honor mean if it is just a word used as currency in trade?

The whole universe could be a lie, a twist in the maze of Lady Chaos, a trap that's devoured him. So he holds on to Persephone Lee, and he lets her hold on to him, because she's warm and right and that at least is something he can embrace.

"I don't know what I am anymore," he says.

"What do you mean, Zizou?" Her pronunciation is off, but his battle name sounds sweet that way. It's easier to speak because he can't see her face, because he took everything at face value before, and now he has to find a way forward without the landmarks he's always recognized.

"I was so proud to be chosen. I worked so hard to be worthy. We were always told we were valued allies of the Phene, but it was never true. Our own families sell us off like trash they have no more room for. And the Phene use us up and throw us out."

Her chest rises and falls against his torso, the press of her body and her heat as ardent as her anger. "You haven't changed. You've just discovered the truth."

"Is this the truth?" he asks bitterly. He thinks of his squad. Did they survive or were they easy to discard, being of no more use to anyone?

"Do any of us know the truth? Probably not." Her head rests against his shoulder. Her breath is a soft measure along the bare skin of his neck. "I guess the truth can change us, or maybe it just helps us understand where we stand."

"What if there is no truth? Just discord and confusion?"

"As long as you have people you can trust, you have ground to stand on." She coughs. Her flinch of pain strikes him like a wound to the heart.

"I hurt you, Persephone Lee."

"No." She coughs again, squeezes a hand up between their bodies to rub at her throat. "No, you didn't hurt me. They hurt me. They want you to think you are master of your own fate, because it gives you the illusion of control, and that feeds their purpose. But they controlled you. I won't blame you for the attacks on me. That's on them. Do you understand?"

He sighs.

"Zizou, you have a choice."

"What choice is that?" He tenses.

"If you want to go home I'll find a way to get you out of here."

"War is my home now."

"Is that what you want?"

"It's what I trained for. It's my purpose."

"It's the purpose they want you to have." The space they stand in is vast, and no one stands near them, but she keeps her voice low, secretive, intimate. "Do you want to go with Prince João?"

"I have to go with him. He is a Royal. So is Princess Sun. I will do as they command."

"That's not what I meant. I mean, do you want to see if this leash can be taken off you? So the Phene can never again compel you to do anything against your will."

"What they do to the banner soldiers under their care is wrong," he agrees. "I am not a puppet. I am an honorable man."

Cautiously he tips his head just enough to rest against the top of her hair. He could stand here forever, like this, but he's also a little embarrassed because he's starting to feel aroused by their closeness and by the way her hand strokes his back in a manner perhaps meant to be soothing or perhaps meant as a caress. She can certainly perceive the changing contours of his body—she's pressed close enough, that's for sure—but she doesn't pull away.

He murmurs, lips at her ear, "If the leash were taken off me, then I could see your face."

He feels her smile. She tilts back and whispers, "You don't need to see my face to do this."

Because he cannot see, his other senses have sharpened: the scent of cinnamon from a saint's alcove; the coarse cloth of her sleeve brushing over the fingers of his right hand; the scuff of her foot on the floor as she shifts her hips to press against his; the tickling taste of her hair as strands trail over his mouth. Her cheek brushes his chin. He bends his head down to the face he cannot see and hasn't really ever truly seen. But it isn't by a face that you know a person.

Her lips are all promise. Her heat is a vow. They stand in a place of worship, attended by the silent avatars of a faith neither of them follow, and yet these are their witnesses, the watchful guardians of protection, duty, ingenuity, loyalty, healing, and all the qualities and trials that human beings seek to emulate or endure or become. Among them there stands a guardian to love and passion, an adventurous and joyous spirit, and maybe this is she come to life in his arms.

He has to breathe.

He says—

"This is all very endearing, but we need to go immediately before our presence here is discovered."

Both he and Persephone jolt back. He's so jarred by the unexpected voice breaking into their embrace that he sparks with a burst of energy along his neural pathways.

"Whoa," says Persephone. "That's vivid."

Prince João adds sardonically, "Zizou, you'll find your lovers like it when that happens. It's an autonomic response to high levels of arousal, something akin to an erection in people who have penises, but naturally a sexual partner can't help but congratulate themselves on bringing it out in you."

"Oh," murmurs Persephone in a tone that makes Zizou flush, wondering if she's visually checking out the awkward silhouette of his clothing.

"Last we met, Persephone Lee," remarks the Royal, "I forgot to mention how much I admired and respected the noble sacrifice of your eight-times-worthy sister. You look just like her."

"So I'm told, Your Highness, although I don't see the resemblance as anything but superficial." Persephone's tone has turned from molasses to acid.

"I can see why Sun likes you."

"Where is Princess Sun?" Zizou asks.

"It's impressive how in the heat of passion one can become completely immune to sense and observation. She and the others have left."

Touching the ring, Zizou recalls that he can always check her position. She has moved out onto the plaza together with her other Companions and the soldier Isis.

"You're coming with me, Zizou." The prince taps him with an implement. By the buzz that resonates in his flesh, he recognizes it as the wand the Rider used to control him. "I intend to free the banners from this leash."

"For Chaonia?" Persephone asks.

"No, not for Chaonia. For humanity's sake. The banner fleets formed long ago to salvage people from the wreck of bondage. It's outrageous the councils of some of the banner fleets pretend they haven't revived the very evil we once fought against. I will end it. There, you've had your speech for the day. And your kiss. Come along, Zizou."

The prince does not wait. Zizou is given no chance for a proper goodbye, for anything but a touch of his hands to her hands. He doesn't even know what to say. To him, a parting means forever.

She says, "Oh fuck, I almost forgot," and thrusts a small wrapped bundle into his hand.

"Come along," repeats the prince, voice more distant because he's walking away.

Zizou obeys the Royal. He leaves behind the basilica with its harsh memory of the Rider leashing him forward and its sweet memory of the mysterious transcendence of the embrace. He leaves behind the flash and its subsequent void of memory, when whatever the Phene did to him caused him to attack her, again.

It's better this way. Despite himself he'll kill her if he doesn't leave. It's not worth the risk. But it still hurts.

Yet he cherishes the pain. He doesn't try to mute its blend of piquancy and hope. The little package is still in his hand as he's guided into a conveyance. A door is slammed shut. The vehicle vibrates as it begins to move.

"Can I take off the blindfold?" he asks.

"No. Not until I say."

There are others in the conveyance with them. They don't speak, but he can smell their sweat and anxiety, taste a hint of metal shavings and wood dust, hear restless movement and, once, a woman's voice say, "Sit still, Kas."

He waits with the patience he learned as a child waiting for his ration, as a youth getting lost in the maze of Lady Chaos and knowing they will let him die there if he does not keep his wits about him and find his way out, as a young man in the endless drills that taught him a soldier's discipline. Waiting is a form of discipline.

After a while the vehicle stops and they disembark. Now they are outside in the windblown, gritty air of the moon. Again the prince guides him, fingers hooked around his elbow. They go up a ramp into another vehicle. They strap into acceleration couches. Still blindfolded, he waits as the shuttle takes off, as g-forces push him into the couch, as they hit the high atmosphere and lose gravity. He thinks of Persephone Lee, replays in his mind every interaction, seeking the hints she gave and emotions she felt that he could not see but that he nevertheless experienced. He also thinks about his squad, and Colonel Evans, and the banner soldiers in the lab and all the ones who have come before him. Every child in the banners is born with the neural pathway. According to tradition it's the legacy of their flight out of the Apsaras Convergence eight hundred years ago, but now he wonders if what he was taught is true. If truth can ever be settled, or sure. A life becomes unmoored when its anchor is shorn away.

With a clang of docking clamps the shuttle arrives at a ship.

Once again he waits as the unseen others disembark. When all are gone except for him, the prince guides him out. By now he recognizes the scent of vanilla as a perfume the man wears.

"Who was with us?" he asks.

"Why, just the lifepods and consoles."

"Not just them."

"Don't ask again."

After they clear the hiss and pressure of the airlock, walk for a bit, and take several turns, the prince unties the blindfold. "Make your proper greetings to the captain."

Zizou blinks as his eyes adjust to the lighting. Some of the tubes aren't lit. The gray paint on the walls is chipped as if maintenance has not done its job. The air has a musty smell that indicates the filters need cleaning.

As a child he memorized all the various classes of ships from the simplest planet-bound Swallow to the massive wheelships of the banner fleet to the heavy cruisers that anchor the fighting fleets of the great confederacies. So he recognizes the command center of a very large knnu-drive ship.

"A Titan!" he exclaims, then sees women seated on a long bench. They are sizing him up.

He approaches, opening his hands to present them palms out. "Warmest greetings, Grandmother and Aunts. My battle name is Zizou. The name my grandmother calls me is Kurash. I offer it to you as thanks for opening your home to me. May I know where I have come?"

The oldest of the women has seen a long life, that is clear from her age-weighted face and the braces that shore up her limbs. Her voice is firm and her dignity unimpaired.

"Kurash, I am Commander Rahaba. You are welcome here aboard the *Keoe*." She looks him up and down. "We're a bit shopworn, still tidying up. This ship came out of a mothballed yard."

"I am a good worker, Grandmother. I can swab decks, paint, clean filters and ventilation systems, repair filtration lines in the hydroponic vaults, and cook." He smiles. "I'd be grateful for a chance to pitch in. It's how we did things at home."

Her imperious expression softens. "What a good boy you are. I see in you the hand of an affectionate upbringing. Someone loved you enough to share with you a love of community and many hands working together. What's that you're carrying?"

He glances down at the package, wrapped in yellow silk, tied in a cunning knot that reminds him of *her*. For an instant he hesitates. But hesitation is so unlike him. It's unworthy of his battle name. So he plucks it open, slipping the smooth cloth free. Inside, neatly folded, rest the socks his grandmother knit for him.

48

A DISPATCH FROM THE ENEMY

Dear Mom,
Why didn't you tell me? Can it be possible you never knew?

"Another game, Lieutenant At Sabao?" Admiral Manu propelled himself into the crash seat next to her with the hearty smile he used to bludgeon people into agreement.

Apama was hungry, stinky, and exceedingly grouchy after five days of being crammed into a courier ship meant for twelve and currently housing twenty hungry, stinky, grouchy Phene military and one egregiously cheerful Yele admiral. Military discipline, and the presence of the Rider they were tasked to get to safety, kept her focused. So instead of pummeling his beaming face she crossed both pairs of arms and imagined herself restfully basking in a lovely sun-warmed glade in the Grove.

"We've already played nine games, Admiral."

"Yes, and you've won six." He clipped himself into the straps so he wouldn't float away. "Give me a chance to catch up."

"If I lose on purpose, will you stop asking me to play?"

He dipped his head, hiding his mouth behind a hand.

"What's so funny?" she demanded.

"You won't lose on purpose. You pilots never do."

With a sigh she triggered a virtual version of the layered boards for four-dimensional chaturanga. "Pilots are chosen for spatial and chronological awareness. We trained at flight school with this game."

"That still doesn't explain why you in particular are so skilled. You're even better than I am."

"Your brilliance is acknowledged by everyone, Admiral. But in the game you have a certain predictability." Especially when his pride was at stake, but she knew better than to say so out loud. "I use your patterns against you, while you haven't figured out what's predictable about my moves."

"You love defeating me with your drunken elephant gambits, do you not?"

"No. I'm not in love with victory for its own sake."

"That wasn't what I meant, but it does suggest another question."

She said nothing, wondering if he would go away, although of course there was nowhere to go. When their courier ship with its precious Rider had fled Molossia System, they'd been meant to join up with the Tanarctus Fleet in Troia System and celebrate a great victory.

Instead they'd been hiding for days in Troia System's outer asteroid belt, powered down with full baffles on and all comms off as Chaonian patrols swept past in the wake of *their* victory to make sure no pockets of Phene ships had been left behind after the Phene retreat to Aspera and Karnos.

"What, or whom, *are* you in love with?" Manu's conspiratorial wink snapped clean the last of her usually copious store of patience that five days stuck on the courier ship had whittled down to a brittle twig.

"Such a question is inappropriate—"

An adjutant slumped in the crash seat opposite stirred. "Huy! Could you two keep it down with your teledrama flirting?" He opened his eyes. "Oh! Apologies, Admiral."

"No need for apologies. We're all exhausted by this confinement." Manu flashed the most genial of expressions toward the adjutant, who was startled into a smile in reply. Their knees were almost touching across the narrow aisle. There was nothing anyone could do to claim personal space or privacy, except the Rider, who had requisitioned the single berthing cabin for himself.

The adjutant adjusted his collar and said, a trifle nervously, "If I may say so, Admiral, didn't you just come from speaking to the Rider?"

"I did, indeed!" Manu smiled as if delighted to be reminded of this exceptional piece of good fortune. "Good news is afoot. We can expect a rendezvous within six hours."

"A rendezvous with who?" Apama asked.

"*Whom* is correct. Without proper grammar, we lose not just proper language but really the foundation of our own selves." He winked at the adjutant, an individual older than Apama but younger than he was. "Youth these days, am I right? Lieutenant At Sabao, six hours is plenty of time for another game."

Plenty of time.

She beat him twice.

Or she would have beaten him the second time. Their game was interrupted by a proximity chime: the expected rendezvous. Everyone donned a protective membrane and weapons were passed out, although there weren't enough to go around. Weaponless, Apama took her place in formation last in the line of precedence. The door to the berthing opened and the Rider emerged, wearing the sleeved mantle of the Rider Council and a steel diadem as a circle around his foreheads.

Gravity took hold between one breath and the next. After so many days in free fall the idea of ground had become disorienting and uncomfortable, but there wasn't time to adjust. Grapples thudded onto the exterior. Fresh, oxygen-rich air was vented in. With a jolt the courier came to rest. A green light signaled a clear airlock.

The commander of the courier ship took point at the airlock, followed by Admiral Manu, two individuals wearing the uniform of the Incorruptibles, and the Rider.

The commander said, "I am Captain Nabua Te Mamaril of the *Certain Swift*. Permission to come aboard for reasons of military security."

The airlock opened to reveal a Yele woman dressed in the

flamboyant colors of a Yele merchant guild. Her gaze touched on the commander but flashed past to note the Rider. "Permission to come aboard."

She stepped aside to reveal a Yele man standing behind her, dressed in soberly colored clothing. Of indeterminate age, he had a slightly sardonic but generally inoffensive expression on his pleasant face.

"Welcome, Your Eminence. I have a comfortable cabin waiting for you."

"Aloysius Voy!" Manu swore. "A trap! You traitor!"

He pushed past the commander and barged onto the entry gangway with such unexpected vigor that everyone gaped as he punched the other man in the face. Apama slid past the others and, since no one stopped her, hurried through the open airlock and onto the gangway just in time to grab Manu's arm before he could punch the other man again.

"Admiral! As I said before, your attacks are predictable. That's why I keep beating you."

The anger in Manu's face relaxed, and he laughed.

"What have I ever done to you?" demanded the other man as he dabbed blood from his nose with the back of a hand.

"To me? Nothing to me personally, since I have never fallen under the sway of your golden tongue. What your glib words and specious arguments have done to Yele is a different matter."

"I have done nothing except to save Yele from being burned to ashes, as you would understand if you could but understand the perilous conditions that faced us when Eirene first began to seize our outposts and outer territories, which had become vulnerable because of our own apathy and arrogance."

"I was involved in those battles while you were prancing around the theater stage declaiming speeches."

"Scorn me if you wish. But at the time, when we were on the brink of losing not just the war but our precious autonomy, a policy of tolerance and cooperation seemed a prudent price to pay as a temporary measure, until such time as we might discover better options."

The Rider walked forward. "I see the truth of the accusation that the Yele like nothing as much as speeches and parsing grammar. Baron Voy, I was promised an immediate report."

"He can't be trusted," said Manu to the Rider.

"*You* don't trust him. I have my own goals, which differ from yours."

The admiral had the pent-up buzz of a disturbed hornet. "He urged the League to make peace with Eirene despite all evidence to the contrary. Then he carved out a cozy sinecure for himself by marrying her, all the while assuring us that Chaonian goals were congruent with Yele goals. But of course—"

"Please desist. I have more urgent matters than your internecine disputes. Or do I need to remind you that your alliance with the Rider Council is deemed traitorous by your own people?"

"We're on the same side now." Baron Voy addressed Manu, showing no sign of rancor despite his bloodied nose.

"I doubt that." But Manu took a step back, his concession to a truce.

When Apama realized he was perfectly happy for her to keep holding on to his arm, she let go.

Baron Voy fished a monogrammed handkerchief out of a pocket and wiped his face clean. "This way."

"You have the information you promised me?" asked the Rider.

"I do, but you won't like it."

The Yele guildswoman worked very hard not to flinch as the Rider walked past. Yet his interest in her was minimal. The gaze of his riding face sought and found Apama. Only her years of training and a quick downward glance of the eyes kept her from an instinctive wince. Phene did not commonly see Riders in public spaces.

"Lieutenant At Sabao will attend me," he said before following Baron Voy along the gangway.

All the Phene peering out of the airlock, eager to see where they'd fetched up, looked at her with a fresh quiver of curiosity. She'd heard them whispering, trying to figure out why a junior lieutenant had first made it off a crippled dreadnought when her squadron was left behind, then escaped the death throes of the Styraconyx flagship, and finally evaded the disaster in Molossia when so many more deserving others had not. It was easier to fall into step behind Manu and the two silent Incorruptibles. It was always easier to keep moving forward when you didn't have any answers.

The gangway dropped them into a passage that overlooked the central cavern of a Remora freighter. The courier was nestled among in-system merchant freighters bearing the various external markers of member systems of the Yele League: Takshashila, Al-Quaraouiyine, Gondishapur, Padua. No non-Yele ships were present. That was unusual because Remoras needed full bellies to clear a profit, and half the slips were vacated. Even more unusual was the complete lack of people in the passage or visible anywhere in the vast hold.

By the time Baron Voy showed them into a cabin, she'd remembered who he was, which only deepened the mystery. The cabin had a pragmatic Yele look, fitted with a conference table and a sideboard folded down from the wall laden with platters of food. An open hatch offered a view into a spacious berthing with a double-wide rack, a desk, and a cushioned seating nook. A young Yele man wearing the robes of a religious order stood discreetly to one side.

Apama remained standing beside the Incorruptibles as the Rider, the baron, and the admiral sat. The young man poured coffee, set out a tray of biscuits and samosas, and stepped back. Briefly he covered his nose with a sleeve. His eyes flickered to Apama, and he colored. She offered him a wry smile, hoping he would understand she knew they all had a ripe smell, but he flushed more deeply and fixed his gaze to the bland gray floor.

The Rider seated himself on an armless stool and turned to address Baron Voy with his riding face. If this disconcerted the baron, he gave no sign. His poise had an admirable polish.

"I remained behind at great risk to myself in order to rescue one of my Rider colleagues after her ship was disabled. She arranged the matter, she vouched for your trustworthiness, and our associates promised they would deliver her safely to me. Now my colleague has fallen silent. What has happened?"

"I have unfortunate news, Your Eminence. Your colleague has been captured by Princess Sun."

"That's not possible."

Manu picked up his cup and held it like an orator's baton that gave him the floor. "I know it scarcely seems possible that Choki's Molossia campaign fell apart when numbers and surprise should have given it a crushing advantage. And yet it did. Because of Princess Sun."

"The attack did a great deal of damage," said the baron. "It will take Chaonia years to rebuild. In that way it was a success."

"I'm glad to hear it," replied Manu with a drawl that veered into mockery before he snapped to a brisk, angry tone. "The Chaonians should have been utterly routed and demoralized in Molossia System. Instead, even with all the damage their fleet and emplacements took, they came away with a stunning victory. I spent many of the long hours in the last five days trying to reconstruct how Princess Sun used the splintered Chaonian fleet to create an opening for herself. I must say, I am impressed by her speed, relentlessness, and audacity." He sipped at the coffee, lowered the cup to stare at the liquid in surprise, and added, "This is quite good."

"Sun Shān is a child," said the Rider. "Barely twenty."

"Don't underestimate her, Your Eminence," said the baron. "The Yele League underestimated Eirene, back in the day, when her brother died and she became queen-marshal at a mere twenty-four years of age with every strike against her. Sun is Eirene's heir. It remains to be seen if she has Eirene's gifts."

"I was assured Sun Shān would be eliminated," said the Rider.

Baron Voy rocked back in surprise. "Were those attempts arranged by the Phene?"

"By our associates."

"Who are . . . ?" the baron asked.

"Fishing for information so you can run it back to Eirene?" Manu shook a cream biscuit in the baron's direction. "That won't wash with me, Aloysius."

"Do you know?" the baron asked Manu. "Were you a part of the assassination plot?"

"I thought you knew everything. So your speeches have always suggested." Manu took a bite of the biscuit and took his time relishing its consistency and flavor.

"This bickering does not amuse us," said the Rider. "Our associates arranged the attempts on the life of Sun Shān via their own channels in order to upset any smooth transfer of power should Queen-Marshal Eirene meet the same fate in battle as her older brothers did. But the threefold promises of these associates have all proved barren. In this circumstance most of all. Why are you here, Baron? What do you offer me? Or do you mean to capture me and turn me over to Eirene Shān?"

"Yes," interposed Manu, "what's with this change of heart, Aloysius?"

"I have had no change of heart. I have always acted with Yele's interest foremost in my mind. A treaty with Chaonia benefited Yele at first. It buffered us from the Phene Empire, if you'll excuse my saying so, Your Eminence."

"Stop calling me that," said the Rider. "We don't use titles among the Phene. It smacks of aristocracy, the vilest of systems which so many fled the Celestial Empire to escape."

"I don't know your name."

"No, you don't, nor will you ever. You need not bother with niceties or formalities. We are not friends. We associate for mutual benefit due to the exigencies of these desperate circumstances. Why are you here?"

"The more powerful Chaonia becomes, the more they intend to grasp."

"You know their plans?"

"That Eirene is intending an assault on Karnos System?"

"This we already comprehend according to her conquests of Troia, Kanesh, and the Hatti territories as well as intelligence we've collected. Tell me something new."

"More and more she scorns outsiders in favor of Chaonian nativism."

"Oh, I see," Manu broke in as he snagged another cream biscuit. "You're jealous she's taken a new consort and you've lost your preeminent position in the palace."

"The marriage to that young woman is entirely unnecessary, it's true. Lust and its pastel of romantic love is never a good reason for an alliance. But the marriage is also dangerous to the cause of Yele. What has transpired before this—economically, militarily—has benefited both Yele and Chaonia. But now the injuries to Yele will increase. Chaonia will drain our treasury for their benefit."

"I am quite heartened by your change of heart," said Manu with a laugh. He plucked up a third cream biscuit, paused, looked over at Apama, and held it out to her. She shook her head, not liking the way the Rider studied her with his riding face, so shallow in its lineaments and yet never fathomable.

The Rider turned back to Baron Voy. "Is my colleague dead?"

"I believe she was captured alive, possibly injured, and is in a stasis pod of some kind. She was captured in a basilica."

The Rider nodded. "That explains it, then."

"Explains what?" Manu asked.

"By what means they were able to capture her. Very well. What assurances can you give me, Baron Voy?"

"I can see you delivered safely back to Phene space. Eirene's fast counterattack forced the Tanarctus Fleet and remnants of the Styraconyx Fleet to retreat from Aspera to Karnos."

"I already know this."

"Of course you do. Here's something you don't know. I can offer you information about Nona Lee."

The riding eyes opened wide, as with an enraged shout. "What news?" he hissed.

Apama pressed back against the wall, feeling stabbed by this unexpected display of anger.

"She's alive," said the baron.

"We know that."

"But I know where she was last seen."

The eyes of the riding face closed, lips pressed tight. When the eyes flickered open again, the mouth spoke with a kind of layered hoarseness as of many voices combined to make one. *"Where?"*

"She must have been working in the outer reaches of Hellion Terminus recently because a young Gatoi soldier was captured there when his squad attacked a ship that she captained. He was brought to Chaonia Prime."

"Yes, we know of the soldier. Where is he now?"

"Also in the custody of Princess Sun. Did you know she cloned herself?"

"Princess Sun?" Manu asked with a guffaw. "Eirene's self-regard is far too rigid to allow herself to be used for any such illegal and unethical experiment. She gave ample proof that Sun was born from her womb, not any other organic or artificial."

"Nona Lee," said the baron impatiently. He turned his attention back to the Rider. "All the daughters of Lee House born after her disappearance may be clones of her. If that matters to you."

Manu whistled. "Does that include Eirene's new consort?"

"What is it you want?" asked the Rider.

"In exchange for working together to bring about Chaonia's downfall? The independence of the Yele League, once Chaonia falls. No tithing, no taxation, no Phene garrisons in Yele territory, boundaries fixed by treaty, and full trade rights for Yele merchants throughout the Phene Empire."

The Rider stood, so the two Yele men stood. "Deliver me safely to the Rider Council, as you have promised, and I will bring the matter up at council. That is all I can offer for now."

"Agreed," said Baron Voy.

"Leave the food. Admiral Manu, I will consult with you later about the Styraconyx fiasco. Lieutenant At Sabao, you will remain."

A glance passed from Baron Voy to Admiral Manu, their antipathy forgotten as Voy arched an eyebrow in a question and the admiral shook his head in negation and gave a puzzled shrug. Then they cleared out. The young religious cleared out. The Incorruptibles set blast charges and sonic disrupters at intervals around the two chambers and cleared out.

The Rider sat back down and indicated a chair. Apama sat. It was very awkward, the legs being too short for her height and it having only two armrests instead of four. She did not want to rudely set her upper arms on the table or, worse, atop her lowers like some kind of crude sewer dweller.

"You are hungry," said the Rider. "Eat. Afterward you may wash off the stink of that unpleasant interlude. I will arrange for clean clothing if there is anything on this vessel that can be tailored to our purposes."

"My thanks," she said cautiously, not going to the sideboard.

He rose, and his other face, his ordinary face, went to the sideboard just as any person would and carefully selected food in prudent portions. Returning to the table he sat to her right, shoved the plate farther right, and angled his body so he could eat. The riding face now looked directly at her, a mere arm's length away.

She focused on her breathing: in five counts, held five counts, out five counts, empty five counts, and repeat.

"Do you know why you are here?" his riding face said in that whisper voice.

Horrible thoughts crowded her head. She was ashamed of thinking them, and yet repulsed by what possibilities swarmed to the front of her mind. She could not look him in those eyes, knowing that what he saw other Riders could see, or so rumor had it. Only Riders knew for sure.

Duty was strength. Among the Phene, children were raised to learn a skill that would aid society and to tell the truth. So she told truth as a bare scaffolding of events, one fact strung to the next to create a path linking her from there to here.

"Colonel Ir Charpentier asked me to ferry you to the flagship. Then I was brought to the courier ship. Then we came here. That's all I know."

"She didn't tell you?"

"That's right. The colonel did not tell me why she chose me to undertake the evacuation."

"I mean the woman who birthed you. She did not tell you?"

The Phene concerned themselves with adaptation and selection. Every child had people who raised them, hopefully with love and careful attention. Every child also inherited genetic traits and information from two or in a few cases three genetic parents. The identity of those progenitors was always logged. It was shameful not to know and especially disgraceful not to reveal.

She knew her mother, of course. Her close kin of the At Sabao line had all died in the terrible accident at Tranquility Harbor. As for whomever else had brought her forth, there was nothing in her birth log, only the stigma of a blank.

"Yes," said the Rider, with something resembling a smile stretching thin lips like a pencil extending the half-finished sketch of a mouth. "It was not possible before for me to claim my part in it. But after the debacle at Na Iri the current ruling faction on the council have lost their majority. We are going to vote in a change of rule. And once we do, I need hide you no longer. I sired you, Apama At Sabao."

In every life there may come a moment when the throat is bared to the knife and there is no means to fight back. She sat for a long interval, too afraid to speak. The Rider's ordinary face kept eating in a tidy, deliberate manner, while the riding face, who never ate and didn't breathe, watched her with the patience of a creature who is used to waiting and who sees all with a thousand thousand eyes.

The silence finally emboldened her. "Did my mother know?"

"That is for you to discuss with her."

"What will happen now?"

"I am taking you to Axiom so you can be formally recognized as my daughter."

"What if I don't want that?" she blurted out.

The Rider stopped eating. Everything tensed, caught in the stillness between the pin being drawn from a grenade and the explosion that will come.

"You'll change your mind once you see how your new status benefits you. It will benefit your mother too, Apama. She's worked hard to keep you clothed, fed, and in school, hasn't she? Don't you want to make life easier for her? I can make that happen. In case you haven't understood me, I'm not offering you a choice."

49

The Cost of Victory

The wide white path led to the sea and the nightly pyres at Autumn West. People flooded out of Orange Line Station, walking in orderly silence toward the flickering red flames along the shore. Some conveyed their deceased on a stretcher, some in a hoverbag, and some on a wheeled death-wagon. Many more came to honor the dead. They stepped back to make way for those carrying a sheet-wrapped corpse, and held aloft lit candles like so many bright ancestor souls come to witness.

Sun walked in silence with her Companions and their cee-cees around her, still limping from the injury to her thigh, although by her expression she gave no hint the wound pained her. She wore the clothes she had fought in. They had been carefully laundered to leave in a few stubborn bloodstains.

The crowd parted before her to create a path to the sea.

Opposite the plaza a large pyre had been built on a stubby peninsula of polished granite. On it lay the wrapped corpses of the thirty-five cadets and two chiefs who had died defending the industrial park. Gentle waves washed the revetment with unceasing sighs.

Sun greeted the families first, taking her time about it. Some of the wounded cadets had also made the journey to pay their respects to their lost comrades. These she also spoke to, asking about their injuries and their deeds. At length the families sprinkled incense over the pyre, speaking the names of the dead. Last of all Sun mounted a platform to address the crowd and of course all of Chaonia.

"Behold the cost of victory. These brave cadets stood up when they might have ducked their heads down and run to shelter. Because of them we have driven off the worst Phene attack on the very soil of the republic since the days of my great-great-grandfather Queen-Marshal Yǔ. Because of these brave cadets and because of the enlisted and officers of the fleet and the citizens working tirelessly in the depots and shipyards, we have sustained hard damage and yet we have triumphed. There is no limit to our courage and our strength. Let me tell you of Cadet Arabesque Chén Alsanfotsi, who was armed with only a raptor gun and yet advanced fearlessly down an open boulevard toward an entrenched position of Phene raiders. Let me tell you of Chief Alejandro Bu Alargos, who led his unarmed gulls against the merciless weaponry of a Phene gunship. Let me tell you of Ensign Imani Yún Alyorvik. She went outside her trapped ship in a vac suit to manually release the docking clamps so the *Asphodel Crane* could escape the destruction of the Naval Command Orbital Station Pánlóngchéng. Let me tell you of Deck Apprentice Skybright Lê Alkabah, who held a light to enable crewmates to escape a collapsing section of Elm Shipyards. Let us fulfill our vow to give them an honorable rite of passage."

She paused as a distant movement from the direction of the Orange Line stirred the crowd like the sweep of a sword. Hetty, standing at the base of the platform, looked questioningly up at her, but Sun merely smiled. A large procession made its slow way through the packed assembly and into the plaza.

Queen-Marshal Eirene had come straight from battle, having chased the Phene into Aspera and left Crane Marshal Qìngzhī there to restore Chaonian control over the system and its crucial habitats and beacons. Yet the queen-marshal had taken care to change into a dress uniform. When she climbed onto the platform she greeted her daughter with her most ironic arch of eyebrow. A red gleam flashed in her obsidian eye.

"So, Sun, I see you are number one in the rankings on Idol Faire."

"Of course."

"Zàofù tells me the stasis pod with the Rider has been delivered to the palace."

"Of course."

"And your father?"

"The arrangement you two made had nothing to do with me, so you'll have to take up any new circumstances with him." Sun paused before adding, "You're not intimidated by him, are you?"

"Really, Sun, don't try that with me since I have sparred with far more experienced opponents. By the way, Moira wants Persephone back. She means to appoint her as governor-in-training of Lee House. She needs an heir too."

"Moira Lee can't have Persephone. I have the right not to release her."

The queen-marshal glanced down to where Alika, James, Hetty, and Isis stood at the bottom of the steps. "It's ultimately up to Persephone Lee, is it not? I see she is not here with you." She examined Candace, with her fans clipped to her belt and her lower body encased in a wheeled bracing frame to support her broken legs and hip, then caught sight of Jade Kim waiting at parade rest a step behind the others. "Effulgent Heaven! Who is that gorgeous young person? I don't think I've seen them before. Have you finally discovered your libido, Sun? It's about time."

Sun ignored the irritating tangent. "I sent Persephone as my representative to the memorial being held at CeDCA. It seemed appropriate for her to go, since that's where she came from."

"Hhn." The queen-marshal's soft grunt was sometimes a measure of annoyance and sometimes just a measure, since Eirene was known as a cunning strategist who never played her hand too soon or too openly. "We shall see for how long this republic has space for the both of us. But for now, Sun, you have done well. I'm proud of you."

The admission, spoken so blandly, crashed a shock wave through Sun's fierce heart.

The queen-marshal settled an appraising gaze on her daughter, waiting, although for what Sun wasn't quite certain. But she was absolutely sure she wasn't about to let her mother see how much that scrap of praise mattered to her. Allowing none of her exultation to show, she dipped her chin dutifully, child to parent, the gesture as brief as the last flash of the solar disc when its rim crosses the sea's horizon with its reminder, its promise, its portent, of a return.

She offered a glass pitcher of scented oil to her mother, who emptied the oil over the wood. A laser shot from the queen-marshal's obsidian eye kindled flame amid the dry tinder.

The families came forward to set additional fires within the stacks of wood. Heat rose, spreading the scent of sandalwood into the night air.

Alika took a place halfway up the steps to the platform and led the crowd in the Hymn of Leaving. The sound coming from so many throats was raw with the texture of grief and yet also vibrant with pride.

Crossing the ocean of stars we leave our home behind us.
We are the spears cast at the furious heaven
And we will burn one by one into ashes
As with the last sparks we vanish.
This memory we carry to our own death which awaits us
And from which none of us will return.
Do not forget. Goodbye forever.

In Which the Wily Persephone Takes the Last Shot

Solomon and I sit side by side on the train, waiting as the rest of the passenger cars fill up with matriculated cadets headed home for a truncated ten-days' leave before they join the fleet. Chaonia's military has a lot of rebuilding to do.

We got into this car at the back of the train first, courtesy of not having to pack our things and clear out our racks after the graduation ceremonies and banquet. Solomon sits to my right with perfect straight posture and feet flat on the floor, eyes forward, wearing his performance ribbons and third-in-class award like the star cadet he is. I'm leaning left, bumping shoulders with Ti, craning my head so I can see her scroll mail, a flexible tablet she has unrolled in order to watch a video burned on it and sent by her family. Their situation is now so top secret that no trace of them remains on the net, courtesy of James.

She smiles at me, then returns her attention to the image of her little brother. Kas is wearing a new cap and new clothes, but what he's really thrilled by is a stand of bamboo in the family's living quarters. Ti has an ear-wire attached to the scroll so I can't hear what he's saying as he reverently holds a branch while excitedly describing its leaves to her. Nor do I try to listen in. My attention has fixed on a shelf in the background with ten books set on it. The map is going on a journey, and it makes me itch to think I once touched it and it's sliding out of my reach.

Zizou is on the ship too. I can't get that kiss out of my mind. It shook me. I'm all about physical infatuation. I've been down that road more than once, only to discover that appetite fades and then you're stuck figuring how much you didn't really like that asshole after all. Or maybe I'm the asshole. Sun's not wrong about me.

But it shook me. I can't stop thinking about him.

"You're thinking about him," remarks Solomon. "You get this melty look on your face like you're undergoing a phase transition into lovestruck marshmallow soup. It's definitely sweet but also creepy."

"Fuck you, Solomon."

"Weak ass, Perse."

I just smile. This isn't a simulation of an exam, but I have a surprise waiting for him anyway, a little piece of revenge. He won't see my victory coming until it hits him square in the face.

A flood of cadets pours onto the platform. As they start boarding the train Ti slips off her wire and tucks the scroll into her travel bag. She quickly checks her makeup in a mirror built into her sleeve. People board our car and start taking seats. With my status as a Companion I could have reserved the whole car for myself, but I attended the memorial and the matriculation ceremony in the dress uniform I wore as Persephone Lï Alargos, and I mean to finish this part of my life in the way I began it.

Despite the number of graduates cramming onto the train, despite the Stone Barracks members greeting Solomon and, after a hesitation, me, not one asks if the bench opposite us is free. Nor do they ask why I have a nonregulation silk scarf tied around my neck, although probably they're envying the clever twist-knot Ti used to hide my bruises because they surely believe it's there only to give a bit of vogue flair.

They'll never see me as one of them ever again, and I never was anyway. Sure, I came by the scores to get into CeDCA honestly, but I had Kadmos as my private tutor, his entire life dedicated to educating the children of Lee House, and at the time there were only four of us in the main line and thus under his primary care. The Republic of Chaonia provides education to all its citizens—it would be foolish and counterproductive not to—but no one would argue that the average cadet got the same level of preparation I did, much less a provisional citizen like Solomon, who had to scrape and claw for every minute of every additional post–standard level course. I'm not sure I could have graduated in the top tier of our class even if I'd tried. As a student I focused all my efforts on the beacon qualifications and settled for a solid seventy-third percentile most everywhere else. Solomon may have cheated by making a deal to get in, but he earned his third-in-class award by being exemplary in every way.

Maybe the truth helps us understand where we stand. I'm just grateful I have people I can trust.

"What hey!" Our rack-mates, now ensigns, Hồng Minh Lê Altadmor, Ikenna Sì Alluòyì, and Ay Jí Alimerishu sashay up the aisle and shove onto the bench opposite. But then they hesitate, looking at me for permission. The gesture makes me wince.

Solomon says, "Sit down!"

Relaxing, they sit. Ti's met them already, but she fusses over them, making them comfortable by asking Ikenna about his glasses, admiring Ay's painted hands, and laughing when Minh teasingly pinches her sleeve with the new surgical forceps she just got added to her multi-tool prosthetic hand.

The departure chime rings. The doors close. The train leaves the station and begins its slow climb up the ridge.

I am departing the academy for what may well be the last time. When I look back I see the debris field left by the Phene attack but also the fields where I'd played rugby and the classrooms where I'd kicked at Solomon's ankles under the table when I got bored. He was my Perseus, because they took Percy away from me. That's what Lee House does—they take and they take and they take.

Just then, as if it's read my mind, a message packet pings into my 🌑 mailbox. The sender's symbol is the emerald tree that designates the governor of Lee House.

"What's wrong?" Solomon asks, ever attuned to my moods.

"Give me a moment." I arrange my expression to something bland and false before I rise and walk down the aisle to the end of the car and into the vestibule. The door into the caboose is closed, and a pair of cadets are leaning up against it, making out. I cough.

They startle and then, seeing my uniform which is the same as theirs, shrug and wave me away.

The Honorable Persephone Lee of Lee House gives them a brusque two-handed *withdraw* gesture. This time they get out fast.

Bracing myself, I open the packet, only to be shunted into a direct link to Aunt Moira.

"Persephone? It's about time. Now that everything is sorted out, I expect you to come home immediately."

"I'm not coming home."

"You have to come home. If you don't start preparing to become governor after me, the position will pass to Marduk's line. You know what happens when one branch of the family loses power. Our line, and your life, will be sidelined forever, exiled to some backwater terminus. Is that what you want?"

"I'm not coming home. I'm Companion to Princess Sun."

"So was I, once, Companion to Eirene. Those were the most exciting days of my life, although I admit we didn't think of entering Idol Faire. What a lark for you kids! But then, my girl, I grew up and took on my family responsibilities."

"I thought you got imprudently pregnant by Queen-Marshal Nézhā and that's why you had to retire from Companion duties."

"Who told you that?"

"You've imprisoned a royal child, Aunt Moira. Your own child!"

"If not held safely there, then my child would be dead. You must return to Lee House. Eirene will back me up if you continue with this stubborn refusal."

"Gosh, then I'll have to tell Queen-Marshal Eirene that my father, who as you recall was allowed and even encouraged to marry into Lee House, was complicit in the smuggling operations of the seers of Iros."

"Eirene already knows. I told her myself, and I was glad to do it since I never favored that marriage. Is this the best you can do, Persephone? Because now that I think about it, it's a mystery how Kiran was able to escape on Tjeker. I wonder if you aided him."

"I did not! I was choked out."

She smiles at my defensiveness. "So we've been told. You have no proof."

"Zizou was there."

"The testimony of Gatoi is inadmissible in Chaonian courts. As I said, I expect you to return to begin your training as heir to the governorship of Lee House."

"I'll also tell Eirene that my father shot Octavian while conspiring with my mother to assassinate her heir."

"The discovery of illegal tech and a store of late bloomer syrup in the Tjeker hermitage points to the seers and their Phene allies as the instigators of the assassination attempt against Sun. There's no proof Aisa was ever anything but an ignorant dupe of Kiran. Lee House is blameless. If it comes to your word against mine, Eirene will believe me, not you."

Eirene will believe Aunt Moira over me. The surge of fury and frustration that blasts through me could surely power the academy for a full year.

She clucks her tongue pityingly. "Really, Persephone, I have far more experience with this than you do. So that's settled. I'll expect you home tomorrow."

I should have known better than to think my family would let me go. Tears fill my eyes. My chest aches and my throat hurts, and I can tell I'm about burst into a harsh, snotty cry.

Then I remember that just as I am not my parents, Sun isn't her mother.

Eirene built the military might and fledgling empire of Chaonia in a mere twenty-five years after the disaster of her older brothers' defeats. She managed it because she is prudent, duplicitous, shrewd, ingenious, subtle, charming, violent, and pragmatic.

But Sun is Sun.

I dry my tears. "You and I know the truth, Aunt Moira. As long as you leave me alone, and never again try to recall me as Companion, I won't tell *Sun* that my parents are the ones responsible for Octavian's death."

My aunt doesn't ask if I would dare betray my parents, much less Lee House, in such a way. We both know the answer. She fumes, considering Sun's temperament and her well-known attachment to her loyal bodyguard. Of course she doesn't know I've already told Sun, but that's not my problem.

I need to be sure, so I take one more shot.

"The thing about Zizou, though, is that even if his testimony isn't admissible, his actions have revealed the thing you must be most desperate to keep secret."

"What are you talking about?" Her tone tightens.

"The Phene don't care about me. They care about Nona Lee, architect of a massacre that killed thousands of innocent Phene civilians as well as dedicated troops. And who knows what else she's been responsible for over the years."

"Nona is dead."

"Sure she is. Which is what makes it weird that the Phene think she's alive. Otherwise they wouldn't have programmed Zizou the way they did. Because you know something else, Aunt Moira. You know that cloning is illegal and has been for hundreds of years. It's so unethical and dangerous that clones are given no legal rights as citizens. Which means that among other things, they can't inherit—let's say—the governorship of a Core House. I mean, if the truth were to come out. And just imagine if people were to discover that the queen-marshal herself has married—"

"You think you're so clever."

"I do think I'm clever!"

I wait.

At last she says, "We'll continue this conversation another time."

"No, Aunt Moira, we won't. I'm not coming home, not today, not tomorrow, not ever. From now on, all communication from you or Lee House will be routed through my cee-cee and Sun's high secretary. I hope you understand me."

I cut the connection.

It takes me a full minute to breathe myself down and stop shaking in time to the rattle and hum of the moving train. When I'm calm enough I open the vestibule's exit door window and stick my head out, looking back down the track. We've hit the top of the ridge and entered the forest, so all I see are coniferous trees and, floating above them, the lonely peaked top of the Sun pagoda where once there were three landmarks rising into the sky full of hopeful promise. There were once three children—Ereshkigal, Perseus, and Persephone—born from the same person's womb, and now there is only me.

If Sun is right, Perseus was the only one who was really the biological child of Aisa and Kiran. But we were still siblings, and that means something in every way that can matter because Resh made sure of it.

I wonder if my big sister suspected the truth. I wonder if the truth really makes you free. But I do know my bonds have loosened and I can finally stretch to see just how very far my reach may go.

The door opens from the carriage. Ti looks in with the efficient and never overwrought concern of an effective cee-cee. She has to pitch her voice louder to be heard over the wheels and the wind.

"Perse? Are you all right? Here, hold on." She closes the window, dabs my tears away with a handkerchief, tidies my windblown hair, and straightens my uniform. "Why does Solomon have so many more service ribbons and awards than you do?"

"Oh! Solomon!" I say brightly. "Let's hurry back so we don't miss the show."

"What show?"

I lead her back into the car. Cadets eye us as we head down the aisle to where the others are seated. I'm not sure what they're most curious and keen on: Tiana's elegant and fashionable presence, my notoriety as a secret House cadet taking up a citizen's place at CeDCA, or the sheen of a first-place ranking on Idol Faire for "Princess Sun and her Companions." Ti's already ordered me a pair of pomegranate-color gloves, not that I could wear them with my military uniform. But on the other hand, I'm a Companion. We make our own style.

I wave Tiana in to the window seat and sit facing my rackmates with a smile.

"That smile bodes trouble," says Solomon.

I look down to the forward end of the car as its connecting door opens. Solomon follows my gaze. He stiffens with shock and awe as his aunt Naomi appears. She heads down the aisle toward us.

"Oh no way. I thought she was gone already."

I point at him with a two-fingered shooting gesture. "You are so dead, Solomon."

Minh jumps up to greet Naomi and introduce her to Ikenna and Ay. Ti and I stand and greet her too. Solomon doesn't move, like he's been struck to stone.

Naomi says, "What a coincidence! Conductor Song served with your uncle Kila in the Twelfth Battalion. We've had quite a nice chat. He says I can borrow the caboose for an hour. You and I need to have a talk, Solomon."

"An *hour*?" gasps Solomon.

"You're right. An hour won't be nearly long enough for everything I have to say you, young man. Two at minimum. Come along."

I smirk in his general direction.

"Dammit," he says to me.

"Your language, Solomon!" scolds his aunt. By the way he flushes to the tips of his ears I can tell she's just getting started on what is going to be an epic smackdown.

I sit, crossing my arms over my chest. "I'll call that even, then."

There's a lot in his expression he doesn't dare say aloud in front of his aunt, but Solomon's not a grudge-holder, not like me. His shoulders drop. His grin breaks out.

"I guess you learned something at CeDCA after all," he says.

He and his aunt head for the back.

"Remind me not to cross you," says Ay.

"You know," I say, "I wasn't sure if you three were going to take your original postings or take the chance with me."

Ikenna makes a *pff* sound between lips and tongue. "You're Companion to Princess Sun. Are you kidding me?"

"Yeah," adds Minh. "Why would we pass up a gift horse like this?"

"You have to call her *Honored Persephone* now," says Ti, deadpan.

"No, you don't," I say, feeling awkward.

She goes on, "*Asshole* is an acceptable alternative."

"Hey!" I shoot her a look as the others chortle.

"It's like we have a full rack again," says Ay.

So it is, except the academy is behind us now. We're headed for unknown territory.

"Well," I say, "I have no idea what's going to happen next, but I would bet anything that it is going to be wild."

ACKNOWLEDGMENTS

Writing and revising *Unconquerable Sun* was a long-haul voyage through some difficult life shoals, but here it is, finally.

I'd like to acknowledge Dr. Jeanne Reames, friend of many years, whose work on the court of Alexander the Great influenced me greatly; she also steered me to the scholars and works that proved most helpful. Petty Officer First Class Alexander M. Rasmussen-Silverstein patiently offered suggestions about military protocol as well as battle strategy and tactics. Shepherd Chandler read the earliest chapters and asked questions that encouraged me to write on. Deirdre Jones saw the first proposal and chapters and recommended I revise my approach, for which I am inexpressibly grateful. Liz Bourke, Aliette de Bodard, and Emmett Baber read pre-final versions and were unflagging cheerleaders when I needed it most. Ken Liu generously and tirelessly answered all my questions. Tade Thompson discovered Tadian and solved cauls as well as codified the Fight Clarity Test and helped me with names. E. K. Johnston dared me to write in verse (even if I could only manage one character speaking in iambic pentameter). Ryan Van Loan gamely offered tips on a last-minute panicked question. Judith Tarr gave me good advice, as always. Jim Davies suggested engineered hallucination. Erik Holmes, Jason Bryant, Krystle Yanagihara, and Tuğçe Bryant bravely dug into the text and offered detailed critiques (their prints are all over the story if you know where to look or in case you're wondering why Alika plays a baritone—not a tenor—ukulele for Idol Faire and composes on a guitar). Other early-days encouragement came from A'ndrea Messer, Wendy Xu, Ann Aguirre, Malinda Lo, and Cindy Pon (thank you, ladies). Ed Yong doesn't know me, but I'm grateful to his book *I Contain Multitudes*. If I forgot someone I apologize; I'm thankful for your help.

Shout-out to Zen Cho, Vida Cruz, Alessa Hinlo, Victor Ocampo, Nene Ormes, Cindy Pon, Rochita Ruiz, Mia Serrano, Aliette de Bodard, and Tade Thompson: you know what you did.

Special thanks to the amazing team at Tor Books: Devi Pillai and Miriam Weinberg for believing, Sanaa Ali-Virani (who also loves maps like I do), map makers Jennifer Hanover and Mary Wirth, and to Steven Bucsok, Sara and Chris Ensey, Christina MacDonald, Hayley Jozwiak, Rafal Gibek, Natassja Haught, Lauren Levite, Peter Lutjen, Caroline Perny, Heather Saunders, Jamie Stafford-Hill, Renata Sweeney, and Becky Yeager.

Finally, to my friends who have had my back, all the <3s.

To Mel and Naci and my fabulous nieces and nephews all: thank you for being there.

Rhi, Alex, and David: you're the best.